The Cornish Cream Tea Bus

Cressida McLaughlin

Cressy grew up in South East London surrounded by books and with a cat named after Lawrence of Arabia. She studied English at the University of East Anglia and now lives in Norwich with her husband David. When she isn't writing, Cressy spends her spare time reading, returning to London or exploring the beautiful Norfolk coastline.

If you'd like to find out more about Cressy, visit her on Twitter and on Facebook. She'd love to hear from you!

f/CressidaMcLaughlinAuthor
𝕏@CressMcLaughlin
📷@CressMcLaughlin

Also by Cressida McLaughlin

Primrose Terrace series
Wellies & Westies
Sunshine & Spaniels
Raincoats & Retrievers
Tinsel & Terriers

A Christmas Tail – The Complete Primrose Terrace Story

The Once in a Blue Moon Guesthouse series
Open For Business
Fully Booked
Do Not Disturb
Wish You Were Here

The Canal Boat Café series
All Aboard
Casting Off
Cabin Fever
Land Ahoy!

The Canal Boat Café Christmas – Port Out
The Canal Boat Café Christmas – Starboard Home

The House of Birds and Butterflies
The Dawn Chorus
The Lovebirds
Twilight Song
Birds of a Feather

The
Cornish
Cream
Tea Bus

Cressida McLaughlin

HarperCollins*Publishers*

HarperCollins*Publishers* Ltd
The News Building
1 London Bridge Street
London SE1 9GF

www.harpercollins.co.uk

This paperback original 2019
1

First published in Great Britain as four separate ebooks in 2019 by HarperCollins*Publishers*

A catalogue record for this book
is available from the British Library

ISBN: 978-0-00-833218-1

Set in Minion by Palimpsest Book Production Limited,
Falkirk, Stirlingshire

Printed and bound by CPI Group (UK) Ltd, Croydon CR0 4YY

To Hannah Ferguson – thank you
for everything that you do

Part 1

Don't Go Baking My Heart

Chapter One

My Dearest Charlie,

Gertie is yours, to do with what you will. I know that you cherish her, but you do not need to keep her. She is a gift, not a millstone around your neck. If the best thing for you is to sell her and go travelling, then that is what you should do.

I have so much to say to you, but my time is running out. I hope that these few words will be enough to show you how much I love you; it's more than I ever thought possible.

Look after yourself, think of all the happy times we spent together, and know that you can do anything if you believe in yourself enough.

Remember, my darling niece, live life to the full – you only get one chance. Make the most of your opportunities and do what is right for you.

All my love, always,

Your Uncle Hal x

Charlie Quilter folded the letter and pushed it into the back pocket of her jeans. She blinked, her eyes adjusting to the gloom, and tried to stop her heart from sinking as her dad stopped beside her in the garage doorway. His sigh was heavy, and not unexpected: he had been sighing a lot lately. She could barely remember a time when his narrow shoulders hadn't been slumped, and she had forgotten what his laughter sounded like. But on this occasion, she felt the same as he did; the sight before them was not inspiring.

The 1960s Routemaster bus, painted cream with green accents, looked more scrapheap than vintage, and Charlie could see that its months left in the garage without Uncle Hal's care and attention had had a serious impact.

'God, Charlie,' Vince Quilter said, stepping inside the garage and finding the light switch, 'what are you – we – I mean . . .' He shrugged, his arms wide, expression forlorn.

Charlie took a deep breath and, despite the February chill at her back, unzipped her coat and unwound her thick maroon scarf. The wind assailed her neck, newly exposed to the elements after the pre-Christmas, post-break-up, chop-it-all-off graduated bob that – she now realized – had been an ill-advised choice for this time of year.

'We're going to fix her,' she said purposefully, putting her bag against the wall and laying her palm flat against the bus's cold paintwork. 'We're going to restore Gertie, aren't we, Dad?' He was staring at the workbench where all Hal's tools were laid out, rubbing his unshaven jaw. Hal's death had hit him harder than anyone else, and while Charlie felt her uncle's loss keenly, she knew it was nothing compared to what Vince was going through. 'Dad?' she prompted.

'Sorry, love. That we are.' He started rolling up the sleeves of his jacket, thought better of it and took it off instead. He switched on the heater and rubbed his hands together.

Charlie felt a surge of hope. She hurried over to her bag and pulled out a flask of coffee and a Tupperware box. 'Here, have a brownie to keep you going. I thought we could do with some sustenance.' She took off the lid, and a glimmer of a smile lit up Vince's face.

'Always thinking ahead, huh?'

'This was never going to be the easiest task in the world, practically or emotionally. Brownies baked with love – and hazelnuts and chocolate chip, because that's your favourite kind.'

'Your food is the best, because it's baked with love and extra calories,' her dad said, taking one of the neatly arranged squares. 'That's what he always said.'

'Yup.' A lump formed unhelpfully at the back of Charlie's throat, as it had been doing at inopportune moments ever since her uncle Hal had been diagnosed with an aggressive cancer at the end of last summer. So many things reminded her of him, and while dealing with practicalities – assessing the state of his beloved Routemaster bus, for example – were easier to focus on without the emotion overwhelming her, his sayings, his nuggets of wisdom, always knocked her off kilter. They were so ingrained in her family now, but it was as if she could hear Hal's voice, his unwavering cheerfulness, whoever was saying the words.

'Love and extra calories,' she repeated, wincing when she noticed a deep gouge in Gertie's side. 'How did he get away with being so sentimental?'

'Because he was straightforward,' her dad said through a mouthful of chocolate and nuts. 'He said everything without embarrassment or affectation. He was a sixty-eight-year-old man who called his bus Gertie. He meant it all, and was never ashamed of who he was.'

Uncle Hal had given scenic tours on Gertie, the vintage double-decker Routemaster, that were legendary throughout the Cotswolds. He was an expert bus driver and a world-class talker. Everyone who took one of his tours left feeling as if they'd made a friend for life, and the testimonials on TripAdvisor were gushing. His untimely death had left a huge hole in the Cotswold tourist trade, as well as his family's life.

And now Gertie belonged to Charlie; left to her in Hal's will, for her to do with whatever she wanted. At that moment, all she could see in the bus's future was being dismantled and sold for spares, but she was not going to let that happen. She couldn't imagine herself taking over her uncle's tours, even though she had spent many hours on them and had been taught to drive the bus as soon as she was old enough. Her expertise was in baking, not talking.

Her dad finished his brownie and started examining Gertie's engine. As a car dealer he knew his way around vehicles, but had admitted to Charlie that he wasn't that knowledgeable about buses. Charlie had argued that it was just a bigger version, and nothing could be that different.

She cleaned the chocolate off her fingers with a paper napkin and climbed on board the bus. It had taken on a musty, unloved smell, and was bone-achingly cold. Charlie walked up the aisle of the lower deck, her fingers trailing along the backs of the forest-green seats, and opened the cab.

Her dad appeared behind her, wiping his hands on a rag. 'The engine seems in good enough shape, but I only know the basics. And in here?' He gave another melancholy sigh.

'It's going to be fine,' she said. 'She needs a bit of sprucing up, that's all. A few things need fixing, there's some cosmetic work, knocking a couple of panels back into shape, and then Gertie will be as good as new.'

'I could give Clive a call,' Vince said, worrying at his scruffy hair, 'get him to come and give her a once-over, see what condition her vital organs are in.'

'And in the meantime, I'll tackle in here. We've got the Hoover, cleaning sprays, and I can make a list of what needs repairing. The toilet probably needs a good flushing out.' Charlie made a face and her dad laughed.

'You sure you want to start that now?' he asked. 'Shouldn't we find out if she's salvageable first? You don't want to waste your time cleaning her if the engine's buggered.'

'Dad, the engine is *not* buggered. She's fine. Hal was driving her right up until . . . he wasn't any more. He never mentioned anything being wrong with her.'

'Yes, but you have to agree she looks—'

'Neglected,' Charlie finished. 'Which is why we're here. I guarantee that once we've given her a bit of love and attention, things will look a hundred times better. Gertie is going back on the road, that's all there is to it.' She grinned, and it wasn't even forced. She had almost convinced herself.

Her dad looked at her fondly. 'You're a wonder, Charlie. Anyone else faced with these circumstances – with this,' he gestured around him, 'and Hal, and everything you've been through with Stuart – would start a lengthy hibernation, and nobody would blame them. Instead you've baked brownies and dragged me here, and you're not going to leave until Gertie's gleaming. You don't even know what you're going to do with her when she's restored!'

Charlie's smile almost slipped at this last point, because that was worrying her far more than the state of Gertie's engine or how many panels needed replacing. What on earth was she going to do with a vintage, double-decker bus, when she worked in a café in Ross-on-Wye and her main skills were baking and eating? 'I'll think of something,' she said brightly. 'One step at a time, Dad. Fix Gertie, and *then* decide what to do with her.'

She put the key in the ignition and a satisfying thrum reverberated, like a heartbeat, through the bus. The engine was working, at least. She cranked the heating up to max – she didn't want her fingers to fall off before she'd polished the metalwork – then turned on the radio.

'Gold' by Spandau Ballet filled the space, and Charlie took her dad's hands and pulled them up in the air with hers. She forced them into an awkward dance down the aisle, bumping into seats as they sashayed from the front of the bus to the back, and sang along at the top of her voice. Soon they were both laughing, and her dad let go of her hands so he could clutch his stomach. She dinged the bell and tried to get her breathing under control. When Vince looked up, Charlie could see the familiar warmth in his eyes that she had been worried was gone for good.

It was impossible not to feel cheered in Gertie's company. Hal had been convinced there was something a little bit magical about her, and while Charlie had always argued that it was Hal who inspired the laughter on his tours, at this moment she wondered if he was right.

They could do this. No question. Despite all that had happened to her over the past few months, she knew she could restore Gertie to her former glory. What came next wasn't so certain but, as she'd said to her dad, they could only take one step at a time. Right now, they needed to focus on bringing the bus back to life.

They worked all morning, and even though Charlie knew the bits they were fixing were only cosmetic, and a small part of her worried that when Clive came round he would tell them that the engine was too old, or there was too much rust in the chassis, or any one of a number of things that meant Gertie would not outlive Hal, she felt so much better for doing it. The radio kept them buoyed, and at one point her dad even whistled along to a Sixties tune, something that, only a day before, Charlie and her mum would both have thought impossible.

The simple act of working on Uncle Hal's bus was taking the edge off their grief. It reminded Charlie how much she had loved spending time with him, a lot of it on board this very bus, and how big an influence he'd been on her. That didn't have to stop just because he was no longer physically with her. Hal would be part of her life for ever.

It was after one o'clock when Vince announced he was going to get sandwiches. Charlie ordered an egg mayo and bacon baguette and, once her dad had strolled out of the garage with his jacket done up to his neck, she climbed to the top deck of the bus. She sat above the cab – her favourite position as a child because she could pretend she was driving – even though, inside the garage, the view was less than inspiring. As she did so, she felt the letter in her back pocket. Hal had left it for her in his will, and it had been folded and reopened so many times the paper had begun to wear thin along the creases.

It no longer made her cry, but the words still affected her deeply. He had never married, had never had a family of his own, so she had been like a daughter to him. Losing him had been a huge blow – his cancer diagnosis a mind-numbing shock followed quickly by practicalities as his condition worsened and he needed more care – but at least she had been able to spend time with him, to let him know how much she loved him and how much he had shaped her life. And she would always have his letter. It was bittersweet, but so much better than the irreversible cut-off of losing someone suddenly.

She was still lost in thought when she heard a woman calling her name, followed by a high-pitched yelp. Charlie ran down Gertie's narrow staircase and out of the open doorway.

'How are you doing?' Juliette asked. Before Charlie had time to reply, Marmite raced up to her, his extendable lead whirring noisily, and put his tiny front paws on Charlie's shins. Charlie scooped the Yorkipoo puppy into her arms and closed her eyes while he licked her chin. However miserable some aspects of life had been recently, Marmite never failed to bring a smile to her face. He was six months old, and more of a terror with every passing day.

'OK, I think,' Charlie said. 'But don't look at the outside, come and see what we've done inside. Dad's getting someone to take a proper look at her, and in the meantime we've been giving her a polish. He's just gone to get lunch.'

'I know,' Juliette said, unclipping Marmite's lead and following Charlie onto the bus. 'I saw him on my way here. He's getting me a sandwich, too.'

'So you can stay for a bit, before you go back to Cornwall this afternoon?'

Juliette nodded. 'It's been so good seeing everyone. But I'm still not sure, Char, how you're really doing. What's going on up here?' She tapped Charlie's forehead. 'You're putting on this amazing front, but I need to know before I go home that you're OK.'

'I'm fine,' Charlie said. 'This morning has helped a lot. Dad was concerned that Gertie wouldn't be salvageable, but just look at her! She might need a bit of work under the bonnet, some patching up, but it's given me hope.'

Juliette surveyed their morning's work, the metal uprights gleaming, the walls clean, the seats vacuumed to within an inch of their lives. 'She looks great, Char, almost as good as new. But I'm not as convinced about you. Since I've been back you've been so busy, working at The Café on the Hill, helping with the catering for the funeral. You haven't stopped, even for a day. You should be taking some time out.'

Charlie groaned. 'Why does everyone think that's best for me? Keeping busy is what helps in this kind of situation.' She led Juliette to a seat halfway down the bus. Some of the chairs were sagging dangerously, but this one, she had discovered earlier, was still fairly firm.

'Are you *sure* you're OK?' Juliette said after a minute. Her voice was low, her slight French accent always adding a seriousness to her words, though in this case it was probably intentional.

Charlie remembered the first time she had heard Juliette speak, on a packed train from London to Cheltenham; she'd been chatting with someone on the other end of her mobile, and had occasionally slipped into French. Charlie had been sitting next to her, and after Juliette had finished her call and offered some expletives in both languages, Charlie had asked her those same words: *Are you OK?* Juliette had been reserved, embarrassed that she'd been entertaining the whole carriage, and so Charlie had told her how *she'd* had a no-holds-barred telephone row with her then-boyfriend in a hotel doorway, not realizing that a wedding party were waiting to get past her into the ballroom, and how some of the guests had looked quite shocked when she'd finally noticed that they were watching her.

She'd made Juliette laugh, and by the time the train had pulled up in Cheltenham, they had swapped numbers and agreed to meet up. That had been almost seven years ago, and their friendship was still strong despite Juliette's move to Cornwall two years before, with her boyfriend Lawrence. Charlie was still touched that Juliette had come back for Hal's funeral, staying for a couple of weeks to catch up with friends in the area. She had been on Gertie countless times when she'd lived in Cheltenham, and Charlie hadn't asked her if *she* was OK.

'I'm not doing too badly,' she said now. 'I've been getting on with stuff, which is better than wallowing in the empty flat, or at Mum and Dad's. Dad's so cut up about losing Hal. Today is the first time I've seen him smile in what feels like for ever.'

'I know you're worried about Vince, but you have to think about yourself, too.' Juliette put a hand on her shoulder. 'Because it isn't just Hal, is it? It's only been a couple of months since you and Stuart . . . finished. And you're in the flat, hosting viewings, unsure where you're going to go once it's sold. I know you don't want to go back to living with your parents, and you can't live on Gertie, as tempting as it is.' She laughed softly.

'That's looking like one of the better options, actually,' Charlie said, chuckling. 'What *am* I going to do with her, Jules? I can't be a tour guide. I'm a baker, a caterer. I don't have the gift of the gab like Hal did. But, despite what he said in his letter, I can't sell her.' She rubbed her hands over her eyes, realizing too late that they were covered in cleaning spray.

'This is why you need time,' Juliette pressed. 'You need to stop thinking for a bit, give yourself some space before you make any big decisions. The place in Newquay wasn't brilliant, but our new house in Porthgolow, it's perfect, Char.

It's so close to the sea. It's beautiful and quiet, and the people in the village are friendly. Come and stay for a couple of weeks. Bea would give you the time off, wouldn't she? The hours you've put into that café, you're probably owed months back in overtime.'

'Working is good for me,' Charlie insisted but, even as she said it, the thought of returning to the café in Ross-on-Wye, even with its spring-themed window display and the ideas she had for seasonal cakes and sandwiches, didn't fill her with as much joy as it should. There were too many other thoughts crowding her mind.

'Take a break,' Juliette continued. 'Come and stay with Lawrence and me. I'm sure Marmite would get on fine with Ray and Benton. They're easy-going cats, and Marmite's still so small. And the most adorable dog in the world, by the way. I'm so glad you've got him to look after you.'

Marmite was sitting on the seat in front of them, scrabbling at the back of the cushion as if there might be a treat hidden somewhere in the fabric. Charlie picked him up and settled him on her lap, rubbing his black-and-tan coat. She pictured the two of them walking along a sandy beach with crystal blue water beyond, to a soundtrack of seagulls and crashing waves. It was certainly a better image than this bland, functional garage or the flat she had shared with Stuart, now empty and soulless. She didn't want to run away from the hard things in life, but she knew her friend was right.

'Let me talk to Bea,' she said decisively. 'I'll see if I can get a couple of weeks off.'

Juliette's face lit up. She ruffled Charlie's hair, which had been enhanced from its natural reddish hue into a vibrant copper at the same time as the drastic haircut. 'The next time you're in the café, you promise me you'll ask her?'

'I will, I—'

'Room for a little one?' Her dad appeared in the doorway, along with the salty tang of bacon.

'Thanks so much, Vince,' Juliette said, accepting her baguette and a coffee.

'You convinced Charlie to come and stay with you yet?' he asked, taking the seat in front and turning to face them.

'Almost,' Juliette said. 'She's agreed to ask Bea for some time off.'

'Bloody hell! You've actually got her considering a holiday? Or have you tempted her down with some sort of Cornish cooking competition?'

'No competition,' Juliette said through a mouthful of cheese sandwich. 'No work. An actual holiday.'

'I am here, you know,' Charlie said, lifting her baguette out of Marmite's reach. The dog put his paws on her chest and sniffed the air, whimpering mournfully.

'It doesn't hurt to hear the unvarnished truth occasionally, love,' Vince replied.

'I've never . . .' she started, then sighed and unwrapped her lunch. She didn't want to argue with her dad, and she knew they both had her best interests at heart, even if they were being irritating about it.

'This is cosy, isn't it?' Juliette said. 'Having a picnic on board Gertie. Hal could have started something like this, including sandwiches and cups of tea on his tours.'

'Enough people brought their own food, didn't they?' Vince laughed. 'He was getting fat on all the sausage rolls and packets of Maltesers that went around.'

'But a few tables in here instead of front-facing seats, a tea urn, the beautiful views outside the windows. It'd be ideal, wouldn't it? If the weather was cold, or you didn't want wasps in your cupcakes.' Juliette grinned. 'You could see the countryside from the comfort of the bus.'

Charlie returned her friend's smile, her synapses pinging. She couldn't be a tour guide. She knew how to drive the bus, she had the right licence and kept up to date with her top-up training, but she hadn't done it every day for the last thirty years; she was inexperienced. But what she could do, almost with her eyes closed, was feed people. She could make cakes and pastries and scones that had customers squealing in pleasure and coming back for thirds.

And Gertie *was* cosy. With a bit more polish and a couple of personal touches, the bus could even look quite homely. It could be somewhere you'd enjoy spending time, and not just for a journey around the winding lanes of the Cotswolds.

'All right, love?' her dad asked, his eyebrows raised quiz-zically.

'Earth to Charlie!' Juliette snapped her fingers, and Marmite let out a tiny growl.

'I think I've got it,' Charlie murmured.

'Got what?' Vince asked.

A smile spread across her face. This might be the answer she had been looking for. If it worked, she would have to reward Juliette for the flash of inspiration, so bright that it was like a meteor sailing across the sky.

'I think I know what I'm going to do,' she said, patting the seat next to her. 'I think I've found a way to keep Gertie on the road.'

Chapter Two

'Have you completely lost it this time, Charlie?'

At least Bea Fishington wasn't one for mincing her words.

'I don't think so,' Charlie replied, following her from the kitchen into the main café, carrying a plate of freshly baked raspberry flapjacks. 'I think this could be a real turning point, for me and Gertie – and for you and The Café on the Hill.'

Bea folded her arms over her large chest, the silk of her cream blouse straining across it. 'Serving cakes on your uncle's bus? I know you're sad about losing him – completely understandable; he was a gentleman – but you're looking for harmony where there is none to be found.'

'I disagree,' Charlie said, sliding the flapjacks into place behind the glass counter. 'It would be a way to get this place known, to expand its range beyond these four walls.' She gestured to the smart, well-appointed café. The walls in question were slate grey, complemented by a black-and-white chequerboard floor. Accents around the room in lemon yellow and sky blue gave it a modern twist. There were high benches in the window and a mixture of squashy sofas and upright chairs, inviting lone workers with laptops, couples, large families and groups of friends.

Early in the morning on a dull Monday at the beginning of March it was quiet, with a couple of post-school-run mums drinking lattes and two men with grey hair sitting by the window sharing a toasted teacake.

Bea glared at her, but Charlie stood up straighter and refused to look away. She had a height advantage over Bea – over most other women, if she was honest – and a determination that had got her into trouble on more than one occasion. But she knew this was a good idea. The area around Cheltenham and Ross-on-Wye, England's glorious, green Cotswolds, was always hosting fairs, festivals and myriad other events, where a beautiful vintage bus selling cakes would be popular. Every time Charlie had moaned to Hal that she had nothing to do at the weekend, that Juliette was with Lawrence or Stuart was staying in London for some posh bankers' do, Hal would reel off a list of all the classic car shows and autumn fêtes and dog owners' carnivals that were happening, leaving her with no room to complain.

'I'm not after world domination,' Bea said, turning to the coffee machine. 'I know you're ambitious, Charlie. I could see that from the moment I met you, and I have no doubt that you'll be running your own café or catering empire before too long. But selling cakes from a bus? It sounds too tricky. How would you store ingredients, make drinks en masse?'

'People live on buses,' Charlie countered. 'They cook and shower and sleep on buses, so selling a few coffees and scones couldn't possibly be a problem.'

'You say that like you've not researched it at all.' Bea frothed the milk, pausing their conversation while a loud whooshing sound filled the space between them.

'That's what Google's for.' She grinned and shrugged, her smile falling when Bea didn't return it. 'I'm going to speak to Clive, one of my dad's friends, tomorrow. He's coming to give Gertie a once-over anyway, and he's refurbished a few buses, so he'll know exactly how I can get a coffee machine and a fridge installed on it.'

Bea handed Charlie a cappuccino, and she sprinkled it with chocolate dusting. 'Is it even laid out like a café?' she asked.

Charlie leaned against the counter and blew on her drink until a dent appeared in the thick froth. 'It's got front-facing seats. But I thought, to begin with, I could just serve from it. People can sit on the bus if they like, but I'll treat it like a takeaway food truck, just to see if it's possible. Then I can think about modifying it properly. The Café on the Hill could have an offshoot, like a cutting from a plant. The Café on the Bus. It has a nice ring to it, doesn't it? And you *know* the food will be good quality; I've never let you down in that respect, have I? Why not spread your wings? Give yourself some wheels, expand your horizons.'

'You have put so many mixed metaphors into that sentence, I don't know where to begin.'

'Begin by saying *yes*, Bea. Just to the Fair on the Field. People in Ross-on-Wye know your café. It's big enough to be a proper test, and small enough that if it all goes hideously wrong – which it won't,' Charlie added quickly – 'then your reputation won't be dented. One event, one chance.' She clasped her hands together in front of her.

'And you're definitely speaking to this Clive person tomorrow? There can be no cut corners with food hygiene or health and safety. Everything has to be done properly.'

'It will be,' Charlie said.

Bea's shoulders dropped, her lips curving into what could almost be considered a smile. 'I'll need to see plans. Exactly how it's going to work. Then I'll make a decision.'

'Of course,' Charlie said, nodding.

'And just the Fair on the Field. One gig, and we'll take it from there, OK?'

'OK. Absolutely. Thank you, Bea. You won't regret it.'

'I'd better not,' she muttered.

Charlie went to adjust the window display where one of her daffodils, lovingly crafted out of tissue paper and card, had drooped and was giving off a despondent air. Her pulse was racing. Serving cakes on Hal's bus, to the general population, at a public event. Somehow, in light of Bea's cold, logical reality, it seemed like the most ludicrous idea on the planet.

But people *did* live on buses. They travelled around in their portable houses, where they had all the mod cons. Some were even luxurious, like tiny five-star hotels. Surely fitting a few basic appliances wasn't too far beyond the realms of possibility? Well, she would find out tomorrow. She hoped that Clive would make it easy for her.

After not having been in Hal's garage for months, Charlie was back there for the second time in less than a week. Today, she had the sun at her back. It was a weak March sun that couldn't cut through the cold, but it was welcome nonetheless, as were the sounds of metal against metal and her dad chatting to Clive while he did something unfathomable to Gertie's engine.

Everything about today was an improvement on last time, except that Juliette wasn't here. She was all the way down in

Cornwall, with Lawrence, her cats and a sea view. Charlie would go and see her – of course she would. But she couldn't go now, not when she had the fire of possibility lighting her up.

Clive had assured her and Vince that Gertie wasn't destined for the scrapheap, and that he would be able to have her back to her best in a day or so. He'd also been more positive than Charlie could have hoped about the other alterations she wanted to make.

'So you really think it's possible?' she asked, when there was a lull in the conversation. 'Putting in a serving hatch and a coffee machine. A fridge, even?'

'Oh, it's doable,' Clive said, standing up. He was a short man with silver hair, ruddy cheeks and cheerful blue eyes. 'I can't get it perfect with your budget and timescales, but for the Fair on the Field it'll see you right.'

'Thank you,' Charlie said. 'And it's safe, is it? What you're going to do?'

Clive chuckled and tapped his spanner against his chin. 'It won't put her at risk of explosion if that's what you're worried about. Ideally, she'd need a generator and an extra water tank, some of the seats ripped out, but you can come to those if it's worth pursuing.'

'That's great!' Charlie did a little jump. Marmite barked and attacked her boot.

'Your mum's going places,' Vince said, picking up the Yorkipoo and rubbing his fur. 'Shame it's not Cornwall, though.' He gave Charlie a sideways glance.

'I'll go and see her,' Charlie protested. 'But the Fair on the Field is the perfect opportunity to test this idea out. I can visit Juliette anytime, and Cornwall will be nicer in the summer. Also, if I do it once the flat's sorted, I'll have more holiday money.'

'It's not gone through yet?' her dad asked, putting Marmite on the floor.

'Nope. We've got buyers, but God knows what Stuart's doing. I need to call the solicitor and see where we're up to.'

'It's a lot to be dealing with, love. Are you sure trying Gertie out for this café bus business is the best step right now? I was surprised that you even wanted to come and look at her so soon, and this new venture is going to be a lot of work. Don't you want a bit of breathing space? Coast along while you sort out the flat and let life . . . settle?'

'I can't let go of this idea now,' she said. 'It's in my head, and I'm going to be *un*settled and fidgety until I've tried it. One event, then I'll have some idea if it's worth more investment – of my time and, maybe, a bit more money. Besides, Bea might have changed her mind by tomorrow. I need to strike while the iron's hot.'

Vince looked at her for a long moment, then nodded. She could see the concern in his eyes, but she knew that he wouldn't push it.

Everyone dealt with loss in different ways. It wasn't great timing that her relationship with Stuart had imploded soon after her uncle had become ill, but at least it couldn't get much worse. And her biggest fear – or the one it was easiest to focus on, at least – Gertie and what would happen to her, was on the way to being solved. Her dad couldn't be against her revitalizing Hal's pride and joy. He was worried about her, but there was no need for him to be.

'Oh,' she said, 'I almost forgot. I brought snacks.' She dug in her bag and pulled out the box of orange and chocolate-chip muffins she'd made early that morning. Clive downed tools immediately. Marmite pawed at her legs, and she gave him a couple of puppy treats.

While they were eating, Charlie took her time to walk slowly around Gertie. Clive still needed to fix the panelling, but with the sunshine hitting her glossy cream paint and reaching through the windscreen to alight on the newly polished metalwork, the bus was looking a lot better. Almost like her old self.

And soon, she would be transformed again. The changes would be small, but significant. They would allow Charlie to give the Routemaster a brand-new lease of life. And everyone deserved a second chance.

As Clive and her dad gave her the thumbs-up for her muffins, she felt the first flutterings of excitement. This could be the start of something great, for her and for Gertie. When you're down, the best course of action is to get up, and aim higher than you've ever aimed before. Charlie Quilter had never been one for wallowing: she was going to prove to everyone just how bad at it she was.

Chapter Three

The Fair on the Field took place at the bottom of the hill on which Ross-on-Wye town centre proudly sat. It was a beautiful spot, with the River Wye wending along the bottom of the field, and the buildings of the town looking down on it from up high. When Charlie had phoned up to book a space, the organizers had assured her that, despite being close to the river, the ground was firm enough for Gertie; they'd had enough food trucks over the years and never had a problem. Even so, her pitch was at the edge closest to the road, where the ground was more solid. But it had rained heavily during the night, and while the sun was shining down on them now, as if the torrential downpour had never happened, Charlie could feel the wheels spinning as she navigated Gertie over the bumpy grass to her slot.

At least she knew how to drive the bus. Her time spent on the vintage Routemaster had started when she was little, Hal teaching her how to steer in car parks from his lap and, once she was old enough to legally drive, being patient with her about turning circles and visibility, how much space she needed to manoeuvre it into a tight spot. He'd encouraged her to take the bus driving test soon after she'd passed her car test with flying colours, and she was proud of her ability to keep the ride as smooth as possible, to not panic when faced with the narrowest of lanes.

'OK, Sal?' she called back into the bus, where Sally, The Café on the Hill's newest staff member, seventeen years old, and with a pile of caramel curls on top of her head, was sitting quietly.

'I'm fine,' she replied, her high voice rising further as they went over a large rut in the grass.

Charlie grinned. They had made it. Clive's hard work had paid off and now, with only the loss of a couple of downstairs seats, she had a small preparation area, and an under-the-counter fridge where she could keep chocolate éclairs and fresh cream cakes. She had made individual portions of Eton Mess and Key Lime pies, and a range of flapjacks, brownies and millionaire's shortbread. Clive had also installed a fresh-water tank. It was small, but it meant she could have a proper coffee machine with a milk frother.

Everything was fairly cramped, but that didn't matter because she wasn't going to invite people onto the bus. What remained of the downstairs seating was taken up with her trays of goodies, and one of the long windows was now a serving hatch. She could unclip it and pull it up, securing it inside the bus while she served through the opening, as with any other food truck. It was perfect.

Gertie was a half-cab Routemaster, with the traditional hobbit-sized door on the driver's side, used to climb into the cab, and the main doorway and stairs at the back of the bus. When Hal had given her a makeover a couple of years ago, he had made the cab accessible from inside the bus – he told Charlie he was getting too old to hoick himself over the wheel arch – and installed a tiny but functional toilet under the stairs. Clive had made Gertie as good as new and, with the extra additions, she had everything she needed, Charlie hoped, to work as a café bus. But this day would prove it either way; she was determined to make a success of it.

She slowed the bus down, and a young man in a fluorescent jacket waved her into position. Sally arranged the trays of bakes strategically around the serving hatch while Charlie jumped down from the bus and, registering nervously how spongy the grass was, slid her menu into the frame Clive had bolted on next to the opening. She was offering a selection of sweet and savoury treats, including a sausage roll with flaky pastry and a herby sausage-meat filling. Ideally they'd be served warm, but they tasted delicious cold as well.

'Ready to go?' she asked Sally, who was smoothing down her apron and staring at the sausage rolls as if they might bite. 'It doesn't open officially for another half an hour, but it may be that other traders will want a snack before the general public arrive.'

Sally had only been working at The Café on the Hill for two weeks, and behaved as if everything was a potential threat. Charlie knew she'd come out of her shell sooner or later, and thought that a day spent at a fair, where almost anything could happen, would be good for her.

'I've arranged all the cakes and pastries,' Sally said, giving Charlie a nervous smile.

'They look great. Shall we go and hang the banner up?'

She'd had it made at one of the local printer's; a beautiful sign in tarpaulin-weight material that would run the length of the vehicle, declaring it to be The Café on the Bus in burgundy writing on a cream background. Beneath it, in a forest-green font, it read: *An offshoot of The Café on the Hill.* It had brass-capped eyelets threaded through with thick chord, so she could attach it easily over the upper deck windows. Even Bea had widened her eyes appreciatively when she had showed her, rolling it out along the tabletops in the café.

She had also added a couple of photos of Gertie to The Café on the Hill's Instagram page, and had received 117 likes on the picture she'd posted yesterday. It needed work, but it was a solid start.

Now Charlie led the way up the narrow staircase, the metal rail cool under her hand, and passed one end of the banner to Sally.

'We're going to have to hang it out of that end window, and then I'm going to have to grab it and unroll it outside, going to each window in turn to get it running the whole length of the bus. So just hold on, OK?'

'OK,' Sally parroted back.

It was hard going. She had to lean her arms out of adjacent windows so she could hold it up and then unfurl it further, but after ten minutes of sweating and muttered swearing, she was tying her end of the banner firmly onto the window. It was the right way round. It wasn't upside down. Quietly triumphant, they rushed outside to look at their handiwork, and Charlie grinned. 'The Café on the Bus,' she declared. 'We are open for business!'

Within two minutes of the banner going up, she had a queue of five people looking eagerly up at her through the serving hatch.

'What's this, love,' said an old man with a flat cap pulled low over his eyes. 'Hal's old bus getting a new lease of life?'

'Absolutely,' she replied. 'He left it to me, and I'm giving it a fresh start as a food truck. What do you think?'

'I think my Daphne will miss the tours,' he said, accepting a sausage roll and a black coffee in a sturdy takeaway cup. Charlie hadn't had time to get them branded, but had picked out cream and green cups to tie in with the bus's colour scheme.

'Lots of people will,' Charlie admitted. 'Hal ran brilliant tours, but I can't do that.'

'Someone else could mebbe take them on, then,' he added thoughtfully, and bit into the sausage roll. He eyed it appraisingly, and then her, and then shrugged. 'Not sure it's meant to be a café bus, like.'

Charlie kept her smile fixed. 'I'm just giving it a go. This is our first outing together.' She patted the side of the bus, feeling like something out of a cheesy Sixties film.

'I say good luck to you,' called a tall man in a navy fleece from further back in the queue. 'Coffee out of a bus is a marvellous idea. Gives it a bit of individuality. You going to serve three-course dinners from your little window, too?'

'Oh, shush your mouth, Bill Withers,' said a bright-faced, plump lady Charlie recognized from the chemist's in town. 'This young lass is using her initiative. Would you rather the bus stayed locked away in a garage until it rusted to nothing? We all know Hal wouldn't have wanted that.'

'I just think it's hilarious,' Bill countered, while Charlie tried to serve and not let embarrassment overwhelm her. 'Serving food from Hal's old bus. Whatever next? Driving to work in the Indian takeaway?' He laughed a loud, unbridled laugh that had several people turning in their direction.

'Oh, don't mind him,' the woman said as she reached the front of the queue. 'He's so far stuck in the past he should

27

be wearing black and white.' She rolled her eyes, and this time Charlie's smile was genuine.

'It was only an idea,' she replied. 'Hal left me the bus, and I wanted to put it to good use, to have it out in the open, like you said. I'm a baker, so I thought I could combine the two.'

'And it's a *grand* idea,' her supporter said, accepting a slightly haphazard-looking Eton Mess that was living up a bit too well to its name – Charlie would have to do something to keep her puddings upright when they were driving across rough ground. 'You iron out a few . . . wrinkles, and it'll be a triumph. Don't listen to the naysayers. You do *you*, and let everyone else worry about themselves.'

'I will,' Charlie said. 'Thank you for the vote of confidence.'

The morning passed quickly, and Charlie had a constant stream of people buying coffees, flapjacks and Bakewell tarts, and the sausage-roll stock was depleting quickly. Music had started up from somewhere, and there were families and groups of friends, people with dogs on leads milling about the field. A falconry demonstration was taking place in the cordoned-off square they were calling the arena, and Charlie knew that, despite all the hustle and noise, Gertie stood out. She was taller than most of the other food trucks, striking with her cream and green paintwork and, if nothing else, word of mouth was doing its job regarding her cakes.

'What do you think, Sal?' she asked. 'Are you enjoying yourself?'

'It's great,' Sally squeaked. Charlie would have to work on her confidence once they were back in the café.

She turned to the hatch, her head full of strategies for female empowerment, and her smile fell. There, first in the queue, was Stuart Morstein. He looked effortlessly handsome in his jeans, white shirt and navy jacket, his light brown hair pushed away from his forehead. He grinned at Charlie, and her insides shrivelled.

'A cheese scone and a latte, thanks, Charlie. Can I have the scone buttered?'

'No problem,' she said, through lips that wouldn't work properly. What was he doing here? Was it something to do with their flat? If so, why hadn't he called her? The last time she had spoken to the solicitor she had said the sale was going through, they were just waiting on some final paperwork. It was a typically vague answer, and she should have gone to Stuart to begin with, but she was avoiding him at all possible costs. He was obviously not affording her the same courtesy.

'How's it going?' he asked, while Charlie frothed the milk and Sally buttered a scone and put it in a paper bag with a green napkin and some Parmesan crisps.

'Good, thanks,' she said, wondering where Annalise, her replacement, was. Charlie wouldn't be surprised to discover she was too proud to come to the countryside, and lived her life entirely in London or on holiday in the Maldives. At least, she thought as she gazed at the man who until four months ago had been her boyfriend, being in the bus meant she could look down on *him* for a change.

Sally handed her the bag. Charlie leant out of the hatch to pass Stuart his coffee and scone, and the bus lurched forwards. Charlie was thrown sideways, scalding latte covering her hand, her shoulder bashing against the window frame. Behind her, Sally screamed, and Stuart took a step backwards, his features contorting in alarm.

'Shit.' Charlie tried to right herself and the bus lurched again, this time sending up a thick spurt of mud from the front wheel onto Stuart's jeans.

'We're *sinking!*' Sally screamed. 'Is it a sinkhole? Oh my

29

God, oh my God, oh my God!' She ran through the bus and flew down the steps.

Charlie tried again to pull herself up and Gertie lurched for a third time, the front left-hand wheel sinking further into the mud. Stuart's latte cup was almost empty now, most of it dripping over Charlie's hand, and she had dropped the scone after lurch number two. Stuart was standing back, looking at her as if she'd turned into a monster, and he wasn't the only one.

A crowd had formed, and as Charlie scanned the faces of the people who were standing and staring, rather than helping, she saw that their expressions ranged between horror and glee.

After the third lurch the bus seemed to settle, and Charlie dragged herself to standing, which was difficult now that the ground below her was tilted.

'Jesus Christ, Charlie,' Stuart said, somewhat pompously, she thought. 'This bus is a death trap! Anyone could have been standing at the front.'

'The ground's too soft, that's all. And nobody would have got hurt even if they *had* been standing at the front. It hasn't rolled. It's just . . . sunk a bit.' She peered out of the hatch and looked at her submerged wheel. Would she be able to drive it out? Would anyone help with planks?

Her ex took a step closer, his hands on his hips. This was classic Stuart: he would rescue her, fix her calamities and errors of judgement like the wonderful, patient human being that he was, and expect her to be eternally grateful. Charlie narrowed her eyes, preparing to do the opposite of whatever he suggested, when there was a flapping sound and the banner, which they had secured so tightly at the beginning of the morning, came free of its restraints and fell towards the ground. Except that Stuart was in the way, so it landed, quite expertly, on top of him, as if he was a fire that needed extinguishing.

'For fuck's sake, Charlie!' came Stuart's muffled voice from somewhere beneath the banner. Even though Charlie's audience seemed less than approving of her, and poor Gertie was clearly wedged quite solidly in the mud, and this probably meant that her time running The Café on the Bus was already at an end – the shortest-lived career in history – Charlie started laughing. Once she'd started, she couldn't stop, tears of mirth pouring down her cheeks as she surveyed the carnage from the hatch window, trying to keep her footing on the lopsided floor. As Stuart emerged, flustered and fuming, Charlie hid inside her bus, where scones and flapjacks were scattered like autumn leaves, and the coffee machine was beginning to leak.

'Shit,' she said. 'Shitting hell.' The sight was sobering, and her laughter left her as suddenly as it had started.

She heard footsteps and looked up, prepared to brace herself against her ex-boyfriend's anger, and found another man standing in the doorway, his movements hesitant as he tried not to succumb to gravity and fall into her.

'Hello,' she said, wiping her eyes. 'How can I help?' In the circumstances, it was a ridiculous thing to say. She wasn't in a position to help anyone.

'Are you all right?' He had dark blond hair crafted into some sort of quiff, and was wearing a denim jacket over dark cords and a black T-shirt with a green logo on it. His skin looked impossibly smooth above the designer stubble, and his hazel eyes were warm.

'I'm OK,' she said, raising her arms hopelessly.

'I've had this happen before.' He edged forward and held

out his hand. 'Oliver Chase. I run The Marauding Mojito.' He gestured over his left shoulder. 'I've got experience of sinking, leaking, wasp swarms – you think it up, I've had it happen. But this is your first time?'

'First and last, I should think,' Charlie said, shaking his hand.

He gave her a gentle smile. 'No need to be so dramatic. First thing we need to do is get her upright. And I'd like to say I can help, but I'm a man, not a god. So . . . recovery?'

'I have a number in my phone.' Charlie walked hesitantly to the cab, holding onto anything she could, and took her phone out of the valuables box. She didn't know Oliver or The Marauding Mojito, but she was grateful for his calmness. Of course she would have made this decision on her own, but it was as if he'd sucked all her panic away.

He was peering out of the hatch towards the site of the submergence. Some of the crowd was still there, and Stuart was tersely dusting himself down, his ego more bruised than anything else. Charlie took a deep breath. It was a hiccup, nothing more. She could still do this.

And then there were more footsteps. She and Oliver both turned to see who else had come to help, and were met with a face that was very familiar to Charlie, and yet stormier than she had ever seen it.

Bea Fishington gripped onto the walls of the bus as if it was a sinking boat, still rocking violently.

'Oh Charlie,' she said, her expression a mixture of pity and distress, 'what on earth has happened here?'

Chapter Four

'A sabbatical? But I—'
  Bea held a hand up to shush her, picked one of the fallen sausage rolls off a seat, dusted it down and bit into it. Charlie glanced out of the window and was relieved to see that the crowd had mostly dispersed now the action seemed to be over. They were waiting for recovery to come and haul them out of the mud.

'My niece, Nora, is coming to stay with me over the summer,' Bea said. 'I know that's a way off, but I can train Sally up. She may be timid, but she's got baking experience and a willing attitude.'

'But you can't do without me,' Charlie replied, failing to keep the shock out of her voice.

'Charlie,' Bea sighed and lowered herself into a tilting seat, 'you're taking on too much. This would have been a good idea, I think, if you had been able to give more time and thought to its execution, but I'm just not sure you're capable of that at the moment. Losing Hal, breaking up with Stuart and having the responsibility of the bus, too. You're trying to run at a hundred miles an hour when, really, you should be slowing down.'

'I don't need to slow down,' Charlie said. 'I need to keep working, to stay busy and—'

'Sometimes we have to let other people decide what's best for us,' Bea cut in, 'and I am telling you to take a break. Come back to the café after the summer. Spend time looking for a new place to live, go and see Juliette or go and lie by a pool, somewhere hot. But stop thinking about work. Give yourself time to heal.'

Charlie opened her mouth to respond, but Bea's warning look said it all. Instead, she slumped into a chair and surveyed the destruction around her.

Most of her stock had fallen onto the floor, the coffee machine was broken and the fridge was making a strange whirring noise. She could hear people outside, shouting for other stalls to be moved out of the way in anticipation of the rescue truck's arrival.

She should be grateful that Bea was being so lenient, even if her appearance had made Oliver retreat so hastily that she could only offer a shouted 'thank you' as he hurried away. Stuart seemed to have stalked off to nurse his wounded pride, though she wasn't about to check. She would be happy if she never saw him again.

In the quiet that followed, Charlie thought back to their final argument. She had found out from Andrew, one of Stuart's friends, that her boyfriend had been cheating on her with Annalise, a sultry, dark-haired analyst who worked at the same bank as him in London. She hadn't confronted him immediately. She hadn't wanted to believe he'd been cheating.

She'd gone into Cheltenham and found a beautiful teapot shaped like a narwhal. In the midst of her worries, it had made her smile, so she'd bought it and taken it back to the flat. Stuart had told her it was hideous, and that she couldn't have it out on display while he was there. She had flipped, and it had all come spilling out. He hadn't seemed remotely sorry for betraying her, and he certainly hadn't uttered the 's' word. Stuart Morstein was the definition of unapologetic.

Charlie sighed. She felt weary all of a sudden. Maybe they were all right; Bea and her dad and Juliette. Some time away from it all would do her good. *Forget the mistake*, Hal had often said to her. *Remember the lesson*. Could that be what today's disaster was telling her? Get away from it all, change your perspective. Don't take on too much all at once.

She heard the beeps of the approaching tow truck, stood up as best she could on Gertie's off-centre floor, and went to greet the poor person who was going to have to pull them out of the mud.

'Oh goodness,' Juliette squeaked down the phone once Charlie had recounted the whole sorry incident to her. 'Please, *please* come. Stay for two weeks – four, six – whatever you want. We can go on boat tours and for fish and chips in Padstow, and take Marmite for long, character-building walks on the beach. You won't regret it – Porthgolow is the perfect place. It's so picturesque. And,' she added, laughing, 'it's Cornwall, so, you know, *full* of tourists. You could even do a recce, see if it's somewhere you think your café bus could work in the future.'

Charlie peered out of her bedroom window. It was her old room in her mum and dad's house, but it had been turned into a guest bedroom, with yellow-flocked wallpaper and a peacock blue vanity stand. Outside, her dad was walking slowly round the garden, on the phone to someone, a cigarette dangling from his fingers. Marmite trailed behind him, racing back on himself whenever he got too close to the smoke. Vince had only started smoking again since Hal had died, and she wondered if she could use her dog as a reason to guilt him into stopping again.

'Char?' Juliette prompted. 'What do you think?'

'The café bus was a disaster.'

'You were bound to have teething problems. Besides, they shouldn't do any kind of event on that field. It used to flood all the time. Gertie didn't stand a chance.'

'But she will in Porth-whatsit?'

'Porthgolow. We have all sorts of fairs and shows in Cornwall, and the variety of food trucks I've seen beats the Cotswolds hands down. But I've never seen a bus, so you'd be unique.'

'Gertie needs a lot of work. The stuff Clive did would have been OK for today if it hadn't been for the whole sinking issue, but if it's going to be a proper café bus, with tables and an oven and storage and a serving hatch, then it needs a full makeover.'

Charlie heard a chirrup down the phone and wondered whether it was Ray or Benton. She had only met the cats once – Ray a Siamese, Benton a white Persian – when she'd made the trip down to Juliette's old house in Newquay the previous year. She wondered if they'd mind a Yorkipoo invading their space.

'We can talk about Gertie when you're here,' Juliette said. 'How feasible, and expensive, all this conversion business is. Come and have a holiday. You've dealt with so much recently, Char. Losing Hal . . .'

'Losing my boyfriend and my uncle in quick succession, and being forced into a break by my boss because I'm too calamitous to be trusted?'

'You've also gained a bus,' Juliette added enthusiastically. 'But it can't be easy at the moment, and I'm not sure you've taken time to process it all. Come and dip your toes in our beautiful blue waters, soak up the salt and the spray. Rejuvenate, revitalize.'

'Do a whole load of yoga?' Charlie asked.

'The benefits are incredible,' Juliette pressed. 'You've never given it a chance.'

'I promise I will. This time.'

She heard Juliette's sharp breath. 'So you're coming, then? Soon?'

Charlie watched a couple of starlings wheeling in the grey sky. 'Yes,' she said, her stomach lurching at the suddenness of her decision. 'I'm coming. How does next week sound?'

She wasn't sure if the noise was one of the cats, or Juliette squeaking with delight.

'Next week sounds perfect. God, Charlie. I can't wait to introduce you to my beautiful village. You're going to fall in love with it, just like we have.'

Charlie hugged her mum and dad goodbye the following Monday morning. She was expecting an outpouring of emotion, but their smiles were warm and, she thought, a little on the smug side.

'Goodbye, darling.' She was swept into her mum's perfumed embrace.

'Take care, my girl,' her dad said, squeezing her shoulders. 'Of you and that dog and that bus. Are you sure you want to take it?'

Charlie turned to look at Hal's bus. *Her* bus. She had not survived her mud bath unscathed, and looked as bad as she had before Clive had worked his magic, if not worse. There was some scratching along the bumper where the tow truck had got hold of her, and the makeshift serving area had come away from the wall. Everything was dishevelled, splattered with dirt or coffee stains, broken or dented.

Charlie had vowed that she would fix her up, and do it properly this time. She had decided, at the last minute, that she would take her down to Cornwall instead of her old Golf. Juliette had told her that she needed time away from everything to think, but how could she make any decisions when she was in Cornwall and the bus was here, in the garage? If she had Gertie with her, then they could give it a second run, somewhere with beachside car parks and market squares with firm, unyielding concrete. She was sure there would be somewhere in Juliette's village where she could park a vintage bus.

'I'm going to take her,' she said confidently. 'I know it's a long drive, but we'll stop on the way. And it'll be worth it once we get there.'

'All right then, treasure. Be safe.'

'I will, Dad. And you look after yourselves. Don't do anything I wouldn't.'

As Charlie put Marmite in his crate, then lifted herself into the driver's seat, she wondered if her parents would be OK without her. Her dad was still so upset about Hal, and her mum did such a good job of appearing capable and brusque, she was worried they would circumnavigate their large house entirely separately, dealing with problems in their own ways. And, aside from everything else, without her to make tray bakes and muffins and Scotch eggs, what would they actually eat?

Charlie found the drive to Cornwall cathartic. She knew all Gertie's quirks, the slight catch of the gearbox and the way the left indicator stuck occasionally. The heater blew alternate hot and cold air for the first hour, and Marmite yowled plaintively about not being allowed to sit on her lap, but as she drove south the sun rose higher in the sky, white clouds puffed in attractive streaks across a pure, fresh day, and she began to relax.

The roads were busy with weekday traffic, salespeople's hatchbacks and trucks ferrying goods to destinations across the country. Gertie got several hoots, as she always did, and Charlie waved back, touched that people still took time to delight in the vintage bus and weren't entirely distracted by the miles of tarmac they were eating through.

They took a rest-stop at a farmhouse-style restaurant with benches outside, warped and dusty from years of soaking up the elements, and Charlie demolished a cheese toastie while Marmite ran in ever-decreasing circles and then fell asleep at her feet. Her senses were alive, as if anticipating all the new sights, sounds and feelings that would wash over her in the coming weeks; her brain had switched to holiday mode. But, she reminded herself, she was also hoping to give Gertie a second run. The café bus wasn't dead in the water just yet.

Porthgolow was on Cornwall's north coast, between Padstow and Newquay, where the most spectacular, wild coastline was. She'd never heard of the village until Juliette had moved there, and wondered if it had anything to set it apart, like the artists and culture in St Ives, the fish restaurants of Padstow or the surfing and nightlife in Newquay. She turned off the main road and wended her way carefully down narrow, hedge-lined lanes with fields and dotted farmhouses beyond. She could see the point where the world ended, a deep blue strip of sea cutting through the pale grey-blue of the hazy spring sky.

She reached a T-junction, peered at the road signs, and turned left when she realized the faded, weather-beaten sign read: *Porthgolow, half a mile*.

She drove slowly, the sea to her right, beyond only a few metres of cliff top. And then, suddenly, the village appeared below her, cut into a typical Cornish cove, houses rising steeply up the cliff that faced a sandy, crescent-moon beach. There was a stone jetty at the far side of the sand with buildings beyond, including a single, primrose-yellow house out on a jutting lower promontory. Charlie could imagine a large wave sweeping it off the cliff in a single, devastating moment. How did anyone survive out there?

A sleek black BMW shot out of a driveway on her right, and Charlie slammed on the brakes. As it disappeared down the steep incline ahead of her, without a honk or wave of thanks, she peered at the gap through which the car had come.

The walls were high and smart, made out of sandy brick, and an understated brass sign read: The Crystal Waters Spa Hotel. The building beyond had a glass-fronted entrance; two bay-tree lollipops with twisted stems stood either side of the doors. She could see all the way through to the glass walls at the back of what must be the reception area, the glint of water beyond. It was a perfect sea-view haven, built on top of the cliff. It looked exclusive and unattainable.

A horn sounded behind her and Charlie raised her foot off the brake, taking the steep road into Porthgolow at a snail's pace, her insides light with excitement at the thought of seeing her best friend. As she got closer to the heart of the village, she noticed that some of the buildings had considerable sea damage, their stone and paintwork battered and warped. She passed a small convenience store, the windows crammed with beach balls and nets for rock pooling. A local newspaper board advertised a *Ten-page spring events pull-out inside!* One of the houses on the front had a B&B sign swinging outside it, black lettering against a dirty-white background. A wooden board in one of the blind-covered windows announced they had vacancies.

At the bottom of the cliff, below the luxurious glass hotel, between the road and the sand, there was a patch of concrete with a couple of cars parked facing the beach. Charlie swung the bus onto it and brought it to a halt. Leaving Marmite sleeping in his crate, she went out to look at the charges. She had to read it twice before she realized that parking was free out of season. That was a bonus: she had anticipated paying a fortune to park Gertie until she found somewhere more permanent.

She stood, hand on hips, and surveyed her surroundings.

A woman and a young boy stood close to the waves, as if they hadn't quite committed to paddling. Otherwise, the beach was empty. Charlie did a slow circle, taking in the stone jetty glistening under the weak sun, the houses rising in layers of small, neat roads up the cliff. Juliette had said to her. '*We're one road back from the beach, a two-minute walk. We can see the sea from one corner of the garden.*' The road she had driven in on passed along the sea front and then rose, equally steeply, on the other side of the cove, travelling out of the village again and, no doubt, joining the main coastal route once more. A second road cut up the middle of the cliff, at right angles to the beach, straight through the houses. Charlie assumed it was this one that would take her to Juliette's place.

She leaned back to look up at The Crystal Waters Spa Hotel, but from her position could only see the very edge of the building, a hint of space-aged glass contrasting with the dark grey rock below it. She snapped a couple of photos on her phone, catching the glint of sun on the water, the spray as it hit the edge of the jetty. She would post them on her Instagram page, but what would the caption be? *Time for a new start.* Was that what this was?

She sighed, feeling unsettled. It was beautiful, as Juliette had told her it would be. It was quaint and picturesque; it had all the elements of a perfect seaside village. And it was still early in the year – of course it wouldn't be busy right now. She let Marmite out of his crate and took his lead, pulled out the handle of her wheelie suitcase and made sure that Gertie was secure, locking the door Hal had added so that the back of the bus wasn't permanently open.

As she followed the directions Juliette had given her to their terraced house, a seagull wheeled in the sky above her, letting out a plaintive, haunting cry, and Charlie landed on the word she'd been searching for. It was a word that took her back to that moment, in Hal's garage, when she'd first seen Gertie after her uncle's death. Forgotten.

Porthgolow looked forgotten.

Chapter Five

Charlie knocked on the navy front door of Juliette and Lawrence's terraced house and waited, inhaling the salty freshness of the sea air, feeling it whisper at her neck. It took only a few moments and then Lawrence was standing there, his eyes and smile widening at the same time. He flung his arms around her.

'Charlie, awesome to see you! We've been so looking forward to having you to stay.' It sounded over the top, even with Lawrence's soft, Scottish accent, but Charlie knew he wasn't being false – he was incapable of it. 'Come in, both of you.' He glanced at Marmite, asleep in Charlie's arms, then took her suitcase.

'Thanks so much for having me, L.' She followed him down a narrow hallway towards the back of the house, which opened up into an airy but modest kitchen and dining room. It was modern, with white walls and cupboards, and accents in lime green. A back door with a glass partition looked out onto a neat garden with a patio and a lawn edged with flowerbeds. Charlie wondered which corner the sea was visible from.

Lawrence put the kettle on. He was a compact man, with muscular arms and a slightly ruddy complexion, his hair a mess of dirty blond. His eyes were blue, and he was rarely without a smile. Charlie had thought, the moment Juliette introduced him to her, that they complemented each other perfectly: Juliette petite and dark, often reserved, and Lawrence happily chaotic.

'Tea or coffee? I know it's getting on for four, but we don't stand on ceremony in this house, so you can even have a glass of wine if you'd like.'

Charlie laughed. 'Coffee would be great, thanks. It's been a long drive.'

'I'll bet. Jules has nipped to the supermarket to get some stuff in, but I thought we could go to the pub tonight, anyway. Give you the Porthgolow tour. You can pop Marmite on a chair, by the way. Ray and Benton are in the front room, and I doubt they'll give him much trouble.'

'Thanks, but it's not them I'm worried about.'

'He's a mischief, is he? Looks like butter wouldn't melt.'

'That's because he's asleep,' Charlie said. She put Marmite gently on one of the dining-room chairs and gratefully accepted a mug of coffee. 'How's business going?'

Lawrence worked for a marquee company, Got it Covered, loaning out and putting up tents and marquees for events across Cornwall. He loved being outside, working with his hands, and had the physique to spend days wrestling temporary buildings into place.

'Ah, it's great,' he said. 'Every day there's something new to see, someone else to chat to, and it's a small company but we're doing pretty well, regardless. I can't think—'

'I'm home!'

'There she is.' Lawrence grinned.

Charlie raced down the corridor to meet her friend, who was straining under the weight of her bags. Charlie took them, passed them to Lawrence and then, when all the shopping was in the kitchen and Juliette had removed her coat, gave her friend a hug.

'You made it,' Juliette said. 'What do you think of Porthgolow?'

'It's lovely,' Charlie rushed. 'So pretty – the beach is gorgeous. And it's . . . nice that it's not too packed out with tourists.'

Lawrence made a choking sound, which Charlie realized was a stifled laugh.

'It's a bit tired in parts,' Juliette admitted, 'but it's a great place to live.'

'We've not been here during summer yet, Jules,' Lawrence said. 'It could be heaving, the roads constant gridlock. It could be a nightmare. Empty in winter, jam-packed in the summer.'

Charlie pictured the old-fashioned shop front and the other, weathered buildings. She tried to imagine it full of holidaymakers. The beach was beautiful, and it had a large enough car park, but it still had distinct ghost-town vibes.

'How are you?' Charlie asked, lifting Marmite onto her lap as they sat down. 'It's so good to be here.'

'This is the perfect place to recharge your batteries. You will not be disappointed, I promise.' Juliette took Lawrence's hand across the table.

'So what's the plan?' Charlie asked. 'I've left Gertie in the car park by the beach. I can't believe it's free – I thought beaches charged through the nose all year round.'

Juliette looked at her as if she'd started speaking Spanish.

'Jules?' Charlie laughed nervously. 'I'm not trying to be negative, I—'

'You bought *Gertie?*' Juliette hissed. 'Is this an April Fool's joke?'

'It's after midday.' Lawrence glanced at his watch. 'So technically it wouldn't count.'

'I thought that's what you wanted?' Charlie said. 'You said my café bus idea could work, but it needed more thought. There's no way we can do that with the bus stuck in Gloucestershire. What if we needed to measure the interior for appliances?'

'I meant more generally,' Juliette said. 'That this could be a chance for you to *relax*, Char, to let the ideas percolate. Not start working on some kind of café bus action plan.'

'What's wrong with an action plan?' she asked. Marmite lifted his head, his tail twitching as he took in the new surroundings.

Juliette sighed. 'Nothing is wrong with an action plan. I use them all the time for my marketing projects. It's only that I thought this could be a proper break for you. You've got your sabbatical, and I thought you were finally coming round to the idea of having an actual *holiday*.'

Charlie was about to respond when her dog jumped onto the table. 'Marmite, no!'

But Juliette reached over and scooped him into her arms. 'He's so gorgeous, Char. Small and fluffy, and funny.' Marmite wriggled in an endearing way. 'Ray and Benton will love him.'

'If he doesn't torment them. I should apologize now for whatever ridiculous hijinks my puppy gets up to.'

'That little mite can be forgiven anything,' Lawrence said, ruffling his fur.

'That is exactly the problem.'

They left for Porthgolow's pub early that evening. As they turned left at the end of the road, to head towards the seafront and The Seven Stars, Charlie's breath caught in her throat. The sun was hovering above the sea, the red, pink and peach of the sky intensely vivid. The whole of Porthgolow seemed trapped in its glow, as if the cliffs weren't grey but golden, the windows of the houses catching hold of the sunset like fireflies.

'Bloody hell,' Charlie said softly, faltering so that Marmite walked into her and started fighting with her boot buckle.

'I know,' Juliette breathed.

'It's fucking awesome, is what it is,' Lawrence finished. 'The best thing about living here.'

'Porthgolow means cove of illumination,' Juliette explained as they continued towards the pub, their steps slow and deliberate against the steep decline of the hill. 'There's something about this particular spot on the coast, the way the cliffs curve inwards like a hug, that means it holds the light in a certain way as the sun sets. It always looks spectacular in the evenings, even in winter.'

'It's stunning,' Charlie said. 'I know that sunlight usually shows up every flaw, but somehow, here, it hides the cracks. It makes this place look magical.'

'It *is* magical,' Juliette replied. 'You've only been here a few hours; you haven't seen it properly yet.'

'First impressions are important, though.' Charlie thought of the hours she had spent crafting the window displays in The Café on the Hill, hoping to entice visitors inside.

The Seven Stars was on the seafront at the south side of the cove, its dark stone façade camouflaged against the cliff.

Charlie saw again the strange yellow house beyond the jetty. In the sunset's glow it looked almost fluorescent, and she wondered what it was like inside, with all the rooms full of overpowering light.

'Here we are,' Lawrence said cheerfully as he held open the door, and Charlie followed Juliette in. In contrast to its dark exterior, the inside of the pub had cream walls and rustic wooden furniture, booths with seats covered in burnt-orange fabric. It was simple and welcoming, and Charlie could imagine long cosy evenings drinking wine by the fire, or the windows thrust open, walls reflecting the water in summer. There were a few people enjoying an early evening drink, and it might have been her imagination, but she thought that the volume of conversation dipped as they made their way to the bar. Juliette and Lawrence didn't seem to notice, so Charlie focused on the gleaming optics and the over-riding smell of cooking fish. She inhaled deeply, her stomach rumbling on cue.

'All right, Hugh?' Lawrence asked.

'Not too bad,' said the man behind the counter. He was tall and slender, his ears sticking out below dark hair that was receding on top. Charlie thought he must be in his early fifties. 'And who's this with you and Jules?'

'Hi.' She held out her hand, trying not to smile at his Cornish lilt. 'I'm Charlie, one of Juliette's friends.'

'My *best* friend,' Juliette corrected, slipping her arm through Charlie's. 'She's here for a few weeks, and we thought it was only fair to introduce her to your fisherman's pie.'

'Ooh, that sounds great. The smell is incredible.'

'Charlie's a cook – a baker,' Juliette continued.

'Oh?' Hugh's eyebrow went skywards. 'D'you work in a restaurant?'

'A café,' Charlie admitted. 'Is your fish pie fresh?'

Hugh grinned, and she silently berated herself. They were in Cornwall – literally on the seafront.

'It's a melting pot every evenin', whatever the catch brings in.'

'And Hugh's sauce – that's why it's so good!' Juliette added.

'It's not my sauce, technically, but . . . a family recipe.' He tapped the side of his nose.

'I can't wait to try it. I'm starving!'

They ordered a bottle of wine and took it to a booth, a few heads turning to watch them go. The window had small, thick panes, the glass old and warped so that the sun came through it in whorls of colour. Charlie unzipped her boots and wriggled her toes free, and Marmite, happy to explore beneath the table, pounced on them and chewed gently. She was used to it, and his teeth were still too small to cause any damage.

As Juliette poured the wine and they clinked glasses, contentment washed over her. She shouldn't be worrying about what Juliette's village looked like, or whether the people were all going to be as welcoming as Hugh. She was here to relax.

'This pub is lovely,' she said, sipping her wine. 'And clearly it has great food. I'm going to indulge in it all while I'm here – fish pie, wine, ice creams. I might have a couple of treatments in that posh spa on top of the hill.'

Juliette bristled, and Lawrence gave her a sideways glance.

'What?' Charlie asked.

'That place,' Juliette said, 'is a menace.'

Charlie frowned. 'How can a *place* be a menace?'

'Because it sits up there on the cliff top, catering for people who are prepared to pay three hundred pounds a night for sea-view rooms, God knows what in the restaurant and on spa treatments, and it doesn't serve Porthgolow at all. The rich people hurtle through the village in their oversized cars, and they don't use the beach or the shop or come in here. It's like they want Porthgolow's landscape and climate, but the thought of stepping outside that glass box and into the real world is too disgusting for them to bear.' Juliette took a breath, and then a large gulp of wine.

'Wow,' Charlie said. 'You're not a fan, then?' She remembered the BMW pushing out of the driveway ahead of her.

Lawrence laughed. 'Nope.'

'*None* of the villagers are,' Juliette continued. 'I've learnt all about it. It even has a private beach so the guests don't have to mingle with *normal* people. You'd think a business like that would want to help the local economy, use local suppliers, be a part of the village. It's hard enough being a newcomer in a tightknit place like this; you have to make an effort, not do everything you can to alienate yourself.'

Charlie chewed her lip. She hadn't heard Juliette get this worked up since their gym in Cheltenham had stopped running advanced yoga on a Thursday evening. 'What about the owners? Don't they come from the village?'

Juliette shrugged.

'Daniel Harper,' Lawrence confirmed. 'He lives here, a couple of roads back from ours, I think. But he's pretty much at the hotel all day. And it only opened a few years ago; he came here from Sussex or Surrey, somewhere like that. He's not born and bred Porthgolow.'

'You know him?'

'Bumped into him here and there,' Lawrence said vaguely.

Charlie shot him a perplexed look and Lawrence gave the smallest shake of his head.

The kitchen door thwacked open and Hugh approached, carrying steaming bowls of fish pie, and the tension was shattered as they soaked up the smell and the steam, the pies' potato tops perfectly golden and crunchy. A satisfied quiet fell over them as they dug in, blowing on their forks as if that would cool the contents instantly. Marmite scrabbled onto the seat, put his paw on Charlie's thigh and looked at her beseechingly. Charlie shook her head.

Hugh returned with bowls of peas, cauliflower and carrots. He laughed when he saw Marmite, and a couple of peas spilled off the dish before he'd put it down.

'Oh God,' Charlie said, 'I'm so sorry! I didn't even ask if dogs were allowed in here.'

'I would have said if they weren't,' Juliette mumbled through a mouthful of pie.

'It's a dog-friendly pub,' Hugh confirmed. 'I'd get hardly any custom if I banned four-legged friends. D'you want me to see if I've got any treats out back? He's clearly got FOMO.'

'That would be brilliant. Thanks, Hugh.' Charlie felt a flush of pleasure as he walked away. She hadn't even been here a day and already, it seemed, she was making friends.

After they'd scraped their bowls clean and finished hero-worshipping Hugh's pie, Lawrence nudged the conversation back to Gertie.

'Do you want me to take a look at her?' he asked. 'Juliette said that after the fair she's looking a bit banged up.'

Charlie sighed. 'I was far too slapdash about the whole project. I got the alterations rushed through, and I didn't stop to consider whether the Fair on the Field was the right place to launch the café bus. It wasn't fair on Gertie, or the customers.' She pictured Stuart fighting to rid himself of the banner, and then Oliver with his calm, concerned expression.

'But I had an email today. The sale on my and Stuart's flat is *finally* going through. I should get confirmation in the next couple of days. We had a bit of equity, so . . .'

'You want to put that into the bus, rather than a new place to live?' Juliette asked gently. She knew all the ins and outs of Charlie and Stuart's doomed relationship. 'What about a deposit on somewhere to rent?'

Charlie folded her arms. 'I can't live with Mum and Dad for much longer, and now I'm without a job for the next few months, I can spread my wings. Part of me thinks a fresh start, in every sense, would be best. But I know it's too soon to decide that,' she added when Juliette frowned. 'What I *do* know is that I can't sell Hal's bus. And if I can somehow combine my baking skills with bus tours, pitching up at festivals, then I would love to give it a go. I won't spend all the money on doing her up, but I think it's worth investing a bit and seeing what happens.'

'I know a guy in Newquay who converts old camper vans,' Lawrence said. 'He'll have a good idea about pimping her up, and I bet he's never done a double-decker before. He'd probably be thrilled to have it as a project.'

'Thanks, Lawrence. See, wasn't it a good idea bringing Gertie down here?' She grinned at Juliette, and her friend punched her on the arm. 'We could even—'

The door banged open, and Marmite leapt onto Charlie's lap and started barking. Juliette looked up, and as Lawrence turned in his seat and saw who had walked in, he let out a low 'Ooooh.'

'What is it?' Charlie asked. She followed Juliette's stern gaze, to where a man was resting both palms on the bar, leaning forward as if anxious to be served. The sleeves of his grey shirt were rolled up, revealing tanned forearms, and his dark hair was cut short around his neck. Standing patiently at his feet, tongue lolling out, was a sleek German shepherd. Charlie couldn't see the man's face, but there was something commanding about the way he stood.

'Hugh?' he called, his deep voice carrying. 'Hugh, are you there?'

Hugh bustled through from the kitchen, smiling when he saw who it was. 'Ah, Daniel, owaree?'

'Good, thanks,' Daniel replied. 'I don't have long, I just wondered if you knew anything about a bus that's parked in the beach car park? It's a vintage-style double-decker, but it's pretty shabby. I don't think it's been there long, but . . .' He sighed. 'I'm keen for it to be moved to somewhere more . . . appropriate. I'm worried somebody's dumped it there.'

Charlie flashed Juliette a look. 'Who is this joker?'

'That,' Juliette replied, 'if you haven't yet worked it out, is Daniel Harper. Esteemed owner of The Crystal Waters Spa Hotel. Isn't he charming?' Her voice was dripping with sarcasm, which was so unlike her that Charlie felt completely upended.

'I'm not sure, Daniel,' Hugh was saying. 'I hadn't noticed a bus, but I've been here all day. Mebbe . . .' His eyes slid towards their table.

Anyone could have made the deduction. A new face in the pub, an unexpected vehicle in the car park.

Daniel followed his gaze, and Charlie was pinioned to her seat by a pair of very dark, very direct eyes. She thought she saw Daniel flinch, but that might have been her imagination, or maybe she was the one who had reacted. Her cheeks burned. Her consternation at his unkind words about Gertie, his imperiousness and his direct stare, in a face that was, Charlie was just about capable of noticing, seriously, sternly handsome, all combined to make her feel even more at sea.

Daniel Harper turned fully to face their table, leaned against the bar and folded his arms across a wide, strong chest. His hair was slightly longer at the front, a curl of it softening the line of his forehead. 'Do you know anything about that bus?' he asked, without any hesitation, any introductions, or an ounce of embarrassment.

'Nice to meet you too,' Charlie said, finding her voice. 'Now, what is it that you think I can help you with?'

Chapter Six

'So you do know about the bus? Is it yours?' Daniel took a step towards their table, his dog following loyally, and Marmite's yelps increased in pitch. Daniel looked in alarm at the Yorkipoo, who was now pawing frantically at Charlie's jumper. It was not, she thought, the best way to start what was clearly going to be an uncomfortable conversation.

'Yes, it's mine. I'm Charlie, by the way.' She half stood, keeping a firm grip on Marmite, and held out her hand.

Daniel leaned forward and shook it, then stepped back again. He glanced at Lawrence and then Juliette, nodding briefly.

'Daniel,' Lawrence said, in a low, serious voice that sounded very unlike him.

'Hi,' Juliette mumbled.

'You were saying something to Hugh about me having to move it?' Charlie said. 'The car park is open to the public and free, unless I've read the signs wrong.'

'It doesn't look right there,' Daniel replied. 'I'm sorry, but it's true. It almost looks abandoned.'

'It doesn't look abandoned! I had an accident last week and she needs patching up, but Gertie is a beautiful bus and she's in very good condition, considering her age.' His lips twitched at her impassioned use of the bus's name, but she kept going. 'It's not like she's taking up space that would otherwise be occupied, and unless you've got a bus phobia then I can't see how it's causing you a problem.'

'It couldn't be parked outside wherever you're staying? For . . . how many days?'

Charlie rolled her eyes.

'She's staying with us,' Juliette said, putting her hand on Charlie's arm. 'And our road's far too narrow to park the bus. She's going to be here for at least a couple of weeks—'

'Probably longer,' Lawrence added.

'So that's good, isn't it?' Juliette beamed, and Daniel's eyebrows knitted together.

'There's nowhere else it can go?'

'I don't see why it has to,' Charlie said. 'Do you *own* the village? Are you the mayor or something? You certainly act like you're in charge.'

'No, of course not,' Daniel said. 'But my hotel is—'

'More important than anything else?'

Daniel folded his arms and stared at her. In the ensuing silence, his dog took a few steps forward, angling his nose up towards Marmite. Marmite whimpered and burrowed into Charlie's armpit.

'You're staying in Porthgolow for a few weeks?' he asked eventually.

'Possibly the whole summer,' Juliette replied for her.

'Great.' Daniel's gaze didn't leave Charlie's, and she knew

that she couldn't look away; she couldn't let him win.

'I'm really looking forward to getting to know everyone here,' Charlie told him.

'And I can't wait to see what the locals think of the bus.' Daniel's eyes shone. 'They're quite protective of their way of life. You'll find that out sooner rather than later.'

'Oh, I think I already have. Thanks for the lesson.' She smiled sweetly.

Daniel shook his head and sighed. He tugged on the German shepherd's lead just as Marmite inched forwards, his fear fading. 'Nice to meet you, Charlie. Lawrence, Juliette.' He nodded a brief goodbye and led his dog away.

'See what I mean?' Juliette said, once the door had closed behind Daniel. 'He is selfish, obsessed with that hotel and completely uncaring.' She folded her arms, and Lawrence reached over and squeezed her hand.

Charlie sipped her drink. Her friend was so mild-mannered and always saw the good in people, so for her to be so vehemently against Daniel was unusual. He certainly hadn't endeared himself to Charlie, but he hadn't come across as a monster, either. He was obviously passionate about his hotel, and confident to the point of arrogance, but she had seen amusement and intelligence in his eyes, and couldn't believe he was entirely thoughtless. She was sure there was something more personal to Juliette's dislike of him – something that she was reluctant to share. She wondered how she could tease the answer out of her.

'So, back to Gertie,' Juliette said, topping up their glasses. 'When do we start work on her?'

It was a week later and Gertie was gone from the car park.

Charlie walked down the hill with Marmite, the sun almost

absent today, just a weak pulse behind rolling clouds as if it was trying to push open a heavy door. She glanced up at Crystal Waters, and wondered if Daniel had thrown himself a party when she'd driven Gertie out of Porthgolow. Then again, from what little she'd seen, he didn't seem like the partying kind. He'd more likely poured himself a large whisky in his walnut-panelled office and thrown fish chum to the sharks swimming in the glass tank underneath the floor. Charlie shook her head to clear the image; she'd been watching too many Bond films with Lawrence and Juliette.

But Gertie wasn't gone because of what Daniel had said in the pub, or because he'd subsequently pulled strings with some Cornwall government cronies. Gertie was gone because Lawrence's friend, Pete, who ran a surfing supplies shop in Newquay and refurbished camper vans in his spare time, had taken on Charlie's project with gusto. He had listened to her and Juliette's ideas in a hipster café overlooking Newquay sands while they drank coffee out of Kilner jars, and turned around the plans within a couple of days.

His realization of her ideas was amazing, and Charlie had been in a perpetual state of excitement ever since, picturing the tables with cup-holders built in, so that Charlie could drive the bus with customers on it but without fear of spillage; the scarlet and royal-blue seat covers, the kitchen area downstairs complete with sink, fridge and compact oven; a built-in coffee machine that would have no chance of slipping off the counter. The plans were as breathtaking as the price of the renovations, but once Charlie had heard them, she couldn't imagine anything less for Gertie.

The sale of the flat had gone through, and she'd been able to put down the deposit for the work. Now Gertie had gone to stay in Pete's workshop for the next month, to be gutted and rebuilt, with the necessary water tanks and generators, everything plumbed in, fixed and decorated. Charlie was looking forward to the final result with a heady mix of excitement and extreme nerves. At the same time she had been applying for her food handlers permit and her trading consent. Her food hygiene was up to date from working in The Café on the Hill, and even though she had concerns – mainly from the reactions of some of the locals – that she wouldn't be welcome in Porthgolow, Cornwall Council seemed happy for her to have a pitch on the hard-packed sand at the top of the beach. Charlie couldn't help but wonder if that was because, even in their eyes, the village needed livening up.

She pushed open the door of the Porthgolow Pop-In, the general store which, beyond the milk, bread and newspapers, was a treasure trove of weird and wonderful objects. Myrtle Gordon looked up from the Jackie Collins paperback she was reading, her glasses low on her nose.

'Hi Myrtle,' Charlie called tentatively.

'Your dog, 'ees not peeing on my paintwork, is 'ee?' she called. 'If 'ee is, you can pay for it.'

Charlie felt herself blush. 'He won't, he's just been— he'll be fine.'

'Good to know,' Myrtle replied coldly, and went back to her book.

Charlie walked down the narrow aisles, marvelling at the Matchbox tin cars, the intricately designed thimbles and the Houdini-themed playing cards that looked as if they'd been there for at least thirty years. *Antiques Roadshow* would have a field day in here, she realized, as she picked up a figurine of a ballet dancer. It was heavy, possibly pewter, and she wondered who would want it as a souvenir of their time in a Cornish village. Not that she had the nerve to ask Myrtle about her shop-stocking policy. It was clear that the older woman wasn't a fan of newcomers to the village. Or, at least, not a fan of her.

'What y'after?' Myrtle called, after a couple of minutes.

'Picking up some biscuits,' Charlie called back.

'Not down there. Over by the tea and coffee.'

Charlie was about to respond when the bell dinged and a young voice said, 'Morning Mrs Gordon.'

Myrtle's voice softened. 'Myttin da, Jonah. What can I help you with?'

Charlie had established, after a couple of confusing encounters, that "myttin da" meant good morning in Cornish.

'We need some more sun lotion,' Jonah said. 'Dad asked me to come and get it.'

'Next to the toilet paper.'

'Cheers. How are you anyway, Mrs Gordon?' Charlie thought Jonah sounded far too young to be asking such polite questions.

'Not too bad, cheel. And yourself?'

'I'm grand, thanks.'

Charlie peered around the corner of her aisle. Jonah, the cheel – or child, looked about eleven, with his blond hair spiky at the front, a bold yellow T-shirt and his legs, below shorts, as thin as sticks.

Jonah turned towards her and held his arm out. 'I'm Jonah. My mum and dad run SeaKing Safaris from the jetty. Nice to meet you. You're staying with Juliette and Lawrence, aren't you? It's your bus that's caused a stir, isn't it?'

'Wow. News travels fast here.' Charlie shook his hand.

'Bleedin' bus,' Myrtle muttered. 'What's it for, anyway? Driving grockles around?'

Charlie frowned.

'She means tourists,' Jonah said, grinning. 'We take the grockles out on the water, and you're going to drive them around in your bus.'

'Unless you are one,' Myrtle added, drumming her fingers on the table. 'Juliette said you were staying a few weeks. Tha' right? Not longer?'

'I'm going to see how it goes,' Charlie said, her palms suddenly slick with sweat. Why was everyone so keen for her to leave so quickly? So much for a relaxing holiday.

'What's your dog's name?' Jonah asked. 'He's a Yorkipoo isn't he? A cross between a Yorkshire terrier and a poodle.'

'That's right. He's called Marmite.'

'Great name,' Jonah said, laughing.

'Bleddy ridiculous if y'ask me,' Myrtle muttered. 'Dog and name.'

Charlie wondered if she really needed biscuits after all.

'You should come on one of our SeaKing trips, if you're staying for a while,' Jonah said. 'They're great fun, and you get to see all sorts of wildlife. Here's a card.' He turned back to the shop counter where Myrtle had a plastic stand full of local business cards and leaflets: The Eden Project, Land's End, Trebah Garden and SeaKing Safaris.

'I'd like that,' Charlie said, taking the card. It seemed Jonah knew how to ride above Myrtle's curtness. He might only be young, but she could learn a thing or two from him.

'We're not too busy during the week,' he added, not meeting her eye. 'But if you're desperate for a weekend slot, I'm sure we could fit you in then, too. Now that you're local.'

'Great. I'll check my calendar.'

Charlie waited while he paid for the sun cream and left, flashing her and Myrtle a winning smile as he closed the door behind him. She put her biscuits on the counter.

'Lovely lad, that one,' Myrtle said. 'Solid head on young shoulders.'

'Are the safaris any good?' Charlie blurted, shocked that she was suddenly being spoken to like an equal.

'Never bin,' Myrtle admitted. 'Don't particularly have sea legs, which isn't ideal, I know, living somewhere like here. But they've a good reputation. You should take 'im up on it. They could do with a few more customers.'

'I got that impression,' Charlie said quietly.

The weather had been typical for April; flashes of bright sunshine chased down by heavy rain showers that seemed to linger in the cove. Charlie had already been walking in the rain, sheltering inside a large orange mac, the hood pulled low, the plasticky fabric making her skin sweat. She loved watching the rain patter onto the sea, and had walked to the end of the jetty while the waves churned and broiled around it, the horizon a wavering line of charcoal.

It was understandable that the beach was quiet; it wasn't swimming weather, unless you were incredibly hardy, and while there was Myrtle's shop and the pub, a bed and breakfast and SeaKing Safaris, there was no ice-cream shack or café; nothing for families who wanted to spend a whole day on the sand and have the necessary amenities at hand.

'Aren't there any public toilets?' she asked, and Myrtle looked up from her book.

'Why? You caught short? I've one out back if you're desperate.'

'Oh no, I just . . . wondered.'

'There was a block at the edge of the car park,' she said, tapping her fingers against her lips. 'A while ago. But it got so run-down the council demolished it. No funds for a replacement, supposedly, despite a few of us makin' noise.

You'd think Mister High-and-Mighty in his sparklin' palace might have helped, but no such luck.'

'Daniel Harper, you mean?'

Myrtle wafted a hand in the vague direction of Crystal Waters. 'It's out of place, I reckon. All cold glass and metal in a simple seaside village. He could've gone to the Seychelles if he wanted to charge sky-high prices. Or Padstow. He's an outsider, knows nothin' about the place. I can see Porthgolow for what it is. Some areas could do with an update. But we're friendly enough,' Myrtle added, and Charlie tried not to snort. 'He's tarnishin' that reputation, turnin' it into a village of two halves. Anyway,' she said, tapping Charlie's hand. 'These your biscuits, then?'

Charlie nodded. Myrtle put her custard creams and bourbons in a brown paper bag, *Porthgolow Pop-In* stamped on the side. As she strolled back to Juliette's house, detouring to take Marmite onto the beach and throw a sea-smoothed stick for him over the damp sand, Charlie thought she might have made progress with Porthgolow's general-store owner. It seemed that – in a place where not all the locals were happy with an influx of new, younger residents – Daniel Harper was the ultimate enemy. And if even Juliette thought he was bad news, then there must be something to it.

Charlie blinked and gasped as a huge plume of sea spray hit her in the face.

'Whoa, that was a big one!' Paul called above the sound of the engine. He was steering and, on this breezy Wednesday morning, Charlie, Juliette and Jonah were the only passengers. Charlie needed to have a word with him about being business savvy. She had insisted on paying for her and Juliette's tickets, even though he had at first protested, saying she was

Juliette's friend and needed to be shown Porthgolow from the sea. But even then, the tour was in no way viable.

Hal, the kindest man she'd ever known, hadn't run his tour if there were less than eight customers, otherwise he wouldn't break even, let alone make a profit. Charlie couldn't imagine how much the fuel for this trip was costing, let alone Paul's time, the fact that he could be promoting his business instead of taking out a couple of residents – one of whom had already been on the tour – and his son. Juliette had also told her that Paul had recently had to get a part-time job as a courier – a time-consuming occupation in Cornwall – to supplement the income the Kerrs were getting from their main business. This seemed especially sad when the SeaKing Safaris experience was so brilliant; Charlie had seen seals, cormorants and razorbills, and even a pod of five dolphins that had swum alongside the boat for a while as if they were in some kind of Disney adventure.

Jonah hadn't held back, and she now knew more than she'd ever thought possible about common and bottlenose dolphins. Thousands of people would love this tour. Why weren't they coming? Charlie was sure it was mainly because they didn't know about it.

'Have you offered your marketing services to them?' Charlie asked Juliette out of the corner of her mouth.

'Yes,' Juliette hissed back. 'Paul and Amanda said they'd think about it, but I'm not sure they have the money at the moment. I've even offered mates' rates, but I can't go any lower because then I'd be losing out.'

'Vicious circle,' Charlie said, nodding. Juliette was a digital marketer, producing websites, social media plans and campaigns for small businesses. Charlie knew the jobs she liked best were working with people local to her, so she could meet face to face even if what she produced was online. Charlie could see already that several of the businesses in Porthgolow would benefit from Juliette's services; she just needed to find a magical pot of money to pay for it all.

'It's much bumpier at the front,' Jonah said as Charlie was hit with another face-full of water. 'This type of boat is called a RIB – Rigid Inflatable Boat, and because of the design, the bow cuts through the waves and it's light, too, so it sort of rides them.' He was leaning against the side of the boat, looking calm and authoritative in a blue waterproof coat, his lifejacket black and stylish as opposed to Charlie and Juliette's, which were the colour of road cones.

'Bumpy is fun!' Charlie said. And it was. Salt was good for the skin too, wasn't it? Loads of expensive products used sea salt. Perhaps after a day on the waves she would have a perfectly exfoliated, dewy complexion. Chance would be a fine thing.

Paul turned the RIB around, and Charlie took in the coastline, heading north towards Padstow, south towards Newquay, and then the cove of Porthgolow, cut out as if with a hole punch from the land. She could see the clusters of houses, the pale strip of the beach, the spray rising up as waves battered the rocks on either side. She also had an excellent view of Crystal Waters, which sat snugly against the cliff, its gardens running down to the very edge. She wondered how much work had gone into securing the foundations. There had obviously been no expense spared.

And then Charlie's gaze was drawn to the other side of the cove, and the little yellow hut.

Jonah must have followed her eye-line, because he said, 'That's Reenie's place. She's an old mermaid who lost her tail and has been cursed to live out her days in the sea-shanty cottage. She never speaks to anyone.'

'Jonah,' Paul called, 'don't talk rubbish!'

Charlie was taken aback. She had believed Jonah was a fountain of knowledge, gathering facts like pebbles. But he believed in *mermaids*?

'It's *true*,' Jonah protested.

'According to who?' his dad asked, steering the RIB towards the jetty.

Jonah dropped his head and shrugged. 'She's strange.'

'Eccentric, maybe,' Paul called. 'But that doesn't mean you have the right to make up stories about her.'

'Flora liked it!'

'Flora is six and obsessed with *The Little Mermaid*.' Paul laughed, giving Juliette and Charlie a good-humoured eye-roll.

'Well,' Jonah said, folding his arms. 'I've seen her, early in the morning and in the evening, standing on the edge of the cliff and signalling with some sort of light. I think she's communicating with her mermaid friends who are all still underwater. That's why she doesn't talk to anyone in the village.'

'Of course she does.' Paul lined the boat up against the jetty and waited for his son to jump onto the stone so he could throw him the rope. 'She talks to Myrtle, and she pops into The Seven Stars occasionally for a cheeky half. She's a normal, probably very lovely woman, who likes to keep to herself. Anyway,' he added, jumping onto the jetty and helping first Juliette, then Charlie, onto dry land. 'When have you been up early enough to see her winking her mermaid light at dawn?'

'There's a lot you don't know about me, Dad,' Jonah said, and stalked off towards the road.

Paul took his baseball cap off and ran his hand through salt-and-pepper hair. 'Don't know what to make of that one sometimes,' he admitted. 'Now, did you enjoy your tour? Anytime you want a repeat trip, just let me know. As you can see, the boats aren't exactly heaving.'

As they walked home, Juliette gave Charlie a pointed look. 'Don't say anything.'

'I wasn't going to say a word.' Charlie gave her friend a butter-wouldn't-melt smile, and felt her insides knot with excitement. Soon, her café bus would be ready, and she had decided – almost the first day she had arrived, if she was honest – that she was going to use it to bring life back to Porthgolow. She only hoped that the village residents – so far a mix of friendly and fearsome – would be on board with her idea.

Chapter Seven

Charlie breathed in the paint fumes and decided it was the most glorious smell in the world, because that smell was responsible for the miracle that was Gertie, gleaming like a precious jewel against the grey, oil-stained interior of the garage. So far it was just the base coat, but the vintage bus had gone from cream with forest-green accents to shiny, original, pillar-box red, and the difference it made was startling. She peered in through a window, smiling as she saw the new seating arrangement.

'Uh uh,' Pete said. 'I'm not done yet. When I'm done, you can look. Wouldn't want to ruin the grand unveiling, would you?'

'What if I hate it, though?' she asked.

Pete let out an incredulous laugh. 'You won't hate it.'

She grinned at him. She knew – from the peek she'd just allowed herself – that he was right.

'And what's all this, on the front?' She walked round to

where a winch had been attached, discreet but still notice-able, to the bumper.

'Comes as standard on all my designs,' Pete said, glancing at some paperwork on his chaotic desk. 'Cornwall is a sandy place, and even if you're not going to drive it onto the beach to sleep on it, it's a safety precaution.'

'I've actually got permission from the council to park it on the beach in Porthgolow. There's a long stretch above the tideline, and the sand is almost as hard as tarmac. Paul, one of the locals, who takes boats out, says it's perfectly safe for Gertie to live there.'

'But sand is unpredictable,' Pete said, waggling his pen. 'Many folks before you have found it invaluable, and it'll give you an extra sense of security. It's included, regardless. Top-notch design, top-notch health and safety.'

'Right then.' Charlie was oddly touched at Pete's concern for her and her bus, and certainly wasn't going to complain about having such a good piece of kit included. She had a sudden flashback to the Fair on the Field and shuddered. He was right: a winch could well come in handy.

'You're one hundred per cent sure about the name and colours?' Pete asked. 'Because a repaint will add a fair amount to the bill.'

She watched him ferreting through bits of paper, a calcu-lator and a spanner sticking out of the pockets of his jeans.

'I'm certain,' she said. 'Colours and name. Jules and I had a brainstorming session – even Lawrence got in on it. And now I've seen the gorgeous red paint on Gertie, I know it's perfect.'

'Right, then. Sorted. See you again at the end of the week?'

'You'll be done by then?' Charlie bit her lip, not daring to hope.

'Scheduled to finish a week today, as we agreed. But these progress checks are good for both of us. Not to mention seeing this guy.' He crouched, and Marmite scampered forward on his lead. Pete laughed as he was covered in puppy licks.

'It's looking brilliant, Pete,' she said when he and Marmite had finished their love-in.

'You wait until it's finished. It'll blow your mind.'

Once they'd said goodbye, Charlie stepped outside into a brisk, sunny day. Pete's garage was close to the sea, which gleamed invitingly in shades of cobalt and aquamarine, the waves nothing more than ruffles on the surface. Seagulls cawed overhead and there was a sweetness to the air that spoke of spring and sunshine and the bliss of the summer to come. And this summer was going to include one very special addition, launching on the May bank holiday weekend. She just hoped that Cornwall was ready for it.

Charlie spent Friday morning turning Juliette and Lawrence's kitchen into a cake factory. She had been working hard on tempting treats to delight her new customers, although the standard Cornish cream tea – with jam before cream, of course – would be the foundation of her menu. Today she was trying out scones with chocolate chips, a savoury version with red onion and cheddar, and a lightly spiced mix that she would serve with a cardamom and lime cream. But the kitchens in both The Café on the Hill and her parents' house were at least three times the size of Juliette's, and within an hour she had various bowls of mix and trays of cooling scones covering every surface.

Marmite, Ray and Benton had been shut in the front room with Juliette, who was working on the marketing for a new restaurant in Truro. Her dog had expressed his disappointment at not being allowed to help, but Charlie was glad of the freedom to make a complete mess all by herself. Her timer went off and she opened the oven door, a wave of heat hitting her face. She pulled the tray of choc-chip scones out, the chocolate bubbling in places, and searched for a surface to put them on.

The doorbell rang, and she heard Juliette call out that she'd get it. Charlie was wondering whether she could balance the tray on top of the mixer tap when she was distracted by the patter of tiny paws.

Marmite yelped as he skidded on the flour-strewn tiles.

'Marmite, no,' she said, raising the tray of scones above her head as he bounced up at her. And then Ray and Benton appeared. Ray leapt onto the table and dipped his paw into a bowl of spicy scone mix. 'Ray, please,' she said, 'you can't eat that.' She scooped the cat up with her free hand, his long Siamese body dangling limply like a soft toy. Benton started to lick the flour from the floor, and Marmite decided that playing with the Persian's tail was the most fun he could have, even though it had earned him a swipe or two already. 'Shit.' Charlie edged around the fight on the floor and made it to the corridor just as Juliette appeared.

'That was only the post, but I . . .' She stopped, her eyes widening as she took in the carnage, and then wordlessly took Ray out of Charlie's arms.

She leaned on the doorframe, her shoulders shaking.

'What?' Charlie asked. 'To create real culinary art requires great sacrifice.'

'You're sacrificing my kitchen?' Juliette managed, her laughter no longer silent.

'I'm not used to being so . . . contained.'

Juliette stared at her, then at Benton and Marmite tussling on the floor, and then at Ray, stalking off down the corridor, leaving floury paw prints in his wake. 'Charlie,' she said, 'you're about to open a café on a bus. I know you won't be baking from scratch there, but you can't get much more contained than that.'

This thought had been a constant niggle in Charlie's head. 'Fair point,' she replied.

'Anyway. Carry on. Marmite! Benton! This way.' Her voice was sharp, and the pets stopped their fight and skittered out of the kitchen. As Juliette left, giving Charlie a winning smile, she took a chocolate-chip scone from the tray. 'I'll let you know what I think.'

'Thank you,' Charlie called, and then turned back to survey the mess. She remembered one of Hal's mantras: *If you find yourself on a sticky wicket, just stop. Stop, breathe, take a moment to compose yourself and then try again. There is nothing that can't be overcome if you believe in yourself enough.* She did believe in herself, and she believed in her bus. She dusted off her floury hands, and got back to her baking.

On Saturday morning, with her friends' kitchen restored to its original beauty, Charlie, Juliette and Marmite headed purposefully out of the house. Charlie had set up social media accounts for her new business venture, but as Gertie had been approved a pitch on the beach, she thought it only right to approach the other business owners in the village face to face. Besides, there was nothing better than word of mouth, and she had already established that some of the locals were suspicious of her and her bus. Instagram wasn't going to help her build those bridges.

'You didn't have to come,' she said to Juliette as they made their way down the hill. It was a fresh day, the sea sparkling as it was whipped up by the wind, and Charlie was glad she'd worn a warm jumper. 'It's not like Porthgolow's huge.'

Juliette shrugged. 'Lawrence had to work at the last minute, and I could have stayed inside ruing our missed trip to Penzance, or I can come with you instead and be useful.'

'I'm sorry.'

'That's OK.' Juliette waved her concern away with a hand. 'We always knew he'd have to be flexible, and lots of the work is at weekends. Anyway, you can't tackle this whole place on your own.'

Charlie was about to reply when Amanda Kerr, Jonah's mum, intercepted them on the seafront.

'Hi girls,' she said, slightly out of breath. 'How are you?'

'Good thanks, Amanda.' Juliette replied. 'We were coming to see you, actually.' She glanced at Charlie to continue.

'We wanted to tell you about The Cornish Cream Tea Bus.' It was the first time she'd spoken the name aloud to someone other than Juliette, Lawrence or Pete.

Amanda frowned. 'What's that, then?'

'My bus,' Charlie continued, feeling a stab of uncertainty. 'The one I drove down in. It's getting a makeover, coming back to Porthgolow as The Cornish Cream Tea Bus. We thought, as a fellow business owner here, you should know about it. We're having a grand opening on the beach next weekend.'

'Based *here*?'

'For the time being,' Charlie said. 'I'll spend some time travelling round, but it'll be parked on the beach over the summer. Serving a selection of sweet and savoury treats, hot drinks—'

Amanda groaned and pushed her dark curls away from her face. 'So there'll be somewhere in the village we can buy a decent coffee? God. Hugh is a sweetheart, but he doesn't open until eleven and his machine makes some fancy kind of instant. You have no idea how many times I've come off the boat with numb fingers, dying for a hot, sweet latte. Jonah said you were an asset to the village, and he does go over the top, but on this occasion he might be right. Grand opening next Saturday? The Kerr family will be there, don't you worry.' She squeezed Charlie's shoulder and walked away.

Charlie waited until Amanda was out of earshot, then squealed and grabbed Juliette's hand, bouncing up and down so that Marmite got overexcited and wrapped himself up in his lead. 'She's coming! They all are! That's *five* people, Jules, even if Jem is only two. Let's split up. Which direction do you want to go in?'

Charlie wasn't surprised when Juliette said she would work her way round the south side of the village, towards the jetty and The Seven Stars. Charlie was a bit disappointed – she had been intrigued by Jonah's story, and had wanted to see Reenie for herself; though not because she believed for one second she was an ex-mermaid. Charlie didn't know that she *wasn't* a business owner, and it would surely be a courtesy to tell her about the village's new café.

But Charlie didn't think asking Juliette to have a civil conversation with Daniel was a recipe for success, and besides, Charlie might have been intrigued about Reenie, but she was equally keen to see Daniel again, not to mention the inside of his luxurious spa hotel.

The walk up Porthgolow's north cliff was calf-crunchingly steep, and by the time she had reached the top, there was a trickle of sweat running down her back. She'd also had to carry Marmite for the last bit because he'd started whining, and he was a lot heavier than he looked, especially when scaling such a severe hill.

She found a gate built into the stone wall and pushed it open. A chalky, golden path meandered through gravel interspersed with shrubs and herbs, and there were solar lights spaced along the paving slabs for when it got dark. It smelt fresh and aromatic, and Marmite scrabbled to be put down so he could investigate.

The path wound its way round to the sliding glass doors and the bay trees that Charlie had noticed on her journey into the village. She peered into the wide, polished foyer, and the doors opened. A woman stood behind the pale stone reception desk, her dark hair pulled into a neat ponytail, her high cheekbones expertly defined with pearlescent blusher. Their eyes met, and then the woman saw Marmite.

'No dogs allowed, I'm afraid,' she said. 'But you can tie him up outside.' Charlie saw a metal railing and a bowl of water. She spent a few minutes fussing over her dog, and then stepped inside The Crystal Waters Spa Hotel.

It was beyond luxurious, in natural, calming colours of pale stone, sage green and cobalt blue. There was an expansive curved sofa, and a low table that looked like a giant pebble. The wall opposite the main doors was also glass, looking out over more spruce garden, a sunken swimming pool and then the sea, shimmering invitingly beyond. Discreet screens flush with the walls played images of beautiful people having massages, lazing in the outdoor hot tub or smothered in mud masks, intermingled with close-ups of exquisitely delicate plates of food and sunsets over the water.

The floor looked like granite, pale grey with a hint of quartz gleaming through, except that in the centre of the space there was some kind of design. Gleaming golden stones were embedded in the rock, set in a concentric circle, their sizes decreasing towards the centre. It was like the reflection of a beautiful chandelier, though the room was lit by discreet spotlights set into the ceiling. Charlie was almost scared to take another step.

'How can I help you today?' the woman at reception asked. Her voice was as polished as her appearance, but Charlie detected a hint of a Cornish accent.

'I'm looking for Daniel Harper,' she said, forcing confidence into her voice.

'I'm afraid Daniel's not here. Is there anything I can help with?'

Charlie read her nametag: *Lauren Purview.*

'It's something I need to see Daniel about, if that's OK?'

Lauren gave her a friendly smile. 'Of course. He should be back within the next half an hour, if you'd like to wait? I can get you a coffee, or—'

'Could I have a look outside?' Charlie blurted.

'Certainly.' Lauren consulted the screen on her desk. 'We have nobody booked for the hot tub, so you're very welcome to look around this level of the gardens. Just use that door to the right of the seating.'

'Thank you.' Charlie did as she was told, and found herself standing beyond the glass, on yet another winding path.

None of the shrubs was tall – she imagined so they didn't block the view from reception – and the gravel was almost purple. She breathed in the fresh, buffeting air, the sea stretching ahead of her like a blue canvas. The path wound round to the right, to where the garden ended and a few steps led down to the tiled edge of the outdoor pool. The wind was too cutting for it to be comfortable, but even deserted it looked inviting. Mirroring the outdoor pool, beyond yet another glass wall, was an indoor pool. It was on a floor below the foyer, and from this viewpoint Charlie could see how the building had been expertly moulded into the cliff, using its various contours and levels. Inside, people lay on loungers, and she glimpsed the curved edge of a Jacuzzi.

She stepped back, not wanting to pry, and returned to the garden, spotting the hot tub Lauren had mentioned and that she'd seen in the pictures screened on the reception wall.

It was close to the edge of the cliff, and looked terrifying rather than relaxing. She edged forward and saw, to her relief, that beyond it the drop wasn't sheer, but a gentle slope down to a ledge a few feet below. Beyond that ledge, the ground fell steeply to the water. She decided, then, that she might be able to enjoy herself, perhaps with a glass of bubbly to calm her nerves, were she to win the lottery and convince Juliette to overcome her hatred of the hotel's owner and join her. She tiptoed forwards, wondering how scary the view was when you were actually *in* the hot tub.

'Hello.'

Charlie jumped and jolted forward. Her heart started pounding.

'Lauren said there was someone outside who wanted to see me, and I believe that must be you, seeing as you're the only person here.'

Charlie turned to find Daniel Harper, his dark eyes amused, arms folded over his chest, wearing a shirt the colour of cornflowers.

'I did – I do. This is a lovely spot.'

'There's nothing like it.'

Charlie wondered if, beyond the trace of mockery in his eyes, he was actually capable of smiling. 'And your guests don't find it . . . scary? Being so close to the edge?'

He peered down, his gaze following her pointing finger, as if he'd never seen the view before. 'I don't think so. I haven't had any complaints, and nobody's thrown themselves into the sea. So on the whole I'd say it was fine. But what can I do for you? I did wonder if you were still here; your bus has disappeared from the car park, which was absolutely the right thing to do. I'm glad that you—'

'It's coming back,' Charlie rushed. 'But to the beach this time. I'm launching it next weekend as The Cornish Cream Tea Bus.'

She watched his face closely.

'The Cornish Cream Tea Bus,' he repeated slowly. 'Is it for children?'

'It's for everyone.'

'It's staying in Porthgolow?' His eyes had lost their amusement.

'I'm going to travel round Cornwall, but I'm launching it here, and I won't be out and about the whole time. It's going to be a new feature of the village.'

'It will ruin the atmosphere.'

Laughter came spilling out of her. 'What atmosphere? It's as dead as a dodo, and we're only a week from the May bank holiday. This village needs livening up. It needs something bright and friendly and affordable to draw the crowds. It's such a beautiful place, but it's not being loved enough.'

'How would you know that?' Daniel's voice was sharp. 'You've only been here a few weeks.'

She hesitated. 'You can't deny that it's looking a bit tired.' She gestured in the direction of the cove, then gasped as she teetered off balance a mere ten feet from the cliff edge. 'Crystal Waters may be modern and glossy and immaculate, but you can't say the same for the pop-in and the B&B, or even Hugh's pub. Gertie is going to help bring Porthgolow back to life.'

Daniel rolled his eyes, which was the most expressive thing she'd seen him do. 'Gertie belongs in a fun fair.'

'We are going to go to fairs and festivals, but most of the time she'll be here. And before you go and check – ' she held up a finger, silencing him before he'd opened his mouth – 'I have got my trading consent. It's all legal, so you can't go looking for ways to shut me down.'

'I wasn't going to . . .' he started, then sighed. 'This is unexpected, OK? And it's not in keeping with Crystal Waters.'

'Why not? Because everyone who stays here is allergic to carbohydrates? I'm selling Cornish cream teas.'

'I guessed that.'

'And who can resist a good Cornish cream tea?' she continued. 'Hot, crumbly scones with thick, slightly sweet clotted cream and fresh strawberry jam. I'm going to do some flavoured creams with a hint of rose, lavender or honey. Earl Grey and Assam tea. All with those views of the cove, the way the sun curves into every crease of it.' Excitement bubbled inside her.

Daniel didn't reply immediately, and Charlie thought she'd won him over. He was staring out to sea, a wistful expression on his face. Eventually, he met her gaze.

'On a bus?'

'Not just any bus. The Cornish Cream Tea Bus. Gertie reborn. You have to come and see her, she's going to be magnificent!'

'Not sure I'd put the words "bus" and "magnificent" together in a sentence.'

'But you'll come?'

'I'll have to see how busy we are,' he said.

Charlie resisted the urge to do a fist pump. 'You'll be the quietest you've ever been, because all your guests will be down in the village, eating cream teas.'

Daniel shook his head slowly, as if dealing with a tiresome toddler, but a flicker of a smile dented his features. 'I very much doubt that.'

'At least follow me on Instagram.' She pulled her phone out of her pocket and scrolled to the app, where her new account, @CornishCreamTeaBus, had four photos: arty shots that she'd taken in the garage, of Gertie's headlights, showing off the glorious red paint, and a couple she'd snapped in Juliette's kitchen of her new scones. #OneWeekToGo and #CornishCreamTeaBusLaunch adorned her captions, and she'd spent a solid hour the previous evening following Cornwall and foodie-related accounts, including Crystal Waters which, she had to admit, had a stunning grid.

She felt warm breath on her cheek, and turned her head slightly. Daniel was looking over her shoulder, close enough that she could see each individual eyelash. She willed her heart to stop pounding. Chances were, he could hear how fast it was going.

'What do you think?' she asked.

'Your photos are good,' he admitted. 'The bus is red now?'

'Back to her original colour. I thought it would stand out more.'

'It almost matches your hair.'

It was a throwaway comment, but the fact that he was telling her he'd noticed her appearance made her insides flutter.

'Do you follow Porthgolow Hideaway?' she asked, tapping it into the search bar and holding up the page for Daniel to see. 'I found it last night, and I wondered who was behind it.' It was a page dedicated to pictures of the village: stunning sunsets and sunrises, the sea and sky in every conceivable mood – stormy, calm, wild and vibrant. It highlighted the very best of Porthgolow, each picture charming or atmospheric. And it had over twenty thousand followers.

'I follow it,' he said. 'But I've no idea who's taking the photos. I don't have time to be a social media spy, but if you do, then go ahead, and let me know when you find out. I might be able to set up some kind of partnership with them.'

'You want me to do all the work so you can have all the glory?'

'I get to *pay* for all the glory. That's how a partnership works.'

Charlie gritted her teeth and stared at the sea, telling herself to calm down. She turned to find him busy on his own phone, and a moment later a notification appeared on her screen: @*CrystalWatersCornwall started following you*.

'Thank you,' she said grudgingly.

'How did you get the villagers to agree to this, anyway?'

'What do you mean, get them to agree? I want the community onside, but I didn't realise that I needed them to give me permission.' Charlie frowned. 'Paul Kerr was the one who suggested the beach would be the best place to park, and the council have agreed to my pitch and given me my trading consent. And as for everyone else, that's what today is about. Letting the locals know my plans, and telling them about the launch. I'm not sure what else I can do.'

Daniel slid his phone in his pocket and grinned at her. Charlie couldn't believe how much it lit up his face. His eyes were no longer suspicious and calculating, but he still looked wolfish; he was still completely sure of himself. 'What about Myrtle? She's going to be at the front of the queue on Saturday, is she?'

Charlie sighed. 'Not everyone's convinced yet, but it's only a matter of time. Once the bus is here, once people can sample what I'm selling, they'll be smitten.'

'I can almost believe that,' Daniel said. 'Still, Porthgolow can be a tough crowd—'

'Says the man who just told me my bus belongs in a fun fair.'

'I'm prepared to defer my judgement.'

'How very gracious of you.'

Daniel laughed. 'Fancy a tour of the hotel? I could show you the spa facilities, the restaurant. We have a five-course à la carte menu.'

'Sometimes people just want a bit of stodgy, sugary cake.'

'And sometimes,' he said, stepping closer, 'they want something more extravagant. Sometimes they want the best.'

'I am the best.' Charlie lifted her chin in defiance, and immediately felt stupid. What was this? A pre-boxing-match showdown? She waited for Daniel's pithy reply but it didn't come. He looked at her coolly and then turned away.

'I need to get on,' he called as he walked. 'Is there anything else I can do for you?'

'Uhm, not at the moment. Thanks.' She followed him back through the beautiful gardens and into the foyer, where he promptly said goodbye and disappeared through a door behind the reception desk.

Charlie said goodbye to Lauren and went to find Marmite. As she made her way down the hill, a snoozing puppy in her arms, all in all she felt relieved with the way her visit had gone.

It was understandable that Daniel was sceptical about the charms of The Cornish Cream Tea Bus; it wasn't anything like his slice of cliff-top luxury. But he hadn't turned her away. He'd said her photos were good and he'd followed her on Instagram; he hadn't discounted coming to the launch on Saturday.

As she reached the bottom of the hill, eager to see how Juliette had got on, she wondered why Daniel's approval mattered to her so much. Did she want to show Juliette that he wasn't as evil as she thought he was, or was it simply that he had been against her bus from the start, and she wanted to prove him wrong? All she knew was that standing close to the edge of the cliff, at the same time as standing close to Daniel, had done nothing for her levels of composure.

Chapter Eight

Charlie stood on the end of Porthgolow's jetty, looking back at the village that, in the last few weeks, had become her home. She didn't know for how long – Juliette had told her she could stay as long as she liked – but she knew she wasn't ready to go back to Ross-on-Wye, or her parents' house. She crouched alongside Marmite, who was peering over the edge of the jetty, and looked at the sea spilling out in every direction. Porthgolow's quaint, haphazard vista was behind her, Reenie's yellow hut to her left, Daniel's shimmering empire at her right side.

Soon, there would be a new addition to the landscape. She was picking Gertie up later that day. Her Cornish Cream Tea Bus was finished, and she had heard the pride in Pete's voice when he'd called to tell her it was ready. She couldn't wait to see it. But Lawrence was working and Juliette had a meeting, and she needed one of them to drive her to the garage, so she would have to be patient.

She stood up and tugged gently on Marmite's lead, and a flash of light caught her attention. A short woman was standing in front of the primrose-yellow cottage, long dark hair straggling out behind her. She was holding something, and it was that object that had caught the light. Charlie couldn't see what it was from this distance, but she found herself raising a hand in greeting. She held her breath, and watched as Reenie's arm rose into the air, mirroring Charlie's gesture. Then she turned and, in a moment, had disappeared inside her precarious little house.

Charlie made her way back to Juliette's with a spring in her step.

'A wave,' she said to her friend as they hefted tins of scones and cookies, cakes and doughnuts first into Lawrence's arms and then their own, and walked out into the fresh air. 'An actual wave. It reminded me a bit of the perplexed greeting Tom Hanks gives Meg Ryan at the end of *Sleepless in Seattle*.'

'I think Reenie's more *Castaway* than *Sleepless*,' Juliette said, grimacing under the weight of her boxes. 'But a wave's more than I got. I think she was pretending not to be in when I tried to talk to her the other day, which was a bit harsh considering her place isn't the easiest to get to. There's not a path all the way, you have to navigate over rocks, and if it's damp they can be treacherous.'

'Has anyone ever seen her leave the house?' Lawrence asked. 'Seen her in the pub or the shop or anywhere?'

They reached the bottom of the hill and Lawrence's question was forgotten as Gertie, in her new, Cornish-Cream-Tea-Bus glory, came into view.

The three of them paused to gaze at her.

The day of the grand opening was calm, hardly any wind

to whip the waves into a fervour, but the cloud cover was thicker than Charlie would have liked. There was a break over the horizon, where opaque rays spilled out and raced down to meet the sea's surface. Charlie's dad called them the fingers of God, though he wasn't remotely religious. But at this point, with the still, blue water, the cliffs rising up either side, and Gertie, resplendent in her new red coat and gleaming with possibility on the sand, it did seem almost magical.

'Let's stock her up, then, shall we?' Lawrence grinned and, despite his boxes, managed to give Hugh, who had appeared at the door of The Seven Stars, a quick wave. 'Coming to have a look, Hugh?'

'Of course,' the landlord replied. 'I've held off having coffee so I can sample some of Charlie's, along with a slice of carrot cake, if there's any?'

'Carrot cake is here somewhere,' Charlie said, raising her stack of boxes. 'Give us ten minutes to set up and I'll give you the grand tour.'

'I'll be over dreckly,' he called.

She resisted the urge to hug Hugh, and wondered if his enthusiasm would spread through the village. Her chat with Myrtle had been chilly to say the least, and the young woman who had answered the door of the bed and breakfast seemed distracted and uninterested. Charlie had been left sleepless the night before, imagining her and Gertie sitting, deserted, on the beach, while villagers passed by as if she didn't exist.

But being here, seeing the bus in situ, and with her arms full of fresh cakes, her worries seemed laughable.

The inside of Gertie was as impressive as her exterior. As Charlie unlocked the door she was delighted all over again by the transformation. On the lower deck, at the end where customers got on, there were four tables. The benches were padded with red fabric on one side, blue on the other, and the cream tables had elegantly curved edges. The walls had been repainted in fresh, bright cream, and the light from the large windows added to the airy feel.

Beyond the tables was Charlie's kitchen. It had a countertop and sink, with a small oven below for heating up scones and sausage rolls, and a fridge for storing perishables. Next to the driver's cab there was a shiny new coffee machine, with mugs in red and blue stacked up alongside it. The bottoms of the mugs perfectly fitted the cup-holders in the tables, and they had plastic lids that could be used when the bus was moving.

Around the roof of the lower deck, and again on the upper, were glowing, LED fairy lights. With wall space at a premium, Charlie had wanted something special for when the days were dull and the sun failed to shine brightly.

'Just beautiful,' Juliette murmured, as they placed their cake boxes on the counter. Charlie started up the coffee machine, checked the filter was full of beans, ran the tap in the sink and switched the oven on. She still marvelled at how all these mod cons could work on her uncle's bus as easily as if she was in a house.

'Check upstairs?' Juliette asked.

'You go,' Charlie said. 'I want to make sure everything's ready here. Can you fill the vases?' They had bought clutches of red carnations and vibrant cornflowers, perfect for the vases that slotted into the circular cut-outs in the middle of each table. Their primary role was for teapots – the teapots themselves designed specially so they would fit snugly in – but when people didn't want a whole pot, or wanted coffee or a cold drink, a spray of flowers would brighten up the tables.

Between them, they had thought of everything. Pete had

improved the tiny toilet behind the stairs, had ensured the layout on the top deck – where the majority of customers would sit – had as much seating as possible without it seeming crowded. Marmite had his own crate below the driver's seat in the cab, so when Charlie brought him on board he wouldn't stray into the kitchen. An old-style bell-pull had been installed – replacing the more modern buttons – so that guests could get Charlie's attention from anywhere on the bus.

She had even got an old-fashioned ticket machine so that customers could go away with a reminder of their visit on board The Cornish Cream Tea Bus. It had been an expensive renovation, but worth every penny. Now all she had to do was make a success of it.

She began snapping photos, adding them to her Instagram story, all with her custom hashtag: #CornishCreamTea BusLaunch. She arranged the cakes and scones and took photos of them on their stands, snapped an arty shot of the sea out of the windscreen, and another of the row of gleaming mugs stacked on top of the coffee machine. She had two different tea options on her menu: one was simply scones, cream and jam – the traditional Cornish cream tea – and one that was more like a full afternoon tea, with sandwiches to start, mini cakes and puddings, and then the scones to finish.

'Hello?' a voice called, as she was putting the cheddar and red onion scones in the oven to heat up. 'Can we come aboard?'

Charlie recognized the woman, who had platinum hair cinched in waves around her face, from the bed and breakfast. She had obviously been paying more attention than Charlie had thought. She was accompanied by a man whose skin was as dark as hers was pale, his deep brown eyes warm with kindness.

'Of course,' she said. 'Welcome to The Cornish Cream Tea Bus. Take a seat, either down here, or there's lots of space upstairs. I'll come and take your order in a moment.'

The woman looked around approvingly. 'I must say, it looks wonderful.'

'Thank you,' Charlie beamed. 'I'm very happy with it.'

'Almost puts our dining room to shame,' the man added, reaching up and pulling on the cord running round the top of the windows. A clear bell sounded, and he laughed even as he apologized. 'I'm sorry, I couldn't resist. I haven't seen one of these in years.'

Charlie waved away his apology. 'It's very tempting to pull it – I'm going to have to get used to false alarms. Maybe I need a sign explaining what the cord is for.'

'It's so nostalgic,' the woman added. 'What made you want to do this? A café on a bus?'

Charlie leaned against the counter. 'The bus was my uncle's. He ran tours on it, but he died earlier this year. He left me Gertie – the bus – and I'm a baker, so while I was happy to have it, I knew I couldn't just take over from him. But cakes, afternoon tea . . . I thought I could combine the two.'

'It's ingenuous,' the man said. 'We went for a traditional style for the B&B, but after four years . . . well, I wonder if we need some sort of overhaul?' He looked at his wife. 'Do something a bit different?'

She nodded, her smile slipping. 'We haven't even intro-duced ourselves. I'm Stella, and this is Anton. You're staying with Juliette, aren't you?'

'That's right. I'm Charlie. Juliette invited me here for a holiday. This . . .' She spread her arms wide, laughing self-consciously. 'I'm not that great at taking time off, and I can always drive the bus home again. But I thought that, while

I'm here, Porthgolow could do with a bit of brightening up.'

The vigorous nods from Stella and Anton suggested that they agreed with her.

An hour later and Gertie was a hive of activity. Paul and Amanda had brought Jonah, and their two daughters Flora and Jem, and had commandeered one of the tables downstairs, which meant that every time a new customer appeared, Jonah was able to regale them with facts about the bus – both what Charlie had told him after extensive interrogation, and what he already seemed to have in his young, encyclopaedic mind. Charlie and Juliette tried not to giggle while they frothed cappuccinos and prepared cream teas. Even though it was only half past ten, her signature Cornish cream tea was destined to be the most popular item on the menu.

'You know,' Juliette whispered, as she filled a stoneware pot with clotted cream and cut a warm fruit scone in half, 'I was a bit sceptical when you said you wanted this part of the bus to be open to customers, but it's perfect. You can prepare the teas and chat to people at the same time.'

'And listen to Jonah?' Charlie said. 'I wonder if I should pay him to come round with me. He's certainly livening things up.'

'And then, what you have to realize,' Jonah was saying to an older couple Charlie had seen a few times in Myrtle's pop-in, 'is that the new Routemaster buses in London only started again in 2012, after Boris Johnson held a design competition. This bus is from the Fifties or Sixties.'

'Nineteen sixty-four,' Charlie called. 'That's when this one was made.'

Jonah beamed, but the couple looked flummoxed by the information overload.

'We'd love a couple of those delicious-looking pastries, please, love,' the old lady said, pointing to Charlie's cannoli. They were a mixture of lemon and hazelnut cream.

Jonah took her change of tack in his stride. 'Of course, there's lots of seating upstairs, if you'd prefer that?'

The man and woman exchanged a glance and decided that yes, they would like to sit upstairs.

'Can I show them, Charlie?' Jonah asked.

'Of course.' She handed him a pad and pen. 'Would you like to find out what drinks they want, too? And whether they want lemon or hazelnut cannoli?'

'No problem!' he grabbed the notepad, ran back to the stairs and paused, waiting for the older couple to follow him.

'You,' Juliette said, 'are shameless. You're definitely going to have to pay him now.'

'I think Charlie's got the measure of him perfectly,' Amanda called, grinning over the top of her latte. Flora, who was six and, as far as Charlie had seen, pretty but incredibly quiet, gave her a sweet smile and hugged her Cabbage Patch doll tighter. Charlie thought they had disappeared in the Eighties, but maybe today was destined to be steeped in nostalgia?

The rush continued up to lunchtime, and Charlie was delighted every time someone new stepped onto the bus, or a car pulled into the car park and the occupants came aboard, their expressions tentative, as if they weren't quite sure what they were getting themselves into. She welcomed everyone warmly and told them about her plans for the bus, that it would travel around Cornwall but have Porthgolow as its base.

She'd watched a few people walk straight past, some of whom she recognized from the village, and Myrtle hadn't made an appearance, but then she was probably working at the pop-in all day. She tried not to feel too disheartened that not everybody was an immediate fan. She had known, and not just because Daniel had told her, that not all the locals would find Gertie charming or desirable. But this was a marathon, not a sprint, and she had time to win them round.

In a moment of quiet, she responded to some of the comments on her Instagram and Facebook posts saying how great the cakes looked, and asking her how far Porthgolow was from Newquay, or Padstow, or Truro. There seemed to be genuine interest, and Charlie thought that, as she took her Cornish Cream Tea Bus around Cornwall, that would only grow.

'We need more drinks upstairs,' Juliette said, hurrying into the kitchen. 'Jonah's spotted a pod of dolphins, so everyone up there wants to stay longer.'

'Ooh really? Pass me the list and I'll bring them up to you. Well done, dolphins! Maybe our resident mermaid put them on specially for us?'

She could hear Juliette laughing all the way up the stairs.

Charlie was adding frothy milk to two cappuccinos when she heard the familiar tread of shoes hitting the metal plate on the bus's step. She looked up, ready to greet a new customer, and found herself smiling at Daniel. He was staring at her intently, as if she was the one who'd had a makeover rather than the bus.

She was suddenly tongue-tied. Everyone had gone upstairs to get a better view of the dolphins, and they were the only two people on the lower deck.

'How's it going?' he asked, after what seemed like hours of silence. He was wearing a purple shirt, grey trousers and black shoes, polished to a high shine.

'It's busy and chaotic,' she replied. 'Everything I'd hoped for.'

He nodded. 'It's looking good. I had no idea a bus could . . . I wasn't sure how it would work.'

'Do you want me to give you a tour? We don't have a spa or an à la carte menu, but it's still pretty special.'

There were loud 'oohs' and 'aahs' from upstairs, and Charlie guessed they must be able to see the dolphins clearly.

Daniel shook his head. 'Lauren needs me back at the hotel. Another time, maybe. Just thought I'd . . . check in.'

'Check I wasn't ruining the atmosphere of Porthgolow, you mean?'

'I told you I'd reserve judgement until today.' He gave her a long, lazy smile, then reached up and pulled the cord. The bell dinged. 'Bloody hell. I didn't know buses still had these.'

'Most don't,' she said. 'I wanted to bring some of the original features back. Here.' She picked up the ticket machine, pressing the button so a piece of paper spewed out of the bottom. It was a replica, and modified so that she could amend what was printed or add a short message alongside the date. 'Have a memento.' She tore off the ticket that said: *Cornish Cream Tea Bus. Grand opening, 4 May, Porthgolow.* She held it out to him and, after a pause, he took it. 'That'll be a piece of history one day,' she said. 'When Gertie is famous for travelling throughout Cornwall and perking up the village.'

'You're staying then?' he asked. He was still looking at the ticket, though surely he could have read what was printed on it at least ten times over by now.

'What, in Cornwall?'

'Here, in Porthgolow.' He met her gaze.

Charlie felt like a fried egg stuck under a heat lamp. 'I don't know yet,' she admitted. 'The great thing about Gertie is that she's mobile. But then, I love being with Juliette and

Lawrence; it's so much more relaxed than my parents' place – even though they're brilliant, too – and Marmite, that's my Yorkipoo that you met in the pub, *loves* the beach. There are no beaches in Herefordshire. And Porthgolow is . . . it's beautiful. So . . .'

'So? That was a lot of words without any kind of conclusion. But it sounds as if you like it here.'

Charlie folded her arms, embarrassed at all the detail she'd spilled out. 'I do. I don't know how long I'll be staying, but I like it here.'

His expression was unreadable.

'So it looks like you're going to be stuck with my shabby bus for a while longer,' she added, to fill the silence.

'Looks like it.'

She waited for him to correct her, to tell her it wasn't shabby any more, but he didn't.

'Ooh, we need a photo,' she said, hoping this, at least, would break the tension.

'A photo?'

'I'm taking them with all of my customers, to show that there were actually some people here on launch day. I'll put it online and tag you, and then—'

'It'll look like I'm endorsing your bus.'

Charlie suppressed a smile and, turning her phone to selfie mode, stood next to him. She could smell his aftershave, something woody and fresh with citrus. She held the phone up and Daniel leaned his head towards hers, resting his hand lightly on her shoulder.

Charlie inhaled, and took the photo, then she moved quickly away from him, back into the kitchen.

'Thanks, Daniel. Thanks for coming.'

'I thought I'd better check out my competition,' he said.

'And?' Her mouth was suddenly dry.

'It suits you. The red.'

'Gertie's paint job, or—?' she put a hand up to her hair, remembering how he'd mentioned it in the gardens of his hotel.

He didn't reply, but simply turned and walked towards the door, giving Charlie a perfect view of his wide shoulders in the purple shirt, the snug fit of his grey trousers. He reached up and pulled the bell cord again, and then jogged down onto the sand and disappeared out of sight, the ding echoing in his wake.

Charlie swept crumbs into the bin and cleaned the counter with a ferociousness it didn't need. He was utterly maddening. Had he really come to see if the bus was suited to the village? It wasn't as if she had loud music playing or had invited Lawrence to set up marquees along the entire beach. It wasn't a bloody carnival. It was one bus, with a very lovely café on it.

While everyone upstairs focused on the dolphins, Charlie sat at one of the downstairs tables and added the photo of her and Daniel to Instagram. She bigged him up in the caption: *Daniel Harper, Esteemed owner of Porthgolow's luxury spa hotel, Crystal Waters*. She made it sound very much as if he had endorsed her bus. She tagged the hotel account, added the hashtags she hoped would widen the reach of the post, and linked it to Facebook and Twitter. She looked at the photo of the two of them, her smile a bit too wide, his cool and composed, even though she'd caught him off-guard.

She pushed her phone away and stared out of the window. The sun was trying to make an effort, and the surface of the water glistened invitingly. She tried to picture Daniel's face if she *did* bring a festival to Porthgolow beach, with food trucks and music, the sheltered cove full of people and laughter, dogs running on the sand and children paddling. An ice-cream van with an old-fashioned jingle – the Popeye theme or 'Greensleeves' – maybe even a mobile bar. This wide, hard-packed strip of sand was the perfect location for a fair.

Charlie smiled. The idea was so clear that she knew she had to try it. The council had approved her pitch on the beach, so they might well consent to allowing more, as long as they weren't all permanent. The weather was warming up, she had her bus and her fledgling social media pages, she was living with a brilliant digital marketer and an expert marquee-wrangler. It would be a crime if she didn't use all that to her advantage.

She had hoped Gertie would liven up her adopted village, and today it certainly felt buzzier, but what about tomorrow? The Kerrs, Anton and Stella and Hugh had all turned up. They might make it a regular thing, treat her like any other local café, but they wouldn't come every day. And if the bus had failed to inspire some of the villagers, would a festival, with a wider choice of refreshments, do the trick? Hal had used themes to brighten up his tours, and she could put on special events, create new flavours and products to tie in with celebration days, but she needed to make an even bigger splash if she wanted Porthgolow to have the attention it deserved.

She realized she had an answer to Daniel's question. Yes, she was going to stay in Porthgolow. As long as Juliette and Lawrence would have her, she could see about turning this festival idea into reality.

Jonah ran down the stairs, his eyes alive with the excitement of seeing the dolphins, and beckoned her to come with him. Charlie put the drinks on a tray and followed. She found Juliette and several customers peering out of the windows at the front of the bus.

'They've been in the bay for half an hour,' Jonah said.

'Come and look,' Juliette added.

Charlie knelt on the bench alongside her friend, and within seconds she could see them, their bodies arching out of the water, their fins cutting through the spume.

'Aren't they magnificent?' Juliette murmured.

'They are,' Charlie replied emphatically, thanking her lucky stars that she had given in to her friend's requests to come and stay with her.

Here, Charlie knew, she had found purpose. Porthgolow was one of the most beautiful places she'd ever visited: it had a charm that was recognizable as a British seaside village, but also its own, individual character. She loved that she could stand on the end of the jetty and gaze back at the seafront, the houses that looked as if they were almost carved out of the cliff. She was intrigued by the mystery of Reenie and her yellow house, and she couldn't deny that she wanted to go back to Crystal Waters, to take Daniel up on his offer of a tour of his hotel and, most of all, convince him how wonderful Gertie was.

If she stayed, she could run The Cornish Cream Tea Bus, walk Marmite along the beach, spend time with her friends and, hopefully, make a real difference. Daniel's amused, handsome face flashed into her mind, distracting her from Juliette and the dolphins. When the bell sounded, she raced downstairs to greet her next customer.

It didn't matter who might be against her, what challenges she would encounter. She was prepared – willing, even – to face them all down.

'Bring it on,' Charlie whispered to herself as she ground coffee beans for the young couple's espressos, 'I'm ready.'

Part 2

The Éclair Affair

Chapter Nine

Charlie squinted into the sun that was coming in through the windscreen of the vintage double-decker Routemaster like a searchlight, and ran her palms down her skirt. It was early on a Saturday morning, but already the light was filling the bay of Porthgolow, making the water glitter encouragingly. And right now, in the midst of a meeting that she had called, but which was beginning to feel like a very bad idea, Charlie needed encouragement.

'Do you want this place to survive, or don't you?' said Hugh, more impassioned than Charlie had ever seen him.

'It's not falling into the bleddy sea, is it?' Myrtle Gordon shot back. Myrtle had taken against Charlie and her bus the moment she arrived in the village, so she wasn't surprised to learn that her new suggestion wasn't getting a seal of approval either.

'No, of course not,' Juliette said in a calm, even tone. 'But what Charlie – *we're* – suggesting, is simply a way to bring a few more businesses to Porthgolow. A small festival to brighten up the beach. The bus has been well-received, mostly, and this seems like an obvious next step.'

'Obvious for you, mebbe. You young things, coming here and taking over. Emmets, the lot o'you.' Myrtle picked up a mini toffee tart and popped it in her mouth, then turned purposefully towards the window.

Charlie had heard the term several times over the last couple of months. It meant interlopers – non-Cornish people who'd moved to the county. She couldn't deny that she was one, even if Porthgolow was only her temporary home, and the term wasn't exactly friendly. She was wondering how to follow Myrtle's outburst when Daniel Harper caught her eye and her entire vocabulary deserted her.

After the successful launch of The Cornish Cream Tea Bus the week before, Charlie's active mind had conjured up the next step of her plan to revitalize the quaint Cornish village that seemed forlorn and unloved, despite all its potential. A festival. Every Saturday. Down on the sand.

Her bus had been embraced by a lot of the locals, and with a few more food trucks, a wider selection of culinary delights and some intense online marketing, she knew she could bring people flocking to the village. But she couldn't do that without agreement from the residents. She had already discovered that they weren't all easy to please, and although she had gone ahead with The Cornish Cream Tea Bus regardless of what anyone else thought, for something that would potentially have a huge impact on the village, she wanted to tread carefully.

Juliette had added her to the village businesses' WhatsApp group, and she had invited them all to join her this morning, providing hot drinks and some of her bakes as a sweetener. The mood didn't feel very sweet at the moment.

The Instagram photo she had posted, of the bus's interior with her treats laid out and the caption: *Planning something exciting on the #CornishCreamTeaBus this morning* now seemed wildly over-optimistic. It was doubtful whether they'd manage to agree on anything at all.

The group was split in the same way they had been about her bus. Hugh, the Kerr family (today represented by Paul and his son Jonah, because Amanda had taken an early tour out), and Stella and Anton from the bed and breakfast – they were all enthusiastic about her beach festival idea. Myrtle was not. She had bought her friend Rose for support, and the woman, with honey-blonde hair rolled under her chin in an immovable bob, had barely greeted Charlie and was sitting like a thundercloud, her jaw set. Myrtle had probably told her to behave like that.

Daniel Harper had turned up with his colleague Lauren. They were sitting at the back, and had contributed little, but Daniel kept sending glances Charlie's way, exuding his usual amused demeanour that, so far, hadn't failed to put her hackles up.

She had spent hours making mini toffee and lemon tarts, muffins with gooey chocolate-ganache centres, blueberry jam or orange cream, as well as ginger biscuits thick with crystallized ginger pieces. They were all going down a lot better than her festival proposal.

'Myrtle,' she said, clasping her hands together. 'I do understand why you're not keen on the idea, and why you don't think Porthgolow needs an influx—'

'Invasion,' Myrtle shot back.

'Needs a . . . a—'

'I think what Charlie is trying to say,' Daniel cut in, 'is that from her point of view, seeing this village as a newcomer, she has spotted some areas where it could do with livening up. And from a business perspective, that's entirely sound.'

Charlie resisted the urge to hug him. Even without his supportive words, he was a rather huggable prospect, in jeans and a black T-shirt, the sleeves tightening over his biceps when he folded his arms. His hair was wavy on the top, a few strands falling over his left eyebrow.

'Sound how?' Myrtle asked. 'She wants to take over, is all.'

'Daniel's right,' Hugh said. 'The more people who come to Porthgolow, the more they'll use the pub and your pop-in. They'll see Stella and Anton's B&B, maybe book a stay there. Crystal Waters will undoubtedly get more custom.'

'Gis-on! From royals and celebrities, mebbe. But they're not goin' to come to a scruffy little festival, are they?' Myrtle was unrepentant. She picked up one of Charlie's cream-filled muffins and started to devour it methodically. Irritation flashed across Daniel's face.

'It will attract all sorts of people,' Charlie said. 'I've made some contacts since setting up social media for the bus, and I'm off to the St Agnes Head Festival in a couple of weeks, so I'll talk to other vendors there. Couldn't we try it once and see what happens? If it doesn't work, or if it all goes wrong or nobody turns up, or if the village is damaged in any way, then I won't do it again. But where's the harm in putting on one festival, just to see how it goes? I promise I'll be careful about noise and rubbish and parking; I'll draw up a set of guidelines all the vendors have to follow.'

'I think it's going to be ace,' Jonah said. 'Are you going to get a Mexican food stand? Burritos are my favourite.'

'I'll see, Jonah. I've got lots of people I can ask.'

'It's a mistake,' Myrtle said, 'mark my words.'

'Mine too,' Rose added, raising her head and then quickly dropping it again.

'It is going to make this place very noisy, very crowded.' Daniel snapped a ginger biscuit in two, examined it and then put one half in his mouth. 'Porthgolow won't feel tranquil, like it does now.' He gestured outside, and everyone turned to look. The water was flat, blue and glistening. The sand was empty apart from a couple walking an enthusiastic spaniel. There were murmurs of agreement.

Charlie rubbed her head. 'You just said it was a good idea.'

'It is, from a business perspective. I'm examining all the arguments.'

'Out *loud?*' She couldn't believe it.

'What's the point of having a meeting to discuss this idea, if we don't look at it from every angle?' He raised an eyebrow and Charlie wanted to push it back down his smug face.

'Our guests won't be happy if it starts too early,' Stella mused.

'I get a few delivery drop-offs on a Saturday morning,' Hugh added, rubbing his chin. 'If the place is gridlocked, that'll make the drivers angry.'

'We run a mindfulness session at Crystal Waters on a Saturday morning,' Lauren said, scribbling in a notebook she'd brought with her. 'Do you think it will impact on that?' She touched Daniel's hand and pursed her lips.

'I really don't know, Lauren.' He sighed dramatically. 'It is a risk, though, isn't it?'

'Oh, for God's sake!' Juliette muttered. She began refilling mugs, the milk frother whistling noisily.

'I'm not going to start it at 7 a.m.,' Charlie said. 'I was

thinking about ten o'clock, so it'll miss early morning wake-ups and deliveries and mindfulness sessions. It's a few food trucks, a bit of fun and laughter on the beach. I honestly think you'll thank me once it's here. Give me one chance, one Saturday in June. A trial run.' Her heart pounded as she waited for their verdict. 'If it gets in the way of anything or causes problems, I won't do it again.'

She had been prepared for opposition, having lots of questions to answer about her idea, but she hadn't anticipated having to plead quite so hard. She was pretty sure the only reason she had ended up on the verge of begging was stirring his coffee slowly, nodding abstractedly at something Lauren was saying and keeping his eyes trained on Charlie. He was definitely smirking.

The answer, when it came, was less than enthusiastic. She could try her festival, once, and they would see if they approved. She had hoped to end the meeting feeling slightly more positive, with at least some of the locals embracing her flash of inspiration and excited about the future of their village. That, clearly, had been a pipe dream.

As everyone filtered off the bus, Daniel lingered. 'If you need any help organizing it, let me know.'

Charlie folded her arms. 'And will that help be actual help, or will it be meddling?'

'I do think it's a good idea,' he said, leaning on the doorframe. 'But you have to consider how it's going to change the village. Not everyone is a fan of change.'

'You don't need to mansplain progress to me, Daniel, I get it.' She hadn't meant to snap, but he was as relaxed as ever and, on this occasion, probably right – which made it worse. She had been daydreaming about being the saviour of the village with her brilliant festival plan, but it was only logical that some people were sceptical. Daniel had simply been trying to bring her back down to earth.

He grinned and leant towards her. For a moment, Charlie thought he was going to kiss her cheek, but he reached over the back of the seat and pinched one of the few remaining lemon tarts. 'These are great, by the way,' he said, hopping down onto the sand. 'I can see them being part of the taster menu at Crystal Waters. We should discuss that sometime. Catch you later, Charlie.' He disappeared in a waft of after-shave and confidence.

Charlie turned to find Juliette watching her, a disapproving look on her face.

Within half an hour of being at the St Agnes Head Festival, Charlie was rushed off her feet. It was her first large event since the disastrous Fair on the Field, but any fears she'd had about sinking were allayed when a smart young woman with a clipboard greeted her on arrival and directed her to the refreshments area, where various food trucks, ice-cream vans and hot-dog stands were laid out in a large semi-circle. Charlie's was the only double-decker bus, but she felt a lot more confident than she had in Ross-on-Wye.

Gertie wasn't pretending to be a café any more – she was the real deal. Her journey had also been less hair-raising than it might have been. Pete had tinkered with the engine and the ride was smoother, not to mention that the lanes she'd driven down were on the large side for Cornwall, and she hadn't got stuck in any hedges.

While she'd been setting up, laying out her cakes and scones and uploading photos to Instagram, she'd heard a few appreciative exclamations outside, people praising Gertie's glossiness or intrigued by her café on a double-decker bus.

She even heard one person say, 'I saw that on Facebook last week, we'll have to check it out.' The Cornish Cream Tea Bus, it seemed, was already getting a reputation.

As a family arrived and she directed them upstairs, telling them she'd be up in a moment to take their order, she glanced at her watch. Juliette was joining her at lunchtime so Charlie could have a break. She could have done with her friend's help all day, but Lawrence had surprised her that morning with two tickets to an exhibition at The Eden Project, and there was no way Charlie was going to get in the way of that. Besides, she'd single-handedly managed The Café on the Hill on more than one occasion when it was full of summer tourists. She could do this. And she would do it well if Marmite stayed asleep in his crate like a good little Yorkipoo.

'That was wonderful,' said a woman wearing a ladybird scarf, as she paid for her and her son's cream teas. 'You don't often get café food at these places, and he's getting a bit of a burger habit.'

'Like cream and jam's any healthier than burgers,' mumbled the boy, who was excelling at being a grumpy teenager.

'Having a cream tea with your mum is much more civilized than wolfing down a burger while we walk round,' the woman countered. 'Don't mind him,' she turned back to Charlie, 'he loved it, but he can't show a single ounce of happiness. It's in the game plan.' She winked, and Charlie laughed.

'Understood.' They said goodbye, and Charlie was left wondering if Jonah would ever be a sullen teenager.

She was doing a stock-take of the items in her fridge when the bell sounded. She stood up quickly, just missing hitting her head on the counter.

'Sorry,' said a voice. 'I didn't know how else to get your attention.'

'Is everything OK?' Her words drifted away as she saw who the voice belonged to.

'Small world, huh?' Oliver's smile was broad. 'And the bus is looking *much* better than the last time I saw it. Very shiny and red.'

Charlie shook his proffered hand. He was wearing a sand-coloured jacket over a black T-shirt emblazoned with *The Marauding Mojito* logo in mint green. 'Oliver! I never got a chance to thank you properly, after the field.'

Oliver laughed. 'You say that like it was an ominous field.'

'It *was* ominous,' Charlie said. 'How are you and The Marauding Mojito anyway?'

'You remembered.'

'Of course I did. You rescued me. But it is also on your T-shirt. What are you doing in Cornwall?'

He shrugged. 'I go where the work is. This festival has always been busy, cocktails are popular, and it's not hard to spend time in this part of the world. How come you're all the way down here? And what happened to the bus? It looks like a fairy godmother waved her wand.'

'That's fairly accurate,' Charlie said. 'Only the fairy godmother is called Pete, and he didn't do it out of the goodness of his heart, but was persuaded by quite a lot of cold, hard cash.'

'Aren't they all. Got some time off? Want to come and see the rest of the fair?'

'Give me half an hour? My friend should be here then and I can sneak away.'

109

'Sounds good.' He gave her a wide grin and sauntered off the bus.

Forty-five minutes later, with Juliette and Lawrence in charge of The Cornish Cream Tea Bus, Charlie and Marmite went to find Oliver. He handed his apron to a man with ginger hair, and hopped down from the cocktail stand.

'So,' he said, crouching to greet a still-sleepy Marmite, 'tell me everything. The bus, Cornwall, what happened after that fateful day. Were you banished from the Cotswolds by that woman, what was her name, Bea?'

Charlie laughed as they fell in step. 'No, she was kind, actually. She forced me to take a few months away from the café, and at first I was furious, but she was just looking out for me, I think. And then – for various reasons – coming to Cornwall seemed like a good idea. It was supposed to be a holiday, but God, I've been here nearly two months, staying with Juliette and Lawrence.' She chewed her lip. There had been no indication that she'd outstayed her welcome, but it was much longer than they'd first anticipated. She would have to talk to them.

'What various reasons?' Oliver asked. 'You seem to be doing a lot better than you were back then.'

His smile was so warm, his attention so touching, that Charlie found herself telling him everything. About Hal and Stuart, about her dad's grief and Gertie's resurrection. They walked round the festival, which was huge and busily cheerful, with traders selling all sorts of products from organic local honey to ride-on lawnmowers to massage chairs, and the day, while not as warm as it could have been for the end of May, was crisp and sunny, the sea breeze wafting over Charlie every now and then, so that she longed to be back on Porthgolow beach, soothing her aching feet in the cool water.

'So you're a bit of a nomad, are you?' Charlie asked once she'd got to the end of her story.

Oliver shrugged, his hands deep in his pockets. 'Not really. I live in Bristol, which is a great base. There are lots of places I can get to easily, and Cornwall, Devon and Somerset have enough going on to keep me busy. Are you planning to travel with your bus, or stay in this area?'

'I haven't decided yet,' Charlie admitted. 'But I'm organizing a festival in Porthgolow. It's a beautiful village, but it could – oh!' Her eye snagged on a smart logo, pale purple writing on a slate-grey background. 'Oh,' she said again, and came to a halt.

Ahead of her, next to a vendor selling Jacuzzis, was a sign that read *The Crystal Waters Spa Hotel*. Beyond it were three large pods made out of glass and wood, with cushioned benches running round the inside and circular tables in the middle, arranged with place settings for a beautiful alfresco dinner. She had seen something similar in her mum's John Lewis catalogue. A few thousand pounds on a mini conservatory that you could place anywhere in your garden. She hadn't noticed any at Crystal Waters, but she could see how they would fit perfectly with the surroundings.

'You OK?' Oliver asked.

'Yes, fine.' A man and woman were standing in front of the pods, wearing navy suits and crisp white shirts. She didn't recognize either of them. After her initial surprise, her next emotion was disappointment.

'Should we be heading back?' Oliver pressed, touching her lightly on the arm.

'Of course. Sorry, it's just that Crystal Waters is in

Porthgolow.' She smiled at Oliver in an attempt to cover her strange reaction.

She was about to turn away when Daniel appeared, shaking hands with the dark-suited man and woman. He was dressed casually, in a grey T-shirt, jeans and a battered leather jacket. Charlie had time to notice this before Marmite, perhaps encouraged by the familiar face, launched himself at the closest pod and the beautifully laid-out table within. Charlie froze, unable to think or move as her dog, his extendable lead whirring, set gleefully about his task, taking a matter of seconds to demolish the luxurious, and no doubt expensive, display.

Chapter Ten

'Oh my God!'
    'What the hell?'
'Whose dog is that?'

The last exclamation, from the man in the navy suit, was surely unnecessary, Charlie thought as she raced forward and scooped Marmite into her arms, trying not to look at the pod's now less-than-elegant display. Marmite licked her face, his tail wagging, as if he'd just achieved something magnificent. Navy Suit Woman stared at what was left of the dinner table, while the man, having found the answer to his question, strode towards her.

Charlie shrank back, covering Marmite with her arms, but before the man could reach her, Daniel placed a hand on his chest and spoke to him in a low voice that didn't carry. She scuttled back to Oliver's side and saw that he was laughing silently, his hands over his mouth, his head bowed.

'Not helping,' she whispered, and had to bite down on her bottom lip so as not to be infected by his laughter.

Navy Suit Man retreated, and Daniel approached her. His fingers were flexing at his sides and she wondered if that was some kind of calming technique, the same way Juliette had taught her how to take deep, even breaths that expanded her entire torso before reacting to a situation. She could do with a few deep breaths right now.

'Daniel, I am *so* sorry,' she said instead. 'I'll pay for any damages, of course.' She prayed that they amounted to table-cloths and a couple of plates, and that Marmite hadn't smashed any of the cut-glass crystal or the glass of the pod itself.

Daniel looked from her to Marmite, then Oliver. He frowned. 'I know you're determined, but I hadn't expected sabotage. I can see I'm going to have to be on my guard from now on.'

'Daniel, I honestly didn't mean for that to happen.'

His serious expression cracked into a grin.

'Wait, you're not—?'

'We're covered for accidents at these shows,' he said. 'It's probably a good idea to have one pod empty anyway, so customers can imagine something that's more to their style. Not everyone goes in for silver cutlery and Royal Doulton.'

'Royal Doulton?' Charlie murmured. 'Shit.'

'I know. Didn't take that into consideration when you were planning to set your dog on me, did you? You should always budget properly for attacks of vandalism. You're lucky I'm such a generous guy.' He glanced at Oliver, his smile slipping, and held out his hand. 'I'm Daniel Harper, owner of The Crystal Waters Spa Hotel.'

'Ollie, The Marauding Mojito.' Oliver shook his hand. 'This all looks pretty swanky.'

'It did, until Charlie came along.' Daniel ruffled Marmite's ears. 'Are you and your dog always this accident prone?'

'No,' Charlie said quickly. 'And just because my dog's a tearaway, doesn't mean I'm clumsy.'

'The first time I met her, the bus had had a bit of an accident,' Oliver said. 'It was actually pretty spectacular, the way—'

'We don't need to get into that,' Charlie said, grabbing his arm. 'I'm sure Daniel doesn't have time to stand here gossiping.'

'I just came to see how Mark and Ali were doing. I left Jasper in the car because I thought he might cause trouble.' He glanced behind him, where Ali was crouched inside the pod, retrieving bits of broken crockery. 'Clearly a precaution I needn't have taken.'

'Maybe our dogs should get together for a doggy date.' She didn't know why she'd said it – maybe to distract him from what Oliver had said about Gertie's accident. She couldn't cope with the two of them ganging up on her.

'Doggy *date?*' Daniel laughed, and Charlie felt her cheeks burn.

'God, is that the time?' she said. 'I've left Juliette and Lawrence for far too long. Nice to see you, Daniel, sorry again about Marmite. Your pods are beautiful, by the way. I didn't see them in the garden that time.'

'They're new,' Daniel said. 'Been installed a week.'

'Great. Lovely. I'll have to . . . drop in.' She started to pull Oliver away.

'I'm looking forward to your festival even more now,' Daniel called, giving her a wave when she glanced behind her. She was unable to stop herself from waving back.

'He's in the village where you're staying?' Oliver asked,

when they were out of sight of the Crystal Waters stand.

'Yes, he is,' Charlie said. 'And he's infuriating. He's clearly only looking forward to my event because he thinks it's going to be a disaster and he can watch me make a fool of myself.'

Oliver's brows knitted together. 'Or because he wants to pay you back for destroying his beautifully laid-out display?'

'Oh God, I hadn't thought of that. Do you really think he'd act out some kind of retribution? He said he was insured!'

Oliver shook his head. 'I have no idea, but I'm glad that I'm going to be there.'

'You are?'

He gave her a warm smile. 'If you're having a festival in this idyllic seaside village, The Marauding Mojito needs to be a part of it. And you need to watch your back around that Daniel guy. There was something about him I didn't trust.'

'Are you really coming to my festival?' Charlie asked.

He nodded.

She had her first official booking. It might actually happen: instead of her and her bus and an empty marquee that she'd forced Lawrence to promise to put up to make it look busy, she might actually have other food stalls there. One down, only about twenty more to go. 'Thank you, Oliver,' she said. 'You won't regret it, I promise.'

She waved cheerily at Juliette as they approached the bus, and wondered what Oliver had seen in Daniel that made him wary. He was undoubtedly annoying, and he spoke his mind regardless of who it might offend. But untrustworthy? She didn't know him well enough to determine that, so how could Oliver pass judgement? And she couldn't ignore the skip of happiness she'd felt when Daniel had said he was looking forward to her festival. He was coming, so she needed to try even harder to make it a success. She couldn't look like an idiot in front of Daniel Harper twice.

Charlie poured a generous measure of wine into her and Juliette's glasses. 'Here's to a first successful fair for The Cornish Cream Tea Bus. Thank you so much for helping me today, you and Lawrence. I wouldn't have managed a whole day by myself. Or, I would have, but—'

'But you wouldn't have been able to skive off with that delicious Oliver bloke.' Juliette clinked her glass against Charlie's.

'Delicious?' Charlie frowned. 'He's not unattractive, but . . .'

'But?'

'He seems too chirpy, somehow. As if he's a cartoon character rather than a real person.'

'Says Charlie Quilter, queen of Glass Half-Full. You don't have the right to say that anyone's too chirpy.'

'Hey! I can be miserable. I was a mess after I found out about Stuart. And then, with Hal . . .' She glanced out of the pub window, watching the waves, distorted by the warped glass.

'But you make the best out of everything,' Juliette said. 'You've had some horrible stuff happen recently, but you're not in your pyjamas watching *Friends* reruns, you've started up your own business. If you and Oliver got together you'd be a positive force to be reckoned with. If he asks you out for a drink, will you say yes?'

Charlie nodded, absent-mindedly stroking Marmite, who was snuffling happily on the seat next to her. Oliver was good-looking, and kind – he'd sought her out twice, first to help and then to say hello. But maybe that was his nature, being friendly with other traders; one of those people who managed to build a community despite doing something transient. But she *would* like to see him again. He was good company – and now they had travelling food businesses in common.

'I saw Daniel today,' she said, deftly changing the subject, although her feelings about him were even less straightforward and, by the look on Juliette's face, she wasn't the only one. 'He was promoting Crystal Waters, though I don't think he was supposed to be there, he just popped in and . . . what is it about him, Jules? I get that he's smug and overconfident, but that wouldn't normally be enough for you to be so utterly opposed to someone.'

'He's selfish, and he's shitty about everything.'

'But is he really like that? What has he done, other than run a luxury hotel on the cliff and not spend a huge amount of time in the village? Marmite rushed in and destroyed a very expensive display, and he would have been well within his rights to be furious with me, or at the very least get me to pay for the damages, but he just teased me. That doesn't fall under the banner of "shitty about everything", so what has he done to you?'

'It's what he hasn't done that's the crime.'

'What hasn't he done, then? God, Jules, don't be so exasperating!'

'He didn't use me for his marketing, OK?' Juliette made a low growl in the back of her throat, shook her head and offered Charlie a weak smile. 'Sorry, but it makes me so mad. Still. It was just after we'd moved here. I heard that he was going to rebrand everything, so I put myself forward. It was a huge contract, very well paid, and it was stuff I could really do well. I was excited about it. Coming up with a new logo, revamping their website. Daniel wanted a complete overhaul and we had this meeting, and I basically thought it was a done deal. And then, a week later, I got this terse, professional email saying that he'd gone with someone else, that he was very sorry but he wouldn't be using me.'

'Wow.'

'Maybe I'm making more of it than I should be. But we had finalized everything, even the work schedule. I was waiting for him to sign the contract. It was mine, and then suddenly it wasn't. I'd turned down a couple of other clients in order to take it on, and then I got this email. His apology was so formal, so cold, especially considering how friendly he'd been at our meeting.'

'He never gave you a proper explanation?'

Juliette shook her head. 'And he's been so . . . distant since then. He knows what he did was awful, but he won't try and bridge the gap. And he lives here, but Myrtle never sees him in the shop and he doesn't drink in here. Everything for his hotel comes from elsewhere. He could promote SeaKing Safaris, do some kind of deal with them for his guests, but he doesn't. If Porthgolow isn't good enough for him, then why is he running his hotel here? A place isn't just its scenery, it's all the people that make it.'

'It is,' Charlie murmured. Now that she'd heard Juliette's explanation, she was puzzled. Daniel hadn't given her an easy ride, but other than saying some hurtful things about Gertie before her transformation, he hadn't been hostile. She wondered why he'd blown so hot and cold towards Juliette, especially when it was clear he valued his hotel and his reputation. It wasn't her business, but Juliette was her friend, and she hated the thought of someone upsetting her. She would have to try and find out what was going on.

The Newquay Surf Festival at the beginning of June turned out to be a hotbed of cream-tea lovers. At half past three, once the competition had ended for the day, Charlie's bus was full of athletic men in wetsuits or tight-fitting T-shirts, a few in only swimming shorts and flip-flops. She would have to spend that evening vacuuming the sand out of the bus, but on this occasion it was worth it.

'Top coffee,' said a man with mirrored sunglasses perched over his dark hair. 'Your bus going to be in Newquay often?'

She resisted the urge to say 'as often as you want', and instead told him about Porthgolow. 'I'm organizing a festival on the beach. There will be other food trucks, hopefully a party atmosphere.'

'Awesome. What's your Insta? You anything to do with the Porthgolow Hideaway account?' He pulled his phone out of his pocket.

'That's definitely not me, though I'd love to know who's running it.' They swapped details, and Charlie resisted the urge to scroll down his grid to see just how many surfing selfies he put up there. Judging by the way all the surfers strutted about with their pecs out, she was fairly hopeful. Charlie waved as he left the bus, Marmite looking at her quizzically from his crate.

'You wouldn't understand, puppy,' she said quietly, as two wetsuit-clad women came down the stairs to pay, their long hair still dripping.

Her customers lingered, all laid-back now the competition was over, and it was after six when she drove Gertie back to Porthgolow.

The sun was kissing the cliffs, and the glass of Crystal Waters shone like an oversized diamond. Charlie thought of Daniel and what Juliette had told her. She wanted to know why he'd dropped her friend so quickly, and with no real explanation. And there was something else that was drawing her to him, something that she hadn't felt for a long time, not since her relationship with Stuart had been good. But it had been a while, and it was only normal to crave some intimacy. Trust her to have those feelings about the most irritating man she'd encountered in months.

When she and Oliver had parted ways at St Agnes Head, she had told him she would be in touch about her – much smaller – festival. He was fun and friendly, so why couldn't she conjure up the same level of interest for him as she could for Daniel? Maybe it wasn't attraction, but an inner competitiveness that didn't want to see Daniel get the better of her. Perhaps, once she'd outsmarted him, she'd stop thinking about him.

As she hopped down from the bus, she saw Anton push open the door of the B&B, his head down, his dark suit smart, but somehow too severe for the sunshine. The door slammed, echoing in the quiet. Myrtle appeared in the doorway of the pop-in, and their eyes met.

'Been at the bank, has Anton,' Myrtle said, as Charlie crossed the road to greet her. She reasoned that any contact with the older woman, however frosty, was a step closer to getting her on side. 'Bet they'll be as tight as bleddy always.'

'Stella and Anton aren't doing well?' Charlie asked, dropping her voice.

'Got some fancy ideas about revamping the B&B, but it isn't going to compete, is it?' She gestured towards the cliff. 'Not with pools and spas and eight-course menus.'

'Not everyone can afford Crystal Waters,' Charlie said. 'Of course there's room for them both in Porthgolow. I would have thought a cosy, affordable B&B would be busier than the spa, if I'm honest.'

'Shows what you know,' Myrtle said, giving her a wry smile.

'Think your festival's goin' to fix it all? Perk this village up till it's shiny and new as Daniel's boots?'

Charlie folded her arms. 'It's a start. And it's more than anyone else seems to be doing.'

'Don't see the need for it meself. Do what you will, maid. I'm too old to stand in your way.'

It wasn't the most gracious acceptance Charlie had ever heard, but she was touched, nonetheless. 'Thank you, Myrtle. I won't let Porthgolow down, I promise.'

Myrtle's benevolent expression evaporated, but Charlie couldn't resist hugging her.

'Get off,' she muttered, squirming in Charlie's embrace. 'Idiot cheel.'

Charlie released her. 'Goodbye, Myrtle, see you later!'

'Make sure you warn 'em all 'bout Crumblin' Cliff, up above Reenie's place,' the old woman called after her. 'You fill Porthgolow with cars, it's an accident waitin' to happen.'

Charlie waved to let Myrtle know she'd heard, and then went back to Juliette's to get the dust-buster and rid her bus of the surfers' sand.

Chapter Eleven

Charlie groaned and stretched her legs out, her bare feet sliding along the beach. 'Oh, this is bliss.'

'I thought you'd like it.' Oliver turned on his side so he was looking at her. His blond hair was tousled, less rigid today, and the blue T-shirt showed off his tanned skin.

Charlie put her hand above her eyes, shielding them from the sun. 'A pub actually *on* the beach,' she said. 'I feel like I'm in Spain.'

The pub in question was a ten-minute drive up the coast road, nestled in a hidden cove only accessible by walking over sand dunes. Its windows were open to the sea, but Charlie and Oliver had taken their drinks and found a spot a little way from the building.

'They should change the name, though,' Charlie said. 'Sea View sounds far too Seventies, and they could have loads of fun with it. Even something cheesy like Seaside Shack would be better. They need to get Juliette on the case.'

'Your friend from last weekend? The one you're staying with?'

Charlie nodded. 'She's a digital marketer. She's been so helpful with Gertie.'

'The Cornish Cream Tea Bus is a great idea, and perfect for this time of year. Have you got many more gigs lined up?'

'A few. The weekends are packed with events now summer's here, and there's a lot I want to do in Porthgolow, too.' Charlie sat up and rested her elbows on her knees. 'It needs a new lease of life. At the moment it's like stepping back in time, and I reckon this festival could give it a boost. I want it to be a weekly event, like a regular market, good enough that people keep coming back. I've got a great selection of food trucks booked for the first one, and I can keep improving, making it bigger and better.'

Oliver laughed. It was a lovely laugh, warm and unashamed.

'What?' Charlie said, smiling. 'Why is that so funny?'

'It's not. It's . . . you.'

'*I'm* funny?'

'Not funny. You're not . . .' He took a deep breath, and waited a beat before continuing. 'You're so relentless. After that first time when it all went wrong, I thought I wouldn't see you again. Or, at least, I didn't expect to see the bus. But you didn't give up.'

'Giving up's for losers.' Charlie wrinkled her nose. 'No, that's not fair. It depends on the circumstances. But I didn't give up because I had to do something with my uncle's bus. I had to honour his memory. And he always told me to live life to the full. You only get one chance, so make the most of it – he was forever saying that to me. If everyone stopped the moment something went wrong, nobody would stick at anything. You told me you had teething problems with The Marauding Mojito?'

'It wasn't all plain sailing, which is why I came to help you out. I know what it's like to feel out of your depth.'

'And now you're an old hand. Old and wizened.' She laughed at her own joke. Oliver looked so fresh-faced she could imagine he had a painting locked away in an attic somewhere. 'You are over twenty-one, right?'

Oliver gave her an incredulous look. 'I'm thirty-three.'

'Ah. Must be all those mojitos. Do they have magic properties?'

'Of course. I only sell the best.'

'Clearly I need to hang out with you more, then. See if a bit of your magic will rub off on me.' She held his gaze, and the atmosphere shifted. His eyes looked almost golden against the sunset. 'Shall we go for a walk?' she asked.

'Sure.'

He helped her up and they took their glasses back to the bar. They strolled towards the water, and Charlie wished she'd brought Marmite with her. He would have loved this wide beach with its flat sand and rippling breakers. But Juliette had insisted on babysitting him, because Marmite had a habit of getting in the middle of everything. Still, he would have been a useful buffer, especially a moment ago when the space between them had felt charged.

Oliver told her about setting up the cocktail stand with his sister and how she'd sold her share to him when her new husband got a job in Hong Kong. 'I've never had ambitions for anything more,' he admitted, as they rolled up their jeans and took off their shoes and socks. 'I get to travel, talk to people all day, sell them delicious mojitos and see them happy. It's a great life.'

'You don't want to settle down, then?' Charlie dipped her foot in the water. It was cold, despite the lingering heat of the day.

'Not at the moment. But it doesn't mean that I'm not interested in doing it eventually. I'm just open to seeing what happens, making the most of what's out there.'

Charlie nodded and stared at the horizon, the glistening water picking up tones of peach and cherry from the sky.

'How about you?' Oliver asked, coming to stand next to her. 'Have you got any idea what you and your bus are going to do after Cornwall?'

'After Cornwall?' She still hadn't had the conversation with Juliette about staying on, about how she and Lawrence really felt about it. But she had the bit between her teeth now, and the thought of driving out of Porthgolow, leaving her plan only half executed, felt like a betrayal. Everyone had been so nice to her – even Myrtle had started to thaw – and she was sure she had it within her power to help them.

'You can't live with your friends for ever.'

'No, I can't. But . . . I'll see how this festival goes. If I do it once and it flops, then at least I've tried. Anyway, I'd rather not think about my future career as a nomad, thank you very much. I love Gertie, but I don't want to end up *living* on her, even if Pete did make sure one of the benches upstairs folds out into a bed in case I ever get stuck some- where overnight.'

'Smart thinking,' Oliver said, following her deeper into the water. 'Lots of people *do* live on buses.'

'I'm not knocking it. I just don't think it's for me. I like my creature comforts, and I like having space.' She flung her arms in the air and walked backwards, beckoning him deeper. He obliged.

'Some people would say that living on a bus you have more space than you know what to do with. You could park up somewhere like here, wake up to this view every morning.' He gestured for Charlie to stop, but she kept going.

'Porthgolow has amazing views, and you can see the sea from one corner of Juliette's garden.'

'But it's Juliette's garden, not yours. Stop now, Charlie, you're too close to the waves.'

Charlie saw the panic on his face, and laughed. 'I could get my own place in Porthgolow, if this all works out. I could be the Cornish Indiana Jones, bringing life back to the village like at the end of *Temple of Doom*, when he returns the stone to its rightful place.'

'Has Porthgolow lost all its children to an ancient evil cult? You're going to get soaked.'

'No, but some people are standing in the way of it flourishing. I get that with the locals who've lived there a long time. It's not easy to watch your home change, to have newcomers – emmets – coming in and making decisions about where you live. That's why I'm trying to include everyone. But . . .' She thought about Juliette's admission, and the way Daniel had argued for and then against her festival idea at the meeting. She couldn't quite work out his motivations. Was he as protective of his hotel as some people made out? With people like Myrtle taking against it simply because it was a shiny, new building in their traditional village, she could see why he might be. She was certainly protective of Gertie.

'But what?' Oliver asked.

'It doesn't matter. Most of the villagers have been nothing but—' Her word turned to a gasp as an ice-cold wave crashed into her back, knocking the breath out of her. She staggered forward, and Oliver caught her before she fell, laughing as he pulled her out of the sea and up the beach.

She was still gasping, still trying to catch her breath, and Oliver was trying very hard to master a serious expression.

'I told you not to go any further.'

'Th-the waves didn't look that big,' she stuttered.

'Do you have a towel in your car? I've borrowed a mate's – easier than bringing the Mojito truck – and I don't think he's got anything as civilized.'

'There's one in the boot.' She had been using it to dry Marmite down whenever he'd had a dip in the sea, and she didn't want to get Juliette's seats wet. 'God, what an idiot.' She wiped her face, cold droplets making her shiver as they ran down her back.

'You got carried away, that's all.' Oliver smiled. 'And it was pretty funny.'

'Glad I amuse you,' she said, grinning back. 'Ugh, everything feels clingy and cold.'

'You'd best go back and get dry.'

'I better had.'

'I've had fun this evening,' he said softly.

'Me too. Rogue waves aside.'

'Another time, then?'

'I'd like that.' And she would, she realized, as they strolled back to the car park, Charlie's jeans rubbing with every step. She didn't feel a burning attraction towards Oliver, but she enjoyed his company, and who knew what would happen as they got to know each other?

'I'm counting down to the Porthgolow festival,' he said when they reached her car. 'I can't wait to see you in the role of event-organizer extraordinaire.'

'Hopefully a world away from the first time you found us. '

'Undoubtedly. Night, then.' He kissed her on the cheek. He smelt of sandalwood and sunshine.

'Goodnight, Ollie.'

'Give my love to Gertie and Marmite.'

'I will.' She watched him walk away, his blond hair dancing in the breeze.

'I need to have a serious talk with you,' Charlie said the following morning. 'And ideally it should be with you and Lawrence, but he's at work already, isn't he?'

'It's just going to get busier from now on, too. I love that he's found a job he's happy with, but sometimes it's hard to get any time together.' Juliette typed something on her laptop and then put it aside, giving her full attention to Charlie. She was wearing a thin summer dressing gown with songbirds all over it that Charlie loved. 'Anyway, tell me this serious thing, and I can talk to Lawrence about it this evening.'

'OK.' Charlie sat down opposite her and stared at her plate. Her toast was covered in Nutella, but she suddenly had no appetite. 'I've been here since April, which is two months – over two months – and you don't have that much space to begin with, so—'

'You're going back home? But what about this Porthgolow festival? All your plans for The Cornish Cream Tea Bus?' Juliette's eyes were wide. 'I was looking forward to having you around, to us doing more together.'

'So was I,' Charlie said, relief coursing through her. 'I wasn't planning on going home.'

'You weren't? So then why—'

'Because I was worried I'd outstayed my welcome. I love being here, and so does Marmite. And I want to do all those things you said: organize a festival on the beach, take Gertie

129

around Cornwall selling traditional Cornish cream teas. But I don't want to be merrily enjoying my life here when all the time you and Lawrence are wondering how to come up with a polite way to send me packing.'

'Oh God, Charlie! That is not how it is at all. We love having you here – I promise. Stay for ever!'

'For ever?'

'As long as you want. The summer, at least. I want to be a part of the Porthgolow festival.'

'You do?'

'Definitely.'

'That's brilliant, Jules. And thank you. You have no idea how much it means that I can stay. I feel so much more positive since I've been here with you.'

'I told you, didn't I? You needed a break. And,' she added ruefully, picking up her marmalade-laden toast, 'if your kind of break involves starting up a brand-new business and planning to take over the whole of Cornwall, then far be it from me to stand in your way.'

Charlie grinned. 'Let's start with Porthgolow, shall we? Once we've got this place back on track we can think about where to conquer next.'

'I wouldn't underestimate the challenge ahead, though,' Juliette said. 'However cool he was in that meeting, Daniel Harper's not going to be happy if you ruin the peace and quiet of the village with a full-blown festival. He promises his guests seclusion and exclusivity.'

Charlie shrugged. 'I'm not here to please Daniel Harper. Besides,' she said, 'he told me he was looking forward to it. He can't have it both ways, and he can't control what anyone else does, as much as he'd like to.'

'I'll raise my coffee to that,' Juliette said.

Charlie clinked her mug against her friend's and bit into her toast. She wanted to bring life back to Porthgolow, and the thought of clashing with Daniel again didn't fill her with as much dread as, perhaps, it should have done.

Chapter Twelve

This time, Charlie wanted to see Reenie's cottage for herself.

She left Juliette in her yoga gear and took Marmite with her. She was opening The Cornish Cream Tea Bus at around ten – she had discovered that her custom was limited before then, and while the quiet time meant she could polish the bus until it gleamed, it sometimes got boring. She only opened earlier when Paul or Amanda had an early boat trip, knowing that they, and their customers, would welcome a hot drink when they came in off the water.

She walked along Porthgolow's main road, past The Seven Stars on her left and the beach, the jetty and Gertie on her right, and when the road started rising out of the village, she turned down a dusty track that looked as though it led nowhere. Marmite bounced at her heels, excited by the unusual terrain. The morning was sunny and clear, with only a few puffs of cloud breaking up the blue of the sky. The track was precarious, and close enough to the edge of the cliffs that sea spray frequently hit her face. Marmite yelped at each new wave, and it wasn't long before he was soaked.

'All right Marmite?' she asked. He barked and bounded a few steps ahead.

And then the path ended and the yellow house stood in front of them. For the last part of the journey, she had to clamber over rocks. How was it possible for anyone – let alone an older woman, as she understood Reenie to be – to live out here? Carefully, Charlie stepped across them, pulling Marmite close, watching her footing carefully.

After the rocks came firm concrete, the foundations of the house much more stable than their surroundings. Close up, the walls were worn, but the yellow paint was thick, as if it was given frequent new coats.

Charlie walked round to the front of the building, feeling more confident now the ground below her was solid and flat. Had this been an old outpost, somewhere to watch the water from, or a weather station? There were often odd little buildings nestled along the very edge of the coastline but, as far as Charlie knew, they were rarely residential. Reenie's house had two floors, four windows at the front and a white door, though there was no number or name. What had she been expecting? *Mermaid Cottage?*

On the small patch of ground between the house and the cliff edge, there were a few terracotta pots containing blue and pink plants that Charlie couldn't name, and a wind chime hung from a hook screwed into a window frame. Charlie wondered how any of it survived; was Reenie forever replacing pots lost to the wind? Did the waves batter against her front door like unwelcome visitors?

She knocked; two loud raps that she was sure would be

heard, even above the churn of the water below. She waited, staring out at the sea, and was about to knock again when the door swung inwards, and Charlie found herself staring into the sharp eyes of Reenie the mermaid.

'Hello,' she said.

Reenie was shorter than her and had long, grey hair streaked through with white. She was wearing a red shirt and jeans, and her feet were bare. No wispy dresses, trails of seaweed or signs of fish scales. Charlie was disappointed that she was wearing jeans; it seemed too ordinary, somehow.

'Hello,' Reenie echoed. Her voice was light, as if it might float away on the wind.

'I'm Charlie Quilter.' She held out her hand. 'I'm staying in Porthgolow, with Juliette and Lawrence. I've just started up a new business, running the—'

'Cornish Cream Tea Bus. Yes, I've seen it. It's hard to miss.' She turned her head, and Charlie looked back towards the bay, but the corner of Reenie's house was between her and a view of the bus.

'Ah. OK. And this is Marmite.' She gestured towards her dog, and Marmite, as if being given permission, pattered forward and put a paw on Reenie's leg.

Reenie made no move to stroke him. 'Hello, Marmite.'

'So, I came to see you because—'

'Don't start your sentences with *so*, girl. Horrendous habit. You wouldn't start a conversation with *therefore*, would you? *Therefore I have come to see you.* Speak sense; I assume you have got something to say, seeing as you've bothered to come all the way out here?'

'I have.' Charlie's voice sounded as small as she felt. She would have to give Jonah a few home truths about his mysterious mermaid. 'I'm holding a festival in Porthgolow,' she continued, 'in the next couple of weeks. I know you're part of the WhatsApp group, but you didn't come to my meeting, and I wanted to make sure you were OK with it.'

Reenie stared at her, and Charlie had to look away. She glanced behind the older woman, trying to see inside her house.

'Eyes front, Charlene. Or are you Charlotte?'

'Charlene, but everyone calls me Charlie. It seems less—'

'Whiny? Charlene is the sort of name you can only say with a whine. Charlie it is, then. Charlie, I am not remotely against you having a festival on the beach – goodness knows the village could do with a bit of sprucing up. I have no desire to be part of it, but I do appreciate the opportunity. It has been a pleasure to meet you. Goodbye.'

She moved back, one hand on the door, and Charlie stepped forward. 'Would you like to come?'

Reenie paused, as if considering it. 'No, thank you. But it was lovely of you to ask. I wonder if you could do something for me, seeing as you've no option but to go back into the village? The council isn't keen on disposing of my rubbish, so I have to do it myself. Would you be so kind?' She disappeared inside, but before Charlie could take another peek she was back, hefting a large carrier bag. 'This is only recycling, nothing soiled. It would save me a trip.'

'I, uhm . . .' Reenie pushed the bag towards her, and Charlie instinctively held her arms out to take it.

'Thank you, Charlie. Very generous of you.' She closed the door.

Charlie gazed at it for a moment, then walked back around the side of the house and slowly navigated over the rocks, her job made more difficult by the unwieldy bag she was carrying. She felt too stunned to be put out. She had been imagining a

135

recluse, someone who was timid, afraid of human company. Reenie seemed like nothing of the sort and, despite her brusqueness, Charlie had found herself warming to her. She wanted to get to know her better.

As her feet found the dusty, solid track and Marmite bounded ahead, she tried to conjure up reasons to return to the yellow house.

They reached the main road and Marmite dashed in the direction of the beach. Surprised by the sudden movement, Charlie lost her grip on Reenie's recycling. The bag tipped out of her hands and she lunged into the road to grab it just as a BMW shot down the hill, going far too fast. She heard the long *beeeeeeeeep* of its horn, the squeal as the driver slammed on the brakes. She managed to twist her body away from it, and staggered a few steps before righting herself, her heart hammering in her chest. Bits of paper and cardboard drifted in all directions, turning over and over in the breeze, but she was too shocked to chase after them.

Marmite was suddenly at her feet, barking loudly and scrabbling at her shins.

'What the hell were you doing in the road?'

She hadn't noticed the car come to a stop, or Daniel climb out of it, but now he was bearing down on her, leaving his driver's door wide open. His voice was sharp, his usual cool nowhere to be found.

'Don't worry,' she said through shaky breaths, 'I'm not going to sue you.'

'You stepped right out in front of me. I could have killed you!'

'Because you were going too fast,' she shot back. 'What if it had been a child? Or Marmite? Maybe I shouldn't have been there, but there's no need to drive like that in the village.'

Marmite was excited now, bounding over to Daniel and pawing at his trousers. He didn't seem to notice.

'And you need to watch where you're going,' he replied. 'That hill's pretty steep, in case you hadn't noticed. Not everyone has brakes as good as mine.'

'Of *course* you've got the best brakes,' she snapped. How could he accuse her of being in the wrong?

'What's that supposed to mean?' He stormed up to her, his jaw set, but when he cupped his hand around her shoulder his touch was gentle. She could feel the warmth of his skin through her thin top. 'You're OK, though, aren't you?'

She saw that it wasn't anger in his eyes, but shock. Concern, even. 'I'm fine,' she said, though his touch had cancelled out the calm that had started to return, and a lump bubbled up in her throat. She put Reenie's bag on the floor, breaking contact, and pointlessly dusted down her jeans.

Daniel took the bag, picked up what flyaway bits of paper he could and shoved them inside it. 'You're right. I shouldn't have been driving that fast. But you need to be more careful.'

Charlie took him in, standing there in a dark suit and white shirt, looking ridiculously handsome and stern, clutching a bag of rubbish. She grinned. 'We're both to blame. You *were* going too fast, but I wasn't paying attention, and this one,' she gestured to Marmite, 'was being an idiot, as always. So I'd say it's about fifty-fifty. Except you were driving a powerful vehicle with killing potential, so your apology is more valid.'

'Fair enough. Do you want this back?' He lifted the bag.

'Thanks.' He handed it to her, but her hands were still shaking, and it slipped. Daniel took it back.

'I'll bring it over to the bus. Promise me that you're all right?'

'I'm fine. Come and have a coffee,' she added impulsively.

'I need to get to the hotel.'

'If you'd actually hit me, you would have been stuck here for ages. Waiting for the ambulance, giving a statement, watching while they scraped me off the tarmac . . .'

'OK, OK. One coffee. I'll meet you there.'

'The beach is twenty yards away.'

'I can't leave my car here, can I? I'll put it in the car park.'

'Fair point. I'll go and open up.'

Daniel sat at one of the downstairs tables facing the kitchen while Charlie turned on the coffee machine, oven and fairy lights. He'd draped his jacket over the seat next to him and rolled his shirtsleeves up, but his hands were clasped tightly together on the table, and there was visible tension in his broad shoulders. Marmite had clearly noticed too, because before Charlie could put him in his crate he had bounced onto the chair and inserted himself on Daniel's lap, his head popping up between Daniel's arms. Charlie refilled the coffee-bean holder and watched them surreptitiously. Daniel ruffled the dog's head with his thumb.

'What were you doing, anyway?' he asked. 'Trying to win the villagers over with a litter-pick?'

'What – oh, you mean the bag? No, that's Reenie's rubbish.' She laughed. 'I went to see her and ended up as honorary waste collector.'

'Reenie's a hard nut to crack. She must like you if she's trusted you with her rubbish.'

'That's a bit backwards, isn't it? Rubbish isn't usually a gift bestowed on someone you're fond of. Also, how could she like me after two minutes of chat? A chat during which, by the way, she managed to be pretty cutting.' Charlie wrinkled her nose at the memory.

'What did she say?'

'She told me that I shouldn't start my sentences with *so*, and that Charlene was a whiny name.'

Daniel laughed. 'That's typical Reenie. She's like a shit fortune-teller, giving you all the truths you don't want to hear.'

'Do you know her well? I got the impression she was a bit of an enigma. Jonah says she's a mermaid who's lost her tail.'

'The Kerr boy? That figures.'

Charlie brought their coffees to the table, along with two scones, perfectly topped with jam and cream. She sat opposite him. 'Listen to you – *The Kerr boy*. It's like you're auditioning for Scrooge. This is for you.' She pushed the scone towards him.

Daniel sipped his coffee. His expression was lighter, and the amused glint was back in his eyes. Charlie had started to relax, too. Her palms had stopped sweating and she was grateful that he had agreed to join her. Conversely, he was helping take her mind off the fact that he'd almost mown her down.

'He's a boy and his parents are Paul and Amanda Kerr. It's not inaccurate. I just had breakfast.' He nudged the scone back across the table.

'It's impersonal, though. They're your neighbours. Live a little. It's one scone, and you didn't seem that reluctant with my lemon tarts.' She pushed the plate towards him again.

'Jonah can be very irritating.' Daniel picked up one half of the scone and took a bite.

'Has he given you lots of facts about your hotel?'

'Yup,' Daniel mumbled, then finished his mouthful. 'I got the entire history of the old Clifftop Hotel – which stood where Crystal Waters is now – even though his family moved to Porthgolow after I did. I also know how Jacuzzis are made, and why sea salt is used in high-end beauty treatments. This is delicious, by the way.'

'I know, that's why I gave it to you. I'm glad Jonah and his family are on my side. I can imagine he could cause quite a few problems if he set his mind to it.'

'Why are you thinking about it like that? Everyone taking sides?'

'Isn't that how you think about it?' Charlie bit into her own scone, and followed it with a sip of cappuccino.

'Not at all,' Daniel said. 'I've got a business to run in Porthgolow, and it doesn't bother me whether the locals like it or not. You're being far too generous giving them your consideration, asking what they think about you running a festival.'

'You were happy enough to give me your opinion at that meeting!'

'That's because you gave me the opportunity. I wasn't going to pass it up.'

Charlie huffed in frustration. 'You really think the best way to run your business is to ignore everyone else and be selfish?'

Daniel put his hand over hers on the table. 'No, of course not. But you had the right idea with this place. You might have listened to what a few people thought about your bus being in the village, but you ignored any negativity and did it anyway.' He gave her a glimmer of a smile, acknowledging that he had been part of the negativity. 'You can tell them how it's going to work and what it's going to look like until you're blue in the face, but none of them will change their minds until they see it in action. I'm sure that you've convinced a few sceptics since your bus has been open, and the same will be true of your event. Show them how brilliant it is, and Myrtle and Rose and all those other moaners will be forced to eat their words.'

'Is that what you do, then?' Charlie asked, trying to focus on what he was saying instead of the feel of his skin against hers.

He nodded. 'Try to, anyway, though it's not always quite that straightforward. My guests aren't all millionaire socialites. People save up for these breaks, they get treated to weekends or overnight stays. They're not superior. I just always wanted my hotel to go the extra mile. To set high standards.'

'But to the detriment of the rest of Porthgolow?'

'What do you mean?' Daniel frowned. 'I haven't done anything to harm anyone in Porthgolow.'

'What about Juliette? She said that you offered her some work and then it fell through.'

Daniel didn't reply immediately and she didn't jump in. Not only because she thought her silence would pressure him into an explanation, but also because when he looked at her like that, from so close, she didn't want to do anything that might make him stop.

'The thing with Juliette was a mistake,' he said, 'and I'm truly sorry it happened. I had spoken to a friend of Lauren's, had a look at his work, and while I was exploring other options, Lauren got a contract drawn up. She thought I'd given him the go-ahead and it was confirmed without my say-so.'

'How? It's your hotel.'

Daniel sighed. She could feel his thumb moving against her skin, and wondered if he was doing it consciously. 'Lauren brought in a pile of papers for me to sign. It was late one Friday night, I was knackered and I wanted to go home, so I signed it without reading it properly. When I realized what I'd done, and what I'd promised Juliette, I—'

141

'You didn't want to tell her the truth, because it would show her you'd messed up.'

'I took my eye off the ball. It won't happen again.'

'So why not tell her now? Admit that you're human. Juliette and Lawrence are great people. If you're not trying to make enemies, then why not just apologize and explain what happened? She'd forgive you the moment she knew.'

'What, that I was weak?'

'That you're a normal person who makes mistakes. My uncle Hal, who gave me Gertie, always said to me that you should forget the mistake but remember the lesson it taught you.'

Daniel laughed. 'Is he a life coach?'

'He ran tours around the Cotswolds on here.' Charlie tapped the table. 'He died in February and left me the bus in his will.'

Daniel squeezed her hand. 'I'm sorry. He obviously cared about you.'

Charlie nodded. 'And I cared about him, too. That's why I have to make a success of this.'

'Oh, I've no doubt you'll do that,' he said softly. 'Not even my BMW haring down the hill towards you has dented your smile. Are you sure you're OK?' He turned her hand over and ran his fingers slowly down her palm, until his fingertips rested on hers.

Charlie swallowed. 'I'm OK. The shock's faded.'

'I really am sorry, Charlie. If I'd hit you . . .' He didn't finish the sentence.

'It's fine,' she mumbled. But it wasn't fine. She shouldn't be sitting here with Daniel, letting him twist her thoughts like this, touch her so tenderly when all he'd done up until this point was rile and infuriate her.

She tried to think back to what it had felt like when

Oliver had touched her. *Had* he touched her during their date? She couldn't remember. And if he had, then she hadn't responded in the way she was now, to Daniel's fingertips pressed against hers.

'I should get going,' he said, taking his hand away. Charlie's fingers fizzed, as if mourning their loss. 'Thank you for the coffee and the scone. Bye, little guy, see you soon.'

He lifted Marmite onto the seat, stood up and stepped out from behind the table, took a moment to brush the crumbs and Yorkipoo fur off his trousers, and then grinned at her. The effect, with the smart suit and the neat hair, a single wave falling over his forehead – along with the lingering memory of his touch – was almost too much.

'Can I buy a spa voucher?' she asked impulsively.

'Of course.' Daniel took a step towards her. 'You know, I give a pretty good massage. Let me know when you're booking in and, if I'm not too busy, I'll look after you person-ally. To make up for earlier.'

'It's not for me,' Charlie said. 'It's for Juliette and Lawrence. I want to thank them for letting me stay so long, and I figured that if I told her why you bailed on your marketing agreement, she wouldn't have a reason to be cross with you any more. Are you happy for me to tell her?'

'Sure.' He stepped closer. 'But let me gift it to them, as an apology for what happened. It won't make up for losing a contract, but you're right, I should have explained it straight away.'

'Good.' Charlie smiled. 'Glad I could help.'

'And if you do fancy coming to Crystal Waters one evening, there's always a spectacular view of the sunset from the hot tub.'

She could feel his breath against her cheek. 'I thought you were going to give me a massage,' she whispered.

'I could give you a massage *in* the hot tub. We could have champagne to celebrate your first, successful Porthgolow festival. If it *is* successful.'

'Of course it's going to be successful,' Charlie said, closing down the vision he was creating in her head. The sunset, the hot bubbles around them and the cool bubbles of the champagne, his hands on her skin . . .

Daniel grinned. 'I'll get Juliette's voucher to you in the next few days. Catch you later, Charlie.'

He turned and, as he left the bus, dinged the bell cord.

Charlie slumped against the counter, her gaze falling on Reenie's bag of rubbish, still on the bench where Daniel had left it. She had found out why he'd let Juliette down and now she could tell her friend and resolve the animosity between them. He'd been honest with her, and offered up a day at the spa by way of an apology. Charlie should be punching the air with delight at having worked her way under Daniel's cool exterior. But when she compared it to the way he'd got inside her head, it seemed utterly insignificant.

She'd been on a date with Oliver and was seeing him again at the festival. They were small, tentative steps towards getting back on her emotional feet after Stuart's betrayal and losing Hal. Ollie seemed safe and kind and comforting. Exactly what she needed. Daniel had got her attention on her very first night in Porthgolow and since then he'd been toying with her feelings. He was the antithesis of safe: the word 'tentative' probably wasn't even in his vocabulary.

She glanced at her hand, tried to recreate the feel of his fingers touching hers, the way it had tingled through her whole body, and then, cursing herself, she put her hands in the sink and ran the hot tap until her flesh went pink.

Chapter Thirteen

It was the day after the summer solstice, and the sun was making its presence known. Charlie stood in the doorway of The Cornish Cream Tea Bus, the smell of red-onion chutney and sausage rolls competing with the fresh sea air. When she had been planning the first Porthgolow festival, she hadn't paid much attention to the significance of the date, but as she'd brought her cake tins down from Juliette's house that morning, she'd heard a couple standing on the edge of the beach, muttering loudly about *disrespect* and *sacred time*.

She was trying her hardest to make friends, and instead she was being accused of stomping all over a significant celebration. If only they would give her a chance they would see that she was adding to the festivities rather than disregarding them.

And she had to admit that, despite all her worries, her hours of online networking seemed to have paid off. The inaugural Porthgolow food festival didn't look entirely hopeless. It was bright, colourful and had a buzz to it, and that was before any punters appeared.

The black and green paintwork of The Marauding Mojito gleamed, as did the Mexican burrito stand, painted in a dizzying array of colours that looked like a carnival all on its own. There was a Japanese food van, the scents of its delicate spices wafting across the sand towards her, and a Gourmet Falafels truck that she had encountered at the St Agnes Head Festival. A pastel ice-cream van and Cornish Fudge stall catered for those with a sweet tooth, and along with Oliver's cocktails and juices, there was an old, corrugated metal Citroën van that had been converted into a coffee stall.

The festival was opening in half an hour and she was missing Benji's Burgers and, possibly the most important offering, The Travelling Cornish Pasty Shack. She was hoping to win the villagers round with some local fairings – if everything felt completely alien, she wasn't sure she stood a chance.

Checking Marmite was secured in his crate at the front of the bus, Charlie hopped onto the sand. She greeted everyone, taking short videos to upload to her Instagram stories, all with the hashtag #PorthgolowFoodFest. She had circulated it to her street-food comrades in the run-up to the day, hoping they would use it and help build the online buzz. They all seemed happy to be here, complimenting the view and admiring Charlie's bus, and there was no hint of annoyance or incredulity that she'd picked the wrong date to run her event.

'If you need anything, just shout,' she told a young woman called Megu who was running the Japanese food stand. 'I've advertised the start as eleven, but people could turn up any time.'

'No worries,' Megu said. 'I've learnt to be ready as soon

as possible. Once people smell the food they're like vultures, which can only be good.' She laughed.

'Very good,' Charlie said, snapping a photo. She hoped Megu was right, and had a sudden image of the Porthgolow residents descending on the beach like a herd of ravenous zombies.

'Charlie.' A hand landed on her arm, and she spun to find Oliver smiling at her. 'It's looking great!'

'Thank you! It all smells so delicious, I'm sure I'll end up buying something from every stall.'

Oliver tapped his trim stomach. 'Occupational hazard. It's a good thing our jobs mean we have to keep moving, or our waistlines would be in trouble.'

'Looking grand, Charlie,' Amanda called, crossing the road to join them. 'Can I nab a coffee before my tour?'

'Your usual latte? Have you got a full schedule of boats going out today?'

'As many as the tide allows. We've been pushing the festival on our website—'

'I saw that, thank you,' Charlie cut in.

'And we're hoping it will bring more customers in our direction at the same time.'

'I'll make sure I mention your trips to everyone who comes aboard, and you'll do the same, won't you, Ollie?'

'No problem,' he said. 'You launch from the jetty, don't you?'

'That's right. Nice to meet you, Ollie.'

'You too,' he said. 'See you later, Charlie.'

Charlie said goodbye to Oliver and walked with Amanda to the bus.

'He's a good-looking chap,' Amanda said, pushing her wayward curls out of her face and leaning against a table. 'Where did you cook him up from?'

'I met him in Ross-on-Wye, actually. At my first, disastrous event, before Gertie looked anything like this. He was kind to me, and it looks like he's spending the summer in Cornwall, too.'

'Oh?' Amanda raised an eyebrow. 'That's rather coincidental.'

'He runs The Marauding Mojito. Cornwall is a prime spot for summer fairs and festivals, so it's not that surprising he's ended up here.' She offered Amanda one of her warm sausage rolls.

'But maybe there's more to it,' Amanda said, cupping her palm under the pastry crumbs and trying to hide a grin. 'And there's no harm in a summer fling, is there?'

Charlie thought of her fun evening on the beach with Oliver, and then Daniel inviting her to Crystal Waters for a dip in the hot tub. Was she ready for a fling? It had been over six months since she'd broken up with Stuart, but there was still a dull ache whenever her mind returned to his casual betrayal, how much she'd loved and trusted him, and how quickly he'd shattered everything between them. She wasn't sure her heart was ready, even for something fun and impermanent.

As Amanda left the bus, Charlie was relieved to see Benji's Burgers trundle slowly onto the sand, followed shortly afterwards by The Travelling Cornish Pasty Shack. Everyone was here. It was time to open the festival.

An hour later, the beach was a melting pot of some of the most delicious smells that had ever assaulted Charlie's nose. The sun was high in the sky, the steep landscape of Porthgolow acted as an attractive backdrop, and the sea sparkled ahead of them. It was a perfect day to be outdoors, trying new culinary delights then walking them off along the sand, but still the stand-holders outnumbered the customers.

There was a middle-aged couple Charlie thought she recognized buying falafel wraps, and Juliette's next-door neighbour was pondering the different fudge flavours, but other than that, everything was quiet.

She felt sick. She had put so much time and energy into organizing this festival, promoting it online, being positive and energetic, and now all these business owners had come to sell their burgers and sushi and delicious Cornish pasties, and there was nobody here to buy them.

When she saw Juliette and Lawrence approaching, she waved manically.

'Quick!' she said, 'go round, buy everything.'

Lawrence whistled, and Juliette turned in a full, slow circle. 'It looks fantastic, Char,' she said softly.

'It's the first-ever ghost festival. At least it will be remembered for something, but unfortunately it's not going to be for my Cornish cream teas, which I've spent hours making.'

Her friends followed her onto the bus and she gestured forlornly to the cake stands, the miniature slices of raspberry and white-chocolate cake, bus-shaped gingerbread biscuits with red and white icing, and tiny doughnuts filled with cream. Her fruit scones were waiting to go in the oven when customers were ready for them, and mini pots of jam and cream, along with tiny finger sandwiches filled with smoked salmon and cucumber, egg and cress and peppered beef and mustard were sitting in the fridge. It was all going to be wasted.

'There's some kind of meeting in the pub,' Lawrence said, pulling out his phone. 'I didn't look properly at the message, but I reckon that's why none of the locals are here.' He opened

WhatsApp and read it out: 'Important. Someone lit a solstice bonfire at Crumbling Cliff last night. Meeting at 11.00 in The Seven Stars. We can't let this sort of vandalism happen.'

'Who wrote it?' Once all her food trucks had arrived, Charlie hadn't even glanced at her messages.

'Myrtle,' Juliette said. 'Crumbling Cliff is dangerous, so I can understand why she's worried. Nobody should be on the grass between the road and the edge, even if it is the perfect place for a solstice bonfire.'

'Ugh.' Charlie rested her elbows on the counter. 'Maybe I've done this all wrong, and now the solstice is paying me back for having my food fest today.'

'Um, Char,' Lawrence said, pinching a sausage roll from the plate, 'how can a day of the year wreak revenge?'

Charlie shrugged. 'It's mystical, isn't it? It has lots of meaning, especially down here, and it's supposed to be honoured. I heard a couple of villagers muttering about disrespect as I passed them earlier.'

Juliette rolled her eyes. 'Don't listen to the naysayers. Some people are against anything new on principle. Once those tantalizing smells reach them, they'll be down here like a shot. It's a shame about Hugh, though. I know he was looking forward to coming.'

'What about Jonah?' Charlie asked. 'He can't have been called to the meeting.'

'If Myrtle's in charge, then I bet he can.' Lawrence wiped his hands down his jeans. 'But it can't go on all afternoon. She's bound to let them out eventually.'

'In the meantime,' Charlie said, 'go and find something to eat. I want to take a photo of you being glamorous festival attendees. I'll zoom in so nobody can see you're the only people here.'

150

'I want a burrito,' Juliette said immediately.

'I'm up for that.' Lawrence kissed her on the forehead.

Charlie followed them as they walked hand in hand to the Mexican food truck, and took a photo of them being handed their burritos by the owner, George, whose smile was as bright as his multicoloured apron.

She uploaded it to Instagram, Twitter and Facebook, with her hashtag and location tag, and HAPPENING NOW in capital letters.

This *couldn't* fail. She couldn't breeze in to this beautiful, hopeful village with her shiny bus, promise them new life, tackle the doubters, and then deliver absolutely nothing. Myrtle would have a field day. Daniel wouldn't offer her champagne, but instead would give her a pitying look and say something clever and scathing about how Gertie and Porthgolow didn't belong together.

As she returned to the bus, Oliver gave her a sympathetic smile, and she forced herself to smile back. She didn't want sympathy; she wanted success.

She wondered who had gone to Myrtle's meeting. It seemed like a huge coincidence that it was happening right that moment. She understood the importance of looking after the village, and if people were messing about somewhere dangerous then it needed to be addressed, but did it have to happen that morning?

She had thought Myrtle was beginning to soften towards her. The older woman obviously had some clout in Porthgolow, with most villagers visiting the pop-in on a regular basis. She could drip-feed her opinions and the latest gossip to everyone who walked through the door, and would be trusted more than an over-eager stranger who ran a café on a vintage bus.

Oliver jumped down from his truck and Charlie watched

as he struck up a conversation with Megu, resting his arms on the counter of her stall. She could hear Megu's delicate laughter as she responded to something he said. None of them would come back if it stayed like this all day, not even Oliver.

A comment popped up on her Instagram post and she pounced on it like a hungry wolf. It was from SurfsUpSeb, the man with mirrored sunglasses she'd met at the surfing competition, and read: '*This happening today? Cool!*' She replied: '*Come down, bring all your friends!*' and crossed her fingers.

And then a couple appeared at the edge of the beach. They were young, mid-twenties at most, and looked nervous about stepping into the middle of a deserted food festival. Charlie was wondering whether it would seem too overbearing to go and say hello, when Lawrence bounded over to them and started pointing out the different trucks. The couple smiled and glanced around, and then headed her way.

'Welcome to The Cornish Cream Tea Bus,' she beamed, handing them menus. 'Feel free to pick a table down here, or upstairs, where there are great views over the sea.'

'We'll go upstairs, I think,' the young man said, and the woman nodded her agreement.

'I'll be up to take your order in a moment.'

She waited until they had climbed the stairs, then rushed up to the front of the bus. 'High-five!' she said to Marmite, but he just tipped his head on one side, so she ruffled his fur instead. She was going to teach him to be a high-fiving dog. If she could make this festival work, then she could do anything she set her mind to.

Half an hour later there was a loud cacophony outside, as if a Harley-Davidson crew were rolling into Porthgolow. Charlie pressed her face against the window and watched as a convoy of cars and vans, some slightly battered, some with colourful decals or paint jobs, drove down the hill and into the car park. People began to emerge, walking across the sand towards the cluster of food trucks.

A familiar man with mirrored sunglasses appeared in the doorway of her bus.

'Surf's Up Seb, it's so lovely to see you.' She held out her hand.

'Likewise, Charlie.' He took her hand and leaned in to kiss her on the cheek. He smelt of vanilla and sea salt.

'I'm so glad you came!'

He gave a laconic shrug. 'You asked. It looks great. And this place is a gem,' he said, turning to face the sea. 'It's not got the right currents to create a big enough surf for us, which is a shame because the lookout is rosy as hell.'

'There are boat trips running from the jetty all day.' He raised an eyebrow and she added, 'RIBs. They're fast, fun – it's exhilarating.'

'I'll be sure to check it out.'

'Go, enjoy – and don't forget to come back for a coffee!'

'How could I forget?' He gestured at the bus, gleaming proudly in the sunshine, and Charlie laughed.

Seb wandered back to his friends and Charlie noticed Oliver watching her from the mojito stand. She gave him a wave and went to see if the young couple wanted more tea.

The surfers were loud and cheerful and their laughter and good-natured noise filled up the space, making it seem busy and vibrant. They might all be one large party, but that didn't make it any less of a success. And the photos she had taken, of the various food trucks busy with customers, and the bus surrounded by people, were bound to encourage more to come to the next event. She tagged Seb in some of the posts, hoping he'd get the hint and add his own to social media.

'So, this is the first Porthgolow festival?'

Charlie looked up from the cake stand she was rearranging, her mini doughnuts temporarily forgotten.

Daniel was wearing jeans and a navy T-shirt, his eyes narrowed against the sun. Behind him were Lauren and Hugh, and Jonah almost running, Paul keeping a hand on his shoulder to slow him down. Behind them, miraculously, was Myrtle. Her walk was more of a trudge, and her expression suggested she was being led towards the fiery pits of hell rather than a festival on a sunny beach, but she was here.

Charlie was at the door in seconds. 'Hello.'

Daniel smiled and approached, while Lauren made a beeline for the sushi truck. 'Hi,' he said. 'It's looking busy.' He didn't try to hide the surprise in his voice.

'Did you ever doubt it?' Charlie asked, silently thanking Seb and his crew. 'I told you it would be a success. How was the meeting?'

Daniel sighed and tipped his head back. 'Tedious. I understand that it's a problem if teenagers are messing about up there, especially in the dark, but I don't know what we can do except petition the council for some kind of barrier. I've told Myrtle that I've already done that and I'm waiting to hear back, but either she doesn't believe me or she doesn't think it's enough. But whatever the answer, it didn't need a two-hour meeting, and definitely not today.'

'It did seem a bit coincidental.'

Daniel laughed. 'Don't take it to heart. Myrtle isn't backwards in showing her disapproval, but she's like that with anyone who was born more than a mile away. She's certainly not *my* biggest fan, even when I give up my Saturday mornings to attend her meetings. Anyway, she's here now.'

'Is that your doing, though?'

Daniel glanced at the sea. 'I just told everyone that I'd had enough and I was coming to check out the festival. I wasn't the only one who was keen, and if there's anything that Myrtle hates more than usurpers, it's being left out.'

Charlie wondered if that was true, or if he'd been more persuasive. Whatever it was, she was touched. 'Thank you.'

'What for? I haven't done anything.'

'I feel like . . . as if you might be on my side.'

'It's still not about taking sides, Charlie. You've done something new in Porthgolow. Some people will like it, some will hate it. You shouldn't take it so personally.'

'You sound like Uncle Hal.'

He narrowed his eyes. 'Should I take that as a compliment? I know he was a big part of your life, but—'

'You approve of all this, do you Daniel?' Myrtle appeared at his side, her gaze fixed firmly on Charlie. 'Figures.'

'Come on Myrtle, you know it makes sense to bring more life to the village. What have you got against it?'

Charlie had thought that Daniel would have been shrewder than to give the older woman an open platform, but it was too late.

'It's mucking up the beach, and it's not the right way to celebrate the solstice. At least those idiots on Crumblin' Cliff had the right idea, even if they chose the wrong place. Lauren should have beaten 'em with her handbag. The size of it, she could've given 'em a proper hidin'.'

'Lauren?' Charlie asked.

'She saw the bonfire on the cliff on her way home from work,' Daniel said. 'She spoke to Myrtle about it first thing and Myrtle called the meeting. I wasn't going to go, but Lauren wanted the moral support.'

'Bleddy lot of use that did,' Myrtle said. 'And now this!' She flung her arm wide, and a couple of Seb's friends glanced in their direction.

'So if this isn't the right way to celebrate the solstice, what is?' Daniel asked.

Charlie shot him a warning look but he just smiled back, amused.

'You want a good fire to symbolize the longest day,' Myrtle said. 'I know it was technically last night, but in Penzance they have fireworks and a festival and all sorts, running over the whole weekend.'

'Well,' Daniel said, laughing, 'we've got the festival. If I can rustle up a bonfire and some fireworks – even if it's a day late – will you be satisfied?'

'Daniel, I—' Charlie felt a swell of panic.

'Where'd you light it?' Myrtle folded her arms.

'We could do it further down the beach now the tide's going out,' Daniel said. 'And I've put on fireworks displays up at the hotel before now – I can get in touch with the team I've used in the past and see if they have availability at short notice. We can launch them from the end of the jetty. Celebrate the solstice and Charlie's first festival at the same time. It won't be as big as Penzance, but it will be unique to Porthgolow. What do you think?'

'You can organize all of that in such a short space of time?' Charlie felt control slipping away from her. How could Daniel be so calm about lighting a huge fire? What if the smoke overwhelmed the food stalls?

'Leave it with me,' Daniel said. 'Only if Myrtle approves, of course.'

Myrtle's suspicious gaze flicked between Daniel and Charlie for what seemed like hours. Then she nodded. 'I'll go and tell Rose.' She shuffled off in the direction of the pop-in.

'Daniel,' Charlie said, as soon as Myrtle was out of earshot, 'do you really think this is a sensible idea? Are we even allowed to light fires on the beach?'

'Come on, Charlie, live a little. You've worked hard for today and this will ensure it's remembered. And I've done this sort of thing before. I can promise you that bonfires are allowed on this particular beach, and I'll even telephone the fire authority and let them know what's happening. I know what I'm doing.'

Charlie didn't doubt that for one second, which was partly why she felt so apprehensive. At the moment the festival was her initiative, the one thing she was contributing to the village. If she let Daniel take control of that too, then she was worried she would be powerless against him. But it was a great idea, and if it made some of the reluctant villagers warm to her, then it would be worth it.

'All right,' she said. 'Let's celebrate the summer solstice in style. I'd better go and tell everyone what's happening.'

She asked Juliette to cover the bus while she updated vendors and customers alike, wondering, not for the first time, if she should invest in a loud-hailer. She watched as Daniel went to talk to Lauren at the edge of the beach, the receptionist's pretty face twisting into a frown at his words. The black handbag on her arm was huge, just as Myrtle had said.

Chuckling to herself, Charlie went to give Oliver the good news.

Chapter Fourteen

By the time Charlie locked up The Cornish Cream Tea Bus, the sun was a mere glimmer over the sea, a line of burning amber below a sky of endless blue. Above her, she could see the first few pinpricks of stars.

Some of the other food trucks were still open – there was more appetite for burgers and burritos than evening cream teas – and The Marauding Mojito queue was longer than Charlie had ever seen it. Seb and his friends had stayed on, and their number had slowly grown until there was an unmistakable buzz that spread along the whole beach.

'Wow, this is gorgeous!'

Charlie turned to find a young woman with a pixie crop taking a photo of Gertie. 'Is she a London bus?' she asked.

'Yes, a vintage Routemaster, though the paintwork and most of the interior were redone this year. If she was still in her original state she would struggle to get admiring looks.'

'I'm sad we've arrived just as you're closing. Where will you be next?'

'I'm open here most days,' Charlie said. 'And I'll be travelling around Cornwall too. Look up The Cornish Cream Tea Bus online and you'll find me. Are you heading down to the bonfire?'

'Yup, meeting my friends by the burger stand, then we're going to wait for the fireworks on the beach.'

'It should be a good display.' With Daniel in charge, she couldn't imagine anything else.

Charlie could hardly believe that, on her first day as festival proprietor, people were already arranging to meet their friends here. Of course, that was mostly down to Daniel's quick thinking, finding a way to placate Myrtle while also turning the first Porthgolow Food Fest into something bigger.

There had been definite interest when she'd told the other vendors and visitors about the bonfire and fireworks display, and she didn't think it was solely Seb's friends filling up the beach. Word was getting around that the day was due to end in spectacular fashion. She couldn't imagine anyone back home being as enthusiastic at such short notice, and wondered whether it was something about Cornwall, with its wildness and holiday atmosphere, that exuded a sense of freedom and spontaneity.

Charlie walked further down the sand, towards where the large bonfire was crackling noisily, sparks and flames shooting up into the darkening sky. It had been cordoned off by netting and metal poles, and gave the impression of being planned and professional, rather than something that had only been dreamed up that afternoon. There was someone playing a folk tune on a ukulele, and a group of friends were braving the shallows, lit by the glow of the fire.

'Charlie!' She turned at the sound of her name and saw Juliette waving, Lawrence standing behind her with a bottle of beer. She went to join them.

'God, Charlie,' Juliette said, 'did you ever imagine it would be like this? It's magnificent! Look at all the people. Look at the size of those flames!' It was hard to ignore the way they shimmied and danced against the backdrop of the inky sea. There was someone standing inside the wide cordon, no more than a silhouette, but Charlie didn't think it was Daniel – perhaps one of the team he'd mentioned earlier.

'It's brilliant.' Charlie took a beer and sat next to Juliette, pulling Marmite onto her lap. He didn't seem anxious about the fire, but it would be the first time he'd encountered fireworks, and she was worried he would be terrified. 'Though it's not how I imagined tonight panning out, if I'm honest,' she continued. 'I thought we'd be packed up by eight and celebrating at home or in The Seven Stars.'

'You don't regret this happening, do you?'

'Not at all. I'm just . . . surprised that Daniel was able to put it together so quickly.'

Juliette was quiet for a moment. 'He really meant to give me that contract? I can't imagine him messing up like that, signing something without reading it properly.' Charlie had given Juliette Daniel's explanation about the marketing mix-up, and told her all about the near miss, the day it had happened.

'I know, but that's what he told me, and I believe him.' It had been the first time she felt as though she'd seen below his armour of confidence and swagger. He was angry with himself for the mistake, and for letting Juliette down, and for some reason he had been able to swallow his pride and admit it to her. 'I'm just not sure why he's doing all this. Why he's gone to the effort.'

'He's not exactly the village's most popular person,' Juliette said. 'Perhaps this is his attempt to give back to the community and show them that he's one of us.'

'One of us,' Lawrence intoned in an emotionless voice. 'Sounds like something from *Invasion of the Body Snatchers*.'

'More like *The Wicker Man*.' Charlie gestured to the bonfire and they laughed.

Night settled around them, the crackling flames and churn of the waves the backdrop to their conversation. Jonah made a fuss of Marmite until Paul decided it was his bedtime and they left with only a minimal amount of protest. Stella and Anton came and sat with them, sharing a bottle of red wine that they'd brought from home.

'I've never seen it like this,' Stella admitted. 'The beach is always so quiet in the evenings; it's such a sleepy little cove. This reminds me of Australia. We partied all night and then went to watch the sun come up on a beach near Sydney. It was as busy as if it was midday, just like now.'

'We missed out on the food, Charlie,' Anton said, 'but we'll be there next time. I never turn down the chance of a fully loaded burger.'

'That's what I'm having next weekend, for sure.' Lawrence clinked his bottle against Anton's wine glass, and Charlie watched the flames flicker over their faces, playing with their features. She heard a burst of laughter and turned to see Myrtle talking to a tall gentleman wearing a grey windbreaker. She was holding a mojito and clutching his arm while her body shook with mirth. Charlie had to force herself to stop staring, sure that when she turned back they would be gone: a figment of her imagination appearing in the bonfire's heat haze.

Juliette stretched her arms up to the sky. 'When are the fireworks kicking off?'

'Give me a chance,' said a voice from behind them. Daniel crouched on the sand between Charlie and Juliette and rested his elbows on his knees. 'Half an hour,' he added. 'They're just doing the final safety checks.'

'I wasn't being impatient,' Juliette said hurriedly, 'I was just wondering.'

'I know that.'

Charlie could hear the smile in his voice, could feel the warmth of his shoulder pressed against hers.

'And look, Juliette, I don't know if Charlie mentioned to you—'

'She has,' Juliette said. 'You don't need to explain.'

'Great. Good. Thanks, Charlie. And I really am sorry, Jules. I should have had all my ducks in a row, and I didn't. I'll be more careful in future. I hope this will go a little way towards making up for it. It was Charlie's idea.' He handed her an envelope, and Juliette squinted at it in the gloom. 'It's a spa voucher, for you and Lawrence. Come and have a pampering session.'

'Daniel, you didn't—'

'It's the least I could do. Just call reception when you want to book in and we'll sort everything out. I'd better go and check on the fireworks, seeing as some people are so impatient for them.' He used Charlie's shoulder as leverage to help him stand.

'Daniel—' she called.

He turned to face her, and she could see the fire reflected in his eyes.

'Thank you, for all this. It's wonderful.'

'If it gets us in Myrtle's good books, then I'll be happy.' He strode over to the jetty, where several powerful torch beams lit up a hive of activity.

'That's not the only reason he's done it,' Juliette said, filling the space Daniel had just vacated. 'He's never bothered trying to placate Myrtle before. And he's never, ever looked like he was even capable of offering an apology until today. I wonder if you might have something to do with it?' Her voice was light and amused, but it made Charlie's stomach churn.

She had been thinking about their previous conversation a lot in the days leading up to the festival. His offer of a massage, his hand over hers on the table. Her mind kept pinging between that and Oliver on the beach, the way he had come to her rescue in March, and Stuart; Stuart who had been so smooth and sure of himself – similar to Daniel in that one way – and who had then discarded her like a used-up chew toy. It was an uncontrollable game of Ping-pong that she couldn't seem to put an end to.

She hadn't come to Cornwall to find romance. She was wholly focused on her bus, on giving Gertie the future she deserved and, since she'd arrived in Porthgolow and fallen for its quaint beauty, on bringing life back to the village.

Love wasn't on the cards for her: she wasn't ready. But as the first firework shot up into the sky above them and Charlie held her quivering puppy against her chest, soothing him and kissing his fur, she found herself focusing, not on the sparkling display in the night sky, but on the jetty, wondering which of the silhouettes was him.

The online response to the first Porthgolow food festival was beyond Charlie's wildest dreams. She lay in bed the following morning and scrolled through her phone, looking at the photos and videos that had been uploaded and reading the comments below her posts. The hashtag #PorthgolowFoodFest had been shared hundreds of times.

Even the Porthgolow Hideaway account had got in on the act, taking a shot of the festival from above – it looked like from the top of the south cliff – that showed the colourful trucks bright in the sunshine.

She thought of Daniel's involvement, and how much smaller the event would have been if he hadn't stepped in. Had he been driven by self-interest, getting the villagers on side so there was less animosity towards him, too? He'd promoted the fireworks and bonfire on the hotel's social media pages, which had no doubt spread its reach even further.

Charlie sighed and closed her eyes. She should be feeling triumphant. There were no bonfire accidents, the fireworks had been spectacular, and she'd seen Myrtle laughing. It was miraculous. And yet Daniel's involvement – and his motivations – unsettled her. She had wanted the villagers to be involved, for the event to be for, and owned by, all of them. But as soon as Daniel started to take over, anxiety had crept in. She knew that was probably more about her than him, about wanting to regain control of a life that had, in the space of six months, changed completely, but that realization didn't make her feel any better.

If she wanted her events to be truly successful then she would have to loosen the reins a little bit, even if that meant allowing Daniel to help. After all, he clearly knew what he was doing.

Later that morning, the WhatsApp messages started. First it was Hugh, singing Charlie's praises and saying his pub had been busier last night than he'd seen it in a long time, though understandably it had emptied out just before the fireworks. Amanda and Paul had nothing but praise, and Stella and Anton had received three new booking enquiries for the B&B that morning. Even Myrtle had got in on the act: *A very fitting solstice event. Thank you.* A genuine thank you – Charlie couldn't believe it! But, she had also hastened to point out in her reply that Daniel was responsible for a lot of it. She couldn't take all the credit for the way people had flocked to Porthgolow as the sun started to set, even though Seb's crowd of chilled-out twenty-somethings had been down to her.

There was no reply from Daniel, which, Charlie thought, was unusual for a man who wasn't shy about throwing his weight around. But she didn't have too long to mull over it, because the comments and enquiries she'd had since last night were going to keep her busy for the rest of the week.

Her fledgling idea was spreading its wings and she was already adapting it, thinking how to root it, firmly, in Porthgolow culture. Last night, with the added entertainment and the summer solstice background, it had definitely been a festival. But without those, it was more like a weekly food market. Something people could drop in on to simply pick up lunch, or spend the whole day at, browsing the stalls, enjoying the tastes and smells and spending time on the beach. If she promoted it like that, she thought it would build up more of a regular customer base, locals who knew they could come and get something a bit different, as well as attracting tourists.

Charlie updated the village WhatsApp group and let her fellow vendors know. The Porthgolow Food Market. It had a great ring to it, and she hoped that, before too long, it would be known across the whole of Cornwall.

The following Saturday the weather was even hotter, and Charlie, Juliette and Lawrence were on the beach early to help every food truck manoeuvre into the right space. Marmite danced about their feet, and while her friends laughed each time they almost fell face-first into the sand, Charlie ended up putting him in his crate.

'You can come out later,' she said, 'once you've calmed down.' Now all she needed to do was follow her own advice. The bus was gleaming, her scones, cakes and pastries were fresh and raring to go, and she had double the number of food trucks taking part today. There was already a buzz on social media, and there was no reason to suspect anything would go wrong. But she was still running on nerves.

Everything started off well. George in the Mexican burrito van, Megu and her Japanese food truck and The Travelling Cornish Pasty Shack, run by twins called Rachel and Andie, all greeted her warmly and then acted like old hands, helping some of the newcomers find their feet. Charlie focused on getting vehicles in the right places, and then on her bus. She'd been more ambitious with her cream teas this week, working out how to cook miniature chocolate fondants in Gertie's on-board oven.

The sun baked down on Porthgolow beach and, even before the official opening time, there were people wandering among the stalls. Jeremy and Delia, who lived in the road behind Juliette and who had become semi-regulars on her bus over the last few weeks, ordered a Cornish cream tea for two and went to sit in their favourite spot on the top deck.

Everything was as it should be. The smells were as tantalising as ever, no village meetings had been called, and there were groups of friends taking it in turns to be in a picture with Gertie, each photographer having to crouch and angle the shot so that her red, gleaming bulk fitted into the frame.

Charlie served and wiped down tables, swaying along to the music from the Turkish kebab stall, which added a jaunty soundtrack to the event. There were people further down the sand, stripping to their swimming costumes and running into the waves, and the queue for the ice-cream van snaked out of sight. Charlie found she was chatting and laughing more than she had done in months. Who couldn't fail to be happy on a day like this, working at an event that was providing so much pleasure?

She was assessing her stock levels, wondering whether she needed to make more sandwiches or text Juliette to ask for a hand over lunchtime, when voices close to the open window drifted through to reach her. She'd been hearing snippets of conversation all day: what was showing at Truro cinema and whether it was a crime to go when the weather was so glorious; could two friends get away with swimming in their underwear or would they have to go home and get changed; should Geraint have the double-stack cheeseburger or the New York deli cheeseburger? Charlie had been entertaining herself by silently answering their questions – she had just managed to stop herself suggesting Geraint had a cream tea instead.

But these voices were different. They didn't sound light or carefree, they sounded annoyed. The hairs prickled on the back of Charlie's neck. She stayed crouched next to the fridge, and as she listened to their conversation she stiffened, her mouth drying out. She could barely believe what she was hearing.

Chapter Fifteen

'You have to admit it's grand, Rose.' It was a man speaking, slightly gruff, his low timbre suggesting he wasn't that young. And Charlie knew exactly who Rose was.

'Think what all these cars are doing to the roads, Frank. Crumbling Cliff will be fallin' into the sea in no time. Then there's the pollution, the noise. Not to mention the poor beach. It's all sufferin'. What about my ma's afternoon nap? How can anyone get any rest with all this goin' on?'

Rose was about Myrtle's age, which meant she was over fifty. Charlie wondered how old her mother was, and felt a twinge of guilt at the thought of ruining her nap. But then Frank spoke again.

'Oh well, maybe Daniel was right. It won't last long. A flash in the pan, that's what 'ee said. A few weeks and the maid'll be gone, scatterbrain that she is. She's already changed the name of it – festival or food market, what difference does it make? No, she'll soon be off again, back home or somewhere

168

else with this bloody great thing.' Charlie heard him pound his hand against the side of the bus. It was as loud as her heart thumping in her ears.

'A flash in the pan,' she whispered to herself. 'Scatterbrain?' She imagined Daniel giving the villagers a lecture at the meeting last week – or had he said all this since then? '*Don't worry, everybody. Humour her for a little while; she'll soon be gone.*' Was that what he had been doing? Rage fired through her, hotter than the heat of the day, but Rose and Frank weren't done yet.

'Weren't you here having a cream tea yerseln' last Saturday?' Rose asked.

'I was,' Frank admitted, sighing. 'And it was great. But,' he added quickly, and Charlie imagined the daggers Rose was giving him over her silver-rimmed glasses, 'if Daniel's going to be doing cream teas on a Saturday, then we won't feel the loss of this place.'

'Daniel's just as bad,' Rose said. 'Young yuppie comin' in and swaggering about as if he owns the village.'

'But Crystal Waters isn't going anywhere, is it?' Frank said. 'May as well make the most of it. Now, are you off home?'

'In a bit,' Rose replied. 'Goin' to pick my ma up some fudge, and mebbe take a look at those Cornish pasties.'

'I wanted to look at the tea stall, see about getting some of that Cornish blend. Truro's the closest place other than here. I could stock up if this is all going to be ending soon.'

'Let's go there first, as that's the closest one,' Rose said. 'Just over here, past the curry place. Don't those spices smell amazin'?'

Charlie waited a few minutes for Frank's reply, but it didn't come and she realized they had gone. Off to enjoy the food market they hated so much and couldn't wait to get rid of. She stood and dusted down her skirt, the anger bubbling inside her. Never mind Rose and Frank's hypocrisy, how dare Daniel be supportive to her face while he was plotting her downfall with the villagers? Did he really think she was scatterbrained? She had done nothing to warrant that insult. And as for him adding cream teas to his menu to spite her, she—

'Excuse me, but would we be able to sit down?'

Charlie turned to find a boy of about fifteen looking at her with alarm. She tried to soften her glare.

'God, yes. Sorry – I was miles away. I think there are a couple of tables upstairs if you'd prefer the view? Here are some menus.'

'Th-thank you.' He took them from her, then almost ran back down the aisle of the bus.

Charlie leant against the counter and closed her eyes. She couldn't let them get the better of her. She didn't mind so much about the older villagers, but after all Daniel had said and done, she wasn't prepared to let him get away with it.

When she finally locked Gertie up and went round the other stalls, thanking everyone for a great event, her feet were throbbing and there was a persistent ache in her lower back. She should feel overjoyed at the success of her second week, but all she could think about was what she had overheard.

'You look like you could do with a cocktail,' Oliver said, as she reached The Marauding Mojito. He seemed as relaxed as ever, despite the sweat on his brow and the detritus of lime peel and mint leaves around him, showing that his day had been as busy as hers.

'I would love to, Ollie, but I've got to go and see someone.'

'Oh. Anyone important?' He came down from the truck.

'Just . . .' She couldn't tell him about Daniel, or why what he'd said had made her so mad. 'I need to clear something up.'

'Of course,' Oliver said, his smile faltering. 'But I'll see you again next week?'

'Definitely! Next Saturday. The Porthgolow food market is here to stay.' If she'd been determined before, then she was absolutely adamant about it now.

'Want to get together sometime soon when we're not working? I could show you this place I know near Helford, or the Eden Project grounds are great this time of year.'

'They both sound lovely. Thank you.' She kissed his cheek.

'I'll be in touch,' he said, squeezing her arm. 'Bye, Marmite.'

The walk up the hill was a struggle, the heat lingering long into the evening, but after a day spent mostly in the cab, Marmite almost bounced to the top of the cliff, and Charlie was spurred on by her dog's enthusiasm and her own anger. She arrived at the retreat with sweat pooling down her spine, her cheeks hot from the exertion. Walking into reception was like being wrapped in a cool blanket, and she breathed a sigh of relief.

'Charlie, hi,' Lauren said. 'How can I help?' She was looking at her curiously, and Charlie wondered if the rage was beaming out of her pores like some kind of aura.

'Is Daniel here? I need to talk to him.'

Lauren glanced at her watch, and Charlie realized that, this late on a Saturday, he might well be somewhere else, enjoying a night out with friends, crowing at how he'd duped the woman who'd arrived in his village with nothing but good intentions and a hearty dose of gullibility.

'I think he's still in the office,' Lauren said. 'Let me check.'

'Thank you.' Charlie shut her eyes for a moment, weariness

171

taking the place of her fading adrenalin, and opened them to find Daniel standing in front of her.

'Hello.' His eyes swept over her. 'How are you?'

'Can we talk?' She kept her voice calm. She didn't want Lauren eavesdropping on their conversation, even though she wouldn't be here if she hadn't been doing exactly that herself. But Rose and Frank had been standing right next to her bus – what had she been supposed to do? Put her hands over her ears and sing 'la la la'?

'Sure,' Daniel said, frowning. 'Want to come into my office?'

'That would be good, thanks.' She was conscious of how she must look, red-faced and sweaty, while he was cool and composed and perfectly at home.

'Isn't Marmite with you?'

'I tied him up outside. There's a bowl of water, but . . .' She trailed off. She should have taken him home first, but she wasn't planning on staying long.

'Don't leave him out there – bring him in.'

'Daniel,' Lauren said. 'I don't think—'

'It's fine, Lauren. He can come into the office. It's much cooler in there.'

'That would be great.' Charlie rushed outside and untied Marmite, reminding herself that Daniel was a master of charm. She couldn't let his show of kindness sway her.

Back inside, Daniel led the way behind the reception desk and into his office. He closed the door behind them.

It had no walnut cupboards or shark tank in the floor, as far as she could see. It was small and neat, with white walls and a pine desk. There was a noticeboard pinned with various letters and leaflets, and a photo in the bottom corner of Jasper, Daniel's German shepherd, as a chunky puppy with his tongue hanging out. A peace lily sat on the desk, and a blue fabric sofa was pushed up against one wall. The high window looked out on the car park, which Charlie thought was a shame when there was such a spectacular view on the other side of the hotel.

'Do you want some water?' Daniel asked, taking Marmite gently out of Charlie's arms and settling him on the sofa. He gestured for her to sit next to her dog.

'I'm . . . uh,' she managed, torn between her raging desire for a cool drink and her need to be strong in the face of his gallantry.

Daniel nodded. 'I'll be back in a moment.'

Charlie sat next to Marmite and stroked him while he chewed the arm of the sofa. She chided him gently, but the dog kept going and she felt a small stab of satisfaction.

'Here you are,' Daniel said, returning with a jug and two glasses. 'You look like you need it.'

'I'm fine,' she snapped, but she took the glass and drained it in a single gulp.

Daniel settled into his chair, wheeled it round to face her, and rested his hands on his stomach. His brows were knitted together, but his mouth was twitching as if he was trying to suppress a smile.

'How can I help you, Charlie?'

'You didn't come to the food market today. Why was that?'

'I've been busy here. Saturdays are one of our main check-in days. Did you expect me to come every week?'

'I bet you've been planning your new afternoon teas, too, haven't you? So you can take over once my "scatterbrain" events peter out. You must have been so pleased when you thought of it; letting me have a few Saturdays on the beach, then filling the void with your upmarket menu once I'd run out of puff.'

Daniel took her glass and refilled it, then pressed it gently

173

back into her grasp. 'I don't know what you're talking about,' he said calmly. 'But something's obviously pissed you off and you've decided I'm the punch bag.'

'Of course you are! You said I was a scatterbrain, that my food markets weren't going to last and that you were going to start serving cream teas in your hotel.'

'When exactly did I say all this?' He leaned back and folded his arms. He'd stopped even trying to hide his smile now, which only made Charlie's heart race faster.

'I don't know! But Rose and Frank were talking about it, right outside Gertie. How ridiculous it was that I'd started calling it a food market instead of a festival, and how they were going to run out of steam and you were waiting to take over once I'd gone back home with my *bloody bus!*'

Daniel stared at her, and then started laughing. He leaned forward and tried to put his hand on her arm, but Charlie pushed herself into the sofa, away from him.

'How can you find this funny?'

'Because it is,' Daniel said. 'Rose and Frank got the wrong end of the stick, that's all. It got lost in translation.'

'Explain.'

Daniel raised an eyebrow at her sharp tone. 'Gladly. I was in The Seven Stars the other night, and bumped into a friend, Evan, who lives in the next village over. I mentioned the food market – which seems an entirely valid thing to call it, by the way – and, in an attempt to encourage him to get his backside along to the next one, said that you didn't live in the area, so I didn't know how long they would last, and that he'd better come while he could.'

Charlie digested that, and nodded. 'I was hoping the markets would continue after I've left Porthgolow. But that's only going to happen if everyone's behind them.'

'You're not staying?' Daniel took a sip of water.

'I don't know how long I'll be here. I can't live with Juliette and Lawrence for ever, can I?' She couldn't seem to moderate her tone and Daniel held a hand up in submission.

'I was only asking,' he said. 'I promise I have never called you a scatterbrain. I may have called you a few other things – I'd had a few beers by this time, which is why I didn't realize I was being listened to so intently – but never scatterbrain.'

'What *did* you call me?'

'What else are you accusing me of?' There was an edge to his voice now, and she wondered whether this was about to escalate into a full-scale argument. She wasn't sure she had the energy for that.

'The fact that you said you were going to start serving cream teas here, at the hotel, in direct competition with me.'

Daniel sighed. 'I'm not sure whether to nominate those two for troublemakers – or idiots – of the year. I was annoyed by the WhatsApp love-in the other day, the fact that you were getting all the credit for the solstice festival.'

'I made *sure* that I gave you the credit, I—'

'Let me finish, Charlie. I was pissed off, I was a bit drunk, and I told Evan I was going to start making a feature of afternoon teas at the hotel. We already serve them, but they can't compete with yours. Our view looks over the sea, you're right on the beach. The restaurant here is pretty smart, you're on a vintage double-decker bus with all its charms and trappings. Is it your sole purpose in life to make me admit my weaknesses to you?' He looked irritated, suddenly. Tired and irritated. Charlie couldn't blame him; it was after eight o'clock on a summery, Saturday night and she had forced him into his shoebox office to have a go at him.

'You already sell cream teas?'

'Yes, Charlie.'

'You're not trying to get rid of me, and you didn't call me a scatterbrain?'

He levelled her with a look, and Charlie dropped her gaze to a snoozing Marmite, who was taking full advantage of the sofa now he'd stopped assaulting it.

'They were so convincing,' Charlie said. 'They didn't know I was listening, and they came out with all this stuff, so I—'

'What is it your uncle Hal said? Forget the mistake, remember the lesson?'

Charlie nodded.

'The lesson here is never to listen to other people's conversations and take them to heart. That goes for Rose and Frank as much as you. Now, are we done? Because I've got much more important things to be doing with my time.'

Charlie nodded, feeling suitably chastised. She should have asked him, rather than going in, all guns blazing. She stood and went to pick up Marmite, but Daniel put his hand on her arm. His skin was warm and dry, and Charlie's breath faltered.

'Leave him,' he said softly.

'I thought you had other things to do,' Charlie whispered.

'I do. They involve you, the hot tub, and the Porthgolow sunset. Come on.'

Charlie held up the black swimming costume. It was simple, not too low or high cut, too frumpy or too exposing. When she had tried to complain, to tell Daniel she couldn't possibly go to the hot tub with him, he had dismissed all her excuses and led her to the spa shop, told her to pick out a costume and showed her where the changing rooms were. Charlie should have said no. She should have thought of some pressing

176

reason why she couldn't stay, but then the thought of those bubbles soothing her event-weary limbs, and the promise of the sunset over the sea, made her hesitate. She didn't want to settle for too long on how important Daniel's presence was in the whole equation.

She changed into the swimming costume, put on the robe and slippers that he had given her, and stepped into the corridor. Daniel was nowhere to be found, but a woman with blonde hair and a nametag that read 'Cherry' over a dark green tunic caught her eye.

'Daniel asked me to take you to the hot tub. He said he'll join you as soon as he can.'

Charlie nodded, and let Cherry lead her along silent corridors and out into the scented garden – past three of the wooden pods that Marmite had taken a misplaced interest to at the St Agnes Head Festival – and down to the hot tub. It was already bubbling and the water looked clear and inviting, the sea beyond contrastingly still. The sun was starting its descent, the horizon a hazy pink after the heat of the day.

Thanking Cherry, Charlie slipped off her robe and slippers. She climbed into the bubbles, sinking down until only her neck and head were above the luxuriously hot water. The cliff-top breeze whispered around her, and the sight of Cornwall's rugged landscape and the endless ocean beyond was breathtaking. She could see why people paid a lot of money to come here. For this experience alone, the hot bubbles, the fresh air and the unbeatable view, it would be worth it.

She leaned her arms on the side of the tub and looked out to sea, laughing at the turn the evening had taken. An hour ago, she'd been hot and flustered and mad as hell with Daniel, and yet, here she was. Putting up little resistance to his suggestion after he'd smoothly addressed all her concerns. Had she been too easy to accept his explanations? She remembered all the times Stuart had dismissed her worries, including the first inklings she'd had that he had been cheating on her. He'd placated her, and at the same time made her sound foolish and neurotic.

She wasn't in a relationship with Daniel – she barely knew him – but that didn't stop the familiar twist of anxiety. She thought of Oliver, his disappointment when she'd turned down his offer of a cocktail to come storming up here.

This was a mistake.

She pushed herself up on her arms, wondering if she could make it inside before Daniel appeared.

She heard a crunch of gravel and turned.

The answer was a resounding no.

Chapter Sixteen

Daniel had two glasses of what looked suspiciously like champagne. He held one out for Charlie, and she reached forward to take it, then sank back into the water.

'Cheers.' He sat on the wooden bench that ran around the outside of the hot tub.

'Cheers.' Charlie clinked glasses with him. 'You're not coming in?'

'We've got a late check-in due to arrive in ten minutes' time, and Lauren's about to go home. I'll join you once they're settled in.'

'Why?' She took a sip of the champagne. It was delicious: fruity but crisp, not too sweet.

'Why, what?'

'Why are we doing this? Do you feel bad about what you sort-of said in the pub?'

He grinned. It was dangerous and sexy, and did strange

things to Charlie's insides that had nothing to do with anxiety. 'You think this is an apology because someone else misinterpreted my words and you got unintentionally offended? No. This is because I told you to come up to the hotel and try out the hot tub – and once you were here it seemed too good an opportunity to miss.'

'An opportunity for what?'

'To get you exactly where I want you.'

She swallowed. Even if she'd wanted to reply, it seemed her mouth had stopped working.

'I've tasted your scones and cakes,' Daniel continued. 'I thought it was about time you sampled the hotel. And this is the best bit.' He gestured towards the view and Charlie turned, spellbound by it all over again.

'It's stunning,' she said.

'And good for relaxing when you've had a busy day, or you're stressed out.'

'I'm less stressed than I was,' she admitted. 'But you can understand why I was so angry.'

'If I'd said those things, then your anger would have been entirely justified.' He glanced at his watch and stood up. 'I'll be back soon. Don't go anywhere.' He went inside, his shoes crunching on the gravel.

Charlie could hear the low murmur of people enjoying the outdoor pool, but the hot tub was on a higher part of the grounds, and not visible from there. She leaned her head back and closed her eyes, letting the bubbles soothe away any last tension.

Ten minutes ago, she had definitely been leaving. Now, she didn't think anything could persuade her to go. A small voice inside her head told her it was because Daniel was coming back. The logical part of her brain reasoned that it was because she would be a fool to pass up something so luxurious, especially after such a busy day.

'I shouldn't really be doing this.' Daniel's voice was low, conspiratorial. Charlie opened her eyes, biting back a gasp when she saw that he was wearing one of the hotel's fluffy robes and holding the bottle of champagne.

'Why not?' Charlie asked him. 'You were the one who invited me here.' Her pulse quickened as he undid the cord of his dressing gown. She turned away, but she had seen the definition of his collarbone, strong shoulders, dark chest hair. She felt the water shift as he joined her, then reached over the side to grab his glass.

'It's unprofessional,' Daniel told her.

'Why? Fraternizing with the guests?'

'Making use of my own facilities.'

'But haven't you booked the hot tub out for me? What if I had invited you in as *my* guest? Nobody else will turn up, and even if they do – so what?'

'All excellent points. I can see you're going to be a bad influence on me.'

Charlie clinked her glass against his for a second time. 'Pretty sure it's the other way around,' she murmured.

The air seemed to bubble between them; everything, on this beautiful evening, was bubbling, especially Charlie's nerves. What was she really doing here? She tried not to think about the answer as Daniel moved round, until he was facing the sea.

'Tell me more about Jasper,' she said. 'Where does he go when you're at work?' It was the first thing she could think of that might put them on safe ground. It all felt a bit dangerous, and not because the hot tub was closer to the cliff edge than she would have liked.

'My neighbour, Lily, looks after him. She's got two Labradors, and they have a great time together, apparently.'

'Oh.' Charlie resisted the urge to ask more about Lily, specifically her age, and how attractive she was. Did Daniel repay her kindness with evenings like this, in the hot tub? She listened to him, laughing as he told her how badly behaved his dog had been as a puppy, and how, initially, Jasper had sent his organized life spinning into chaos.

'So you're a workaholic?' she asked.

'I'm proud of this place. I had a strong idea about how I wanted it to turn out, and I made it happen. Just like you and the food markets.'

'Today's was even better than the first,' she said, smiling. Now she was away from the beach and her anger had been quashed, she could appreciate how well it had gone, how something that had started as a spark of an idea could become an established event in Porthgolow. It was already getting recognition further afield. 'Even if it didn't end with fireworks this time round.'

'I'm sure your Uncle Hal would be proud of you.' Daniel turned to face her. 'You miss him a lot, don't you?'

'All the time,' she said quietly.

'But you have Gertie. She's a beautiful bus – now – very popular, great food. There's something simple and romantic about serving cakes on a bus.'

'*Simple and romantic,*' she echoed. 'Can I quote you on that? I could pop a decal on the side, get posters and banners printed. *Successful local hotelier urges you to come aboard the romantic Cornish Cream Tea Bus.*'

'And,' he continued, ignoring her, 'I reckon you could do worse than ending up here, with this view, to get you back on track after your uncle's death. Porthgolow is soothing to the soul.'

182

'Even if it starts out twisted?' Charlie grinned, then felt instantly guilty. 'Sorry. God, I don't really think that you have a twisted soul.'

Daniel's eyes crinkled at the edges. 'What do you think of me?'

Charlie groaned. 'Why would you ask that? How is anyone meant to answer that question honestly?' He didn't reply. She waited while he poured the remainder of the champagne into their glasses before continuing. 'I don't think you take anything seriously, other than this hotel, which is your pride and joy. I always feel wrong-footed when I'm around you. Are you helping me, or making fun of me? And if you *are* helping me, then why? Is it because you see me as a kindred spirit, someone else in the village who isn't particularly popular? Do you want to be some sort of a team?'

Daniel moved closer. It was only a few inches, but Charlie noticed. 'I think we could be a very good team, if we put our minds to it.'

Charlie inhaled. She could feel the champagne fizzing inside her, lightening her mind, making her stomach dance. Daniel had such strong shoulders, a firm, angular jaw line. Everything about him was solid and real and, at that moment, far too close. She slid further round the hot tub.

'You want us to help each other out?' she asked, hoping she sounded calmer than she felt.

'I'm not making fun of you, Charlie. I'm trying to get to know you. To understand why you've whirled into this village that – I presume – you've never been to before, and have adopted it as if it's a stray puppy. You don't owe Porthgolow anything.'

Charlie pursed her lips, thinking seriously about his question. 'Juliette fell in love with this place as soon as she arrived, and when I got here I could see its charms. And Hal spent his life making other people happy: that was the reason for his tours, for Gertie, for everything he did. I want to keep his legacy alive, and show that, even though he's gone, Gertie can carry on, with me. And once she was up and running I just thought . . .'

Daniel moved closer, reaching up to stroke her damp hair. 'What did you think?'

'I thought that – that holding an event would be a challenge. An adventure.' Her words were rough. She wondered if she was even saying them out loud. 'And I realized I could bring some life back to Porthgolow at the same time.'

His face was inches from hers. He leaned in and, so softly, brushed his lips against hers. Electricity rushed through her. Every part of her responded to his touch and, for a moment, she was kissing him back. Her heart pounded louder than the jets of the Jacuzzi. How could his kiss be tender and commanding, all at once? It felt right. Wonderful. Perfect, but . . . she pulled away from him.

Daniel's eyes were searching. 'Charlie, do you want to—?'

'That shouldn't have happened. Should that have happened?'

She pictured Oliver with his blond hair and *The Marauding Mojito* T-shirt, Stuart knowing exactly what to say and soothing away her worries. Daniel was so sure of himself. What if he *had* said those things in the pub, bad-mouthed her to the other villagers? Accepting Stuart's lies was what had led to her heartbreak in the first place. She didn't know Daniel, but she had let him get close to her; she had encouraged him. And it had felt so good.

'Why shouldn't it have happened?' he asked.

'I'm sorry, Daniel. I should go.' She clambered out of the

hot tub, scrabbled for her robe and pulled it over her wet skin. 'Marmite's still in your office – he's probably going frantic.'

'Charlie!' Daniel stood and hopped out of the hot tub in a single, impressive move. Charlie tried not to look at him standing there dripping, the water, turned golden by the sun, running in rivulets down his toned chest, his arms, his legs. His sodden navy trunks hugged his thighs, and his hair was plastered to his forehead. He looked even more delicious than her chocolate-chip scones. Hal's voice slipped into her head: *Spontaneous moments are always better than planned ones.* It was one of his life lessons that wasn't, at this point, remotely helpful.

'Thank you so much for this, Daniel,' she said. 'I really do appreciate it. And I feel so much more relaxed.' Or she had, until he'd kissed her.

'You're welcome.' The stiffness in his voice told her he'd switched to professional mode. Whatever there had been between them a few moments ago, she'd successfully killed it. 'I'll get Marmite for you.'

'Thank you, that's very kind.'

'We aim to please.' He pulled on his robe and tied it tightly around his waist.

She followed him inside, the sun setting at their backs.

'What did you want to talk to me about?'

Reenie passed Charlie a steaming cup of tea and sat alongside her on the edge of her concrete garden outside her yellow house. Charlie couldn't get over the view, the way the sunlight sprinkled the waves with shimmering pink. In another half an hour, the sea would look like it was on fire. She had thought the end of the jetty was good, but this was something else.

'I couldn't fail to notice your success yesterday,' Reenie continued, when Charlie didn't reply.

'It didn't disturb you, did it?'

'Not at all, girl. It's good to see there's still some life in the old village. Now, tell me what this is about. I can't believe you came here to resume your role as my waste-disposal operative. I have hardly anything to give you – it's not been that long since you took my last load of recycling.'

'No, it's not that. It's . . .' What was it, exactly? The evening after her dip in the hot tub, Charlie's head was so full and, with Juliette and Lawrence having a meal out in Truro, she could only think of one place to come. 'How well do you know Daniel?' she asked.

There was a moment of silence. Then an 'ah'. Then a chuckle.

'What?' Charlie said. 'What does that mean?'

Reenie smirked. 'You want to know more about our resident hotshot hotelier? You've fallen for his charms already, then.'

'He kissed *me*, actually.'

'Good Lord, girl. Things are moving faster than I anticipated.'

Charlie stared at her. 'What do you mean? You *knew* this would happen?'

'Daniel needs someone who can match him for tenacity and stubbornness and, even though he's got a ruthless streak and you're as kind as they come, I thought you might create a few fireworks that had nothing to do with the solstice.'

Charlie shook her head. How could this woman live so far on the edge of society and know so much? She hadn't once seen her anywhere else in the village. 'I thought he'd been talking about me behind my back, so I went up to Crystal

Waters to confront him, and we ended up in the hot tub.' She was trying not to think about it, but her brain seemed intent on doing nothing else. Just the memory of their kiss set her pulse racing.

'This is a turn-up for the books,' Reenie said. 'The Daniel I know would never have let his standards slip.'

Charlie gasped. 'You think he's letting his standards slip by spending time with *me*?'

'Of course not, ridiculous woman. I was talking about him using his own Jacuzzi while the hotel is open. You're messing with his mind if he's encouraging that sort of behaviour.' She laughed, a loud, brazen cackle that was swallowed by the wind.

'Oh, right. So—'

'What are you planning next? He could do with being taken down a peg or two.' She peered at Charlie over the top of her mug.

Charlie sighed. She had no idea why this woman, whom she had only met once before, had been her choice of confidante. Maybe it was precisely because she didn't know her that she felt able to offer up her innermost thoughts, like to a priest in a confessional.

'I don't want to topple him,' she said. 'I want to stop thinking about him. I came to Porthgolow to get away from everything, and I've got Gertie to focus on. Making a success of her and the food market. Most of the villagers are on side now, and I was thinking about doing some cream tea tours; you know, more in the spirit of my uncle Hal, who ran tours in the Cotswolds. Of course, Gertie wasn't a café then so it's more complicated, but—'

'My dear girl,' Reenie said. 'Did you come here to talk *to* me, or *at* me?'

Charlie shrugged. 'I wasn't planning on getting involved with anyone.'

'So back off. Tell Daniel, straight out, that you're not interested. I don't see how it could be any simpler, if you don't have feelings for him. And I'm not sure how you think I can help you.'

Charlie stretched her legs out in front of her. 'When I came here last time I got the impression that you know everything about the village, despite being out here.'

'This isn't a leper colony. I may be on the fringes, but I have eyes and ears, and legs for walking when I choose to.'

'Exactly. It sounds like you're friends with Daniel and I want to know more about him.'

'Ah, so you *do* have feelings for him. My suggestion of simply cutting yourself off isn't the answer you wanted to hear.'

Charlie sipped her too-milky tea. 'In some ways, he reminds me of my last boyfriend – and my last boyfriend cheated on me.'

'I'm sorry to hear that, Charlie. But only you can decide if Daniel's worth taking a risk on. I can tell you that the man I have got to know is kind, beneath all that bluster, but he's not that easy to get close to. He likes being up on that cliff top, away from the centre of everything, and he likes to keep his life simple. Making money, having a good reputation, not getting too attached.

'Daniel is a force to be reckoned with, but now you've muscled in on his patch, and it's good for him. You're knocking down a few of his barriers.' Reenie chuckled and narrowed her eyes, as if she could see something on the horizon, but when Charlie looked, there was only endless sea.

Juliette had said something similar, the night of the solstice.

That Charlie had made an impression on Daniel, forcing an unlikely apology out of him. But if she was adamant she didn't want a relationship with him, why wasn't she just doing what Reenie suggested and backing off? She tugged on Marmite's lead as he strayed towards the edge of the cliff.

'Don't beat yourself up, Charlie. Sometimes it's best not to overthink and just see what happens. I'm assuming Daniel's a good kisser or we wouldn't be having this conversation.' Ignoring Charlie's shocked expression, Reenie stood up and took her mug, even though she hadn't finished her tea. 'Now, off you pop. The rocks aren't easy to navigate in the dark, and I don't have an outside light.' Before Charlie could reply, Reenie went inside her yellow house and closed the door.

Charlie pulled herself to her feet and began to make her way over the rocks, replaying everything the older woman had told her. She'd had no contact from Daniel since the previous night, and she couldn't really blame him after the way she'd left, scrambling out of the hot tub as if she'd been scalded. But she had all her plans for the Cornish Cream Tea Bus to think about, not to mention growing the food market.

When she'd first considered turning Gertie into a café bus, she couldn't have imagined the journey she would come on. She might still have some locals to convince, but she hadn't given up on the possibility of winning them round. Rose and Frank had been torn between wanting to enjoy the market and standing against it, sticking to what they were comfortable with. But this was a new way of life for her too; the difference was that the one she'd come from had been miserable, so she was embracing each day in Cornwall with as much energy and enthusiasm as she could muster.

But did that mean she could consider a new romance, too? She loved how carefree and relaxed Oliver was, how easily she could talk to him. But then her thoughts returned, predictably, to Daniel's kiss. With the briefest touch, he'd made her feel so much; awakened parts of her that had been asleep for so long.

Part of the reason she'd come to Porthgolow was to soothe away the remaining shards of hurt and anger at Stuart's betrayal. Was she ready to risk her heart again? She reached the edge of the beach, and gazed at the last glimmering rays of a spectacular sunset. Gertie's red paintwork was amber, her large windows gleaming gold.

As Charlie turned away from the sea and towards Juliette's house, Marmite skittering along beside her, Hal's voice popped into her head: *Live life to the full, Charlie. You only get one chance.*

But should that chance involve Daniel Harper? That was something all Hal's wisdom combined couldn't decide for her. She was just going to have to come up with the answer herself.

Part 3

Scones Away

Chapter Seventeen

From Charlie's spot on Penzance Harbour, St Michael's Mount was a regal, impressive structure. It sat above the sparkling blue water like a beacon while, around it, a summer mist gave everything a hazy, dreamlike quality. But inside The Cornish Cream Tea Bus, it was anything but dreamlike.

The tables were full, upstairs and down, and Charlie had spent a frantic morning putting scones in the oven, arranging mini Danish pastries – *pains au chocolat*, almond croissants and pecan plaits – on her cake stands to go with cups of strong black coffee or frothy cappuccinos. Penzance was much bigger than Porthgolow, but she hadn't anticipated quite how much attention her bus would get in the town.

There were people taking photos and peering in through the cab window and she'd had to start a waiting list for customers who, when she'd told them the bus was full, said they were happy to sit in the sunshine until a table became available.

Charlie had decided that, in order to promote her bus, and the weekly food markets she had started in Porthgolow, she was going to take Gertie to every town in Cornwall. If the others were even half as busy as this, then it would be worth it. She just wished she'd brought Juliette with her so she wasn't running the bus by herself, but her best friend was at home, working on a marketing project, and had offered to look after Marmite so he wasn't stuck on board. It was the right decision, but Charlie missed having her little terror with her.

'Oh my God, The Cornish Cream Tea Bus!' squealed a voice. Charlie followed it to where a young couple was standing outside, the woman gazing up adoringly at the double-decker. 'This is the one I was telling you about Matt, in Porthgolow? We *have* to go to their food market. Liz and Phil were there last weekend and said it was epic. Just swam and sunbathed and went back for more food whenever they felt like it.'

Charlie smiled to herself as she put her finger sandwiches on a tray and took them to a family sitting upstairs. They had asked for two traditional cream teas and two half-sized ones for their young children. Charlie hadn't thought of doing a children's cream tea until now, but she was going to add it to her repertoire.

'If you need anything else,' she said as she stood back from their table with a flourish, 'just ring the bell.' She pointed at the cord that ran around the edge of the bus. It was one of Gertie's most popular features.

Running The Cornish Cream Tea Bus was a constant learning curve. There were always new possibilities to explore, certain elements needed to be changed or adapted, and ideas popped into her head on a daily basis. It was exhausting and exhilarating at the same time. When she went back downstairs, she added *children's cream teas* to her ever-expanding to-do list.

She closed the bus once the sun had begun its descent, and made the long, winding journey back to Porthgolow, cutting over the lower half of the county, the glistening sea falling out of sight behind rolling green hills, the statuesque towers of wind farms like alien armies on the horizon. As she went, she got honks and waves.

She was getting used to it now, the number of people who noticed her on the roads, and every time she felt a surge of pride, sitting high up in the cab while drivers or cyclists gave her a cheery thumbs-up or sounded their horns. She thought about her uncle Hal, how wide his smile would be if he could see what she'd achieved. Maybe things weren't perfect, but she was going in the right direction. *No regrets, Charlie*, he used to say. *Keep moving forward.*

For the most part, that was what she was doing. She knew that she had to learn from her mistakes to make any kind of progress, but what had happened last weekend, after the market had finished, had been playing on her mind ever since.

She approached Porthgolow from the south side, slowing her speed as she reached the area known as Crumbling Cliff. It was a sharp bend at the highest point above the village, with only a scrubby patch of grass between the road and the drop, which fell at least eighty feet to the promontory where Reenie's little yellow hut sat, then the rocks and churning waves below that.

Ahead of her, beyond the bay of Porthgolow, on the opposite cliff, sat Crystal Waters. The place where, last week, she had allowed Daniel Harper to seduce her into his hot tub, ply her with champagne and kiss her. If she put it like that, she came out as an innocent party, totally at his mercy. But it hadn't been like that at all.

She drove down the hill and parked Gertie in her spot on the hard-packed sand at the top of the beach. The sky was fading from blue to violet, the cloak of twilight settling over Porthgolow. Charlie breathed in the salty, seaside scent, and tried to move her thoughts away from Daniel. The village was quiet, with only a couple of cars in the car park, no sounds besides the churn of the waves and the occasional shout from the last family lingering on the beach. Myrtle's pop-in was closed for the day but, next to it, the windows of the B&B were aglow.

Charlie's gaze was drawn to the sea, as it so often was. She loved the way the light and the waves shifted in harmony with each other; still water mirrored by a placid sky, or a raging sea below racing, thunderous clouds. Out beyond the jetty, the lights were on inside the primrose-coloured cottage. As she watched, Reenie, now only a silhouette, emerged and stood at the edge of the rock. There was a flash, like the flicker of a torch beam, a wink of brightness piercing the dusk.

She stood there for several minutes, the light blinking intermittently. Then she went back inside her yellow house and stillness settled over Porthgolow. Jonah had said that Reenie was a mermaid communicating with her family beneath the waves. Charlie turned away from the sea, her mind racing. She wondered what Reenie was really doing out there.

The third Porthgolow Food Market got off to a good start and Charlie was both touched and relieved to see several locals wandering through the stands, shopping bags in hand, picking up fudge or sushi to take away with them, trying the tasters that the vendors put out to entice customers. Oliver was giving a group of women the full mixologist performance, juggling glasses and lemons and spinning shakers behind his back. The women were entranced, laughing and nudging each other, and it was clear that he was in his element.

'It's great, this,' Amanda said, as she and Paul lifted Jem's pushchair onto the bus, Jonah and Flora following. 'I can't believe the difference it's making to the village. It's like a brand-new place.'

'On a Saturday, anyway,' Jonah added, ever the realist.

'Not true, my son.' Paul ruffled his hair. 'We've seen an increase in bookings during the week as well as on Saturdays. Charlie and her bus are getting Porthgolow's name out there.'

'I'm not the only one who's working hard,' Charlie said.

'But you're going out and promoting it.' Amanda checked Jem was secure in her chair and smoothed Flora's curls behind her ear. 'I follow you on Instagram, and Penzance looked glorious yesterday.'

'It was pretty busy,' Charlie replied. 'I felt as if I'd run a marathon by the time I got home.' She'd forgotten that, by uploading everything on social media, people could see where she was at all times. She wondered if Daniel had watched her videos, made a mental note to check whether the Crystal Waters account appeared in her viewers' list, and then immediately scrubbed it off her virtual to-do list. 'What can I get you, anyway? No boats today?'

'Later this afternoon,' Paul said, 'so we thought we'd squeeze in a cream tea to keep us going.'

'And then we get burgers for dinner on the way home,' Jonah added, peering at the sausage rolls laid out on the cooling racks. 'It's our Saturday tradition.'

'Tradition?' Charlie laughed. 'It's only been three weeks!'

'It's staying, though, right?' Jonah asked, looking worried. 'I can't find a chicken burger with piri-piri sauce anywhere else, and Mum's attempts are *hopeless*.' He rolled his eyes dramatically.

'Hey,' Amanda said, laughing. 'That's a bit harsh, isn't it, Jonah?'

'Would you go back to our homemade ones after Benji's blue cheeseburger?' He pinned his mum with a stare.

Amanda grinned. 'Not a chance. It's definitely our new tradition.'

'And you get on with Benji?' Charlie asked. Out of everyone in Porthgolow, of course it would be Jonah who would make friends.

'He's going to show me how to make the perfect burger, as long as we don't stop going to him. I tried to get him to tell me his piri-piri sauce recipe too, but apparently that's a family secret.'

'Everyone needs a USP,' Paul said.

'What's ours, Dad?' Jonah asked, sliding onto the bench next to him.

'We're the only boat trip that leaves from this beach, so we give a unique view of the Cornish coast to our visitors. And we're right next to this, every Saturday.' He gestured out of the window, where the market was in full swing.

Charlie wished Bea could see what she'd achieved – and maybe even Stuart. Irritation flashed through her at the thought of him, there and then gone. But, even though he was almost out of her system, his betrayal had made her wary. He was being replaced in her thoughts by someone else, but she just wasn't sure exactly what that person was offering, or if she was ready to accept it.

The bus emptied out after tea time and Charlie was

clearing the empty tables on the upper deck when she looked up to find three burly, bearded men standing at the top of the stairs. 'Room for some little ones?' asked the tallest of the three.

'Of course,' she said. 'Come and sit down, browse the menu and I'll be back in a few minutes to take your order.'

Charlie watched as they took instrument cases off their shoulders and laid them carefully on an empty seat.

'Have you come to perform on the beach?' she asked. 'I'm Charlie, I organized the food market, so . . .'

'Charlie, hello! Hugh has told us so much about you.' The man's blue eyes shone out above his curly beard. 'I'm Silas, this is Artem and that's Ken. Along with Hugh we make up the Cornwall Cornflowers. We weren't planning on playing, but we could always be persuaded.'

'Oh, sorry – it's just that you've got your instruments.'

'Band rehearsal,' Artem said. 'We're off to Hugh's after this. We're performing in the pub at the end of the month. One of the villagers has a big birthday, apparently. Hugh said we should come and sample your famous cream teas first.'

'I'm so glad you've come,' Charlie replied. 'You don't know which villager it is, do you? I've only been here a few months, so I'm still getting to know everyone.'

'Someone called Myrtle,' said Ken. 'We've not met her, but she's into the traditional folk songs, so Hugh's arranged a party in the pub and we're going to be the musical entertainment.'

'It sounds wonderful. I'd love to hear you play sometime.'

'Come to the party,' Silas said. 'I'm sure Myrtle will want the whole village there.'

'I'll see what Hugh thinks. Have a look at the menu and I'll be back in a moment to take your order.' Charlie left them to it. She wasn't sure she'd be welcome at Myrtle's birthday celebrations, though she wondered if, in time, the older woman could come to see Gertie and the food markets as one of the local traditions. The Kerrs were already planning their day around it, and it seemed that, despite what some of the more stalwart villagers might think, the Porthgolow food market was starting to put down roots.

The following Thursday, Charlie lay in bed watching light patterns dance on the ceiling, Marmite snoozing quietly on her feet. She had another morning in the bus and then she was spending the afternoon with Oliver, Juliette offering to cover for her while she took some time off.

They walked down the hill in bright sunshine, Charlie mesmerized by the glittering sea, so still and calm, the deep turquoise of Caribbean waters. She didn't realize something was wrong until Juliette's arm-tugging became painful.

'What's—' she started, then her voice disappeared.

Down on the beach, next to where Gertie stood resplendent in the sun, was what looked like a load of cross-legged people, all as still as statues.

'What the hell?' she whispered. 'Is this some kind of bizarre art installation? Are those sculptures?'

'Not sculptures,' Juliette said, 'yogis.'

'*What?*' Charlie rubbed her eyes and looked again. Juliette was right. There were about twenty people sitting perfectly still, wearing leggings and vests or shorts and T-shirts, all facing out to sea. Beneath each person was a brightly coloured mat.

'It's a yoga class,' Juliette said, picking up her pace. 'I've never seen one in Porthgolow before. What's going on?'

'I have no idea,' Charlie said, her pulse returning to normal when she realized it was two days until her next market so they wouldn't get in the way of the food trucks. She realised that, in a short space of time, she had come to think of Porthgolow's beach as hers – at least on a Saturday. She knew she shouldn't be so possessive, but she couldn't help it.

'Let's go and find out.' Juliette grinned and Charlie followed her friend onto the sand.

They waited for a break in the class and introduced themselves to the instructor, who was called Belle and looked like a young Cindy Crawford. The class was called Yoga by the Sea, Belle told them, and it was a popular pursuit in other countries, but rarely happened in the UK due to the unpredictable climate. The current warm weather had made it possible.

'How did you find out about Porthgolow?' Juliette asked Belle, whose perfect figure was sculpted into a sea-blue leotard and fuchsia leggings. 'I had no idea you were coming and I check for new yoga events in Cornwall all the time – especially close to here.'

'Oh, my husband and I stayed up at Crystal Waters a few weeks ago. We got chatting to the owner about Porthgolow and yoga, and this seemed like the perfect spot to try it out.'

'It is beautiful down here,' Charlie said, trying not to react at the mention of Daniel. She hadn't heard from him since the hot tub incident, almost two weeks ago now.

'How long are you here for?' Juliette asked.

'Oh, for a week, all being well,' Belle said.

Charlie's stomach flipped unpleasantly. 'A *week?* Here, on the beach?'

'Sure,' Belle said. 'We can use one of the spaces in the hotel if the weather turns, but from the look of the forecast we're going to be fine. The sea air makes a huge difference.'

'Wow,' Juliette said. 'Can I . . . I mean, I'm busy today, but could I come tomorrow?' She looked like someone had just offered her a million pounds.

'Sure, Juliette. I'd love to have you. What about you, Charlie?'

'I can't,' she said. 'I've got to run the bus.'

'Oh, yeah.' Belle laughed. 'Don't suppose you're serving kale smoothies, are you?'

'We're not, I'm afraid,' Charlie replied calmly. 'We're more full-fat hot chocolates and Cornish cream teas. But there will be a juice bar here on Saturday, when the market is on.'

'Daniel mentioned something about that. It's not noisy or anything, is it?'

Charlie stared at her incredulously. 'It's, uhm, a food market. With people and trucks and ice-cream vans. It's pretty established now, so . . .'

Belle's delicate nose wrinkled. 'I'll have a word with Daniel, but I'm sure it'll be fine. Lovely to meet you guys. So looking forward to welcoming you into the fold, Juliette.'

'Me too,' Juliette said.

'*Into the fold?*' Charlie whispered as she unlocked the bus. 'It sounds more like a cult than a yoga class. And what am I supposed to do? What was Daniel thinking, organizing this yoga week to clash with the food market?'

Juliette gave her a sympathetic look. 'I'm sure he didn't do it on purpose. Maybe he just forgot – or wasn't thinking?'

'You're his biggest fan now, are you?'

'No, but he explained what had happened with the contract, and he gave us that spa voucher. I thought everything was smoothed over. What actually happened when you went to see him at the hotel? You were really vague about it, but you've been distracted ever since. Is everything OK?'

Charlie switched on the oven and the coffee machine, lifted Marmite up and, before putting him in his crate, gave him a hug. 'Everything's fine,' she said. 'Nothing happened at the hotel. We had a misunderstanding and we sorted it out.'

Juliette didn't say anything, but Charlie could tell she wasn't convinced.

She knew that yoga was supposed to do wonders for your mood, but it was having the opposite effect on her. How could Belle's class and the food market happen alongside each other? Yoga was supposed to be calming, serene, and her markets were anything but. As she unloaded fresh scones from her cake tin onto the oven rack, she wondered if she'd have time to go and see Daniel after she got back from her afternoon with Ollie. But the thought of another confrontation wasn't remotely appealing, mainly because she knew he would find a way of smoothing things over. She wasn't prepared for him to upend her argument – and her emotions – all over again.

Chapter Eighteen

'I don't see how it's going to work.' Charlie stared up at the blue sky and the occasional puffy cloud that drifted above her. They were lying on the grass outside the large eco-domes of the Eden Project, their bellies full of Cornish ice cream. She glanced sideways, to where Oliver had his eyes closed.

'Maybe it just will,' he murmured. 'Food trucks and yoga, in harmony with each other.'

Charlie turned her sigh into a deep breath, as Juliette had taught her to do. She didn't want to acknowledge that yoga techniques were helping to calm her down. She had left Juliette on the bus, exchanging waves and smiles with Belle through the window.

'Who holds a week-long yoga class outside anyway? I understand retreats for the truly committed, but Porthgolow is hardly the place, is it?'

'It's a beautiful, tranquil beach.' Oliver held his hands up when Charlie glared at him. 'I'm playing devil's advocate. You've got to think of it from Daniel's point of view, and then you can work out the best response.'

'The best response is to ask all my market people to get there early, so Belle and her yoga class can't stop it happening. I can't believe he's doing this.'

'Can't you?' Oliver rolled onto his stomach, and Charlie did the same. Marmite, who had been snoozing between them, raced forward so he could stand in front of them and be unavoidable. Oliver ruffled his fur and Marmite lay down in front of him.

Charlie thought back to the night of the hot tub and the way Daniel had effortlessly parried all her accusations. How, on the day of her first event, he had placated Myrtle not with words, but with a bonfire and fireworks. He did whatever he wanted. 'I suppose I can,' she admitted.

'So *why* is he doing it?' A robin dropped onto the grass and began investigating the undergrowth, sounding its sharp little call as it went.

'That is the million-dollar question.' She wondered if it was a way of getting back at her for abandoning him after their kiss. But that seemed petty, and unlike him, and certainly not something she could discuss with Oliver. 'Perhaps, even though he claimed to be supportive at the beginning, he doesn't like the food market.'

'Why doesn't he like it?'

'Because his hotel is all about calm and serenity, and the market gets quite noisy. But the cliff's a long way up, and I know sound drifts, but it's not like the hotel walls are made out of paper.'

'But the outdoor swimming pool and gardens will be used a lot now it's summer.'

'It's only one day a week.' Charlie drew herself up to sitting. 'I wonder if he's had complaints from some of the guests? But then he should just come and talk to me about it, or turn it around – advertise it as a feature of Porthgolow and encourage them to take advantage of it. Surely they can't all be so refined that they faint at the sight of a hotdog stand?'

Oliver laughed, stood up and held out his hand. 'I don't know, but I don't think you should let him rile you.'

Charlie let him pull her to her feet. They stood facing each other, Oliver's warm, open expression drawing her closer. She realized she wasn't being fair to him, coming on a date and spending the whole time talking about Daniel. 'You're right,' she said. 'I won't. Not any more. I'll do my thing, and work around him.'

'Exactly.' Oliver's grin flashed, and when they started walking, his hand remained firmly around hers.

They strolled through the gardens, the sun beating down, and Charlie could almost feel her freckles popping to the surface. Oliver told her about his childhood near the Welsh border – not that far from where Charlie had been born – and how he'd loved going to the funfair and country shows as he grew up.

'I loved them all,' he said. 'The atmosphere, that sense of everyone having a good time, finding something interesting or new, or indulging in their passion. I thought about getting involved in the gun dogs for a time. I always watched the trials but, as I grew older, I instinctively moved towards catering. It suited me, and so when Nat – my sister – suggested the cocktail stand, it felt right. I mean,' he added, stopping on a wooden boardwalk that protruded into the middle of a pond, 'who wouldn't want to spend their days around people who are taking time to do something for themselves? Enjoyment, education, whatever it is. It wouldn't be bad working here, would it?'

Charlie looked around, at the families and couples strolling, a woman sitting on a bench pushing a buggy back and forth, licking a green ice cream. 'No,' she agreed, 'it wouldn't. But we have more flexibility with our businesses. We're our own bosses.'

'How are you finding that?'

'Good. Busy, though. I can only call on Juliette so often – she has her own work to do. But I don't know if I'm ready to employ someone else. Everything's a bit fluid – the markets, where I might end up.' She watched as Marmite dangled a tentative paw in the water, got scared when a leaf drifted towards him and hid behind her legs.

'You're not staying in Cornwall?'

'I don't know,' Charlie admitted. 'I can't live with Jules and Lawrence for ever. They need their own space. What about you, anyway? You don't live down here.'

'I've got a few mates,' he said, his eyes sliding away from her. 'As long as I don't outstay my welcome on any one sofa then it's not a problem.'

Charlie laughed. 'You're a proper wanderer.'

'Does that bother you?' His grip on her hand had tightened, his gaze returning to her face.

'No, of course not, but—'

'Charlie?'

'Yes?' She waited, the ice cream suddenly heavy in her stomach. Oliver seemed to be searching for the right words, but then he leaned towards her. His kiss was gentle and Charlie found that, after a beat, she was kissing him back. It felt good, comforting, but nothing like the sensation of

Daniel's lips on hers. That rush of adrenalin and desire. She shouldn't be doing this. She stepped back.

Oliver's smile downgraded from self-assured to tentative. 'Was that OK?'

'It was lovely.' It wasn't a lie.

His smile widened and he took her hand again. They walked off the boardwalk, back onto the path, only to find a small boy giggling up at them. 'You made smoochies,' he said, pointing an unapologetic finger. 'Eww!'

'You won't feel like that when you're older,' Oliver said calmly, and pulled Charlie away.

After Oliver had failed to persuade Charlie to go on the zip wire that hovered terrifyingly over the Eden Project, Charlie drove them back to Newquay, the windows of Juliette's car wound down to let in as much air as possible. When she pulled up outside his temporary digs, he turned to face her.

'Come to the beach with me? There's an area where dogs are allowed.'

'I'm not sure,' Charlie said. 'I left Juliette on the bus, so I should just check . . .' she pulled her phone out of her bag and saw that there was a message from her friend.

Doing an evening session with Belle on the beach. Hope Ollie was fun! Xx

Charlie bristled. 'Beach sounds great,' she said, forcing a smile.

Ten minutes later, she was showing Oliver how to skim stones across the breakers while Marmite bounded in the shallows, treating each new wave as if it was a tiny, Yorkipoo-eating monster.

'You're not holding your hand right. It needs to be more like this.' Charlie stood behind him and twisted his hand.

'And then, in one, fluid motion you need to go like this.' She demonstrated with her own stone, which skipped across the water three times before it disappeared.

'Right.' Oliver narrowed his eyes. 'So I go like this, then like this. And then . . .' He threw his stone, and it skimmed once before disappearing.

'Yes!' Charlie gave him a high-five. 'It can only get better from there.'

'I wouldn't be so sure. I've never been that great at sports.'

'Skimming stones is hardly a sport, though I *can* get competitive about it. I won't today, obviously, as it's your first time. But next time, Oliver, you'd better watch out.'

'Next time?' He took her hand. 'You think there might be a next time?'

Charlie swallowed. 'There could be. If you show enough promise.'

'Then I will try very, very hard.'

They walked at the edge of the sea, their shoes in their hands, while the summer evening played out beautifully around them. Charlie liked Newquay. It was always full of people laughing, surfing, jogging along the beach. There were families paddling, a few still swimming, the sky turning pink just above the horizon. A group of twenty-somethings were trying to light a bonfire on the beach, which made her think of Daniel.

'What is it?' Oliver asked.

'What do you mean?'

'You squeezed my hand.' He released his grip. 'Luckily I still have the use of all my fingers.'

His grin was usually calming, but Charlie couldn't match it.

'No shrugging,' he said. 'What's wrong?'

'Juliette is spending the evening with the yogis.'

'And that's bad because . . .?'

'Because they're Daniel's.'

'Daniel *owns* the yoga group?'

'You know what I mean. I'm sure he set it up to piss me off, and now Jules has gone over to the dark side.'

'You're making this all very black and white.'

'It is! He's suddenly decided he doesn't like my food market, and he's sabotaging me.' They started walking back to the car.

'Or maybe the yoga has been organized for months and he forgot to tell you. Or he's seen the positive impact your events are having on Porthgolow and has decided to put resources in to continue your good work, and bring even more people to the village? Look, I've only met Daniel briefly, and I told you before that there was something about him I didn't like. But if you've got to know him, then why don't you just talk to him? Get everything out in the open.'

'Every time we see each other we end up sniping.'

They had stopped outside Oliver's temporary home, and he glanced at the upstairs window, gave someone a quick wave and then ran his hand through his hair. By the time Charlie looked, there was nobody there.

'Ask him to move the yogis further down the beach,' Oliver said, shrugging. His cheeks were fiercely red, and she wondered if his tanned skin had finally had enough sun. 'Surely it could accommodate you all?'

'If that's the case, why didn't he set them up at the other end of the beach in the first place?'

'Just talk to him, Charlie. And let me know if Saturday's still happening.'

'Of course it is!' Charlie said, aghast. 'There's too much momentum to stop now. You will come, won't you?'

Oliver brushed his lips over her cheek. 'You know that I'm entirely at your disposal.'

'Brilliant! Thank you, Ollie. For that and – and for today.' She smiled, wondering if he would kiss her properly again, wondering if she should let him when, only two weeks ago, she had been kissing someone else. If she really wanted to take things further, she would have to tell him about Daniel, that it had been a one-off, an aberration. But Oliver just squeezed her hand, gave Marmite a quick stroke and let himself into the house.

As Charlie drove back to Porthgolow, her mind refused to settle. Was it just a misunderstanding, another slip from Daniel that had resulted in the yoga group taking up her part of the beach, or was he playing games with her? Of course Oliver was right, and the only way of finding out was by talking to him, but the idea of facing him again after the hot tub evening made her palms clammy. She would just have to go ahead with the food market as usual; they'd been there first and what, realistically, could Daniel do about a whole load of vans and trucks driving onto the beach? If he didn't want a horrible accident on his hands, then he would have to be the one to give way.

The yogis looked serene, sitting on the beach equal distances apart, their shadows stretching long and thin behind them in the evening light. Charlie tried to make Juliette out but, from this distance, she could be any one of a number of dark-haired women. She slowed when she passed Myrtle's pop-in, indicated, and was about to turn up the hill when she saw a figure leaning against Gertie, his attention focused on the water.

His muscled calves were tanned below khaki shorts, his

dark hair blowing in the sea breeze. A German shepherd sat placidly at his side, his tail twitching. Charlie's heart began to pound. She had to face him sometime, and if she did it now they might be able to avert the impending disaster.

She swung into The Seven Stars car park, attached Marmite's lead and climbed out of the car. Daniel's gaze was fixed firmly on the horizon and she felt a stab of satisfaction that she might be surprising him for once, but when she was ten yards away, Marmite barked and raced over, first sniffing Jasper and then putting his paws on Daniel's leg.

He looked down and then crouched to ruffle the ecstatic dog. As he stood, he caught Charlie's eye and grinned. She stopped, taking a moment to compose herself.

'Charlie, I wondered if I might bump into you here.'

'Why, because I'm going to have to spend the next day and a half trying to work out how to fit twenty food trucks in among a group of flexible yogis?'

His lips twitched. 'No, because this is your bus.'

'It's after hours and I had the afternoon off, anyway. I don't know why I'm explaining myself to you. It should be you doing the explaining.'

'Do anything nice?'

Charlie gave him a blank look.

'This afternoon, were you doing anything fun?'

'I went to the Eden Project, with Oliver.'

Daniel's smile wavered. 'It's a great day for it. You've caught the sun.' He stepped closer, his eyes narrowing, and Charlie felt truly scrutinized. She wondered how red her cheeks were, whether her spray of fair-weather freckles had taken up residence across her nose. She forced herself not to look away and Daniel's expression softened.

She took her chance.

'Why did you organize the yoga when you knew my food market was happening this Saturday? If it's because of how we left things before, then . . .' Then what? Should she apologize? She had been well within her rights to back off after their kiss. It had been so sudden, so intense. She was still struggling to work out exactly how she felt.

Daniel dragged his gaze from her lips to her eyes. 'Lauren organized it,' he said. 'She got talking to Belle when she was staying with us and asked if she could put on a course of yoga on the beach. I told her to go for it, because she's a good colleague and I like to encourage initiative. I thought she'd have the common sense to plan it around the market.'

'But she hasn't,' Charlie replied. 'So what are we going to do about it?'

'We? So you think we can try working as a team, now?'

The heat in Charlie's cheeks went up a few degrees. 'The reputations of my events and your hotel rest on the outcome. We could do with working together to come up with a solution.'

'I think you're right,' Daniel said. 'What do you suggest?'

Charlie sighed and leaned against the bus. It was easier being next to him than facing him. 'You definitely have to have yoga on Saturday?'

'Belle has been booked and paid for, and she's got clients for every day that she's here. I'm not sure anyone would be too happy about us cancelling it.'

'And I can't cancel the food market, because it's a sure thing, now. I've got vendors invested in it, and I've promoted it on social media. We could move Belle further down the beach, but it's still going to be noisy and busy. We don't want to risk any yogis being squashed. Not even Belle,' Charlie added, with only a slight trace of bitterness.

Daniel laughed. 'She's not your cup of tea?'

'She simpers,' Charlie replied. 'I mean, she obviously runs a very successful business and Juliette is beyond happy that she's here but I just—'

'You don't think she's on your side.'

'Oi.' She slapped him on the arm. 'You're not being helpful. We need to fix this, for both our sakes.'

'OK,' Daniel said, suddenly serious. 'How about we . . . no, I'm not sure that will work. We could maybe . . .' Charlie glanced at him, but he was shaking his head. 'Oh, I know!' He grabbed her arm and Charlie jumped, feeling the fizz of electricity at his touch.

'What? What could we do?'

'How about, just for Saturday, we have the yoga up in the gardens of Crystal Waters? There's lots of space around the pool, they'll still have the spectacular views, and they're far enough removed from the market for neither to impact on the other. There.' He spread his hands wide. 'Perfect solution.'

Charlie stared at him. His expression was smug, satisfied, but there was something else, too. That laughter bubbling just under the surface. Slowly, realization dawned on her.

'Oh my God,' she murmured. 'Oh my God, Daniel.'

He raised an eyebrow.

'It was always going to be up at the hotel on Saturday, wasn't it? You were never going to be in the way of my food market.'

'It was an easy assumption to make, when they appeared on the beach this morning for a week-long residence. I can see how you could have jumped to the wrong conclusion. I had expected a visit from you earlier, actually. I was looking forward to seeing you.'

Marmite squeaked and hid behind her legs, but a quick

glance showed her that Jasper was still lying patiently at Daniel's feet. Her dog was making something out of nothing, as usual. Charlie wondered if he'd learnt that from her.

'You purposely didn't tell me,' she said through gritted teeth. 'You *let* me think this, let me get worked up about it, when all along you were planning on having it at the hotel on Saturday.'

'All's well that ends well. You need to stop assuming that everyone's against you.'

'How can I, when you keep doing stuff like this? I bet you organized Rose and Frank to put on that little show outside my bus, just so you could set me straight and feel superior about it. You're trying to show me who's in charge, but do you know what?' Her eyes blazed into his.

'What?' he asked. 'Tell me.' He leaned towards her, his breath tickling her cheek. 'I'm all ears.'

They were only inches apart. He smelt good, woody and citrusy. She pushed the thought away.

'I'm not against you, Charlie. I thought I'd made that clear the other night, but if you want to keep believing it, there's nothing I can do.'

She couldn't look away. Daniel's eyes were dark pools of intent and his lips were so close . . . She knew how kissable those lips were . . .

'Hey, Char! Hi, Daniel.' Juliette's voice broke the spell and Charlie jumped backwards, turning to her friend as if she'd been starved of her company.

'Jules! How was it?' Juliette looked happy, her skin glistening, her cheeks bunched into a smile.

'Brilliant. You have to give it a go, Charlie. It's the most wonderful, uplifting feeling, and Belle is a great teacher. Oh, and I meant to text you earlier, but I got caught up on the bus. She found out that they're running all her sessions at the hotel on Saturday, so you don't need to worry. The food market is safe! But Daniel's probably told you that anyway. Want to go up to the house together?'

Charlie forced a smile. She wished, with all her heart, that Juliette had sent that text. 'I've got your car in The Seven Stars car park. I'll drive you up the hill, unless you want to walk?'

'A lift would be lovely. Did you have a good time with Ollie?'

Charlie nodded, aware of Daniel's gaze on her. 'I'll tell you all about it at home.'

'Great. I'm just going to go and say goodbye to Belle, then I'll meet you at the car. Catch you later, Daniel.'

'Bye,' Daniel called. 'There, you see,' he said, once Juliette was out of earshot. 'I wasn't keeping anything from you.'

'I need to get Marmite his dinner,' Charlie said. 'Please don't scratch the paintwork of my bus.'

'Wouldn't dream of it.' Daniel stood up straight. 'Good to see you again, Charlie. Glad we've sorted things out. I'd hate for there to be any animosity between us.' He squeezed her hand briefly, letting go before she could react, and led Jasper down onto the beach.

Marmite whimpered, as if he was upset at the German shepherd's departure, despite clearly being terrified of him. Charlie let out a loud, exasperated sigh and took her dog back to the car.

Chapter Nineteen

Charlie tugged the hair out of her eyes and the wind whipped it straight back. She breathed in a huge, restorative gulp of sea air, and marvelled again at the sheer scope of the view. The water churned all around her except at her back, a mixture of deepest blue and frothy white, the blistering sun adding a sparkle that was almost blinding. Ahead of her in the sea sat The Brisons, large rocks that – Charlie remembered Hugh telling her – people swam out to in an annual race. She shook her head, wondering at the bravery of anyone who was prepared to get into such a tumultuous surf, and licked her strawberry ice cream.

'Would you swim?' she asked Juliette. Their bench was snuggled against the chimney that sat proudly on the top of Cape Cornwall, still here though the tin mine was long gone. Her friend seemed intent on devouring her mint choc chip cone in minimum time, perhaps because the wind seemed equally intent on flinging most of it into her face.

'Not a chance,' Juliette replied. 'The sea is never flat here, because it's where the Atlantic currents divide. I can't ever imagine it being safe. Stunning to look at, though.'

'God, yes. Do you think anyone would mind if I moved The Cornish Cream Tea Bus to Cape Cornwall permanently? I could do this walk at the end of every day, and spend hours looking out at the water.'

'Everyone would mind!' Juliette said, laughing. 'You were lucky the National Trust allowed you to pitch up here for a single day, so I wouldn't push them. And what about poor Porthgolow? Would you move the food markets out here, too?'

'It might be easier,' Charlie murmured. She had reached her cone and took a big, satisfying bite.

'Why easier?' Juliette asked. 'I thought most of the villagers had accepted it now, and even Myrtle's gone a bit quiet. Unless that's because she's plotting something dastardly.'

'It doesn't matter. Forget I said anything.'

The market had gone without a hitch at the weekend because, as promised, Belle and her yoga class had been at the hotel for the whole of Saturday, leaving the beach free for Charlie's gang of food trucks. But she was still annoyed at the way Daniel had let her get worked up about nothing.

She'd even seen him towards the end of the day, strolling along with Jasper and eating a cone of calamari, The Friendly Fish Stall's trademark blue and grey design on the paper. They hadn't spoken, but he'd noticed her looking at him through the window and given her a cheery wave, then a thumbs-up, and pointed in the direction of the hotel. Charlie knew what he was referring to, and it had taken her half an hour to calm down.

From now on she was going to keep her cool, which

wasn't easy when Cornwall was putting on the most glorious summer Charlie could remember, and she was spending most of it on board Gertie, rushing around, making hot drinks and warming scones in the oven.

She loved it, of course, but when, after spending the day serving customers in the Cape Cornwall car park – a spot with arguably as beautiful a view as Porthgolow beach – Juliette had suggested a walk to the top and an ice cream before the long drive home, she had jumped at the idea. Now the heady sea breeze and churning waves were putting everything in perspective. Charlie needed to stop focusing on the minutiae, worrying about matters she couldn't control – namely Daniel – and focus on herself.

'I know what this is about,' Juliette said. 'It's not Myrtle who's bothering you, is it? Could it be something to do with a rather intimate conversation I saw you having next to the bus with a dark-haired hotelier the other day?'

Charlie pressed her fingers to her lips. 'You noticed that?'

'I might have been high on yoga, Char, but I'm not an idiot. I could see there was something going on, but I was waiting for you to tell me. Then there was the food market, and you're always out and about on Gertie, or you're shut away in the kitchen baking up a storm, and I hardly ever see you. I'm glad I could help today, it's been fun; and, more importantly,' she nudged Charlie's shoulder, 'we get a chance to catch up. Which, I think I remember telling you, was part of the reason I wanted you to stay.'

'I never meant for us to be ships that pass in the night, Jules. This whole thing has taken off in a way I didn't anticipate. God, can you imagine if I'd actually called it The Café Bus? What a lame name.'

'Cornwall gave you the perfect inspiration,' Juliette said.

'The Cornish Cream Tea Bus is becoming legendary. Did you hear that group of girls earlier on? The ones who all had hot chocolates with cream and marshmallows? One of them said, I swear to God, "*We're on the ACTUAL Cornish Cream Tea Bus. I can't believe it!*" It was as if they'd found the Holy Grail or something.'

'She was only giving it the reverence it deserves. Gertie *is* legendary. It just took a bit of a spruce-up and some good, hard baking for people to see it.'

'And long may it continue,' Juliette shouted. Her words were swept up and carried away by the wind.

They gazed in silence at the view. The dark hulk of a boat, a liner or trawler, moved slowly along the horizon; black birds flew below them, arcing round the curve of the cape, heading north.

'Choughs,' Juliette said, pointing. 'Did you see their red beaks? They're pretty rare. Apparently this is one of the only places you can see them in the whole of England.'

'When did you turn into an expert birdwatcher?' Charlie asked, standing so she could watch the progress of the birds until they were nothing but dark specs against the cliffs.

'I read the Cape Cornwall info leaflet while I was waiting for a batch of scones to cool.' Juliette grinned. 'Now, tell me what's happening with Daniel.'

'Nothing's happening,' Charlie said, sitting back down. 'He's infuriating me, that's all. I need to ignore him and get on with it.'

'What was Hal's phrase?' Juliette said. '*The only journey you can control is your own*. He used to say that a lot when I was worried about leaving you and everyone else in the Cotswolds and moving down here. He was right, of course, but how is Daniel infuriating you? It's obviously affecting you, and I know that, after what Stuart did . . .' She squeezed Charlie's hand.

'We barely know each other,' Charlie replied quickly, 'so it's not – not like that. I'm over Stuart.'

'I know you are, but I'm not so sure what he did to you hasn't had a more lasting effect. Betrayal's a horrible thing, Char.'

'But Daniel's not . . .' She sighed. 'He winds me up, that's all. He gets involved with stuff. At first it seemed supportive – he must have gone to a lot of trouble to organize the bonfire and fireworks on the solstice at such short notice. But then there was the yoga. He deliberately didn't tell me that he was moving it up to the hotel on Saturday. He let me worry about it and then smoothed everything over, cool as a cucumber. And when I thought he'd been bad-mouthing my event and went up to confront him—'

'He did *what?*'

'But I don't know if he *did* bad-mouth it. He says it was all a misunderstanding. Words that got twisted by Rose and Frank who overheard him, but I'm still not sure.'

'What do you mean?'

Charlie waited until a couple with an English sheepdog had strolled past, and then told Juliette what had happened at the hotel, admitting everything except their kiss in the hot tub. It had barely lasted for more than a couple of seconds anyway, so – she kept telling herself – it didn't really count.

'Oh boy,' Juliette said, when Charlie had finished.

'It's like he's got me on this piece of string. He keeps reeling me in and then letting me back out again. I just feel so . . . hopeless around him.' And exhilarated, and hot in a way that had nothing to do with the Cornish summer.

'You like him,' Juliette said.

Charlie sat up straighter. 'I do not.'

'You're not talking about Myrtle like this. Analysing what she's doing or why she's doing it.'

'That's because she's not behaving like Daniel! She's just someone who's lived here all her life who isn't ready to embrace a shinier, busier Porthgolow. She's not toying with me like he is.'

'Why do you think he's doing it?' Juliette asked. Her voice was light, her dark eyes sparkling.

'I should never have said anything.'

'Oh come on, Char. Don't be mad with *me*. I'm just telling you what I see. You like Daniel, and he likes you. He wouldn't have gone to all the effort on that first Saturday just to please Myrtle.'

'A lot of the villagers are against his fancy hotel, too, you know.'

'And when has he ever given the impression of caring about that? He always does his own thing – I thought to the point of selfishness, until you coaxed the real reason for that marketing mix-up out of him. Which is another point towards my argument, by the way. He talks to you, and not just the odd pleasantry or quip. He puts his heart on his sleeve for you. He invited you into the hot tub, for goodness' sake! I mean, talk about being obvious. Do you want me to write you a list? How does Daniel like you, let me count the ways . . . One, he—'

'OK, OK, there's no need for that. I get it.'

'Do you like him as much as you like Oliver?' Juliette asked. 'I'm guessing more, considering how much you're angsting over him.'

'Shouldn't we be getting back? We've got a long drive ahead of us, and what if Ray, Benton and Marmite have overwhelmed Lawrence and turned him into puppy chow?'

'If Ray and Benton are involved, it'll be cat food. Marmite will only be allowed the scraps.'

'I'm going to have to come back here with Marmite. He'd love it.'

'It is magnificent isn't it?'

They took a few, final moments to drink in the view, and then started the descent, navigating the stone steps cut into the scrubland. Behind them, the tall chimney glowed red in the late afternoon sun. Charlie would have to see about bringing Gertie back here, too. It was a popular spot, and the more she got her bus out and about in Cornwall, the more word of Porthgolow and the food markets spread.

'So what are you going to do about Daniel?' Juliette asked, once they'd tackled the steepest part of the walk and were on gentler ground. 'Putting aside that you like him, you can't let him make you feel hopeless. You have to beat him at his own game.'

'I thought if I ignored him, he might go away.'

'Daniel Harper is the kind of person you need to stand up to,' Juliette said firmly. 'And action is what you're good at. Don't start being passive because he's got you on the back foot.'

Charlie nodded. Juliette was right. She needed to show Daniel that he wasn't in charge – not of her events or her emotions. He had his own business to run; there was no need for him to get involved with hers.

They reached the car park and found a man and woman peering in the window of her bus. They were both grey-haired, and wearing light coats and walking boots covered in sand.

'I'm so sorry,' Charlie said, 'but we're closed for the day. I'll be back in Porthgolow tomorrow, and at the food market there on Saturday.'

'Do you do tours on it?' the woman asked. 'Travelling round an' suchlike?'

'I'm getting around the county, but I'm not running tours at the moment, though that is something I'm planning in the future. Look me up online and you can keep up to date with where The Cornish Cream Tea Bus will be next.'

'Righto,' the woman said, 'Thanks for that.' They headed towards the ice-cream van.

'You know your tours?' Juliette said, once they were on board and Charlie was settled in the cab.

'You mean the ones I haven't even started work on yet? Schools break up soon and I want to make the most of the summer crowds.'

'You need a trial run,' Juliette said. 'You've not done it before. You watched Hal endless times, but you can't tell people all about the Cotswolds while you're driving round Cornwall. That would really confuse them.'

Charlie laughed. 'I've got to learn some facts, write a script and plan an interesting route that won't end up in traffic or stuck down narrow lanes where Gertie can't go. It's a lot of work.'

'But when that's done, you'll need a group of volunteers to test it out, to tell you what's good, and what needs changing. You can't ask Amanda and Stella, because they won't be honest – they'll say it's great whatever. And Myrtle will be *too* honest, probably deliberately negative.'

'If I could get her on board in the first place, which is doubtful.'

'Exactly. Soooo. Where could you find a group of strangers, but people who were already in the holiday vibe, probably willing to try out something like a cream-tea tour on board a vintage Routemaster bus, especially if it was free?'

Their eyes met, and Charlie resisted the urge to jump out of the cab and hug her friend. 'Jules, you are a genius.'

'How do you think Daniel's going to feel if you waltz into Crystal Waters and kidnap all his precious guests to take them for a tour on Gertie?'

'I don't think he'd like it very much. I'd be like the Pied Piper, except with the lure of warm, cream-filled scones instead of music.'

'Exactly.' Jules giggled. 'Oh my God. You have to let me come! Obviously I'll be on the bus during the tour, in charge of serving while you drive. But you have to let me come up to the hotel, too. I cannot wait to see his face!'

'No,' Charlie said, starting the engine and manoeuvring Gertie slowly out of the car park, leaving the beauty of Cape Cornwall behind, 'neither can I.'

Charlie slowed at the top of the hill and indicated left, then swung the bus into the Crystal Waters car park, fitting expertly through the gap in the sandy coloured walls.

'I cannot believe we're doing this,' Juliette said, her voice a whisper even though it was just the two of them on board.

'It was your idea,' Charlie replied, parking Gertie next to a gleaming silver Range Rover.

'I know. I guess I wasn't sure we'd actually go through with it.'

Charlie tried to ignore the fluttering in her stomach at the thought of seeing Daniel. She was determined not to let him tie her in knots this time.

'But you were right,' she said, following Juliette to the door, 'I need to stand up to him, show him how it feels to be on the receiving end of the meddling, and besides, we *do* need people to trial the tours before I start promoting them.'

She had spent the last ten days, since their heart-to-heart at Cape Cornwall – when she wasn't serving at the food market or taking her bus around the county's towns and beauty spots – working on her tour, plotting a route with Lawrence and Google's help, writing a script with details about all the scenic places they would visit, and cooking up new cakes and scone flavours to make the cream teas distinctive from those she was already selling. Now all that hard work was going to be tested.

She wiped her hands down the back of her cropped trousers, and smoothed down her top, pressing out the kinks.

'You're nervous,' Juliette said.

Charlie gave her friend her widest smile. 'I am, but I'm not going to let him see it.'

They walked through the doors of Crystal Waters together.

'Hi, Lauren,' Charlie said, breezing through reception. 'Just nipping to the dining room, if that's OK?'

'No, Charlie – excuse me . . .' She heard the panic in the other woman's voice and kept going, Juliette beside her, eyes fixed firmly to the floor.

Charlie followed the signs on the walls, along wide, airy corridors, until she stepped into a large, open room with glass walls looking out over the sea. The restaurant was at the far end of the building, beyond the swimming pool, as far from reception as it was possible to get. She hoped that would give her the time she needed.

She scanned the room, took in the blue, luxurious carpet, the slate-grey chairs and tables covered in pristine white cloths. The number of empty tables surprised her, though it was just after nine so it was likely many of the guests had already been and gone.

She fixed on a family, a man and woman with two young

daughters, one sitting on a firm cushion so she could reach the bowl of cereal on the table. The mum and dad were laughing over something, their other daughter eating a piece of toast and reading a Harry Potter book. There was an older couple close to the window, and a group of three – two men and one woman – tucking into English breakfasts.

Charlie took a deep breath and clapped her hands together. Everyone looked up.

'Hello,' she said loudly. 'My name is Charlie Quilter, and I'm the owner of The Cornish Cream Tea Bus. You might have seen it in the village, on the beach?'

Nine faces looked blankly back at her. She reminded herself these people were on holiday. They might only have arrived the day before. She swallowed and kept going.

'I'm a fairly new business and I'm running my first Cornish Cream Tea Tour on Monday. It's a scenic route along part of Cornwall's coastline, with an afternoon tea served while we go. Myself and my colleague, Juliette, would be honoured if those of you who are still in the area on Monday would be our very first guests. As it's a new idea, we're running it for free; you will essentially be our guinea pigs, so your feedback will be invaluable and will help shape all future tours. The bus is parked outside, if any of you want to have a look before you make a decision.' She paused, trying to read the faces of the people she had ambushed, and then felt panic rise as footsteps echoed down the corridor behind her. 'What do you say?'

'Can we, Mum?' said the youngest girl. 'I love buses.'

The three friends were exchanging glances and nodding, and the old couple looked positively bemused.

'The tour will start at two o'clock on Mon—'

'Charlie, Juliette,' Daniel cut in, coming to stand in front of them.

Charlie's cheeks flamed, and she tried not to be distracted by the way his blue shirt clung to his torso, the firm body she knew was underneath, or how his dark eyes met hers in a way that seemed to rip through her, exposing all her thoughts.

'Good morning Daniel,' she said. 'I was just inviting your guests to come on our first Cornish Cream Tea Tour on Monday.'

'A tour?' he raised an eyebrow. She could tell he wanted to say more, but that the need to be professional in front of his guests was winning out.

'Their feedback will help us plan the best possible trips in the future. It's a great opportunity.'

'We'd love to,' said the older woman, her voice reaching across the cavernous room. 'We'll still be here, and it does sound good, doesn't it, Elber?' The man nodded his agreement, and the little girl at the table raised her hand as high as it would go.

'Us too!'

'Sounds like a laugh,' added one of the men from the party of three.

'You see,' she said to Daniel. 'Why don't you come, too? It's the least I can offer after all your support with the food markets.'

Daniel seemed rooted to the spot and she knew she'd got him. He could get away with saying he was too busy, but now his guests had agreed, he would want to seem amenable in front of them.

'What do you think?' She squeezed his arm.

He didn't take his eyes off her. She could see the battle going on behind them. The desire to turn her down, to take back control, competing with his need to be the smooth, charming hotel owner.

'Two o'clock on Monday?' he asked.

'Yes. Leaving from here.' Triumph surged through her, and she wondered if this was how sea fishermen felt when they'd hooked a barracuda. 'I'll meet you outside reception,' she said to the wider room. 'Just bring yourselves, your cameras and a healthy appetite. Great.' She grinned, then had to look away from Daniel's unwavering gaze. 'Looking forward to it.'

Chapter Twenty

Before they'd even reached the pub, Charlie could tell that it was packed. The windows were glowing and snippets of conversation and laughter escaped every time the door opened, which was often. It was Sunday evening, and the sun was hovering over the sea, the sky above a rich turquoise. There was the faintest hint of a summer breeze. It tickled Charlie's skin and made the skirt of her green dress whisper against her legs.

Gertie stood proudly in her spot on the sand; around her, the beach was busy with families and groups of friends, dog walkers and lone strollers. It was the end of July, the summer holidays were in full swing and Porthgolow no longer looked forgotten. It looked at ease, somehow, still slightly shabby in places, but accepted for all that it was. Charlie felt that this was exactly how it was supposed to be and a smile bunched her cheeks.

'Earth to Charlie.' Juliette tugged on her arm. 'What's going on with you? Gertie looks fine.'

'I know Gertie's fine,' Charlie said. 'And I'm not worried about anything.'

'Even though we're about to walk into a party organized for the benefit of Myrtle Gordon, arch-nemesis of the Porthgolow food market?'

Charlie rolled her eyes at Lawrence, who had donned a pale blue short-sleeved shirt for the occasion. Juliette was wearing a panel dress in navy and red that suited her slender figure and had tied her dark hair away from her face.

Charlie felt a thrill of anticipation. They'd had lots of evenings in The Seven Stars, but none like this, with a reason to dress up. Since she'd been in Cornwall she'd had no need of her heels, but tonight she had dusted them off, their slow progress to the pub reminding her that they didn't mix well with steep hills.

Juliette pushed open the door and they walked into a wall of heat and light and chatter. It was busier than Charlie had ever seen it, the tables rearranged to make room for a cluster of chairs and music stands against the far wall. She remembered the musicians who had come aboard her bus and realized the set-up was for Hugh and his band, the Cornwall Cornflowers. She searched the room for familiar faces, but Juliette pulled her to the bar.

'Hey, you three.' Amanda lifted her wine glass in welcome. She was wearing a peach-coloured top and jeans, her curls tamed around her face. Paul's dark shirt was slim fitting, and Charlie almost didn't recognize them without their water-proofs and their windblown hair.

'You look great,' Charlie said, kissing Amanda on the cheek.

'Likewise,' Amanda replied. 'I think everyone's made an effort tonight.'

Charlie had to agree. Stella and Anton were talking to another couple over by the window, Stella wearing a pair of impossibly high-heeled, golden shoes that matched the sequins on her top, and Anton in a lemon-yellow shirt that perfectly complemented his dark skin. Rose and Frank – who she now knew by sight as well as voice – were huddled at a table close to the improvised stage area, their heads bowed conspiratorially, and Hugh, for once not behind the bar, was wearing a blue shirt with a design of huge white flowers.

'They look like inverted cornflowers,' Charlie said, pointing.

Amanda laughed. 'That's the kind of thing Jonah would say. Has he been spending a lot of time on your bus?'

'Not as much as I'd hoped, actually,' Charlie admitted. 'He's very helpful when he's on board, acting as the perfect host and keeping up a constant stream of engaging conversation. Was he disappointed about not coming tonight?'

'Actually, no,' Amanda said. 'He's found a new app that's teaching him about marine life. He wants to learn all there is to know about the waters around Cornwall, for when he's a skipper.' She gave Charlie an indulgent grin.

'He'll make a brilliant skipper,' Charlie replied. 'That's already a given.'

'Here you go, Char.' Lawrence handed her a glass full of orange liquid.

'What's this?' She took a sip. The flavours of orange and passion fruit burst on her tongue. 'Wow.'

'It's called a Porthgolow Sunset,' Juliette said, clinking her glass against Charlie's. 'Made up specially for Myrtle's birthday.'

'Speaking of which, where is the birthday girl?' Hugh had

assured them that all the villagers were welcome tonight, but Charlie was fairly sure she wouldn't be the *most* welcome of all Myrtle's guests.

'She'll be fashionably late, of course,' Amanda said. 'Now, go and find a seat before they all get taken.'

They wove their way through the throng to a booth against the back wall, leaving Amanda and Paul to their stools at the bar.

'Cheers!' Lawrence raised his own Porthgolow Sunset. 'Can't believe how busy the pub is, especially on a Sunday night.'

'Apparently Myrtle didn't want to have it on Saturday because of the food market. What do you think about that?' Juliette raised her eyebrows. 'She didn't want you and the others involved to miss out.'

'Or she didn't want the pub to be full of strangers instead of all her friends,' Charlie said. 'I'm not sure I would have been here if she'd had it yesterday. It was so busy!' She couldn't help grinning. The Porthgolow food market was showing no signs of slowing down. She might be exhausted on a Saturday night, but it was worth it to see the beach vibrant and alive, the other vendors making a good living, and Gertie getting the attention that Charlie felt, as Hal's legacy, she deserved.

'Speaking of the market.' Juliette gestured to the door. Oliver was standing there, looking lost and running his hand through his tufty hair.

'Over here,' Charlie called. She waited for him to join them, then gave him a hug. 'Can I get you a drink?'

He kissed the corner of her mouth. 'You look amazing, Charlie. And this place is heaving. What are you drinking?'

'A Porthgolow Sunset,' Juliette said. 'Does it live up to your standards?' She handed him her drink and Oliver sipped it.

'Not bad. A bit sweet for me, but it wouldn't be out of place on The Marauding Mojito menu.'

'You should talk to Hugh,' Charlie said. 'See if you and he can swap ideas.'

Oliver laughed. 'I'm heading to the bar. Everyone OK?'

They all nodded, and as he sauntered away Juliette leaned in towards Charlie. 'So, you and Oliver?'

Charlie sighed. 'I like him, and we see each other every week at the market, but it's finding other time to be together that's the problem.' She also knew that she needed to tell him about her kiss with Daniel. Draw a line under it as a mistake, be honest with Oliver and start afresh. 'He's touring the fairs and shows with his cocktails, and I'm – well, you know what I'm doing. I thought it would be good to see him tonight. I hope Myrtle and Hugh don't mind.'

'Of course they won't,' Juliette said. 'After all, this is still a public venue. It's not like Hugh's put a sign up saying it's closed for a private party.'

'True.' Charlie moved over to let Oliver sit next to her.

'Are you driving?' Lawrence asked, pointing at Oliver's glass.

'Nope. I've got a lift organized. This is a Long Island Iced Tea. Now I'll get to see what Hugh's cocktails are made of. The quality of your Long Island proves how good you really are.'

'Right,' Lawrence said, failing to contain his grin. 'The quality of your *long island*, eh? I'll have to remember that.'

'For God's sake, Lawrence.' Juliette hit him on the arm. Lawrence's mock-innocent expression got them all laughing.

Ten minutes later, Myrtle arrived, wearing a cream and yellow floral dress that made her look soft and summery. The pub erupted into applause and she looked, for a second, like a rabbit frozen in some very bright headlights. Charlie thought she might turn round and walk back out, but Hugh took her hand and, with a sweep of his arm, gestured to a table with a 'reserved' sign, in prime position for the band, and a long set of tables which, Charlie presumed, would at some point have food on them.

After Myrtle had made her way to her seat, and Rose and Frank had joined her, the pub seemed to settle. Charlie could feel Oliver's arm against hers and pressed closer to him. He was handsome, funny and laid-back, and had shown her nothing but kindness. She should be bold and encourage his affections. Her mind tripped a switch, presenting her, traitorously, with an image of Daniel in the hot tub.

'What do you think, Char?' Lawrence asked.

'About what?'

Juliette gave her a bemused smile. 'About whether . . . ooh, Daniel!' Her eyes flickered to the door.

Charlie turned to see that Daniel was, indeed, in the pub, looking even more uncomfortable than Myrtle had as heads swivelled in his direction. Lauren stood behind him, searching for something in her clutch bag. She had on the world's tightest black dress, her dark hair was loose around her shoulders and her eye make-up was dark and sultry. Daniel bent to whisper something in her ear and Lauren grabbed him by the hand and pulled him across the room.

Charlie recognized the hard lump at the base of her throat as jealousy. Daniel was with Lauren. She didn't know if they were there as colleagues, or something more, but she got the sense that it was the two of them against the rest of the pub, the outsiders from the swanky cliff-top hotel taking their chances in the heart of the village. Daniel had told her it wasn't about taking sides, but – despite being here with her

235

friends, and with Oliver – Charlie couldn't help feeling as if she was on the wrong one.

'Another round?' Lawrence asked, and she nodded absent-mindedly.

Lauren led Daniel to a booth next to the window that a family had just vacated, and as Daniel sat down he caught her eye. He was wearing a white linen shirt that brought out his tan, and his dark hair seemed intentionally ruffled. He nodded a welcome, and though he was clearly uncomfortable, she saw that unmistakable twitch of his lips, as if every time he saw her, he remembered how easy she was to fool. Charlie gave him a quick, stilted wave. She wasn't sure she'd breathed for about five minutes. She turned back to her friends and got a smug, knowing smile from Juliette.

The buffet appeared, and while Lawrence and Oliver claimed they were starving and got up immediately, Charlie hung back. The pub had become a battleground, with explosive mines waiting to detonate at every turn. She decided it was best if she got at least one of them out of the way. She was about to go and talk to Myrtle, when she realized the guest of honour was heading towards their table.

'Oh God.' She took a big swig of her drink and moved against the wall, so Myrtle could take Oliver's place. 'Happy Birthday, Myrtle!' she said.

'Good evenin' Charlie, Juliette.'

'Are you having a lovely time?' Juliette asked.

''Tis a bit much, all this.' She gestured around the room. 'But Hugh's a good friend, so I let 'im organize it. And,' she added, smiling, 'it's pretty grand havin' this all for me. It's proper.' She nodded decisively and Charlie and Juliette exchanged a relieved look.

'And I wanted to say somethin' to you, Charlie. My nephew,

Bill, runs this food truck down in Devon. Vegan or some such thing, and he – well, we were *both* wonderin' if he could, mebbe, come to your event. The Porthgolow food market,' she corrected, as if she'd been practising this speech and wanted to get it right. 'You don't have a vegan truck yet, do you?'

'N-no,' Charlie stuttered. 'Not yet. That – that would be wonderful, Myrtle. We'd love to have Bill at the market, and I'm sure he'd be popular. If you give me his details I can talk to him, arrange a start date, make sure I promote him before his first weekend.'

'Good. Right. I'll get his info for you. That's great, then. Enjoy your evenin'.'

Charlie managed to wait until the older woman was back at her table before bursting into overjoyed, incredulous laughter.

'High-five,' Juliette said, looking as shocked as Charlie felt.

'One mine eliminated,' she whispered to herself.

The buffet food, all from Hugh's kitchen, was delicious: mini Cornish pasties, avocados loaded with delicate crab meat, cod goujons and steak baguettes with beef from a local farm. There were Cajun vegetable skewers, tiny halloumi burgers and rolls full of creamy egg mayonnaise. Waiters laid out three huge Pyrex dishes full of Hugh's trademark fisherman pie, all of which were close to empty within minutes. Charlie wondered whether she could convince Hugh to invest in an old camper van and convert it into a Seven Stars food truck.

As the queue at the buffet tables petered out, Silas, Artem and Ken settled in their chairs and tuned their instruments. Hugh took up position, brandishing his ukulele and, as the room hushed for the first time that evening, they launched into their opening number. The music was folky and melodic, at turns upbeat and melancholy, and while Charlie was unfamiliar with the songs, some people sang along.

She had to turn in her seat to watch them and could feel Oliver's breath on her neck. He was being so attentive, touching her hand, checking whether she needed more food or drink, it was as if the four of them were on an impromptu double date. She had laughed a lot, and felt more carefree than she had in a long time.

But that didn't stop her glancing in Daniel's direction. Every time she did, she saw Lauren either talking animatedly to him or tapping away on her phone. He seemed quieter than usual, nodding at Lauren or staring into his pint glass.

Charlie felt suddenly, unexpectedly, sorry for him. He was usually so in control, but she got the sense that, here, he was out of his depth. He wasn't known for integrating with the other villagers. Organizing things – fireworks displays, council staff to come and look at dangerous cliffs – that was fine because he could take charge, but plain, old-fashioned socializing seemed to be out of his comfort zone.

Oliver announced that he was nipping to the gents and, as he left, Charlie watched Lauren stand up, rest her hand on Daniel's shoulder and then walk, slightly unsteadily, towards the bar. She didn't give herself time to think.

'Back in a minute,' she said to Lawrence and Juliette, raising her voice to be heard above the music, and then walked across the pub and slid into Lauren's empty seat.

'Hello,' Daniel said, running his eyes unapologetically over her dress-clad form. 'You look good.'

'Thanks,' she said. 'You look miserable.'

He laughed. 'That obvious?'

She nodded. 'Why did you come if you knew you'd hate it?'

'Because I thought you might be here, wearing something other than jeans and a stripy apron. I'm glad I was right.'

Charlie rolled her eyes. 'Seriously, Daniel. You and Lauren look like a couple on the verge of a break-up. You haven't spoken to anyone else in the entire pub and you seem totally out of sorts. This is meant to be a celebration.'

He leaned towards her. 'Lauren convinced me to come,' he admitted. 'Or rather, she badgered me until I decided it would be a lot less hassle to give in. A few hours' penance to stop her going on at me. This isn't my kind of thing. A quiet drink with a couple of friends, but not this – the band, the buffet, all the forced goodwill for someone most people don't know, and a few definitely don't like.' He shook his head, his jaw clenching.

'So turn it into something better.'

'What do you mean?'

'If you don't like all this, then adapt it. You're obviously not going to have fun if you sit there while Lauren communicates solely through the medium of WhatsApp. If you like having a drink with a few friends, then do that instead. Come and join us. You and Lauren – we can squeeze a couple more people round our table. And the band won't go on for ever.'

Daniel glanced over at Charlie's table. 'With you and Oliver?' he asked drily.

'The six of us,' Charlie confirmed, her heart skipping at Daniel's obvious dislike of her being with Oliver. 'Just try it. If, after twenty minutes, you can't stand our company, then you can come back to self-pity corner. But anything has to be better than this, right?'

Lauren was snaking through the crowd, holding a pint and a large glass of wine aloft, and Oliver had taken up Charlie's seat in the booth with Juliette and Lawrence, his shoulders moving in response to the Cornwall Cornflowers' latest jaunty number.

'Come on.' She held out her hand.

Daniel stared at her, and Charlie was transported back to the hot tub, the moment when he'd lost his flippancy and was entirely, intently focused on her. A small voice in her brain suggested having Daniel and Oliver at the same table might not be the best idea she'd ever had. But it was too late.

Daniel reached out and took her hand.

Chapter Twenty-One

When Charlie brought Lauren and Daniel to their table, pulling over a couple of chairs to stick on the end, there were a few moments of bemused incredulity, until Lawrence stood up, slapped Daniel heartily on the back and kissed Lauren's cheek. Juliette offered to get fresh drinks for those who needed them and the six of them sat around the table while the conversation stalled and stuttered like Gertie after her run-in with the Ross-on-Wye mud. When the band announced they were taking a break, the silence was almost deafening. Charlie wondered if – after putting them in this situation – anyone would believe her if she told them she had to go home and check on Marmite.

'So, Daniel,' Oliver said, taking a sip of his gin cocktail, 'what's it like running that posh hotel on top of the cliff? Was that always what you wanted to do? What do you think of the invasion of the little people on the beach each week, now that Charlie's here?'

Charlie closed her eyes. His question had started off so well. She had thought that Oliver was incapable of having a tone, but clearly she wasn't the only one who found matters less straightforward when it came to Daniel.

'I've always wanted to run a hotel,' Daniel said calmly. 'I started off working as a general dogsbody in a boutique place near where I grew up, then got an apprenticeship at a corporate hotel in London, where I tried my hand at everything, from concierge to waiter to security. But it was always with the intention of starting my own place one day, having it just as I imagined it, no cut corners or compromises.'

'What was it like working in London?' Juliette asked. 'Was it glamorous?'

Daniel laughed. 'The hotel was, but the work most definitely wasn't. You bust your balls to give the impression of perfection, as if there are no wrinkles and it all works like clockwork, when it's often a mad panic just under the surface. Crystal Waters is no different, really. You must feel the same about what you do.' He gestured to Oliver. 'With your cocktails, and with your bus, Charlie.'

'I feel like I've pretty much got my routine sorted,' Oliver said. 'No wrinkles at The Marauding Mojito.'

Juliette levelled Charlie with a look that said: *Why did you do this?* Charlie wished she knew the answer. But she had expected the barbs to come from Daniel, not Oliver.

'You must be very well practised,' Daniel said, sincerely. 'I still feel like I'm learning, and I know I couldn't do it without Lauren and my other colleagues.'

Lauren put her hand on Daniel's arm. 'It's my pleasure,' she cooed. Charlie could see that she was quite drunk, and that, when she was drunk, her flirting was rather unsubtle.

'Why did you pick Porthgolow?' Juliette asked. 'Other than

that it's the perfect place to live.' There was polite laughter round the table.

'My family used to come on holiday here,' Daniel admitted. 'And I loved it, even when I was little. It was always the dream to come back here, to open up a hotel with those views of the coastline, the perfect summer days.' He sounded wistful, and Charlie knew she was seeing that other side to him, the one she'd only had glimpses of up until now. He was a man who had followed his dream, made it happen, and then worked hard to keep hold of it.

Oliver was on Charlie's right, against the wall, and Daniel was at right angles on her left. Under the table, their knees were touching. She pushed hers more firmly against his, and he looked at her, surprised.

'Porthgolow is special,' Charlie said. 'I thought that the moment I drove down the hill that very first day. I had no idea you came here when you were a child.'

'Oh yes,' Daniel replied, laughing. 'I even remember Myrtle before she had grey hair – not that that's made her any more fond of me.'

'Was she always so scathing,' Lawrence asked, 'or did she get like that over time?'

'I remember being in the Porthgolow Pop-In and picking up a toy,' Daniel said, rubbing his jaw. 'It was a Matchbox Porsche, I think. Silver, with yellow headlights and doors that opened. I just wanted to look at it, and she almost bit my head off. I was only about seven and I refused to go back into her shop for the rest of the holiday.'

'Wow, Porthgolow back in the day,' Juliette said.

'It wasn't that long ago,' Daniel replied, mock-hurt. 'Our holiday snaps aren't in sepia or anything.'

'Who else did you know?' Lawrence asked.

'God, I . . .' Daniel blew air out through his lips. 'Well, we used to have dinner with Reenie and her family.'

Juliette almost knocked her glass over.

'Reenie's *family?*' Charlie said. 'But she's . . . she's all on her own, out there in that little house. What happened?' A lump formed in her throat.

Daniel shook his head. 'Look, it's not for me— maybe I shouldn't have said anything. It's—'

Charlie put her hand over his. 'It's OK. Don't tell us if you think you're betraying a confidence. I was just surprised. It's been a while since I saw her, actually. I had wondered if she'd come tonight, but I guess clambering back over the rocks in the darkness wouldn't be much fun.'

Everyone else was quiet and Charlie's laugh sounded far too loud. Daniel pressed his knee against hers under the table, returning the gesture.

'So, Oliver,' Lawrence said, clearing his throat, 'where are you taking your cocktail truck next? Are you staying in Cornwall for the whole summer?'

'Probably,' Oliver admitted. 'It's got a much more tempting outlook than anywhere else at the moment.' He slid his arm along the back of the booth and let his hand rest on Charlie's shoulder.

Charlie glanced at Juliette and saw that she was trying hard not to laugh. She decided that her plan to cheer Daniel up hadn't been as successful as she'd hoped, and yet she knew, with absolute certainty, that she would miss his company at the table more than she would miss Oliver's. It was a sobering thought and she excused herself to go to the ladies.

She took longer than necessary washing and drying her hands, looking at her reflection in the mirror, at her bob which was growing out messily, reaching halfway between her chin and her shoulders, the red dye fading after so much exposure to the sunshine.

'What are you doing, Charlie?' she asked herself. The answer that came back was one of Hal's favourite sayings, one that she had often rolled her eyes at, even though she liked the simplicity of it. *All you can do is follow your heart and see where it leads.* At this moment, her heart was holding a flashing, neon arrow that was pointing straight at Daniel.

When she walked out of the toilets, the change in atmosphere was obvious. Voices were muted, and all eyes had turned in one direction. But it wasn't the direction of the band, and Hugh hadn't suddenly announced there was an open bar for the rest of the night. Everyone was focused on Charlie's table, and she saw that Oliver was standing up, his usually calm face contorted with anger.

She took a few, hesitant steps, expecting to see Daniel facing off with him, then realized that it wasn't Daniel who Oliver was angry with, but Lawrence. Her best friend's boyfriend was wide-eyed, his hands up in submission.

'It's all right mate,' he was saying, 'calm down. It was just a joke.'

Charlie spotted Amanda and made a beeline for her. 'What did Lawrence say?' she whispered.

Amanda shook her head. 'I have no idea; we didn't hear the beginning. Something about his cocktails, I think.'

'Shit.' Oliver was here because of her, and she had invited Daniel and Lauren to their table, so if he was pissed off – even if it was with Lawrence and had more to do with the number of drinks he'd had than anything else – then it was down to her. She exhaled and approached the table.

'Oliver,' she said, 'can we sit down and sort this out?'

He ran a hand through his hair. His gaze was slightly unfocused, and there were points of colour on his cheeks.

'Ollie?' she touched his arm, but he flung her hand off. She tried again. 'Whatever's happened, I'm sure it was just a misunderstanding.'

'It was a fucking insult.'

'I was joking,' Lawrence said. 'I didn't mean anything by it. I loved that Porthgolow Sunset, or whatever it was, earlier. I was just saying that—'

'No need to repeat it,' Juliette murmured, and he nodded, contrite.

'Let's get another tune on, shall we?' Hugh called, and there was a frantic scrambling as the band hastily took up their positions and launched into a loud, upbeat song.

Oliver stared at the table and everyone else waited, poised, to see what he would do. Charlie felt a hand squeeze hers and knew it was Daniel's. It was quick, over in a second, but she felt instantly comforted.

'Oliver,' she said again, 'do you want to go outside and get some air? Walk down to the beach?'

Oliver sighed, his hand worrying the back of his neck. 'I should go.'

'You don't need to . . .' she started, but he nudged her out of the way and made unsteady progress across the pub, the people who hadn't been distracted by the band watching him go. Charlie gave an apologetic smile to the rest of the table and went after him.

Outside, the night-time breeze was refreshing, and the moon hung above the sea, leading a glittering path across the water to the sand. Oliver was trudging across the gravel in the direction of Porthgolow's main car park.

'Oliver,' she called, hurrying after him. 'Ollie, you're not driving!'

He turned, his expression shifting from anger to guilt. 'A mate's picking me up. They're only a few minutes away.'

'I'll wait with you.'

'Charlie, you don't have to. I know I messed up.'

'You're drunk, that's all. Everyone will forgive you.'

'Go back inside,' Oliver said. 'Go back to Daniel.'

Charlie inhaled sharply. 'What do you mean?' She wrapped a hand around herself as the wind picked up, chilling her bare shoulders.

'I saw the way he looked at you. Don't think I didn't.'

'No, Oliver, it isn't . . . look, can we do this another time, when you're—?'

'Yup, sure. Whatever.'

'I know we need to talk, that there's . . . that I need to be straight with you, but I don't think now—'

'I said no problem. Look, here's my lift.' He gestured as a car drove down the hill, and then stopped, idling at the edge of the car park. The driver was a young woman, her long blonde hair highlighted by the light from the dashboard. Oliver climbed into the passenger seat and the woman gave Charlie a quick, angry glance. Charlie wondered who she was – Oliver's sister, Nat, who had started the business with him, or a concerned friend?

The woman did a three-point turn in the middle of the road and then drove back up the hill, past Crystal Waters and out of sight. Charlie stood on the gravel and gazed at the moon, listening to the rhythmic churn of the waves against the sand. It was a sound she loved, but even that couldn't soothe her right now.

'This is exactly why I don't like these kinds of events.'

Charlie turned to find Daniel leaning against the wall of the pub, his hands in his pockets.

'It's a melting pot of people,' he continued. 'Nobody really knows or likes each other, everyone drinks too much to cover up their insecurities, and this is what happens. Are you OK?'

'I'm fine,' she replied. 'And things don't always turn out this way; you're just smug that, on this occasion, you were right. And this is my fault. I asked Oliver to come, then I invited you and Lauren to join us, so . . .' She shrugged.

'Why should that have been a problem?' he asked. 'Oliver's a grown-up. He should be responsible for his own actions.'

'Yes, but I . . . I think he felt threatened by you.'

'By me? Why? That man has no grounds to feel hard done by.'

'Oh, come on, Daniel.' Charlie folded her arms. 'You don't have to be against him on principle.'

'I'm not!' he shot back. 'He's . . .' He looked away from her and rubbed his jaw. 'I'm just concerned that he's not all you think he is.'

'You're really going to—'

'Charlie, stop.' Daniel put his hand on her arm. His palm was hot against her cool skin. 'I'm sorry, OK? Forget I said anything.'

Her mouth was dry. She couldn't deny that Oliver's temper had been a surprise, a complete contrast to the other times she'd been with him. 'What did Lawrence say to upset him?'

A group of friends spilled out of the pub, laughing, and Daniel took her arm and led her round the side of the building, so they were out of sight of the door.

'He said he thought cocktails were for women,' Daniel admitted. 'Though I think he might have used the word "girly". It's a fair enough comment, but Oliver took it to heart.'

'Shit. Poor Lawrence. He doesn't have a malicious bone in his body. He must feel awful.'

'Juliette's looking after him, so I thought I'd better come and see if you were OK.'

'I'm fine. Thank you, though. For checking on me.'

'No problem,' he said softly. 'It's what friends do, isn't it?'

'Friends?'

'That's what you called me, when you were convincing me to come and join your table.'

They were so close that, despite being lit only by the moon, Charlie could see strands of green and amber in his brown eyes.

'Yes, of course—' she started.

'But you think Oliver felt threatened by me?' He ran his thumb lightly down the side of her face. Charlie's breath stalled in her throat, but the rest of her body fizzed into life. 'Why would that be, do you think?'

'Because he believes that you . . .'

'That I what? What is it that I do, Charlie?'

'We should go inside,' she murmured.

'Right now?' He stopped his thumb at the edge of her mouth, and then grazed it over her lips.

'Daniel—'

'We'll go back in a moment.' He replaced his thumb with his mouth, so swiftly that Charlie didn't have time to protest. And once it was happening, there was no part of her that *wanted* to protest. Her mind was a blank, everything focused on the feel of Daniel's kiss, his body warm against hers. There was confidence in his embrace, and she knew that, were it to go further, she would relish him being in control. She craved it.

He pulled back, his breathing heavy. 'Now,' he said. 'We can go inside now, if you want?'

She nodded, trying to gather her composure.

She pictured Oliver stumbling away, hurt and drunk, and realized how unfairly she'd treated him. The hot tub kiss, as brief as it had been, was bad enough, and even though she wasn't sure what was – or had been – happening between her and Oliver, she couldn't keep leading him on. She wouldn't be able to tell him, now, that her kiss with Daniel had been a one-off. She needed to set the record straight, to let him know that, although part of her still couldn't believe it, her intentions were entirely focused elsewhere. Nothing else could happen with Daniel until she'd done that.

She looked at the man who, despite the boldness of his actions, was staring mutely at the sea, as if he was as taken aback by the last few minutes as she was.

'Are you coming?' she asked.

Daniel stared at her, his lips slightly parted. 'Lead the way,' he said.

Together, they went back inside the pub.

Chapter Twenty-Two

Daniel was waiting for her when she pulled into the Crystal Waters car park on Monday afternoon. His guests, those she'd seen in the breakfast room on Friday, plus a couple of others she didn't recognize, hovered next to the entrance. They had no idea how much had changed over the course of the weekend.

When Charlie and Daniel had gone back inside the pub, Lawrence was repentant, worried about how much he'd upset Oliver, and Juliette and Lauren were trying to calm him down. After that, the evening had felt as if it was over and Daniel had called a taxi for Lauren. While they waited, Myrtle had given them each a hug and thanked them for making her birthday so wonderful. Charlie hadn't been able to work out whether she was referring to the added drama, or if she had been genuinely pleased that they had been a part of her celebrations.

Daniel had accompanied them up the hill, and said

251

goodbye at the end of Juliette's road. His brief embrace had felt as charged as the moment outside the pub. Which meant today Charlie had an extra reason to be nervous on what was already a landmark afternoon: her first-ever Cornish Cream Tea Tour aboard Gertie.

'Great to see you all again,' she said, beckoning her guests forward and shaking hands as they passed her. 'The best views are from the upper deck, so if you'd like to make your way up there and find a seat, Juliette will give you all menus. There are tables downstairs if you'd prefer, or if you're not fond of steep staircases.'

'Oh, don't worry about us,' said the older woman who had spoken up on Friday. 'We did the Cornish coastal path last year. This holiday may be a bit more comfortable, but we're good for a few stairs, aren't we, Elber?'

'Indeed,' Elber replied. 'It was an experience, I'll give you that. But Crystal Waters is too, and I don't mind a bit of the high life. I'd pick the king-sized bed and Jacuzzi over tents and hostels any day.'

'I don't think I could do it,' Charlie said.

'Oh, you could,' the woman chimed in. 'A sprightly young thing like you. Fancy thinking of cream teas on a bus, too. I don't know whether you've got sense or stupidity behind all that red hair of yours, but I'm looking forward to finding out.' She patted Charlie on the shoulder and took Elber's hand to climb up onto the bus.

Charlie turned to find Daniel watching her, a smile tugging at his lips.

'Don't mind Helena,' he said. 'She has a knack for putting the younger generation in their place. How are you, after yesterday?'

'Fine,' she said. 'You?'

252

'Not bad. Heard from Oliver?'

Charlie shook her head. She had tried calling and had left several texts, but he had remained resolutely incommunicado. She hoped he was just sleeping off his hangover.

'Maybe he's realized he's not good enough for you,' Daniel said. 'But if he stops hedging his bets and asks to see you, then I think you should be honest with him.'

'Honest? I—'

'You know what I mean,' he whispered. His brushed his hand against her bare arm as he passed.

'Charlie? You coming?' Juliette called from inside the bus.

'Of course!'

As she took her seat and pulled out the detailed route plan she had created, she was relieved to see that all the guests – Daniel included – had chosen to sit upstairs. She could concentrate on driving, on pointing out the highlights of Cornwall's beautiful coastline through the mic system while Juliette arranged the cream teas. There were stopping points along the route, strategically timed to help with serving, but also with spectacular views. She had planned everything down to the last detail.

She needed this tour to be triumphant, and if she'd been lacking any kind of incentive before, then having Daniel on board had given it to her. So far, she had failed spectacularly in her quest to show him she was unflappable. Now it was time to pull it out of the bag. There was no other option but to succeed.

As Charlie navigated the twisting coastal road south from Porthgolow, pointing out the various coves, lighthouses and old mining towers, the sun burnt off the last of that morning's clouds to leave behind a beautiful afternoon. Green hills and fields rolled inland, while to their right was the deep blue of the sea beyond a sheer drop, a craggy cliff face or a sloping, golden beach. The heat was tempered by a brisk breeze, and Charlie had the driver's window open so that it licked deliciously in, cooling her hot cheeks. It was strange, driving the bus, acting as tour guide and talking to guests she couldn't see or interact with. Every time Juliette came downstairs to refill teapots, Charlie asked for an update.

'How's it going?' she asked. 'What's happening?'

'There's lots of laughter,' Juliette said. 'That old couple are holding court, telling everyone their stories from the coastal path walk. I honestly think they'd be a bad influence on us, Char. You want to hear what happened in a pub in Padstow! Lucky that the girls, Sarah and Samantha, don't really understand, but their parents seem pretty laid-back.'

Charlie slowed as a bright green van declaring itself to belong to The Best Pastry Company in Cornwall approached along a particularly narrow bit of road. She waved a thanks to the driver as they passed each other. 'And Daniel?' she asked, keeping her voice casual.

It didn't work. She saw her friend's grin in the mirror. 'He's being well behaved,' Juliette confirmed. 'Joining in with the conversation, complimenting the scones and the mini lemon meringue pies. It was fun with him, in the pub, if you discount the moments of excruciating tension. It was a surprise that he used to come on holiday here as a child. I feel as though I hardly knew anything about him until last night. Did you have fun with him outside, too?'

Charlie kept her gaze on the road. 'I really need to talk to Ollie. He stormed off pretty quickly.'

'Poor Oliver,' Juliette sighed. 'Poor Lawrence, too. Why do men have to be so confrontational?'

'Beats me,' Charlie murmured. 'At least Daniel remained level-headed during the whole thing.' Almost until the very end, she added silently. 'He came outside to see if I was all right.' She spotted the lay-by she had earmarked for their next stop, which had a panoramic view over Hayle Beach, stretching for miles and curving round towards the bay of St Ives. She indicated and pulled gently into it.

'I bet he did.' Juliette's lips flickered into a smile that vanished as soon as it had arrived. 'Just be careful, OK? Remember what you told me about him making you feel hopeless. Don't forget why we're doing this, today, using *his* guests as guinea pigs.'

'I won't, Jules. It's at the forefront of my mind.' Although, after last night, Charlie felt as though she had a better understanding of Daniel and thought that they might have moved beyond game playing.

Juliette sighed, suddenly pensive. 'I don't want you to get your heart broken again, Char. You're here to heal yourself, and obviously your interpretation of that is to throw yourself into this,' she gestured around her, 'but just – just don't get too invested in Daniel.'

'I'm not getting invested in him. I just – after all this back and forth between us, I want him to take me seriously. I want him to see that Gertie is a good thing, for *all* of Porthgolow, including his customers.'

'You're doing that, for sure. Want to come and talk to your adoring clientele?'

Charlie laughed. 'I do want to stretch my legs.'

Charlie gave Marmite a quick stroke and followed Juliette to the upper deck, where everyone, led by her friend, gave her a round of applause.

'I sometimes get nervous driving my Mini along these

255

roads,' Kerry said. She was part of the trio, on holiday with her friends, Luke and Richard. 'And I've been to Cornwall every year since I was twelve. How you're driving a double-decker is beyond me.'

'Not a drop of tea spilled, either,' added Luke, raising his cup in appreciation. 'Have you been a bus driver long?'

Charlie shook her head. 'My uncle Hal used to tour this bus round the Cotswold countryside. I often went with him and he taught me to drive it. I added the café after I inherited it.'

'Great addition,' the father of Sarah and Samantha said. 'I've not had an afternoon tea like this for years. It reminds me of one I had in the Langham in London, decades ago.'

'Oh wow, that's a huge compliment. Thank you.'

'And the views,' added Helena. 'Sublime. It's bringing back memories of our trip last year. You know, I've seen every Cornish beach, and I think Porthgolow is one of the most beautiful. No wonder that Porthgolow Hideaway Instagram account has got so many followers. You must know who runs it, living there?'

'Not a clue,' Charlie said. 'What about you, Jules?'

'I've never been able to work it out, though I have an inkling Daniel might know.'

'Me?' He raised an eyebrow. 'You think I've got time to go sneaking about incognito, snapping photos and uploading them to Instagram?'

'You don't even know who it is?' Juliette asked, deflated.

'Nope. But what about Jonah? He strikes me as the kind of kid who would do something like that.'

'Are you even allowed an Instagram account at twelve?' Juliette asked.

'I wouldn't have thought so,' Helena said, tutting.

'I know the one you mean,' cut in Richard. 'It's partly why I agreed to come to Crystal Waters with Kerry and Luke. They post those Cornish landscapes on the tourist sights and social media and you know you have to see them for yourself.'

Charlie nodded. 'As soon as I drove into Porthgolow, I was blown away by the view. Cornwall couldn't be any more different from Herefordshire.'

They all took a moment to look out at the wide strip of sand and glittering water.

'Did you paint the seagull cookies?' the older of the two girls, Sarah, asked, breaking the silence.

'I did,' Charlie confirmed. 'But with icing. You can use different colours and make any design you want, like the seagull and the shell, and the green one shaped like Cornwall.' She had spent yesterday morning baking the cookies, and she and Juliette had got up early today to ice them, Charlie thankful that she hadn't had too many cocktails the previous night. They were more intricate than any she'd done before.

'And the bus!' Samantha added. 'I love the bus, like this one.'

'The cookies are as pretty as they are delicious,' said a young, beautiful woman who was one of the last-minute additions to the tour. She was there with her partner, their hands clasped across the table. They were the type of guests that Charlie had expected to be staying at Crystal Waters, their clothes, posture and demeanour all refined.

But the rest of them weren't. They were simply people indulging in a bit of luxury for whatever reason. She had allowed the look of the hotel, Daniel's initial coolness, and the gossip in the village to sway her assumptions, and she knew now that she had misjudged.

'Thank you everyone,' she said. 'This is our last stop – the seemingly endless Hayle Beach. I'm in negotiations with the National Trust, which owns lots of the car parks along here, to run a tour that includes a stop closer to the sand. A swim, stroll or paddle to work up an appetite, followed by afternoon tea looking out across the water. There are always new events and initiatives happening on the bus, including the weekly food market in Porthgolow itself. Please keep up to date on our social media pages to find out what's going on and where we'll be next. Now, does anyone need a top-up before we head back to the hotel?'

There were a few murmurs of assent, and she helped Juliette refill the teapots before seating herself behind the wheel and beginning the slow, winding journey back to Porthgolow. She didn't want to count her chickens, but it seemed as if her taster tour had gone well. Now all she had to do was work out how to fit them into her schedule. Her mother's words came to her; a mantra she'd heard so often growing up. *Don't bite off more than you can chew, Charlene. Otherwise it'll get stuck in your gullet and choke you.* She thought how different that was to Hugh's positive affirmations, and pushed the words to the back of her mind. For her, busyness meant happiness, and The Cornish Cream Tea Bus was making her feel more fulfilled than anything had done in a long time.

'Impressive tour,' Daniel said, once Charlie had waved the guests off the bus and was about to head upstairs to help Juliette clean up. He was standing in the doorway, his heels hanging off the step.

'Thank you. I knew if you came, you'd love it.'

'There was never any doubt of that.' He took a step towards her, his polished boots clanging against the metal floor.

Charlie frowned. 'Really? Even after all your posturing with

258

the yoga sessions, muscling in on that first Saturday as if it wouldn't be good enough unless you intervened? What did you think of the lemon meringue pies?'

'Delicious,' he said. 'Everything was. Is that really why you thought I arranged the fireworks? I was trying to help. Why are you picking a fight with me now? Do you regret what happened last night?' Charlie looked away but he touched her cheek, forcing her to face him. 'I believe in your events, Charlie. I believe in you.'

'What about the mix-up with the yoga?'

Daniel's smile was irrepressible. 'OK, that was a bit cruel, but I couldn't help it. I love the fire you have and I wanted to see it unleashed. But the food market was never in danger.'

'You really believe in me?'

'You think I'm still playing games?' He took another step towards her. 'Last night was not a game to me. You've brought a breath of fresh air to Porthgolow, changed it for the better. And as for me . . .' He took her hand.

'What about you?' she managed. She leaned in closer, the scents of orange and cedar wafting over her, his face inches from hers.

'You've got all the way in here.' He brought her hand up and pressed it against his chest.

She swallowed. She could feel his breath against her face, the hard contours of his muscles beneath her palm. When she forced herself to meet his gaze, he was smiling.

'It's not easy for me to admit,' he said, 'and I can see you're having a hard time accepting it, too. So I'm going to prove to you just how much I believe in you, and in Gertie. Maybe then you'll realize.'

'Realize what?'

'That this is meant to happen. Again. And then again. Ad

259

infinitum.' He bent his head towards hers and she closed her eyes, waiting for his kiss.

'*Charlie?*' Her eyes sprang open.

Daniel turned, allowing her to see beyond him, down into the car park where Oliver was standing, his face paler than usual and, at that moment, a mask of shock.

'I saw the bus as I was passing. I wanted to apologize for last night. For what I said to you, accused you of . . .' His words hung in the air.

Charlie was frozen. She tried to speak, but all that came out was a weak stutter. Oliver looked from her, to Daniel, and back again. The seconds ticked past, her pulse like the beat of a metronome. By the time she'd come to her senses, Oliver was climbing back into his van, and Daniel squeezed her hand, giving her a weary, resigned smile as he walked off the bus.

Charlie leaned against the nearest table and wondered what on earth she was meant to do now.

Chapter Twenty-Three

As the food trucks started to drive onto the creamy Porthgolow sand on Saturday morning, Charlie felt sick. She wondered whether Oliver and The Marauding Mojito would even turn up. The raft of unanswered calls and ignored texts suggested that he might be giving it a miss.

On Monday evening she had watched Daniel walk back into the hotel and Oliver drive out of the car park, and at first she hadn't done a thing about either of them. Juliette had remained quiet, as if waiting for Charlie to decide what to tell her, but the truth was Charlie hadn't known what to say.

She had been meaning to speak to Oliver. Between the pub on Sunday night and her tour on Monday afternoon, she hadn't been able to get hold of him, and it was predictably awful timing that he had turned up just as Daniel had been turning her insides to jelly in the doorway of her bus. But she had nobody to be angry with but herself. She should have stayed away from Daniel until after she'd found Oliver. But she hadn't, and now everything was a mess.

Benji drove onto the beach, hopped out of his cab and waved at her, then began opening up his burger stall. Almost on cue, Jonah raced onto the sand and Benji handed him an apron.

'New apprentice,' he called over.

Charlie laughed. 'Wow! Lucky you. Can I steal you back later today, Jonah? I thought you wanted to take orders on my bus?'

'I need to learn how to do these,' Jonah called. 'But maybe I'll come and see you after lunch.'

'I would be honoured,' Charlie said.

The day was too grey for the first Saturday in August, but it perfectly matched Charlie's mood as she performed her usual ritual, laying her cakes and scones out on stands, snapping photos of her daily special – today a custard Danish with local raspberry jam – and uploading them to Instagram, complete with blurred seascape backdrop.

Bill, Myrtle's nephew, was next to arrive in his converted Ford transit van, now called The Versatile Vegan, and Charlie went down to greet him. He was young and enthusiastic and, judging by the reaction when she'd announced the new addition on social media, would be very popular.

As she was walking back to Gertie, The Marauding Mojito drove into place, and her stomach clenched. This should be her opportunity to talk to Oliver, but she was alone on the bus today and she wasn't sure how she'd find the time. She turned to her Victoria sponge tray bake, and began cutting it viciously into squares.

'Table for four?' asked a cheery, sun-reddened woman in the doorway.

'Of course! There are lots of tables upstairs, or these ones down here if you'd prefer.'

'That's grand, thank you. Come on, lads.' She walked onto the bus holding the hand of a boy of about six, two more similarly aged children following behind. One of them looked at her, and then the scones piled on the counter, with wide eyes. Charlie smiled, and the boy hid behind his friend's shoulder. 'Got me neighbours' two as well as me own today,' the woman said. 'Thought I'd treat them.'

'Sounds like the perfect plan. Have you been on the beach?'

The wide-eyed boy shook his head.

'We are, after this!' another piped up. 'But we can't play games unless we have cake first. Cake is magic fuel. Isn't that right, Auntie Katie?'

The woman flushed, her neck matching her red cheeks. 'Well, I—'

'Cake is most definitely magic,' Charlie interjected. 'But which one will you pick, and what kind of magic does it hold?'

Now she had the attention of all three boys, she handed them menus and went through it, inventing magic properties for each item. In the end Auntie Katie asked for a cheese scone, a flapjack, a gingerbread dragon and one of the custard Danishes. She said they would share them all, so that none of them missed out on any magic. Charlie offered to cut each one into four equal slices and, once the group had gone upstairs, she was so engrossed in her task that she didn't notice the footsteps.

She looked up to see Oliver staring at her, his branded T-shirt on, hair swept off his face. He looked tired and anxious, and her heart sank. 'Give me two seconds to serve my customers, and I'll be with you.'

When she returned from doling out her magic cakes, Oliver was slumped at one of the tables.

'Can I get you a coffee?' she asked.

He shook his head. 'No, I'm good thanks. Except – I'm not. Not really.'

Charlie bit her lip. 'What you saw the other day—'

'I know he's a catch,' Oliver said, talking over her. 'He's got his incredible hotel, all the business smarts. I knew I'd seen something between you at the pub that night, but I thought you were at loggerheads. I thought you didn't get on.'

'It's . . . complicated,' she said.

'What I saw didn't look particularly complicated.'

'That was . . .' She shook her head. 'Ollie, I was planning on talking to you. You didn't answer my calls on Monday, and the tour with Daniel's guests was already organized. I never meant for you to see that. I should have been honest with you before now. I am so, so sorry.'

Oliver shook his head, aghast. 'You know, I didn't try to take things further because I was respecting your feelings! I sensed that you weren't ready, so I backed off. Turns out I backed off too far, and someone else got ahead of me.'

'It's not like that.'

'Isn't it? Because when I think about it, every time we're together all you talk about is Daniel and how you need to get one up on him. Now I'm wondering if all the time you'd actually been planning on getting a leg over.'

'Ollie!'

'You should never have led me on like that. I really cared about you.'

'I am so, so sorry.' She felt sick. Everything he was saying was true; she had treated him badly, dithered over her feelings, and had been letting it play out, even while her attraction to Daniel had been growing.

'Forget it, OK?' He stood up just as voices drifted onto the bus. Charlie smoothed her hair back, willing her pulse to settle, but when she realized who her new customers were, it sped up again.

Daniel looked relaxed and tanned in dark jeans and a blue T-shirt. Accompanying him was a woman who wouldn't have been out of place on the cover of a magazine. Her long chestnut hair was straightened to perfection, and while her white shirt and navy skirt were more formal than Daniel's outfit, she still managed to look effortlessly cool.

Charlie could only stare as Daniel noticed Oliver. His eyes narrowed and the air on the bus seemed to constrict.

'Oliver,' Daniel said.

'Daniel Harper,' Oliver replied. Charlie silently prayed that he'd leave, but he leaned against the nearest table and folded his arms. 'It's almost as if there was some kind of magnetic force attracting you to this bus. I would have said it was all down to Charlie, but now I'm not so sure.' He gestured towards Daniel's companion.

'I'm Josie,' she said, holding out her hand. 'Do you work with Charlie?'

Oliver kept his arms crossed. 'No, I don't work with her. I had thought we were destined for a somewhat different relationship, but she has her sights set elsewhere.'

'Ollie,' Charlie said quietly. 'Please don't do this.'

'Don't do what? I'm only stating the facts.'

Charlie glanced at Josie, who was looking distinctly uncomfortable. Daniel was stony-faced, his hands clenched into fists at his sides. Charlie had a sudden urge to turn off the oven and the coffee machine, to lower the uncomfortable temperature.

'You should probably go, Oliver,' Daniel said. 'Before you cause a scene.'

He was staying calm, but Charlie could hear the waver of tension in his voice. She knew that was her fault too; he'd been honest with her about how he felt, but after Oliver had interrupted them, she hadn't gone to find him. She had left him hanging, wanting to speak to Oliver first, to say what she should have told him a while ago. She had been desperate to make matters right, and all she'd done was make the situation worse for everyone.

'I'm not going to cause a scene,' Oliver replied. 'Or I wasn't until you turned up. You just keep rolling back here like a bad penny.'

Daniel gave a minute shake of his head. 'We should go.' He glanced at Josie, who nodded. 'Jasper's waiting outside. We'll come back later, Charlie. Call me if you need me?'

'Oh that's right,' Oliver said, before Charlie had a chance to speak. 'Play the chivalrous hero, why don't you? It'll be a novel role for you, I would have thought. His gallantry's all an act, Charlie. The only person he gives a shit about is himself.'

'Oliver—' Charlie started.

'You really think that I'd hurt her, Daniel?' he continued, his cheeks colouring. 'That I have no regard—'

'So Charlie knows about the woman in Newquay, does she?' Daniel cut in. 'Blonde hair, ripped jeans. The two of you looked very cosy, from what I could see.' His words were clipped, as if he was forcing them out. 'Is she the only one?'

Charlie turned to Oliver. 'What woman?'

Daniel flashed her a quick, pained look. 'I'm sorry, Charlie. I didn't mean to . . .' He ran a hand through his hair. 'Look, we'll go. Leave you to it.' He placed a hand on Josie's shoulder to guide her off the bus.

Once they'd gone, Charlie went to the cab and picked up Marmite, hugging the wriggling dog against her.

'Doesn't he make you mad?' Oliver said, but his eyes wouldn't meet hers.

'What did he mean, about that other woman?' Marmite nuzzled his wet nose into her neck.

Oliver's laugh was forced. 'He must have been mistaken – someone else who looked like me. I don't know what he's talking about.'

She remembered when they'd walked back to his place after the beach, the way he'd waved to someone in the window and his sudden reluctance to kiss her. The woman who had picked him up from the pub on Sunday had had long, blonde hair. Had Oliver told her he was just meeting friends for a few drinks? Is that why she had given Charlie such an angry look when she'd come to get him and found her there, too? 'I don't think Daniel would lie,' she said, slowly.

'Even though he was on the back foot, still wanting you on his good side despite appearing with *her*?' Oliver flung his arm out, and Marmite whimpered.

'Was I the only one, Ollie?' she asked, but from the way he was fidgeting, refusing to meet her gaze, she thought she already knew the answer. She remembered his words at the Eden Project. *I'm just open to seeing what happens, making the most of what's out there.*

'This life, Charlie,' he sighed. 'Never staying in one place, always on the road, it makes relationships difficult.'

'But meeting women easy, right? The ability to pick up and drop off at will, move on to the next one as swiftly as your next event?'

267

'You're making a mistake with Daniel. We could have had a lot of fun.'

She closed her eyes. She hadn't been honest with him but, as it turned out, she wasn't the only one keeping secrets. 'Please can you go?'

'Charlie—'

'Please, Oliver. I think we can safely say that this – whatever it is – is over. I will always be grateful for your help. But now . . .'

'Fine. No worries.' He wiped his hand over his face, let out a dramatic sigh, and walked off the bus.

Charlie turned away from the window. She thought of all the effort he'd gone to, taking her to the beach and the Eden Project, his patience and insight as they'd talked about her new venture. But perhaps that was how he lived his life, giving his attention to a number of women at the same time. He obviously had lots of love to spread around, and in some ways it wasn't even wrong, as long as everyone knew where they stood. But they'd been fooling each other. She had vowed never to be like Stuart and, while she and Oliver had only shared one tentative kiss at the Eden Project, she still felt ashamed that she hadn't been clearer with him.

But she was more shocked that Daniel had brought Josie onto the bus. Had all his attention been part of some bigger scheme to wrong-foot her, or was he just pissed off that she hadn't gone to find him on Monday, after the tour? Was he paying her back for her indecision, showing that he could move on and ruining things with Oliver at the same time? It seemed a bit rich telling her about Oliver when he was there with another woman himself.

When the boys and Auntie Katie left, thanking her profusely – though the look in the woman's eyes told Charlie

268

she'd heard everything – Charlie tried to stay calm. It had been one kiss outside a pub; one heartfelt declaration that, now, she wasn't even sure she could trust. If she was capable of getting it so spectacularly wrong with not one, but two men, it only proved that she wasn't ready for another relationship. She was much better off on her own.

But over the course of the afternoon, while the market continued blithely on and Charlie served families and couples, people wanting to take treats home with them, other vendors looking for a caffeine and sugar pick-me-up at the end of the day, her anger grew.

She watched as, one by one, each of them packed up and drove their food trucks off the beach, her shoulders dropping as The Marauding Mojito turned right and disappeared up the hill. Eventually, Gertie was the only vehicle left. The sea was dark and thrashing, but there was an intense humidity to the air, as if the tension had been building up outside as well as inside her, waiting for the right moment to burst.

She took a sleepy Marmite out of his crate and, checking everything was switched off and ready for another day, locked up the bus. But instead of turning towards Juliette's cottage, she found herself walking up the north side of the cove. The breeze was warm and thick and she got hotter with every step, Marmite stretching his tiny legs to keep up with her. She puffed out her breaths as she climbed, propelled forwards by anger.

Checking that the water bowl was full, she tied Marmite up outside and stepped into the air-conditioned foyer. There was nobody behind reception and, not finding a bell, Charlie was about to call out when Daniel walked out of his office.

His eyes widened. 'Charlie, are you OK? You look—'

'Harassed? Upset? Pissed off? Well, that's OK, because

that's exactly how I feel. What did you think you were doing, bringing your new girlfriend onto the bus this morning?'

'Josie? I—'

She didn't let him continue, didn't fall for the confusion plastered across his handsome face. 'I know I didn't handle it well when Oliver appeared the other evening, but I didn't know what to do. I needed to be honest with him, but at that moment, with you there – it wasn't the right time. And for you to throw it back at me with Josie, to come and show me how easy it is for you to dismiss our – our – oh, what would *you* call what's happened between us?'

Daniel put a warning hand out in front of him. 'Charlie, you need to—'

'Need to what? Weren't you the one who told me I'd got inside here?' She thumped her chest. 'Did you mean it? At the time, it felt as if you did.' Lauren stepped out of a corridor and came to a sudden stop, her mouth falling open. But now Charlie had started, she couldn't stop. 'You told me you'd show me exactly what I meant to you, how much you respected me and what I'm doing here. Was *that* what you meant? Bringing Josie onto the bus? Couldn't you resist making fun of me one more time?'

Daniel dropped his hand and stepped towards her, even though the reception desk remained between them. 'Come and have a cold drink. Let me explain.'

'That's what *I'm* trying to do. Don't you get it? Today, when you appeared, I was trying to tell Oliver the truth, that it wasn't him I had feelings for. And I was doing an awful job of it, believe me, before you told me all about him. How long have you known that he's been seeing other women?'

'I'm so sorry, Charlie, I—'

She shook her head. 'I don't know how to deal with relationships any more. I came to Porthgolow to try and get my head around Hal's death, get over what Stuart did to me. I wanted my life to be simple, and then here you were, with all your confidence and your . . .' She swallowed, trying to push the emotion down.

Daniel walked around the desk and put his hands on her arms. 'Come and sit down.'

'Don't patronize me.' She suddenly felt so hot, despite the air conditioning, that she could hardly breathe. The gold stone pattern in the floor shimmered, as if it was mocking her.

'I'm not. You need to sit down. Have a glass of water.'

She shook her head. 'I'm trying to tell you how I feel!'

Daniel's grip tightened. 'Not right now. I'm sorry about today. I didn't want to tell you about Oliver then, not like that. But right now, you need to—'

'Daniel, is everything OK?' Josie stepped out of Daniel's office.

Charlie felt the anger and the determination leave her in a single, sickening swoop. She swayed slightly, the heat of her stomp up the hill catching up with her. 'I shouldn't have come,' she said. 'This was a mistake.'

'Charlie, let me explain.' Daniel's voice was firm, his gaze locked onto hers.

She shook her head. 'You have company.'

'Charlie, please sit down, just for five minutes. Josie's a journalist!'

'That's lovely,' she said, feeling slightly dazed. 'I hope you'll be very happy together.' She offered what she hoped was a smile, but it might well have been a grimace. She tried to shrug out of his grip. He resisted for a couple of seconds, then let her go. 'Bye.' It seemed such an inadequate word for that moment, but she didn't know what else to say. She walked towards the exit, her head pounding.

'Charlie – wait!' He sounded on the edge of panic, his control slipping.

And then there was another voice, smooth and low and completely in command. 'Daniel, let her go. Maybe now isn't the best time. She's clearly not in the right frame of mind.' It was Josie.

Charlie didn't hear Daniel's reply, but no footsteps followed her towards the glass doors.

She crouched, putting her hand on the wall to steady herself, and then untied Marmite's lead. Her little dog whimpered when he saw her, and she cradled him to her before standing, relieved that the journey home was downhill.

Charlie walked into Porthgolow Bay just as the first rumble of thunder rolled in across the sea.

Chapter Twenty-Four

Apart from a couple walking a red setter along the beach, the village seemed deserted. Charlie reached the bottom of the hill, Marmite skittering ahead of her towards the sand, and she followed him, staring out at a sea that was more grey than blue.

Despite the heaviness in the air, the water around the cliffs was choppy, hinting at the strong currents beneath. Charlie crouched on the sand and dropped her head into her hands. Her phone buzzed, and she pulled it out of her pocket. When she saw it was Daniel, her jaw clenched, but she read it anyway.

Josie is a journalist. I wanted her to cover the food markets and do a profile on you. I thought you could meet each other today, she could get a feel for the event and then set up an interview. I didn't explain myself. I'm sorry. Are you OK? Dx

She read the message several times, trying to equate what she'd seen with Daniel's version of the truth. It was smooth – as always – and complimentary. But they'd made a habit of this: her confronting him, him coming up with a plausible excuse. She no longer knew what to believe.

She watched Marmite chasing the waves back and forth, yelping whenever he misjudged them and got his feet wet. When he tired, they started the journey back to Juliette's. The sky was an oil painting of grey and gold, the sun failing to break free from the clouds.

When she opened the front door, Ray padded down the hallway and stared balefully at Marmite. Charlie rubbed behind his ears, pulled off her shoes and went into the living room. Juliette and Lawrence looked up from the film they were watching.

'Charlie, what's happened?' Juliette asked. 'Did something go wrong today?'

Charlie sank onto the sofa. 'I'm fine,' she said. 'Go back to your film.'

Juliette extracted herself from Lawrence's arms. 'You are not fine. What is it? Did Bill not turn up? Or did . . . did you . . .' her eyes widened. 'Oliver was there?'

Charlie nodded. 'And Daniel. At the same time.'

'Ouch,' Lawrence murmured. 'Bottle of wine?'

Juliette nodded, and he slipped out of the room.

'Tell me what happened, Char.'

Charlie pulled her feet up under her and told Juliette everything. Lawrence returned with a bottle of wine and, half an hour after that, a plate of creamy pasta with bacon and mushrooms that Charlie devoured even though, if she'd been asked, she would have sworn she wasn't hungry. She had reached the mortifying confrontation at Crystal Waters

– the second one, she reminded herself – when her phone buzzed again. It was a second text from Daniel:

I promise I'm not lying to you. At least let me know you're OK. Dx

'What is it?'

She showed her friend the message, and Lawrence peered over Juliette's shoulder to read it too.

'Don't you think you should talk to him?' Juliette asked. 'See what he has to say? If this Josie person really *is* a journalist, and he was planning all that for you . . .'

'It's a pretty good move,' Lawrence added. 'Pretty selfless, coming from Daniel.'

'It is.' Charlie read the words over and over until they blurred into nothing.

'It's understandable you were flustered and upset after what happened with Oliver,' Juliette said. 'But doesn't that make the path clear, now? For you and Daniel? If you want it to be.'

Charlie nodded, but she couldn't meet her friend's gaze. After their kiss on Sunday she had been so sure. She loved how alive she felt with Daniel, even if he sometimes infuriated her, and she wanted to spend more time with him. But now, after he'd used his knowledge about Oliver to score points with her, and after Josie, she didn't know what to think.

She gave her friends her most enthusiastic smile. 'I'll have to sleep on it. Thank you for all of this. I'm sorry I interrupted your evening.'

Juliette waved her apology away, and they watched the second half of *Spy* together, though Charlie paid little attention to what was going on. Then Juliette and Lawrence said goodnight and she listened to them filling glasses with water, the pipes gurgling as they brushed their teeth, the bedroom door shutting.

The house settled and all was still, except for Charlie's mind.

Ray, Benton and Marmite were asleep, Marmite snuffling quietly. Charlie finished the last of her wine and looked at her phone. She reread Daniel's texts, constructed roughly the thousandth reply she had written in her head that evening, and then dismissed it.

She unfurled herself from the sofa, pulled on her shoes and grabbed a light jacket, then stepped outside. The wind had picked up, and the air was heavy with the scent of rain. She walked down to the seafront, where the rhythmic tug of the waves was the only sound. The sea was a vast, dark nothingness framed between the cliffs.

The streetlights picked Porthgolow out in patches, and Gertie's red paintwork shone like a burst of colour in a black-and-white photo. It was too late for Reenie and her mysterious flashing light, and Charlie didn't feel comfortable walking to the end of the jetty when it was so dark and nobody knew where she was.

She wrapped her arms around her waist and headed towards her bus, having some vague notion of sitting on the top deck, watching the waves crash against the shore while she worked out what to do.

As she got closer, she saw that something had been stuck over Gertie's door. It was a large piece of paper, though she couldn't, from this distance, see what was written on it. She picked up her pace. Had Daniel done it when she'd left his texts unanswered? Was it some act of vengeance from Oliver? She turned on the torch app on her phone, holding it over the notice that had been secured with about a roll's worth of masking tape. At first, she couldn't understand what she was reading, but as the words sunk in, she went cold.

STREET TRADING CONSENT REVOKED

She read on, trying to take in the overly formal, legalese phrasing about how she was no longer entitled to sell anything from her Cornish Cream Tea Bus; but the words kept swimming together, so she had to go back and reread them. The consent that she'd applied for, all those months ago when Gertie was being transformed in Pete's workshop, had been taken away. It explained that there would be a reassessment of her original application in light of new facts, but until that had been completed, she was unable to trade.

Her pulse thumped in her temples and she rubbed them, trying to make sense of it. Who had taken time out of their Saturday evening to do this? Who could she talk to about it? It was unlikely that anyone would be at the council until Monday morning.

She scanned down the document, reading to the very bottom where there was a small box. It had two headings: 'Petitioned by' and 'Actioned by'. Under 'Actioned by' it said, unsurprisingly, Cornwall Council, but it was the name and address under 'Petitioned by' that made Charlie's breath catch: *The Crystal Waters Spa Hotel, Cliff Road, Porthgolow.*

She blinked and looked again, hoping there was some mistake. There wasn't. Josie wasn't a journalist, she was from the council. Daniel had brought her onto the bus with some story about how it was dangerous or unhygienic, but the confrontation with Oliver had meant she couldn't shut Charlie down there and then. So she'd waited up at the hotel until everyone was gone, and then, on Daniel's instruction, she had come to the beach and finished the job.

This was what he thought of her events. This was how little respect he had for her. It had been a game to him from the very beginning. He hadn't liked her bus on day one, but had put up with her for months, placating her while she'd set up the food market and brought life back to Porthgolow. He'd distracted her with mind games, and now he'd run out of patience.

Her hands shaking, Charlie opened her messages. No time for mental rewrites now. Her fingers flew across the keyboard:

You lying bastard. How could you do this?

She pressed send and then, her body full of adrenalin, she stomped up to the end of the jetty and stared into the inky water, waves breaking half-heartedly against the sides. She didn't realize she was crying until the first, salty tear reached her lips. Her phone rang and she stared at his name on the screen.

On his third attempt, she answered.

'Charlie, what are you talking about? What's happened?'

He sounded so concerned that her venom dissolved, the anger replaced by hopelessness.

'You've shut down my bus. How could you do that to me? After everything you said?'

There was silence, and then: 'Hang on, what? Your bus . . . what's happened?'

'I've had my consent taken away. I can't trade any more.'

'But . . . *Why?*'

He sounded as confused as she was, and she faltered. 'Why don't you tell me?' she said, wiping her cheeks.

'Are you at Juliette's?'

'The jetty.' A second later she was listening to thin air.

She didn't turn round, didn't watch him jogging down the hill from his house. But she heard his footsteps, the change from dusty road to the solid stone of the jetty beneath his feet.

'Charlie!' He was breathless, and when she turned he was leaning forward, his hands on his knees. He was wearing a navy hoodie and jeans, his dark hair untamed. 'How did this happen? Who called you?'

'Nobody called me. It's there, on the bus. A large, obvious sign.'

'Shit.' He glanced at Gertie, then turned back to her. 'It must be some kind of mistake. You'll be able to fix it on Monday morning.'

'Why did you do it? Why go to all that trouble to get Josie to shut me down, then pretend you were trying to help me?'

His brows knitted together. 'What? I didn't. Of course I didn't. Charlie, you really think I did this?'

'It's right there, on the notice. Petitioned by The Crystal Waters Spa Hotel. You can feign ignorance all you like, but you can't explain your way out of this one.'

His eyes widened. 'I would never . . . Josie is a journalist, I swear it. God, Charlie. Come on. Do you really think that badly of me, that after all of this – everything that's happened over the last few months – I'd just go "fuck it" and slap some kind of revoke notice on your bus?'

Charlie chewed her lip. 'But it says that that's exactly what you did.' She pointed at Gertie. 'Why would it say it if it wasn't down to you? This is just another one of your games, isn't it? The tricks you play so you can stay in control of the village without anyone realizing. And this is the one where you get rid of me for good.'

'That is the last thing I want, I—'

'You offered Juliette that work and then took it away again.' She didn't want to let him speak, not yet. 'You *say* that Lauren booked someone else without you knowing, but is that really plausible? You care so much about your hotel. Were you just throwing your weight around? Showing Juliette how much power you had?

'Then you organized that meeting the morning of my first event, making me think nobody was coming, and then swooped in and put on the fireworks. It's like you *have* to be in charge, manipulating things so they look like they're going wrong, then you rush in and fix them, make everyone – me, especially – so grateful that you're around. That's exactly what you did with the yoga. And now this. Except maybe you didn't realize the council would add your name to the notice, leaving absolutely no doubt about who wanted me shut down. How are you going to solve this one?' She folded her arms over her chest. 'Get them to give me my trading consent back, and expect me to thank you for it? Expect me to fall into your arms?'

Daniel pressed his lips together. 'I didn't do this, Charlie. Whatever it says, whatever it looks like, I am not responsible for putting your bus out of action.'

Her reply lodged in her throat. She had expected him to laugh, to tell her she was right about everything. How could he not, when it was written there in black and white? She opened her mouth but nothing came out. Sea spray hit her face. Behind Daniel, the village was made up of pockets of light and shade, as if it was a mirage slowly appearing out of the mist.

Daniel walked up to her, until he was only inches away. She could smell the linen scent of fresh washing, felt the soft cotton of his jumper as he brought his arm up to stroke her hair off her forehead.

'I have never done anything to intentionally hurt you,' he said. 'I am truly sorry if I've ever given you that impression. I care about you, Charlie. You have to believe me.' He took a final step towards her, bridging the gap. Then he kissed her.

The feel of his lips pushed everything else aside and she parted hers, responding, pressing herself against him. His hand found the back of her head, twisting her hair through his fingers, angling her face up to better meet his. Her body tingled and sang, betraying her anger, and she let it go, imagined it drifting away on the tide. Eventually, Daniel pulled back and untangled his hand from her hair. He ran his thumb tenderly across her cheek, wiping away a droplet of sea spray.

Then he turned and walked away from her, soon lost in the darkness between streetlamps.

Charlie pressed her fingers to her lips. She felt upended. Confused. Dizzy. She walked carefully down the jetty to the soundtrack of thunder, rumbling closer and closer across the sea. She was suddenly desperate for the warmth and light of Juliette's house.

First thing on Monday she would get in touch with the council, see if she could get her trading consent back, and find out who had set the wheels in motion. Daniel's business had been on the form for all to see, but if he had been behind it, then why had he denied it so forcefully? Was he expecting her to blindly accept his version of events, as she had done with Rose and Frank's eavesdropping, and with Belle's yoga class?

281

After that kiss, Charlie couldn't believe it. As she gave her Cornish Cream Tea Bus a final glance, and a silent assurance that she would get it up and running again, she realized that Hal had been right, as always. He had told her that actions spoke louder than words, and Daniel's kiss had given her more insight into his true feelings than any verbal promises could have done.

Charlie was going to find out who had shut Gertie down, and then she was going to apologize to Daniel. She had a strong feeling, more than just a sneaky suspicion, that he might be part of the solution to her own happiness. And she was determined to find out if, on this occasion at least, her instincts were worth trusting.

Part 4

The Icing on the Cake

Chapter Twenty-Five

'Is the council deliberately designed like this, so you go round and round in circles and they somehow make money off all the interminable phone calls?' Charlie resisted the urge to bash her mobile on the table. She'd been sitting in Juliette's kitchen all morning, being pushed from one department to the next, trying to get her trading consent for The Cornish Cream Tea Bus reinstated. It was sitting forlornly on Porthgolow's beach, a gleaming café from which, for the moment, she could not sell a single cup of tea.

'I don't think the council makes money from phone calls,' Juliette said, replacing Charlie's empty mug with a fresh cup of steaming coffee. 'Besides, don't you have free minutes as part of your plan?'

Charlie smiled her thanks and then rolled her eyes as the robotic voice said, for the millionth time, *Please stay on the line; your call is important to us.* 'Is it, though?' Charlie asked her phone. 'Is it really?'

'Tell me again what Daniel said.' Juliette sat opposite her, cradling her mug.

Charlie sighed. 'Why are men so bloody complicated?'

Juliette laughed, and Charlie joined in until there was a pause on the line, and she bit her lip, thinking that she might get to talk to an actual person this time. But no, it was just the tape looping. The electronic voice told her again how important she was.

'So, Daniel,' Charlie said, her stomach twisting when she thought of their recent encounter. 'He told me that he didn't shut down Gertie, despite Crystal Waters being named on the notice, then he kissed me and walked away.'

'On the jetty, in the darkness. It sounds so romantic.'

'Or overly dramatic, depending on how you look at it.'

'And how *do* you look at it?' Juliette asked. 'You and Daniel have been so up and down since you got here, but I can tell you really like him. Though you're being more cautious than you were when you met Stuart; understandably, because he turned out to be a total dickhead.'

'And Daniel had dickhead form before I even met him.'

'Hmmm.' Juliette looked at the table. 'Have you spoken to him at all since Saturday night? Any texts? Aubergine emojis?'

'Nothing. I don't know what to say. I mean, *why was your business on there if you didn't get my bus shut down, and what was that kiss about, and what fabric softener do you use because you smelt really great the other night* doesn't seem like a conversation you can have via text.'

'So go and see him, then.'

Charlie let her head drop to the table, then lifted it up and rubbed her brow. 'I will, but I can't until I find out who was behind this. I will apologize to him if it's all a big misunderstanding, but what if it isn't? What if he's making a fool of me? Again?'

'Char, I don't think he would be *this* cruel.'

'I really hope you're right.' She didn't know what she had with Daniel; she just knew that even the thought of him sent butterflies fluttering through her like she was some kind of hothouse. 'As soon as I . . . oh, hello, is that the licensing department?' she enquired as Electronic Ethel was replaced with a living, breathing human being.

'This is waste and recycling. I can put you through to the licensing department. Please hold.'

'Noooo,' Charlie screamed at her phone. But it was too late. Electronic Ethel was back. *Please stay on the line; your call is important to us.* 'Is it my arse,' Charlie said, while Juliette tried very hard not to laugh.

By the time she stepped outside, into a warm day with a gusty breeze, she felt as though her ear was close to burning off. She had spoken, finally, to a young man in the licensing department. He wouldn't tell her the name of the person who had challenged her consent, only repeated the information that had been written on the notice. But he had assured her that it was only temporary, and once she'd resubmitted the paperwork, answered their additional questions and had someone come to inspect the bus, unless anything untoward cropped up, she'd be back in business in roughly a week.

It was time-consuming and annoying, but she was prepared for that as long as it wasn't fatal to the future of The Cornish Cream Tea Bus. She had gone online and resubmitted the paperwork electronically as soon as the call was over. Now all she had to do was wait.

It seemed that whoever had done this had simply wanted

to make her life more complicated, perhaps send her some kind of warning. What it had done was fire her up. She was overflowing with determination; she felt like Superwoman.

Marmite bounded beside her as they headed to the beach. The water was choppy, the sand whipping up into miniature dust devils. The sun peeped out intermittently between clouds ranging from pure white to darkest grey, and Charlie watched as a couple of young women in wetsuits ran across the sand from a van parked in the car park, no hesitation before they plunged into the waves.

Charlie walked the length of the beach, past Gertie and up towards the car park. She craned her neck to see to the top of the cliff, where Crystal Waters sat, looking out over the village, sea and coastline to the south. She knew she should go and see Daniel, but without all the facts she felt completely unprepared.

She huffed in frustration and turned, retracing her steps across the sand, this time towards the other side of the cove. She had almost reached the jetty, her walk accompanied by the shouts of the women in the sea, when she heard her name being called. To her amazement, she saw Reenie approaching her, her slender frame clad in a flowery shirt and faded jeans, her long hair dancing in the wind.

'Reenie, hi! What are you doing?'

'Out of my cage, you mean?'

Charlie blustered, but the older woman grinned.

'Recycling time again. I've dropped it off with Hugh, who's usually happy to dispose of it for me. But I did want to see you, too.'

'You did?'

Reenie narrowed her eyes. 'I saw you and Daniel on the jetty on Saturday night. I couldn't hear what was being said, but there was no missing the drama of the situation. I need details, especially after finding out what's happened to your bus.'

'You *need* details?' Charlie laughed. 'And what if I don't want to give them to you?'

Reenie held out her hand. 'Of course you do, girl. You might be in denial about it, but you need someone to make sense of it for you.'

Charlie hesitated, wondering if she was prepared to tell this woman everything. This woman who had a weather eye cast over the whole village and, Charlie knew, was close to Daniel.

'If you do,' Reenie continued, 'then I might be able to offer a nugget or two of advice. Perhaps reveal my own secret.'

'That you are, in fact, a mermaid?'

'Don't be so ludicrous. Come and have a cup of tea with me and explain why Daniel Harper kissed you and then left you alone two nights ago. And then I will tell you why I am absolutely, 100 per cent, not a mermaid.'

Charlie glanced at Marmite, who was in the process of digging a hole in the sand. 'OK,' she said, 'but I draw my line about what I tell you.'

'Of course. You are your own woman, after all.'

Charlie followed her, wondering why it didn't feel like that was always the case.

Her line, it turned out, was very low.

With a too-milky tea on the concrete in front of her, Charlie told Reenie everything: about what had happened in the pub; about her first Cornish Cream Tea Tour, and how it had been so successful until Oliver had found her in a compromising position with Daniel. About the confrontation on the bus, and Daniel revealing Oliver's true nature; about Josie – who was either a journalist, or from the council; about her outburst at Crystal Waters and their impassioned conversation that had ended with that kiss on the jetty.

'None of it makes sense, Reenie. Did he shut me down, or not?'

Reenie stretched her legs out, her feet, now bare, dangling over the edge of the cliff. Charlie had thought, with it being particularly windy, she might be invited inside the house, but they were sitting in the same spot, on the edge of the world. Not that she minded; she could stare at this view all day, even if there was zero chance of seeing a mermaid.

'Think of everything you know about him,' Reenie said. 'All the encounters you've had. All you have to do is weigh up the good and the bad and decide whether you think he's responsible. Although I'm sure you already know the answer, deep down.'

'It said it, in black and white, on the revoke notice. The Crystal Waters Spa Hotel.' Charlie took a sip of her tea.

'But situations are rarely ever black and white. If everything was so straightforward, you would never have got into a mix-up with Daniel and Oliver. You would have known how to make your bus successful from day one, and wouldn't have had to work hard to achieve what you have. The shades of grey are where life really happens, Charlie.'

'So you're saying that even though his business is on the notice, someone else could be behind it? But why would anyone else want to close down my bus? Myrtle's nephew is part of the food markets now, and I can't imagine Rose or Frank being so proactive. Oh my God, do you think it's Oliver?' She almost dropped her mug. 'That's it! He's pissed off that I rejected him, he doesn't like that I've got feelings for Daniel, so by naming the complainant as Daniel's hotel, he's found a way to hurt the bus and cause a rift between us at the same time.' She shook her head. 'I can't believe it. God. *Oliver?*'

Reenie frowned. 'He does seem a possible culprit, but are you sure he's the only one? You need to be absolutely certain before you accuse him. There must be a way to find out the truth.'

Charlie nodded. Even though the thought of kind, well-intentioned Oliver being behind it was awful, she still found it more palatable than Daniel being responsible. Reenie was right; she did know, deep down.

'How come you're so wise, Reenie? Hundreds of years at the bottom of the sea?'

'It's mainly my therapist,' Reenie admitted. 'I've spent so many hours with her, unravelling what's going on up here,' she tapped her forehead, 'and in here,' she patted her chest, 'that I feel I have some insight into the minds of other people; especially when it comes to affairs of the heart.'

'I didn't know you had a therapist,' Charlie said. 'But then, I know hardly anything about you.'

Reenie drew her knees up to her chest, a gesture that made her look like a young girl. 'Maybe it's time I told you a thing or two.'

Charlie stayed silent, waiting.

'My husband, Maurice, died ten years ago. He dropped down dead in the post-office queue, of a ruptured brain aneurysm. He'd been entirely healthy up to that point, so it was a complete shock. I fell apart. There are large chunks of the following months that I don't remember. I rejected offers of help from my sister and her family, and stopped going to see her – or anyone.'

'I'm so sorry, Reenie. I had no idea.' She remembered

Daniel mentioning Reenie's family that night in the pub, how everyone at the table had been surprised.

'Why should you? I haven't told you about it up until now.'

'Is that when you moved out here? After he died?'

She shook her head. 'Maurice and I lived here together. I know it's hard to believe, sitting here precariously on the cliff, but it is a stable home. We have a son, Eddie, but he's grown now, with a family of his own out in Sydney. I haven't seen him for several years, though we Skype every other morning. With my therapist, it's once a week.' She gave Charlie a wry look. 'Modern technology has been the making of me – or should I say, *re*making of me. In more ways than one. Come inside.'

She stood suddenly, and Charlie, after waiting for this moment and then unprepared to have it offered up so freely, almost stumbled off the edge of the cliff in her haste to see inside the yellow house.

Reenie pushed open the door and Charlie followed her into a small, open-plan kitchen and living room. The sparse furniture was white-painted pine, everything spick and span: a kitchen table and two chairs, a dresser against the far wall. The sofa and single armchair were grey fabric, cosy and worn, and the coffee table was clear apart from coasters. But it wasn't the furniture Charlie was interested in, or even the sheer quantity of light that flooded the rooms; it was what the light was falling on, covering every wall, making it hard to see the paintwork behind.

There were hundreds and hundreds of photographs. Unframed, A6 size, pinned close together like a mosaic.

Charlie did a slow circle, taking it all in. They were all of Porthgolow, either facing into the village, or out towards sea, the shifting moods and colours of the ocean, the cliffs and the sky. There were some taken from the beach, and others from the top of the hill above the cottage, on Crumbling Cliff. Something snagged in her brain. How many years' worth were here? Suddenly, the lights in the evening made sense. It was a camera's flash.

'How . . .?' she began.

Reenie chuckled. 'It's my obsession. My therapist doesn't think it's healthy, but she's accepted that it may take another two decades – however long I have left – for me to think my way out of it.'

Charlie stepped closer to the nearest wall, taking in the detail. In a few photos she could see The Cornish Cream Tea Bus, the flash of sun reflecting off Crystal Waters. There were several taken during her food markets, with the beach a hive of colourful, vibrant activity.

'Do you take photos every day?'

'Every day,' Reenie echoed. 'I can't bear to let one pass without capturing it. I am the very definition of a dotty old woman.'

'Because of your grief,' Charlie said, moving to look at a cluster where the sea was pearlescent, the light not quite reaching the water's surface. They must be the sunrise, she thought, the sun still low behind the land to the east, but touching everything with its morning glow. 'You couldn't hold onto Maurice, and this is your way of trying to regain control.'

She thought of how often, after Hal's death, she'd had the sensation of falling, trying to grasp hold of something to stop herself, and realizing it would never be there again. The pure, white-hot burst of desolation, of aching to go back to the days before, when everything was as it should be.

'You really are as smart as you look,' Reenie said, amusement in her voice. 'Almost.'

'So you take the photos, then put them up randomly on the walls of the house?'

'My printer works overtime. My biggest expense, even more than electricity on this place, is ink and photo paper. There are albums too, with the older pictures in. But it's my version of knitting or pottery class with the local adult education centre. My way of coping. My therapist—'

'Does she have a name?' Charlie asked, laughing.

'She does, but it's Dolly, so it's best if we gloss over that. She says it's a symptom of my grief, not a part of my recovery. That's usually when I tell her I don't give a toss and end our session early. But she understands. We work well together.'

Charlie grinned. She'd had no idea what this yellow house contained, though the most surprising thing was Reenie herself. 'And you don't . . . do anything . . .' Her voice drifted off as the synapses fired, and the truth hit her like a lightning bolt. 'Oh my God.'

'Shut your mouth girl, you'll catch things bigger than flies.'

'Porthgolow Hideaway,' Charlie said. 'That's where I recognize the photos from. *You're* behind the Porthgolow Hideaway Instagram account? It's got *thousands* of followers.'

'It does seem to be going rather well. And it's nice to have a place where I can chat to people.'

Charlie peered over Reenie's shoulder as the older woman opened her iPhone and then the Instagram app. There it was, @PorthgolowHideaway. The successful Instagram influencer was a reclusive, wise old woman who some people thought might possibly be a mermaid. She remembered Daniel saying he'd like to have some kind of partnership with the account and laughed out loud.

'Daniel doesn't know, does he? He's never been in here?'

'You're the first person to darken this door for a long

while, and whenever I see Daniel, it's up at the hotel. Nobody knew about my foray into the online world up until this very moment, and I'd like to keep it that way, if it's all the same to you.'

'Why?' She could smell Reenie's faint lavender scent and felt a twist of protectiveness towards her, as self-aware and defiant as she was.

'I don't want anyone to know. It's for me, posting the beauty of this place, interacting with people who comment. They don't need to know I'm behind it.'

'Porthgolow Hideaway,' Charlie murmured. 'What made you start it up?'

'Why not?' Reenie said. 'I was taking the photographs anyway, and Dolly said I should connect with people. This is how I choose to do it. I may not have the will to come to one of your markets or socialize in the pub, but I can show people how special this place is. It's how I see Porthgolow. And this,' she gestured to the sea beyond the windows, 'this is our view. Maurice's and mine. If I put my name to it, if the Instagram page isn't anonymous any more, I'd be giving up what Maurice and I had together.'

Charlie put her hand on Reenie's arm and could feel how thin it was, the bone close to the surface. 'You're already sharing it,' she said softly, 'even if nobody knows it's you. And just because you tell them, it doesn't mean it's no longer yours and his. You don't dilute your memories just because you share them with other people. In some ways, I think, it makes them stronger.'

Reenie stared at her, suddenly looking her age. Charlie wouldn't force her to do anything she didn't want to; it was entirely up to her what she did with her photographs. But they had definitely had an influence on her events; the account had put Porthgolow on the social media map before Charlie had even driven into the village. She was sure it had helped build the momentum.

'You know what?' Charlie continued. 'You have been a huge help to me, to the food market, and I didn't realize it. Thank you, Reenie.'

'Oh tush.' Reenie waved her away, but Charlie could see she was pleased. 'Now, never mind all this. What are you going to do about Daniel, and Oliver, and poor, stricken Gertie?'

Charlie chewed her lip. Reenie had solved one of her Porthgolow mysteries, but there was another, more pressing issue she had to get to the bottom of. And the sooner she worked it out, the sooner she could get on with enjoying the rest of her summer.

Chapter Twenty-Six

Charlie put her spatula down and scraped her finger along the edge, her phone tucked under her ear as she listened.

'So I really think we can do some great new things, Charlie, and if your bus wants to be part of it, obviously with a bit of a shift-around, then of course that would be wonderful.' Bea Fishington sounded contrite, but she had no reason to be. The Fair on the Field had been a disaster, but The Cornish Cream Tea Bus was not. Charlie knew that everyone back home was following her success online – her mum and dad had been cooing to her about it on the phone.

'It sounds great,' Charlie murmured. 'I'm glad it's worked out so well with your niece, and that . . . that you're looking forward to having me back.'

'Beginning of September, I think we said, didn't we?'

'Something like that.' Ray jumped effortlessly onto the kitchen table, and Charlie gently lifted him off again.

There was a pause, and then Bea said, 'I'm so glad this

summer's been so good for you, Charlie. You've spread your wings, really found your place in the world. It's brilliant. Let me know when you're back in Ross, or Cheltenham, and we can get together and have a chat before you officially return. I'm sure your mum and dad are dying to see you.'

'They're really looking forward to it,' Charlie confirmed.

They said their goodbyes and Bea rang off. Charlie dropped into one of the kitchen chairs and Ray jumped onto her lap, nuzzling against her hand.

The truth was, the few times she'd spoken to her parents there had been no talk of the end of the summer and her return home. And Bea and The Café on the Hill hadn't been troubling her consciousness while Gertie and her markets were working so well. A part of her had believed that Bea wouldn't want her back. She had seen her sabbatical as an extended period of garden leave, her boss quickly finding a replacement and getting in touch at some point down the line to let her know she was no longer needed.

Could Charlie really leave Porthgolow? Leave her food market to carry on into autumn, attracting more vendors and customers, but without The Cornish Cream Tea Bus at the centre? She tried to imagine it, and found that she couldn't.

While she waited for her trading consent to be reinstated, she had planned to spend her time baking, devising new, delicious cakes and pastries to serve, to take the cream teas for her tours to new culinary heights. And she still would, she decided, spurring herself into action and returning to her bowl of cake batter. She wasn't gone yet.

'You can't run Cornish Cream Tea Tours on your Cornish Cream Tea Bus if you're not in Cornwall,' Juliette said half an hour later, once Charlie had updated her on her conversation with Bea.

Charlie gave her third and final cake mix a gentle fold, and then poured it into the tin. 'So I'll have a name change. The Cotswold Cream Tea Bus works just as well.'

'You wouldn't!' Juliette was acting as if Charlie had committed treason.

'I can't live with you and Lawrence for ever, Jules. This isn't my home. You have been so, *so* generous letting me stay here. It's beyond the bounds of even the closest friendship.'

'It is not—'

'And Bea wants me back. She's excited about what we can do at the café. And on the bus.'

'And you sound equally thrilled,' Juliette replied sarcastically.

'I hadn't thought about it, that's all. I've been so tied up with everything here.' She waved her spatula around and a bit of cake mix landed on Ray's head. He stared at her accusingly.

'That's because things here are *better.*'

'You and Lawrence need your own space, and I have to think seriously about what I'm doing next.'

She could still hear Bea's enthusiastic voice in her ear and wondered how her mum and dad were really doing without her. They always seemed happy on the phone, but how would she know for certain unless she saw them? Maybe it was time to go back: maybe her trading consent being revoked and the mess with Oliver and Daniel were signs that she'd outstayed her welcome here. The Porthgolow food market would remain, but it could run perfectly well without her there.

'I understand that.' Jules wrapped Charlie in a hug. 'Just don't be too rash with your decision. For what it's worth, I love having you here, and can barely imagine the place without you in it. Also, I don't think it's right that you're taking on this Mary Poppins role! Sweeping in, fixing the village with your food market and sweeping out again. I might have to confiscate all your umbrellas – and your bus keys, for that matter. If Gertie can't leave, then neither can you. Besides,' she added, giving Charlie a fierce look, 'you still need to talk to Daniel.'

Charlie stared at the hob, the drifts of flour where she had been less than careful with her ingredients. She made a pattern with her finger. 'I know that,' she muttered. She still had to find out who was responsible for her bus being taken out of action, but the thought of seeing Daniel again, after he'd left her with that kiss burning through her, set her emotions spinning.

'You'll get to see him at the meeting tomorrow, anyway,' Juliette added.

Charlie rolled her eyes. The WhatsApp message had pinged onto her phone that morning, encouraging everyone to attend an urgent meeting and asking whether, as she couldn't open Gertie to paying customers, Charlie would be happy to host it. 'Any idea what Myrtle wants?'

'Nope,' Juliette said. 'But it's bound to be something important.'

'Bound to be,' Charlie echoed. Dread settled in the pit of her stomach as she opened the oven door. Not even the delicate waft of a cooked-to-perfection lemon drizzle cake could lift her spirits.

Everyone was there. Juliette and Lawrence, Rose, Frank and Hugh, the entire Kerr family – including Jem in her buggy and Jonah sitting poised with a pen and notepad. Myrtle had bustled on board, all business, and Lauren had sneaked in and sat at the back, her white shirt and dark skirt in stark contrast to all the colourful T-shirts and shorts of the other villagers.

Anton and Stella had been first to arrive, offering Charlie beaming smiles that made her feel slightly unsettled, as if they knew something she didn't and, just as she was serving pots of tea and laying plates of her lemon drizzle cake on the downstairs tables, Reenie appeared.

'Reenie Teague, as I live and breathe.' Hugh stood up to greet her.

'I'm not the queen,' she said, though she was smiling as she accepted his peck on the cheek.

Charlie looked at all the expectant faces and wiped her sweaty palms down her skirt. But this wasn't her gig; today she wouldn't be the one offering suggestions, trying to change the way things were run in Porthgolow. It didn't stop her being nervous. Maybe whoever had gone to the council was watching and would try to get her shut down permanently this time. She had got in touch with the licensing department just in case, confirming she was entitled to use Gertie for private, unpaid events once Myrtle had asked her to host the meeting. She wasn't taking any chances. But was that why Daniel wasn't here? Was he worried about being seen on board a condemned bus? She took a deep breath and leaned against the kitchen counter.

Myrtle cleared her throat. 'Thank you, all, for comin' today,' she started. She had her hands clasped together in front of her, and Charlie thought that she might not be the only nervous person on board.

'What's this about, Myrtle?' Hugh asked. 'Are we here to find out what's happened to Gertie, why someone is threatening the food market?'

'The market is safe,' Charlie said. 'I won't be able to take part tomorrow, but that doesn't stop everyone else. It's only my bus that can't trade.' She had pulled the notice off the door the day after it had appeared. Not that that would reinstate her consent – and it certainly hadn't stopped the Porthgolow rumour mill from getting hold of the news – but she hadn't wanted to leave it there for everyone to gawp at. Even though she hadn't done anything wrong, she couldn't help feeling ashamed.

'I could be a spy,' Jonah said, raising his hand. 'Follow the clues, do some digging. You like Bond films, don't you, Lawrence? Do you want to team up?' There was a smattering of laughter.

'Sounds grand, Jonah mate,' Lawrence said. 'Let's talk about it later.'

'What has happened to Charlie's bus is a – a *travesty*.' Myrtle bristled. 'When will you be up and running again, d'you know?'

Charlie was momentarily stunned into silence. 'A few days, I think. I've got my inspection on Monday and so as long as that goes well, I should get my consent back straight away.'

'Good, good. You can't keep a Porthgolow maid down, that's what I say. Which means our plan can still go ahead. A three-day food market for the August bank holiday.'

Rose and Frank nodded energetically and Stella gave Charlie a wide, pretty grin.

Charlie gasped, her eyes shooting to Juliette, but her friend looked as surprised as she felt.

'That's a grand idea,' Hugh said. 'It's been going so well. Makes sense to end the summer with a bang.'

'But it's not the end,' Amanda piped up. 'We don't want it to just be a summer thing. It'll be harder in the winter, of course, but we were thinking we could hold them once a month in the off-season. There are foodie treats more suited to autumn and then, of course, there's Christmas. We've done some research on other markets. Well, when I say we, it's all been Jonah.' She held out a folder and Charlie took it, peering inside at the sheaves of paper covered in photos and information.

'You want it to continue?' she asked.

'I know I've not always been the easiest to get on with,' Myrtle said, 'but there's no denying it's brought life to this place. Bill was singin' its praises, and I've, uh, sampled a few bits, here 'n' there.'

'The market is wonderful, Charlie,' Anton said. 'There's no way we could stop it now.'

'Best thing to come to Porthgolow for a long time,' Rose agreed, her arms folded tightly across her chest.

Charlie felt the sting of tears. She couldn't quite take it in. She caught Reenie's eye and the older woman smiled back at her: a knowing, smug little smile that made Charlie want to hug her.

'You think everyone will be on board for three whole days?' she asked. 'It's a lot of work. A lot of effort.'

'Don't be so negative, cheel,' Myrtle chided gently. 'We're all goin' to help. We'll promote it where we can, spruce the village up a bit in preparation. I've cleaned tables in my time, so you won't be on your own in the bus if you don't want to be.'

'Benji's going to create a special Porthgolow burger,' Jonah piped up. 'We're already looking at sauces and recipes. Maybe you could come up with some new cakes, Charlie? Just for that weekend. Like a bank holiday special or something?'

She nodded. 'I could certainly give it a go, Jonah.'

'And I've been brewing my own ale for a while,' Hugh said.

'I could see about having a stand out here on a Saturday. Nothing fancy, mind, but I could launch it on the bank holiday, then sell it in the pub, too. I've been inspired by all those artisan brewers with beards and no socks.' He laughed. 'I want to be a part of it.'

'You've made such a huge difference, Charlie,' Amanda said. 'We want you to know that we appreciate it, that what you're doing here has changed Porthgolow, and we hope it never ends.' A lower-deck full of heads nodded back at her and Charlie smiled, even though her eyes were swimming.

Could she really leave this – all these wonderful people – behind, and go back to Bea and Ross-on-Wye?

'It hasn't just been me,' she said, finding her voice. 'It couldn't have happened without you – without all of your support. That first meeting wasn't . . . well, it wasn't quite as unanimous as this one,' she added, laughing, 'but I still felt encouraged to give it a go.'

She realized then that both she and Daniel had been right. She had needed to show everyone that it could work; that she could turn the empty beach into a thriving hub of activity, but she would never have had the courage to try if everyone had been against it from the start.

'You were brave,' Reenie said. 'You put yourself out there, even though you knew it was a risk.'

Charlie nodded. 'I did, but—'

'It's about time I was brave, too. Let everyone in on my little secret. As you're all here, now seems like the perfect time.'

'Reenie,' Charlie started, 'you don't have—'

'The mermaid thing!' Jonah jumped out of his chair. 'You're going to announce that you're a mermaid, and bring all your mermaid friends up from the sea to say hello.'

'Holy mother o' God,' Myrtle murmured.

Hugh's usually pale face went red, and Amanda and Paul couldn't have looked more embarrassed if Jonah had swept their table clear and climbed on top of it to dance the Macarena.

'Darling boy,' Reenie said, 'if you continue to perpetuate this mermaid myth, then your younger sisters are going to grow up to be very confused individuals.'

'So . . . you're not a mermaid, then?' Jonah looked genuinely confused, and Charlie's heart went out to him.

'No, my love. I am not. But I do have something I can contribute to this bank holiday market.'

'Unicorns are real, though,' Flora interjected.

'That, young lady, is a discussion for another day. No, my contribution is twenty thousand Instagram followers, and my willingness to promote this event on my account in any way you so desire.'

'What on *earth*?' Myrtle asked.

'What did you just say, Reenie?' Stella took another piece of lemon cake.

'Twenty thousand Instagram followers,' Hugh said. 'That's no mean feat.'

'I have one hundred and four,' Jonah declared proudly.

'You're too young to be on Instagram,' Reenie said, and shook her head at Paul and Amanda, who had begun to look as if hiding under the table might be their only option.

As Reenie explained about the Porthgolow Hideaway account, everyone got their phones out to see for themselves, as if somehow by viewing it with this new knowledge, they would be able to find a previously hidden selfie of Reenie standing in front of her cottage for all the world to see.

Charlie got milk out of the fridge, desperate for a cappuccino even though it was gone seven in the evening.

She hadn't thought to bring wine, though it would have been perfectly acceptable in this private gathering. She barely noticed the chatter stop, and almost missed Juliette's sharp intake of breath, but then a slender hand clutched her arm, and Charlie turned to her friend and then followed her gaze to the doorway.

'Sorry I'm late,' Daniel said, glancing at Lauren. 'I got held up.'

Charlie took in his dark jeans and navy hoodie, the way his hair had clearly fought a battle with the wind. It was the first time she'd seen him since their encounter at the jetty.

'Oh Daniel,' Reenie said, rising and holding her arms out. He hugged her and kissed her on the cheek. Reenie's face was flushed with pleasure, and Charlie could see how close they were; perhaps Daniel had partly replaced her distant son, whom she saw only via computer screen. 'Better late than never, though this is a rather important meeting for you to be rocking up so late.'

Charlie hid her smile, inexplicably happy that he didn't escape Reenie's gentle chiding.

'I know, and I'm really sorry. How did our plan go down? What do you think about a bank holiday food market, Charlie?'

Charlie could tell that he wasn't as relaxed as usual; there was a nervous energy about him she wasn't used to. 'I think it's a great plan,' she said. 'A perfect way to end the summer.'

'Good.' He leaned against the back of the bench Reenie was sitting on, his arms folded over his chest, and listened to Myrtle – and Hugh, Amanda, Stella and Jonah – recap what he'd missed, even though, from the sound of it, he'd been in on the idea from the beginning. He showed genuine

306

surprise – and amusement – that Reenie was responsible for the Porthgolow Hideaway account.

Charlie allowed her gaze to drift over his arms, taking in the definition of his biceps, visible despite the hoodie, the length of his legs, his blue Converse, the way an unruly wave of his hair had fallen over his forehead and he'd left it there. She felt the churning, low in her stomach, that appeared whenever she thought of Daniel, ten times stronger now that she was in his presence.

'OK?' Juliette whispered. 'Only the milk's about to over-flow.'

'Oh *fuck*,' Charlie shouted, as the boiling milk she'd been absent-mindedly frothing bubbled to the lip of the jug and cascaded over her fingers.

Juliette took the jug away, turned on the cold tap and pulled Charlie's hand under it.

'Is our fearless leader OK?' Reenie asked.

'I'm fine,' Charlie called, glad that she could stand next to the sink and hide her flaming cheeks.

'A minor milk scald, nothing more,' Juliette confirmed. 'So everything's settled, then? We're all on board for the bank holiday weekend? Three whole days of eventing! Porthgolow won't know what's hit it.'

There were murmurs of assent, whoops and cheers and general jubilation. Daniel stood up and ran his hand through his hair. 'Lauren,' he said. 'Could I have a word with you, outside?'

He'd spoken quietly, but it wasn't the ideal place to have a private conversation. The bus fell silent and everyone's eyes swivelled in Lauren's direction.

She sat up straighter, her gaze wary. 'Shouldn't we wait until the meeting's finished?'

'Just a quick word,' Daniel said. 'It won't take long.'

Lauren relaxed into her seat, but her hands were fidgeting on the table. 'I think we should finish up here first. If this three-day market is really going to happen, then we need to know all the facts so we can manage its impact on the hotel. We don't want to miss anything important.'

'We won't,' Daniel said. 'But I do need to talk to you, quite urgently.'

Lauren shook her head. Charlie was shocked to see her eyes were glistening. Something cold and hard lodged itself under her ribcage.

Daniel rubbed his jaw. 'Listen, I—'

'She did it, didn't she?' Myrtle said quietly. 'That's why you want to talk to her, and she won't come. Because she knows what you're goin' to say.'

'Did what?' Hugh asked, as Lauren stared at the table.

'Went to the council.' Myrtle curled her thin fingers into fists. 'She called the council and got Charlie's bus shut down.'

Chapter Twenty-Seven

The silence that followed was thick with shock.

'She didn't,' Amanda murmured. 'Lauren, you didn't, did you?' She looked at Daniel.

He sighed and sank back onto the edge of the bench. 'Although you know about the bus losing its consent, what you probably don't know, because someone took the notice down pretty quickly, is that it stated that the proprietor of Crystal Waters had raised the petition against it.'

'Holy shit,' Paul muttered. There were murmurs of consternation and confusion around the bus.

'But I didn't do this to Charlie,' Daniel continued. 'I care about her far too much to have put her business in jeopardy.' Everyone fell quiet at that and Daniel stared at the floor. When he looked up, his eyes found Charlie's and his expression softened. 'I've been doing some digging,' he said. 'It turns out the council can be very tight-lipped, even when you're supposedly the person who submitted the form. But

I've just come back from Truro, where I was shown the full petition, the false evidence used to put the claim in, some made-up bullshit about the bus not following health-and-safety guidelines. And it was all submitted by Lauren Purview, apparently on my behalf.'

Lauren's gaze stayed firmly on the tabletop.

'I didn't want to do this in front of everyone,' he said softly. 'But you wouldn't come with me.'

'I bleddy *knew* it!' Myrtle said. 'Untrustworthy eyes, that's the thing.'

Lauren looked up. All signs of her earlier tears had gone. 'I was looking out for your interests – for the hotel. I would never do anything to hurt you, Daniel.'

'You weren't hurting Daniel, though, were you?' Amanda said. 'You were hurting Charlie.'

Lauren drew herself up straight. 'I haven't done anything wrong. I have always been loyal to you, Daniel.'

'There are a few occasions where you might have over-stepped the mark,' he said sadly. 'Come on. Let's go back to the hotel.'

Lauren nodded. She stood and, keeping her head high and her eyes averted, pushed past everyone and walked off the bus.

'I'm sorry, Charlie,' Daniel said. 'If I'd had any idea, then—'

'It's OK, honestly. Thank you for finding out. And I'm so sorry I accused you; I'm sorry for everything I said that night.'

'The hotel's name was on the form. What other conclusion could you have come to?' He squeezed her arm and then, looking decidedly weary, followed Lauren off the bus, leaving a stunned silence in his wake.

Charlie was going to create biscuits in the shape of Porthgolow's landmarks. There would be house-shaped biscuits for the

B&B, Myrtle's pop-in and Reenie's yellow cottage, a pub for The Seven Stars and a lower, longer building decorated to represent Crystal Waters. There would be a biscuit for her bus, and a beachscape with sand, sea and sunset on it. They were her most ambitious designs, but practising in the weeks before the bank holiday would hopefully make them perfect.

Biscuit dough didn't need a whole lot of pounding, but it was getting it anyway. Lauren had closed Charlie's bus down. She'd had a successful inspection and it would be up and running tomorrow, in time for her first Cornish Cream Tea Tour, but that didn't stop her incredulity at the reason it had been shut in the first place.

After Daniel and Lauren had left the bus on Friday, the conjecture had continued, and Charlie had remembered the times the hotel's receptionist had shown initiative: making sure her friend got the marketing contract and organizing a week of yoga on the beach when she knew the food market was happening. Charlie was sure, now, that it had been Daniel who had renegotiated with Belle to move her classes up to the hotel on the Saturday, so that nobody lost out. Had Lauren been manipulating things all along?

'I was a bit suspicious of that claim she had,' Myrtle had said. 'Youths lightin' bonfires on Crumblin' Cliff. Seemed a bit suss to me.'

'But why would she do that, call a false meeting, if nothing had happened?' This had been Amanda.

'Because it was my first event,' Charlie had said, realization hitting her. 'And if you were all tied up in the meeting then nobody would come; it would look like I didn't have your backing. I think she was trying to dent my confidence.'

'But *why*, though?' Stella had asked. 'You've done nothing but good for Porthgolow.'

'And for Daniel Harper.' Everyone had turned to Reenie. 'Isn't it obvious? The girl's in love with him, and as soon as Charlie appeared, his attentions were elsewhere. I know he's never thought of Lauren as anything more than a colleague, but that didn't stop her trying all she could to make him notice her and put a spanner in the works for Charlie and her bus. Obviously, it all got out of hand.'

'Did you know it was Lauren when I came to see you earlier this week?' Charlie had asked.

Reenie had levelled her with a straight stare. 'I had my suspicions, but I wasn't going to start accusing anyone without cold, hard facts. Luckily Daniel didn't let it rest and, as unpleasant as it is, you have your answer. The real question is, what are you going to do about it?'

Charlie knew Reenie hadn't been talking about Lauren. She was quite sure that, as of Friday, the receptionist was no longer an employee of The Crystal Waters Spa Hotel. No, Charlie had to work out what to do about Daniel. She owed him an apology – a proper apology, not a garbled sorry, offered up hurriedly as he went off to fire one of his most valued colleagues. That was the first item on her to-do list. But after that, it was less certain. With Bea's phone call and all its implications running through her mind, she pounded her biscuit dough until her hands ached.

The sun was beating down as Charlie drove back towards Porthgolow after her first, official, Cornish Cream Tea Tour. Since getting the feedback from the Crystal Waters guests on her trial run, she had been honing it to perfection. She had advertised on social media and, with Gertie's reputation preceding her, had had no problems filling up her first outing.

So, two days after she had got her trading consent back,

she and Juliette – who had agreed to accompany her on her tours as it was the one thing she couldn't do alone – had picked up a group of people from Newquay, and a group from Padstow, and driven them up towards Port Isaac and Tintagel, the landscape beginning to show the first signs that summer was ending, patches of russet and yellow among the green.

A family had taken up two of the tables downstairs: a mum, dad and another adult, along with four children, all under ten. They were loud and boisterous, and while Charlie kept up her tour spiel – prepared facts about each of the places they visited – she couldn't help but be drawn towards the laughter.

She had glanced in the mirror, watching in delight as the twin boys – dressed in identical outfits – seemed spellbound by her mini Viennese whirls and cupcakes, the butter icing cream-coloured, with red swirls that matched Gertie's paint-work. The older daughter's giggle was infectious, and by the time the tour had come to an end, Charlie's cheeks ached from smiling.

She had hopped down at the Newquay departure point. 'I don't know if you're still in the area at the end of August,' she said, 'but we're holding a bank holiday food market in Porthgolow. There's guaranteed to be something there for everyone, and hopefully a festival atmosphere.'

'We'll be around,' said the dad, flashing one of the women a quick look. 'But Evie has to head home. She's been staying with us for a couple of weeks, but—'

'I need to get back to real life,' Evie admitted. 'Cornwall doesn't quite feel real, does it? Like some make-believe land full of sea and sunshine and amazing cream teas. I could easily stay here for ever.'

'You can always hang on for another couple of weeks, sis, and we can make a day of it,' the other woman said.

Evie smiled. 'And then another week, and then another. I can't move in with you permanently. It wouldn't be fair.'

'The markets happen every Saturday,' Charlie had said. 'So if you're not here for the bank holiday you could always come this weekend. Summer's not quite over yet.' As she had watched them traipse off the bus, Evie's hand wrapped around the youngest boy's, she had wondered who she was trying to convince.

Now, as Charlie approached Porthgolow from the south, she considered whether she'd been putting real life on hold, too; keeping her feelings about Hal and Stuart at bay by throwing herself into Gertie and her new business. Her mind returned, as it so often did, to the night on the jetty and Daniel's kiss. It had felt like a scene from a fairy tale, and for all their contact since, it might as well have been. But Daniel had taken the first step. He had found out that Lauren was responsible for the temporary closure of her bus; it was her move, so why was she holding back?

Porthgolow looked golden and inviting, and she could see Crystal Waters, on the same level as her, its glass winking from the other side of the cove. The thought of driving onto the beach and heading back to Juliette's empty house was unappealing. She had dropped her off in Padstow on the way home, where she was meeting Lawrence for dinner after he finished a job. Charlie had the evening to herself: just her, her Yorkipoo, and her thoughts.

Not wanting to relinquish the view, she pulled her bus onto the side of the road. There was a dusty verge, and then a small area of grass, between her and the drop. She could find no dark patches where the grass might have been scorched by a bonfire, and wondered whether Lauren had seen anything at all, or if she really had made it up to engineer the meeting and keep everyone away from the beach.

It was hard to get her head around, even if it meant that Oliver had nothing to do with it. She pulled Marmite out of his crate and held him in her arms, relishing the warm, comforting feel of him. Her dog was an idiot, entirely reckless sometimes, but he wasn't complicated. At the moment, it felt like he was the only uncomplicated thing in her life.

There were ten days to go until the bank holiday weekend, less than three weeks until the start of September. If she went back to the Cotswolds, to her mum and dad, Bea and The Café on the Hill, would life be simpler? There was promise of a future for Gertie there, but she wouldn't be close to Juliette and Lawrence any more. She wouldn't be able to spend time with Amanda, Jonah or Stella. She supposed she could Skype Reenie – the old woman was clearly a pro – but she wouldn't see any of them unless she came back to visit.

And was she ready to give up on this view? Her gaze drifted from the blue, undulating sea, to the beach where Gertie usually sat, and back up to Crystal Waters. She wondered what Daniel was doing, how he was coping after Lauren's deceit. Was she really ready to give him up: the way he made her feel and made her think; the passion he had showed her? She felt like she was ready to start something, just as it was coming to an end.

Beeeeeeeeeeeeeeeeeep!

The sound startled her and Marmite scrabbled in her arms, trying to see over her shoulder. She looked out of the window and found a battered old Volvo alongside her, but her higher vantage point meant she couldn't see the driver. It pulled in ahead of her, blocking the road down the hill.

Charlie's mouth went dry. There was some money in the till from the customers who hadn't paid for their tour by card. She wondered if she could lock the back door, hide and then call the police, but before she'd put her plan into action, Frank climbed out of the Volvo, his face like thunder.

'Are you *mad*?' he called. 'What the *hell* are you doin' there, Charlie? Get your bus away from the cliff dreckly!'

'What, I—'

'Crumbling Cliff!' Frank shouted. ''Aven't you been listenin' to us all these months? That cliff is a death trap waitin' to 'appen. You can't stop there in a car, let alone a bloody great two-ton bus!'

'But I thought . . . I mean, I'm not on the grass. I thought it was just the edge, the grass, that's unstable!'

'The whole place! The sandy verge, the bend. You can skid, never mind the landslide you might set off. What if another car comes speedin' round the corner? I only just saw you in time! Get off, this instant! I'll wait until you're safely away.'

He got back in his car and pulled forward, and Charlie lowered Marmite back into his crate. The little dog was whimpering, picking up on her fear.

'It's OK,' she told him. 'We're fine. We'll be off here in a moment.' She glanced outside. Beyond the edge of the cliff, the view was spectacular – endless sea and sky, the promise of a long drop should the ground beneath her give way. But she was in control. She was fine. Marmite looked up at her, his head on one side. Charlie felt a waver of doubt as she put the bus in gear and inchingly, inchingly, turned the wheel, her eyes going from one mirror to the next, to the next. She felt the movement of sand beneath the wheels, felt resistance at the back of the bus as she moved it a fraction and thought, for one horrifying, mouth-drying moment that she was stuck, that she'd made a terrible mistake and put herself and her puppy in danger. She had an image of the ground beneath her crumbling and Gertie plunging straight down, missing Reenie's house by inches and hurtling into the sea, sending them to a watery grave.

Clamping her teeth together, she turned the wheel a fraction more, and then another, and then the front tyres found the road and she pulled gently onto it, off the verge. She began the slow descent into Porthgolow, her palms slick with sweat, Frank keeping pace ahead of her.

'God,' she whispered to herself. 'Oh my God.'

At the bottom of the hill, Frank beeped once and then turned right, up towards the neat roads of houses behind the seafront. Charlie wished he'd waited to talk to her, perhaps offer her a lift up to Juliette's. She drove Gertie onto the sand and into her usual place.

There were a group of friends lounging on the beach and, as she arrived, one of them stood up, waved at her and started snapping photos. Charlie gave them a weak wave back and looked out at the steely water, the clouds pink in a violet, pre-dusk sky. Marmite barked, and she opened the crate and pulled him onto her lap. 'Look at that, puppy,' she said. 'Look how beautiful it is.'

Evie's earlier words played in her mind and she thought of Juliette and Lawrence enjoying a romantic meal out in Padstow. She knew that she was coming to the end of her stay in their house. It wasn't that she had outstayed her welcome, exactly, but it felt as if everything was drawing to a close. Her friends needed their space, regardless of what they told her, how generous and selfless they were prepared to be.

Keeping her dog in her arms, she climbed out of the cab on slightly unsteady legs. Her own stupidity, along with the realization that she had potentially been very close to disaster, made her tearful. She closed her eyes and thought of Hal. What would he have done if he'd found himself up there? What would he have said? *If you find yourself on a sticky wicket, just stop. Stop, breathe, take a moment to compose yourself, then try again. There is nothing that can't be overcome if you believe in yourself enough.*

She may not have composed herself, she might be regulating her breathing now instead of before the event, but she was OK. She wished she wasn't going back to an empty house, wished, for the first time in a while, that she could be wrapped in her mother's sweetly scented embrace, be soothed and comforted and forgiven her moment of stupidity on top of a dangerous cliff while she mooned about the man who was in the hotel on the opposite one. For the first time since arriving in Porthgolow, Charlie wished that she was somewhere else.

Chapter Twenty-Eight

As Charlie walked through the village over the following week, she noticed small changes taking place. Myrtle had put hanging baskets of pink and purple cyclamen and petunias outside the Porthgolow Pop-In, and the sign for SeaKing Safaris, which had been secured to the jetty ever since she'd been there, had been replaced with one twice the size, its blue writing gleaming against a gold background. One morning, when she was taking Marmite for his walk, she saw a notice covering the car park sign, detailing repair works that were happening the following day.

'They're takin' down the streetlamps,' Myrtle said by way of greeting, when Charlie went in to buy a pint of milk.

'That's not good.'

'No, they're takin' them down and replacing them with better ones, those old-fashioned lantern jobbies, with a new type of bulb that's much more powerful, apparently. This place will be less of a black hole at night.'

'You said you were going to get the village spruced up before the bank holiday, but I had no idea you'd go this far,' Charlie said, amused.

'Oh, it's not down to me,' Myrtle replied. 'Some man in a fluorescent vest was measurin' up one of the lights, so I asked him what was goin' on.'

'Did he say why he was doing it?'

Myrtle shrugged. 'Council orders, prob'ly. Seems our little chunk of Cornwall is finally gettin' its place on the map, as it were. Down to all the publicity with your events, no doubt.'

'Maybe.' Charlie chewed her lip.

'I haven't seen crevices that deep since Jonah showed me his book about the Grand Canyon.'

'Sorry?'

'Your forehead's creased like an origami flower. Is there somethin' on your mind?'

'Something's always on my mind, Myrtle. Oh, and talking of the council, do you know if they're doing something about Crumbling Cliff?'

'Not heard anythin', but it would be a good idea. I heard about your near miss the other day.' Her stare was unwavering and Charlie flushed. 'Frank was furious. Said you were just idling on the edge, as if waitin' for the sea to claim you.'

'I'm sorry, I wasn't thinking. I didn't realize . . .'

'There there.' Myrtle leaned over and patted her arm. 'No harm done, but I reckon we do need a barrier put up. Not sure there's time now, before this weekend, but wouldn't hurt to give it another try.'

'Of course,' Charlie said, chastened. 'I'll see what I can do.'

'Why don't you speak to Daniel about it?' she asked. 'He's already asked 'em once – though fat lot o' good it did – but he has been to the council recently. He might have a contact you can talk to.'

'Maybe.'

'How long have you been putting off seein' him?' Myrtle asked.

Charlie fiddled with the packet of Wotsits she was holding. It had been almost two weeks since the meeting on the bus when Lauren had been exposed. Daniel's BMW had driven past a few times, and they had both been an active part of the village WhatsApp group, but that was all event-related. She thought she had seen him going into The Seven Stars one evening on her way home from work, but she had told herself she was too tired to speak to him, that she was focused on getting Gertie prepared for their bank holiday food market. It was only three days away now.

'I know it's far from me to say,' Myrtle started, 'but I'm goin' to anyway. If he's owed an apology, you need to give it to him, however hard it is.'

'I do know that,' Charlie said. 'But it's more complicated than just saying sorry. I know I was in the wrong, but I just . . . I don't know if . . .'

'All your "knows" and your "don't knows". Go and get it over with, lass. Then you can focus on the rest of your life.'

The wind was whipping the sea into a frenzy when Charlie powered up the hill the following evening. It snatched at her hair and the hem of her cardigan and all but pushed her back down again. She hoped it wasn't trying to tell her something.

Myrtle was right. She had put off seeing Daniel for long enough. But it felt like some barrier had come down since the revelation about Lauren and she was scared of stepping forward into unknown territory. First there had been the fact that she had been unwaveringly irritated by him, and then there had been Oliver, and then the possibility that he'd closed her bus down and might have been lying to her all along.

Now all that was left was Daniel – and the undeniable truth that she was hopelessly, overwhelmingly attracted to him. Of course, since she had wrongly accused him of trying to shut down her business, he might never want to speak to her again but, even if there was no chance for them, the least she could do was apologize.

The evening sunlight glinted off the windscreens in the hotel car park, making everything seem polished and shiny. Charlie smoothed down her skirt, wished she had a compact with her to check the wind hadn't made a Picasso of her carefully applied make-up, and headed towards the doors. She had left Marmite with Juliette, not wanting her cute companion to be a distraction.

She stepped into the peaceful foyer and was met by a pretty, mousy-haired woman with a wide smile.

'Welcome to The Crystal Waters Spa Hotel,' she said. 'How can I help you this evening?'

Charlie was caught off guard by the new face. 'I'm looking for Daniel Harper, if he's around?'

'One moment, please.' She picked up her phone, dialled a number and spoke a few quiet words. Then she hung up and gave Charlie the full beam of her attention. 'He's in the restaurant, but he said he'll be here in five minutes. Please take a seat.' She gestured to the low sofa and Charlie did as she was instructed, resting her cake tin primly on her lap, her hands, palm down, on top of it. The lemon tarts had been a moment of inspiration – or desperation – but baking was what she was good at and she hoped Daniel would appreciate the gesture, even if he couldn't forgive her.

The time dragged on. The receptionist gave her a cheery smile. Then a slightly apologetic one, and then, after another five minutes had passed, she picked up the phone again. As she did, Charlie heard footsteps. They were soft, the sound dulled by the thick carpet, but she knew that they were his.

'Oh!' the receptionist said brightly as he appeared. 'There you go.'

Charlie shot to her feet, almost dropping her lemon tarts.

Daniel's lips twitched. 'Charlie Quilter,' he said. 'What a pleasant surprise.'

'Daniel, I . . .' She swallowed. 'I wanted to see you.'

'And here I am. How can I help?'

'Could we, maybe . . .' she gestured in the vague direction of his office.

A frown flickered across his face, there and then gone. 'Sure,' he said.

She followed him across the wide expanse of reception, admiring the way his strong body fitted so snugly into his white shirt and black trousers, acutely aware that, if he was able to forgive her and was his usual, commanding self, then she was really in trouble.

He led her into the neat office with the peace lily and the photo of Jasper and gestured for her to sit on the sofa. He pulled his desk chair round to face her, dropped into it and leaned forward, his elbows on his knees.

'I am so sorry about Lauren,' he said, before she'd had a chance to speak. 'I can understand if you think I should have known about it, but I swear to you I didn't.'

This was not what she'd been expecting. 'I didn't think you should have known. How could you have?'

'Because she was my colleague, my right-hand woman.

323

She was tenacious, had a great work ethic, I just didn't realize that—'

'That she was in love with you?' Charlie said softly.

Daniel rubbed the back of his neck. 'I didn't think she would allow any personal feelings to override her professionalism. I never saw it coming.'

'Well, if it makes you feel any better, neither did I.' Charlie picked at a thread on the hem of her skirt. 'Daniel, I'm here to apologize to you. I even made you some lemon tarts.' She gestured to the box she'd put on the corner of his desk.

'You're bartering for my forgiveness with tarts?'

'You loved them, that first meeting on my bus. They're made with love and extra calories,' she added, her cheeks flushing. 'That's what Hal used to say about my cooking. It never sounded ridiculous coming from him.'

'Made with love?' Daniel echoed.

'I should never have accused you,' Charlie said hurriedly. 'But it was the day Josie appeared, Oliver made it seem like you were—'

He put his hand over hers. 'You don't need to explain. It's not as if I haven't rubbed you up the wrong way occasionally.' His grin cut through his solemn expression. 'Though if it hadn't mentioned Crystal Waters anywhere on that notice, I would have been pretty pissed off if you'd come to the same conclusion.'

'I wouldn't have.' She moved her hand back, so she could lace her fingers through his.

'You promise?' His voice was suddenly rough.

'Promise,' she whispered.

'You think it might be time for us to stop this, now?'

'Stop what?'

'This. Confrontation. Winding each other up.'

'When, Daniel, have *I* ever wound *you* up?' She gave him a withering look, and he laughed.

'So you agree?'

'I agree that there are better things we could be doing with our time together.'

'Oh?' he asked. 'What are those?'

Still holding his hand, she tugged gently, and he took the hint and joined her on the sofa. It was only a narrow two-seater, so his knee was pressed against hers. The top button of his shirt was open and she could see the dark definition of his collarbone, the hollow at the base of his throat.

'We could start with this.' She slid her hand into his hair, pulled him towards her and kissed him. He hesitated, frozen for a second, then he responded, his lips moving against hers. He wrapped his arm around her waist and drew her closer, until her chest was pressed against his. Charlie let the kiss take over, let his touch and his taste overwhelm her. He tasted sweet: sweeter than her clotted cream, sexier than her dark chocolate ganache.

'That,' he said, when they eventually broke apart, 'was a surprise. I had hoped, but never thought—'

'You thought that I had too much sense to ever be truly attracted to you?'

'No, I knew you were attracted to me, I just never pictured you seducing me like this, in my office, of all places. Don't you have any professional boundaries?'

'I do when it comes to my bus, but Crystal Waters? Not so much.'

Daniel laughed softly. 'I suppose that's fair, considering I was the first one to set a bad example.'

'Exactly. Imagine if any of the guests had found you luxuriating in your own hot tub?'

'Want to go back there?' He brushed a strand of hair out of her eyes and pressed a kiss to the side of her mouth.

'Could we guarantee being alone?'

He shook his head.

'Then, no. Not as our . . . next team meeting.' She smiled.

'What are you thinking?'

She took his hand again, rubbing her thumb over his palm. 'I'm thinking your place, Monday night, after this three-day event. When my head is entirely empty of gingerbread cookie designs and fondant recipes.'

'Monday night?' He couldn't hide his disappointment and it was Charlie's turn to laugh.

'I have one full day left to prepare and I want to be able to focus on you,' she said. 'On us. I want The Cornish Cream Tea Bus to be at the back of my mind for once and, as utterly desirable as you are, I can't guarantee that until after the weekend. Do you want to share me with Gertie, or have me all to yourself?'

'As much as I would rather keep you here, and make use of every inch of this sofa, I think I can wait until Monday night. I'll drive back from Sussex as quickly as I can.'

'You're not going to be at the market?'

Daniel shook his head. 'It's my mum's birthday. One thing I can't rearrange or send my apologies to. But I will be back to see you on Monday, and I hope I've made up for my absence in my own small way.'

Charlie frowned, but Daniel just grinned, stood up and pulled her to her feet. 'You'd better get going,' he said, 'before my last thread of willpower snaps.' He left her with a long, lingering kiss and then, when Charlie was feeling a little flustered, and a lot annoyed with herself for not giving in to his suggestion about the sofa, he led her out of the office and back into the foyer.

'Oh Daniel,' the perky receptionist said, 'Mr and Mrs Hathaway have got a hot tub session in half an hour, and the previous user said one of the jets wasn't working. Could you take a look?'

'Of course.' He turned to Charlie, looking entirely composed, only the slight ruffle of his hair where she'd mussed it up giving anything away. 'I trust I've left everything to your satisfaction?'

'Almost,' she said, smiling. 'But I think I'll feel a lot better after our next meeting.'

'I agree. We should be able to tie up those loose ends next time round. I'd better get going, but,' his voice softened, and he squeezed her arm, 'I'll see you soon?'

'You will,' she said. 'Monday night.'

He began walking away, then turned back to her, stopping on the shimmering gold design in the floor. 'And good luck this weekend. Not that you need it, but you know you will always have my full support.'

She did know, and now, Charlie realized, as she stepped out into the last of the day's sunshine, she had so much more than that, too. For once, she couldn't wait for her food market to be over, because there was something even more tempting waiting for her on the other side.

Chapter Twenty-Nine

The day before the bank holiday extravaganza was Charlie's birthday. It was a fact only Juliette and Lawrence knew, and Charlie had thought she had got away with it and would be able to spend her time in Juliette's kitchen, baking everything she needed for Saturday, thinking dreamily about seeing Daniel again. She was wrong.

Juliette bounced into the kitchen, wished her a happy birthday and told her she was booked for two hours over lunch. Charlie protested, but her friend promised to help her with whatever baking she needed to do when they got back and told her she wasn't allowed to spend the whole day working.

Which was how she found herself on board Gertie, a blackboard outside announcing it was 'Closed for a Private Party,' with Amanda, Flora, Jem and Jonah, Reenie, Juliette and Lawrence, and a whole load of food that she hadn't made

There were prawn and mayonnaise sandwiches from

Amanda; Jonah and Flora had made some rather wonky but delicious cheese scones, and some less wonky chocolate-chip cookies, and there was even a Victoria sponge from Reenie. Charlie was beyond touched, a couple of tears threatening to spill out when she'd been pushed to the top deck and they'd all shouted 'surprise!'

The only thing that could have made it better would have been Daniel, but she was holding their rather successful reunion close to her chest, at least until after Monday. Her feelings for him were blooming, but it was a private bloom, a secret garden she wasn't yet ready to share.

'Are you rethinking tomorrow?' Reenie asked as Charlie took a bite of prawn sandwich and murmured appreciatively. 'Bet you're worried your stuff isn't up to scratch, now.'

Amanda chuckled. 'As much as I love my children, I don't think Charlie has anything to worry about.'

'That's only because I've been spending most of my time working on the burger recipe with Benji,' Jonah said. 'These were knocked up in half an hour.'

'Half an hour,' Flora chimed, mimicking his superior tone.

Everybody laughed.

'All the plans are coming together, then,' Amanda said. 'Food for this place, obviously, will be perfect – there are more food trucks than ever before – and SeaKing Safaris has got a full schedule of pre-booked tours.'

'I'm going to skipper one of them,' Jonah said proudly.

Amanda sighed. 'No you're not, Jonah. We've talked about this. You're not old enough, and if you did, our insurance would be invalid. One day, of course. I know you're more than capable, but it just isn't possible.'

Jonah folded his arms. 'I could do it in my sleep.'

'Something I suggest you don't try,' said his mum, ruffling

329

his hair. 'You're still my boy, Jonah. Don't get ahead of yourself. There's plenty of time to be an adult and, believe me, you'll wish you hadn't raced to get there when you realize how tough it can be.'

A contemplative silence fell over the group and Charlie felt the mood drop like a stone in a pond. 'Aren't you with Benji in the burger stand, anyway?' she asked.

'I'm doing both. Organizing the queues for the boat trips and helping Benji with the burgers when I'm free.' Jonah nodded, his young face cast in steely determination.

'A very confident young man,' Reenie said affectionately. 'You've got a touch of Daniel Harper about you, did you know that?'

Amanda laughed. 'I hope you mean that as a compliment!'

'Oh, I do,' Reenie said. 'Most definitely. Keep the cheek to a minimum, Jonah, and you'll have all the good parts and none of the flaws.'

'I did invite him today,' Juliette said, glancing at Charlie. 'But apparently he's away for the weekend. He might not come to the food market at all.'

'I don't suppose he needs to.' Amanda shrugged. 'He's been promoting it on the hotel pages and I'm sure some of his guests will turn up. Though it is a bit of a shame the whole village won't be there.'

'Does anyone want another drink?' Charlie asked, unsure she could hold her poker face while they were talking about Daniel.

She took orders and went downstairs, made fresh cups of tea and coffees, and Amanda's usual sugary latte. She got most of the drinks on a single tray and edged back up the staircase as carefully as she could. She could hear Reenie commanding the attention of everyone else on the bus.

'The council couldn't afford to resurface the car park *and* replace all the streetlights. They probably have that sort of budget for the whole of North Cornwall, never mind a single village.'

'And why do it for a bank holiday food market, anyway?' Amanda added. 'It's only three days.'

'What they should have been focusing on,' Lawrence cut in, 'if they were going to do *anything* for this weekend, was Crumbling Cliff.'

'Oh yes,' Amanda said. 'I heard about Charlie almost getting stuck. It sounds awfully scary.'

'And we don't want any visitors to have the same – or a worse – fate,' Juliette added. 'If they don't know about the dangers, what's to prevent them stopping to look out at the view like she did?'

Charlie slid up the final steps and put the tray on the table. 'I was an idiot. I wasn't thinking clearly about where I was, or what the dangers might be. But I did phone the council a couple of days ago. They admitted they hadn't followed up on Daniel's original enquiry and they couldn't promise anyone would come out to look at it before the weekend, and it's too late now. But didn't you get some cones and tape to rope off that part of the cliff, Lawrence? We just need to stop people being careless when they drive around the bend.'

'I've got a load of stuff from work, and Martin, my boss, is coming round later this afternoon to help me put it up,' Lawrence said. 'It's not as good as something permanent, but it should hold for three days. You know, I never knew running an event like this involved such a humungous bloody to-do list. I just put the tents up.' He grinned, and Juliette rubbed his arm.

Charlie felt a swell of love for her friends, for their kindness over the summer, and for Juliette's insistence, all those months ago, that she come and visit them. She watched as Reenie meticulously cut a cookie into quarters, and Jem stuck her hand in the butter, then brought it forcefully to her face. Jonah was scribbling something in his notebook, his brow furrowed, tongue protruding.

'I've left my drink in the kitchen,' she murmured, but nobody seemed to notice as she slipped back down the stairs.

She leaned against the counter and looked at the text she'd received from her mum an hour ago, a follow-up to the phone call they'd had early that morning. She'd been walking Marmite along the blustery beach when her mum had called her to wish her a happy birthday.

'Your dad's doing a lot better now,' she'd said, once Charlie had told her about her birthday plans – or what she'd believed them to be at the time. 'Your success with Gertie has really perked him up. We went to the summer fair last weekend, you know, down on the field, and people in a couple of the other foodie places were singing your praises about these markets and whatnot.'

'That's great, Mum. I'm so pleased to hear about Dad.'

'And you, darling. Be pleased with yourself, too. What you've achieved is no small thing, and your dad and I can't wait to visit. Which leads me on to my next point.'

'Oh yes?'

'Bea Fishington and The Café on the Hill. It's decision time, Charlie. She's expecting you back in the next couple of weeks.' Charlie's heart had plummeted at her mother's words, and she had chatted on without really listening, while around her the waves crashed and the wind whipped strands of seaweed across the sand. She'd ended the phone call with her mum's words echoing in her head.

Bonnie's follow-up text read: *Just saw Bea. She's looking forward to having you back!! The clock is ticking, C. Lots of love, Mum. xx*

'You can't be a spectre at your own feast.'

Charlie turned and smiled at Reenie. 'Just checking things down here.'

'Well, you've no time for that.'

'Why?'

'Because, in case you've failed to notice, Charlie, it's your birthday. We've moved past the savouries and you're needed back upstairs. That's all there is to it.'

Charlie followed her friend, and as soon as she got to the top deck, the group launched into a rendition of 'Happy Birthday'. She stared at the bus-shaped cake complete with windows, and a smiling stick person and dog visible through the windscreen. She laughed so much she took three attempts to blow out the candles.

'This is incredible,' she said. 'Who made it?'

'We did,' Amanda and Juliette chorused.

'And it took hours,' Amanda groaned. '*Hours,* Charlie. How do you do it?'

'We have to taste it,' Charlie said. 'Where's a knife? Ooh – hang on, photo first.' She took several photos of the cake, and then several more with everyone crowded around behind it. Then Jonah insisted on setting up the timer on Charlie's phone, balancing it precariously on the back of a seat so they could all get in shot.

By the time they sat down to eat the cake, which turned out to be a delicious, light, chocolate sponge, Charlie was wiping tears of mirth off her cheeks.

'Oh my goodness,' she said, when she tasted it. 'Do either of you fancy a job?'

'Why, is there one going?' Juliette asked. 'Here, in Cornwall, on *this* bus?'

Charlie knew what her friend was asking: whether she was staying in Porthgolow, or whether she was going home. She couldn't answer her; not yet. 'This is utterly amazing,' she said instead. 'Thank you, Jules and Amanda, thank you all so much for my birthday lunch.'

'You're welcome,' Juliette replied, but her smile had slipped. Charlie would tell her, in a few, short days – days in which they would all be rushed off their feet anyway – what she had decided. She just needed to do a couple of things first.

As cars streamed into the village on Saturday morning, Charlie realized how a few small alterations, a bit of attention to detail, could change everything. There were the new, Victorian-style street lanterns, the hanging baskets outside Myrtle's shop, the bolder, smarter SeaKing Safaris sign. The pot-holed car park was gone, hidden for ever beneath a layer of smooth, black tarmac. A low railing ran around the edge of the space, and new signs listed the – very reasonable – parking charges. They all helped to make Porthgolow feel up-to-date, welcoming, less faded. They inspired confidence, something the village had been sorely lacking when she arrived.

The weather helped, of course. The cove was holding onto the late August sun, which made the silver water glisten and the sand look thick and inviting. Porthgolow was glowing and, as Charlie peered out of the bus window and watched Myrtle step onto her doorstep and say something to Stella that made her laugh out loud, she realized that, in turn, had made its residents glow.

She picked up the milk-frothing jug, then wiped her hands on a tea towel as it slipped from her grasp. She didn't know why she was so nervous; she had been running these events the whole summer. But she had come a long way from that first, disastrous fair in Ross-on-Wye, and here she valued everyone's opinion. They had all, finally, put their faith in her, and had adopted the food markets as their own, but Charlie still felt that swell of responsibility.

But so far, so good.

The beach was humming with activity, the food trucks and ice-cream vans, burger shacks and sushi bars covering it like a swarm of brightly coloured beetles. There was music and laughter, sizzles and smells, and an energy that seemed entirely unique to the Porthgolow food market. Hugh had set up a stand close to the pub, using one of Lawrence's smallest marquees as his mini beer tent. Charlie watched Benji top a portion of skin-on fries with cheese and wondered when Jonah was going to join him – and what ingredients were in their exclusive Porthgolow burger.

A large family walked past the bus and a young girl, wearing a pink shimmering dress that must have come from the Disney store, raised her fingers in a tentative wave. Charlie waved back and noticed the girl's attention was focused on the tower of cupcakes she'd put in pride of place in the window. She had perfected the silky red icing and topped them with shining white and silver sugar balls. They matched Gertie's paintwork, but they also looked celebratory.

She was taking her afternoon teas to the next level, hoping to achieve both rustic charm and a professionalism that would have people talking about her bus beyond Cornwall's borders. Her ticket machine was set up to print the words: *Porthgolow Bank Holiday Food Market*, marking it out from the previous events they'd held. This one felt special, and not just because it was three days long, but because it signified an important personal turning point, one that, she hoped, might have a bearing on her entire future. *Live life to the full, Charlie*, Hal's voice said, popping into her head. *You only get one chance.*

And it seemed she wasn't the only one who'd decided this bank holiday market was special. It was as if they'd opened some floodgates somewhere and couldn't remember how to shut them. Within half an hour of unlocking the door, the top deck was full, and Charlie spent her time running up and down the stairs, taking orders, filling teapots, and arranging her cream teas in the way she'd practised. She had other items on the menu, but the Cornish cream tea was the most popular, even at half nine in the morning.

She was beyond relieved when, at ten o'clock, Juliette appeared, wearing jeans and a shimmering red T-shirt, her hair swept off her face.

'It's like a carnival out there,' she breathed, her eyes alight. 'And in here, too.' She surveyed the kitchen area, which looked less like a carnival and more like a bombsite. 'Tell me what to do.'

With Juliette, service got easier. Charlie felt less rushed, and they had time to chat to the customers while they worked.

'We're from Bristol,' said a large, burly man wearing an olive green fleece. 'Shirley looks at that Instagram account every night before bed. You know, Porthgolow Hideaway.'

'It calms me down,' she admitted. 'We have my mum staying with us. She's in her nineties and it isn't always easy, but those sunsets, they're bliss.'

'They are very special,' Charlie agreed.

'As soon as it mentioned this event we thought this was our

chance to come and see it in person. We decided to make a weekend of it. Lucky, really, as I think we got the last room.'

'Whereabouts are you staying?'

'Porthgolow B&B,' Shirley said. 'We had that sunset last night, right in the bedroom window. Though of course we came to stand on the beach, watch it until it was out of sight. I don't want to go home, but my brother has to get back to work and can only stay with Mum until Sunday.'

'It's so lovely that you've come,' Charlie said.

'It's a proper slice of magic,' Shirley's husband said, and grinned. 'Exactly what we needed.'

'You must feel so lucky living here,' Shirley added. 'Having that view on your doorstep, the sound of the waves. I can't imagine anyone ever wanting to leave.'

'She's had Rightmove open on her phone most of this morning.' He laughed gently and rubbed his wife's shoulder.

Charlie offered to refill their teapot and hurried back to the kitchen. She didn't admit to the couple that, as she had lain in bed that morning, awake before dawn, Rightmove was what she'd been looking at, too.

She watched out of the window as Jonah corralled a group of people into a straight line next to the jetty, high-fiving them as they waited to board one of the SeaKing RIBs. He was in his element, chatting and gesticulating, no doubt giving his captive audience any number of useful facts.

Charlie waited for the elevenses rush to fade, and then, when it didn't, she resigned herself to the fact that her bus was going to be busy until the end of the day. Myrtle was as good as her word, appearing after lunch and installing herself upstairs, clearing tables and bringing down trays of dirty crockery so Juliette could focus on serving and Charlie could stay in the kitchen, plating up and managing her stock.

She kept up her social media posts, her phone pinging as the comments and likes flooded in, the hashtag sending news of their little food market out into the online world, stretching further and further away from the hub of Porthgolow.

Sometimes her phone buzzed with a more personal message. Daniel's texts were never that long – she had the feeling that, like her, he was full of nervous anticipation about Monday night – but he let her know he'd arrived at his parents' house and had sent her several updates since then. She, in turn, had sent him a few of her photos of the market, and one of the bus birthday cake, to which he'd replied that she was in trouble for not telling him it was her birthday and she'd better expect some sort of retribution for that when he returned.

She saw Reenie and Frank strolling along the sand, plucking chips from cones, and Lawrence chatting with a group of his friends. He had told Charlie and Juliette the previous evening that he was going to keep an eye out, make sure everyone was safe and happy. Juliette had hugged him and then, when he'd left the room, confided to Charlie that he was a bit high on responsibility after putting up the barrier at Crumbling Cliff. Now, Charlie watched him push his sunglasses onto his head and turn towards the sea, and wondered how many lifeguards did their job while eating ice creams.

'Hello.'

Charlie felt a glimmer of recognition at the voice, and turned to find Josie smiling at her. Her cheeks immediately started burning.

'Josie, I—'

'Look, I know you're ridiculously busy, but I just wanted to let you know that I'm profiling the food market this weekend. Daniel said that it would be a good time to cover it and that you might be willing to give me an interview to accompany my piece, sometime next week, when you're quieter.' Her smile was hesitant.

'That would be amazing,' Charlie stammered. 'And I'm so, so sorry about—'

'It was the wrong day.' Josie waved away her apology. 'I could see that, and honestly, it doesn't matter. Daniel encouraged me to come back and I'm glad I did. This place is buzzing and it's getting quite a reputation. I'd love to sit down and chat to you. Give me a call.' She handed Charlie her card.

'Thank you, Josie. I appreciate you giving me another chance.'

'Thank Daniel,' she said, smiling. 'I'm going to go and get some sushi and maybe one of those burritos. I can't accurately write about it unless I've experienced it to the full, can I?'

Charlie laughed and watched her saunter off the bus, shielding her eyes against the sun. She couldn't be cross with Daniel for this particular bit of meddling. She was touched that, despite all that had happened when he'd first arranged for the journalist to see her, he had been willing to try again. And a profile of the Porthgolow food market would, without a doubt, be a huge boost to the event and the village.

If she had been heading back to Ross-on-Wye, to Bea and The Café on the Hill, then she would have been leaving with a happy heart. Heavy, too, because she had made so many friends and would miss them terribly, but she would have known that the market was in safe hands, that the village was busy and bubbling with life. But she didn't have to worry about that, because her enquiry to the estate agent on Rightmove at some ungodly hour of the morning had already had a response.

She'd scanned the message in a one-minute window she'd had while waiting for a new batch of scones to finish warming up. The little terrace house in a road further up the hill from Juliette's was available for rent and the estate agent would be happy to show her round on Tuesday. She was the first one who had enquired and Charlie had decided, then and there, that as long as it wasn't falling down the cliff, rife with mould or full of rats, then she and Marmite would take it. She had a couple more loose ends to tie up, and then she could let Juliette, Reenie – and perhaps one other important person – know the good news.

Chapter Thirty

It was Monday, the last day of the bank holiday food market, and Charlie was in her pyjamas and dressing gown at six thirty in the morning, trying to make a coffee and whispering to her Mum on the phone. Marmite, Ray and Benton were watching her eagerly from various vantage points around the kitchen, hoping that as soon as she'd got her coffee she would turn to the important subject of their breakfast.

Her mum had always been an early riser, but this, on a bank holiday, was ridiculous.

'No, I know, Mum, it's great news.'

'Have you told Bea?'

'I phoned her last night.'

'And?'

'She was shocked more than anything. I don't think she'd ever considered that I might not come back. But she was happy for me, in the end. She wished me well and I'm sure she'll have no trouble replacing me. And if she's serious about expanding, it's not like Gertie is the only bus in the world – though of course she's the best.'

'You're irreplaceable, Charlie, you know that. Gertie too. When are we coming to visit?'

Charlie heard a noise and glanced behind her, but it was just Marmite, who had fallen off the chair when Benton objected to him using his tail as a chew toy.

'Let me check everything is OK with this house first, then once I'm in of course you and Dad can come and see it. I feel bad not telling Juliette right away, but I'm sure once she knows she'll be happy to have this place back: just her, Lawrence and the cats.'

'And when does this event end?'

'Tonight,' Charlie said, blinking at her mum's change of subject. 'Look, you probably think this is all a bit sudden, a bit rushed, but I know it's the right thing to do. Now I've made up my mind, I just want it to happen straight away.'

'Of course you do. Grab life by the throat! Let me know as soon as you've seen this darling little cottage, won't you? I'm sure your dad and I could come and help with the decorating, if it needs any once you're in.'

'Thanks, Mum. I'd better go. I've got loads to do.' She rang off and poured steaming coffee into her cup. When she turned around she noticed that, despite being sure she had closed it, the kitchen door was ajar.

The sky that morning was peppered with thick, puffy clouds. They were mostly white, but a few towards the horizon were darker, threatening bad weather. Their shadows drifted across the sea and the sand, racing each other, and Charlie felt such a strong rush of love for the view that a lump lodged in her throat.

The bus had only been open for ten minutes when a young couple came on board, holding hands. They chose one of the tables downstairs and the woman shrugged off a suede coat and laid it along the bench beside her.

'Hello, welcome aboard The Cornish Cream Tea Bus,' Charlie said. 'Have a look at the menu and I'll be back in a few minutes to take your order.'

'We already know what we want,' said the man. 'Cornish cream tea for two, please.'

'But could I have a cheese scone instead of fruit?' the woman asked.

'Of course; I can do a sweet and savoury selection.'

'Thank you! Cream and jam seems wrong straight after the breakfast we've just had.'

'Are you on holiday here?' Charlie asked.

'Yes, we're staying up at Crystal Waters.' The woman took her partner's hand. 'It's our anniversary, so Adam's treating me. It's spectacular up there.'

'It's beautiful, isn't it?' Charlie said. 'So well designed, everything perfectly in its place. Daniel Harper's worked hard to get it exactly as he wants it.'

'We've not met him, I don't think,' the woman said. 'Only the receptionist and a couple of waiters in the restaurant. We're booked into the hot tub tonight – have you been? It's right on the edge of the cliff. I'm worried it might be a bit scary!'

Charlie smiled at the memory. 'I have been, as it happens. It's one of the best spots in the whole of Cornwall. And don't worry; it's not as terrifying as you think it's going to be. I'm sure you'll love it once you're in there. Let me go and sort out your cream teas.'

She went back to the kitchen, holding the menu over her

chest, as if they might be able to see how quickly her heart was pounding beneath her breastbone. She just had today to get through, and then she would see Daniel again. She was already planning their next visit to the hot tub together.

The clouds thickened, darkened and finally dumped their rain on Porthgolow at two o'clock that afternoon. Charlie had known that the day wasn't going to stay calm, but she hadn't predicted the force of the downpour. People scattered, rushing inside the various undercover areas, and her bus went from cheerfully busy to 'no standing room' in a minute. 'Bloody hell,' Juliette said, peering out at the deluge. 'This wasn't forecast.'

'It doesn't look like it'll last, though.' Charlie pointed to the horizon, where blue shone out between gaps in the clouds. 'Not enough to send everyone away, just enough to steam up the windows.' She glanced around her but, despite the crush, the windows stayed condensation-free. Pete really was a wizard. Not many vintage Routemasters had state-of-the-art air-temperature control, a fully functioning kitchen and a winch on the front. Maybe Gertie *was* irreplaceable, after all.

'Listen,' Juliette said, keeping her voice to a whisper. 'I know this probably isn't the time to be having this conversation, but I can't let you do this, Char.'

Charlie frowned. 'Do what? Load up that plate with raspberry scones? Is there something wrong with them? Too much salt?'

'No,' Juliette huffed. 'Of course not! I overheard . . .' She stopped. 'What on *earth*?'

'What is it?' Charlie looked out of the window, where the rain was still falling but with a gentler patter, and peered at the jetty. The view was partly obscured by food trucks, but not enough to hide what was happening.

'Is he . . .?' Juliette squealed. 'Oh my God!'

A second later they were pushing through the people on the bus, shouting apologies, not caring that they were leaving it unmanned. Because when the rain had started, the queue for SeaKing Safari tours had dissipated, the customers perhaps hoping they would resume when the sun came back out. But what Charlie and Juliette had both seen from the bus was a very confident twelve-year-old boy climbing inside the remaining RIB and pulling his little sister on board with him.

'Jonah!' Charlie called as she ran across the sand. 'Jonah WAIT!' Juliette was shouting too. The sodden sand was heavy, grabbing at her feet with every step, and soon her chest was aching with the effort of running. She could see the RIB hovering at the jetty while Jonah untied the ropes, making a concerted effort, she thought, not to hear their cries.

'Shit,' Juliette said breathlessly, 'he *can't* go. Not just him and Flora.'

'He's so smart,' Charlie gasped, 'why is he doing this? Jonah!' she shouted again. '*Jonah!*'

Soon Paul had joined the pursuit, several steps behind. He was red-cheeked as he called out. 'Jonah, son – wait!'

The sound of the engine cut through the air and, even though she wasn't sure she had anything left, Charlie picked up her pace. Her foot hit the hard, slick stone of the jetty and she almost went flying, but she regained her balance and raced to the end, threw herself down and grabbed hold of the side of the boat, trying to grasp its inflated side as Jonah pushed the throttle.

'Jonah, stop,' she panted. 'Stop, please!'

His lips were pressed together, his brows lowered. He

hesitated, the engine still turning over, and Charlie knew that if he steered away she wouldn't be able to hold on. She reached out to try and grab the rope, and Flora laughed.

'We're going to find mermaids!' she said delightedly.

'Jonah, please,' Charlie tried again. 'Don't go.'

He gave her a cool glance – and then his face crumpled and he screwed his eyes shut. He turned off the engine.

'Oh God, Jonah.' She slid into the boat and, ignoring how soaked she was, pulled him into a hug. 'What were you doing?'

'Jonah, bloody hell!' Paul reached the boat, Juliette just behind him. 'Why on *earth* did you do that? Don't you know how dangerous it is to go out on your own? Especially when the sea is like this! Did you ask me to go and get fudge just so you could take the boat out?'

'*Da-a-d!*' Jonah wailed, his bottom lip trembling.

Paul and Juliette climbed into the boat, and Juliette wrapped her arms around Flora.

'Shit,' Paul muttered, squeezing his son's shoulder. 'Sorry, I'm sorry, Jonah, but . . .' He shook his head.

Jonah was openly crying now. Charlie couldn't bear it.

'Th–they made fun of me,' he said, through his sobs. 'They said I was all high and mighty, high-fiving everyone like an Apple employee, but that I was only in charge of the queue.'

'Who said this?' Charlie asked.

She felt Jonah shrug. 'Some boys.'

Paul met her gaze, his expression a mixture of relief and despair. 'You don't need to worry about them,' he said. 'People can say hurtful things, but most of the time they're just jealous. And they were jealous because you're part of our team – the SeaKing's team. You know more about it than them; you can come on the boats with us whenever you

346

want, and *one day*, you'll be piloting them. Don't let their jealousy get to you. You are a brilliant, funny, caring young man, and your mum and I couldn't be more proud of you.'

Jonah looked at his dad with pooling eyes and sniffed loudly. 'Really?'

'Really,' Paul said. 'You kill it, every single day. You are already living your life, making the most of it. Don't ever change.'

'Are we going to find mermaids now?' Flora asked.

Jonah ruffled her hair. 'Not today, Flora. Maybe Dad will take us out next week, and we can have a look?'

'Absolutely,' Paul said. 'Next week. You two, me, Jem and your mum. We can take a picnic, stop somewhere round the coast and have a proper hunt for these mythical beings. You mustn't be disappointed, though, if we don't find any.' He smiled at his son and Jonah gave him a knowing grin in return.

'OK. Sounds good.'

'High-five!' Flora shouted, raising her arm. Jonah hit her palm, and everyone laughed.

Once they were back on the sand, Jonah flung his arms first round Juliette, and then Charlie. 'Thank you for caring,' he said.

Charlie hugged him back and closed her eyes. 'Your dad's right, you know. You are brilliant – don't ever forget it. I'm lucky to know you, Jonah.'

'I need to get back to the bus,' Charlie said, as she watched the other RIB returning, a very soggy Amanda at the helm, while Paul, Jonah and Flora waited for them on the beach.

'You can't,' Juliette said. 'You did a very impressive slide across that jetty, and you're both soaked and filthy.'

'Can you run home and get us both a change of clothes? The bus is packed and God knows what kind of madness will have descended – there were at least three tables waiting to be served when we left.'

'OK, I'll be as quick as I can. Are you all right?' Juliette narrowed her eyes. 'You know, a moment ago, with Jonah . . . It seemed like you were saying goodbye, or something.'

'What? Of course not. I was just glad he was OK,' Charlie rushed. 'I need to get back. There is something I want to talk to you about, but it'll have to wait until later. See you in a bit?' She gave her friend a quick smile and raced back to her bus to see what carnage had been caused in their absence.

She needn't have worried. Most of her customers had seen what had happened and, when she walked back on board, she was treated to a round of applause, and more understanding than she felt she deserved. It took her a long time to speak to everyone – they all wanted to hear the full story – and by the time Juliette returned with a pair of faded jeans, a T-shirt and a thin, cornflower-blue cardigan, Charlie was shivering. She climbed into the cab and performed one of the most awkward clothes' changes of her life, but when she emerged, leaving her slightly damp phone to dry out on the dashboard, she could already feel the warm, dry layers wrapping themselves around her.

The sun was out again and the crowds had returned, people buying burgers and spicy noodles, packages of Cornish Yarg and boxes of sweets to take home. Hugh was busy at his ale stand and Myrtle was chatting to Bill – and anyone who came to buy a superfood salad, vegan curry or vegetable fajita from his truck. 'We have fireworks sometimes,' Charlie heard Myrtle say. 'Should've thought to organize some for tonight, but our master of ceremonies is away this weekend.'

Not for much longer, Charlie thought, and felt a dizzying rush of anticipation.

'How long are you going to stay open?' Juliette asked.

Charlie shrugged. 'Until custom dwindles. I want to make the most of it.'

'Good. That's great – really great. What can I do to help?'

They worked well, a polished machine after time spent together over the summer. Myrtle and Stella popped in with news of a group of dolphins spotted out by the cliffs below Crystal Waters, and to tell them the cocktails at The Cornish Cocktail Co. were much better than Oliver's had ever been. Unsurprisingly, The Marauding Mojito hadn't been a part of the markets since her confrontation with Oliver a few weeks before. Charlie would have been happy for him to still be involved – she wasn't going to let personal differences encroach on the events. But for this weekend she had found a replacement, safe in the knowledge that Oliver would find more fairs and festivals, and more company, away from Porthgolow.

Myrtle and Stella were in high spirits and Charlie chatted to them in between serving, though she was now on a countdown to when the afternoon was over and Daniel returned. There had been talk of everyone meeting in the pub on the last night. All the vendors were invited and Charlie was looking forward to spending more time with the people who had brought Porthgolow to life over the summer. But she was looking forward to seeing Daniel even more. She wanted to tell him that she was staying; that she and Gertie were going to be a feature of the village for the foreseeable future.

They were still working as the sun began to set. The tarmac was shiny from the earlier rainfall and the sea glimmered outside the windows. People were drifting towards

The Seven Stars, its outdoor light glowing invitingly, the noise and hubbub on the beach beginning to fade. 'Look at our village,' Charlie whispered, placing her hand on the glass. 'What do you think, Marmite? Beautiful, or what?' Her Yorkipoo looked up at her from his spot in the driver's seat and she ruffled him behind the ears.

A couple came down from the top deck and handed Charlie their tray of empty crockery. She wished them goodnight and was about to tell Juliette they could start closing down when her friend rushed up to her and clutched her arms.

'You can't go, Char. I won't let you. Not tonight – not at such short notice!'

'What?' Charlie stepped back. 'Go where?'

'Home. Back to Ross-on-Wye. I don't care if you've found a place, or if—'

'Wait, Juliette. Stop.' She squeezed her arm. 'Why do you think I'm leaving?'

'Because we talked about it. You told me Bea wants you back and I heard you on the phone to your mum this morning, saying Gertie wasn't irreplaceable and that we'd get another bus, that you'd found a house but you didn't want to tell me you were going, even though you're leaving tonight! You belong here, Char, and I *know* you haven't sorted things out with Daniel. You absolutely, categorically, cannot go until you've spoken to him. Think how devastated he'll be if you leave without even saying goodbye.'

As realization dawned on Charlie, of all Juliette had overheard and misinterpreted, she started laughing.

'What?' Juliette folded her arms. 'This is not funny. Shit, Charlie.'

'I'm not going,' she said. 'I'm not leaving Porthgolow.'

'You're . . . you're *not?*'

'Nope. I've found a house here, to rent, potentially. I'm going to look at it tomorrow, but I didn't want to tell you until I knew whether I could have it or not. You've let me stay for such a long time, and—'

'But the bus. You said Gertie was replaceable.'

'For *Bea*. She had been talking about using Gertie for The Café on the Hill, so I was telling Mum that if she really wanted to go ahead, then Gertie wasn't the only vintage Routemaster in the world. Though of course nothing will ever be as good as The Cornish Cream Tea Bus!' She laughed again, but Juliette didn't join in.

'You said you were going tonight.'

'I didn't, I . . .' Charlie frowned. 'Mum was asking me when this market was over, when I could start organizing everything – that must have been what you heard. God, Juliette, I thought *I* was Porthgolow's worst eavesdropper.'

But still her friend didn't look overjoyed.

'Hey, Jules, I'm sorry if you thought that—'

'I called Daniel,' she said.

Charlie froze. 'What?'

'After our rescue at the jetty. You gave Jonah such a heart-felt hug, I was convinced that I'd got it right, and that you were definitely going.'

'You told Daniel I was leaving?' Charlie pressed her hand over her chest to try and stop her heart from galloping. 'W-what did he say?'

'He seemed shocked, Char. *Really* shocked. He said he thought he was seeing you tonight.'

'Oh God.' Charlie checked her pockets, then remembered leaving her phone out to dry when she got back on the bus after Jonah's act of defiance. She looked at the screen and saw she had six missed calls from him. 'Shit.'

'Why is that so bad?' Juliette asked. 'If you're staying, then . . . I mean, he said he was coming back tonight anyway. We can tell him I got it wrong, can't we? If you had arranged to see him, that is. It's just a misunderstanding.'

'Sure,' Charlie said. 'We'll explain it, and it'll be fine.' She dialled his number, but it went straight to voicemail. 'He's probably driving.'

She glanced at the clock. It was time to close. There had been no new customers and some of the other food stalls had already packed up.

'So,' Juliette said, finally smiling, 'do you want to tell me why you're so keen that Daniel knows you're not leaving Porthgolow? I'm sensing there's something you haven't told me.'

Charlie grinned. Her friend had already wheedled one secret out of her and Charlie had been determined to keep her and Daniel under wraps, at least until after tonight. But it seemed Juliette's eavesdropping had inadvertently put paid to that, too.

In the quiet that followed, while she worked out how much to tell her friend, she could hear the seagulls cawing outside, and the rhythmic churn of the waves creeping up the beach as the tide came in.

And then a loud squeal reverberated through the air, followed by a sickening thud. It seemed to echo for ever, ripples of sound filling Charlie's head.

Her breath stalled in her throat. She tried to give the noise a definition: something logical and unthreatening, something perfectly normal.

Juliette's eyes were wide. 'Charlie, what was that?'

Charlie stared at her and shook her head.

There was a commotion outside the window, people

running up the hill beyond the pub and someone running down, arms waving.

Charlie grabbed Marmite and followed Juliette off the bus. They ran towards the south side of the village, passing the remaining trucks, most of them packing up.

'What was that, Charlie?' Benji called out.

'Don't know – going to see,' was her breathless response.

They met Hugh, his arms outstretched towards them at the bottom of the hill.

'What is it?' Juliette gasped. 'What's happened?'

Hugh looked first to her, then Charlie. 'It seems the rain . . . it dislodged some of the loose earth at the top of the cliff.'

'*Crumbling* Cliff? There's been a rockslide? Oh God, Reenie. Did it reach Reenie's house?'

'No, nothing's fallen . . . yet. But he was coming too fast round the corner, slid on the wet road and went through the barrier. He's . . . we've called the emergency services, but there's a barn fire over near Truro; they said they would get someone here as soon as they could. We don't know if—'

'Is it Lawrence?' Juliette squeaked. 'But he's been in the village all weekend. He's here, he's—'

'It's not Lawrence,' Hugh said as Charlie pulled her friend against her, trying to swallow the lump in her throat. 'He saw what happened, but he's OK.'

'Not Lawrence?' Juliette asked, her voice shaky.

'It's Daniel,' Hugh said, his gaze sliding to Charlie. 'He's stuck, hanging over the edge, apparently. I haven't seen for myself, but—'

Charlie didn't listen to the rest. She was already running.

Chapter Thirty-One

There was a group of people at the top of the hill by the time Charlie arrived, Marmite still in her arms, Juliette just behind. They were both panting and Charlie felt as though her lungs might burst out of her chest, but she couldn't stop. And there was Daniel's black BMW, close to the place where, only a couple of weeks earlier, Frank had told her off for idling. She had felt panicky then, but this time it was serious. It was very, very serious.

His car had travelled over the verge and the patch of grass, and its front end was hanging off the edge of the cliff. She could hear the slight creak of metal as the chassis shifted. There were skid marks running from the middle of the damp road to Daniel's current position, and the cordon that Lawrence had put in place was scattered, a strip of hazard tape flapping lazily over the BMW's bonnet.

Frank was crouched at the driver's side, as near as he dared, calling to Daniel through the window. But the driver's door was partly over the edge, so there was no chance of him getting out. The car was balanced, Charlie realized, like a seesaw, but with solid ground at the back end there was only one way it was going to tip. She could see a flash of dark hair, but Frank was obscuring her vision. At that moment, though, she didn't want to see or talk to Daniel. She had to focus.

'What's happening?' she demanded, walking up to the group of people. 'What are we doing about pulling him back onto safe ground?'

A woman she didn't recognize shook her head. 'We have to wait for emergency services, love. They shouldn't be too long. And we've got someone turning cars away if they try to head into the village, so as not to risk upsetting the ground in the meantime.'

'Why can't we just pull the car back?' Charlie asked.

'It's too dangerous,' another man said. 'He could tip and go over at any moment.'

'All the more reason to get him to safety now.' Charlie hugged Marmite against her chest. 'We can't just sit here and watch that happen.' She tried to ignore the fear shivering up her spine. The BMW made a groaning sound and Frank stepped back, his face pale.

'We need proper equipment,' the woman pressed. 'Enough weight behind us. If we don't know what we're doing then we could send him, and the tow car, over the edge. We can't risk it – we have to wait for the experts.'

Charlie turned away from them. They couldn't stand around and wait for someone to decide this was more important than a barn burning down. She spun round. 'It's just about the weight of the tow vehicle? If we had something heavy, we could pull him back with more certainty?'

'A fire engine,' the woman stammered. 'They said on the phone to wait for the emergency services. That's what we have to do.'

'No,' Charlie shook her head. 'No, we don't.'

'Guys!' It was Lawrence, running up the hill, pulling Reenie behind him. She looked horrified.

'Oh God, Charlie.' Reenie flung herself at Charlie, and they embraced. Even though Marmite was between them, she could feel the older woman trembling.

'Apparently we can't try and move him ourselves,' Juliette said to Lawrence, as he wrapped his arm around her. 'We have to wait for the fire engine.'

'It's so risky,' Lawrence replied, glancing at the BMW. 'Hugh's at the bottom of the cliff, telling any traffic that tries to come up here to turn back.' He released Juliette and went over to Daniel's side of the car, crouching down and peering forward. 'You doing OK, Daniel, mate?'

Charlie turned away. She couldn't lose what little composure she had left. She thought of Hal, of the lessons he had taught her, his nuggets of wisdom and inspiration. *If you find yourself on a sticky wicket, just stop. Stop, breathe, take a moment to compose yourself, then try again. There is nothing that can't be overcome if you believe in yourself enough.* Could she do this? Could she ignore the advice of the emergency services, or was it a terrible mistake? No. She believed in herself, and they *had* to overcome this. There was simply no other option

She pushed Marmite into Reenie's arms and called out to Lawrence as she ran. 'Tell Daniel to hold on. We're getting him out of this.'

'Where are you going?' Juliette shouted after her. 'Charlie?!'

But Charlie didn't reply. She ran back down the hill,

past Hugh, past the remaining food trucks, and onto the beach. The sun was falling as she raced back to the bus, which she'd left open in her haste to discover the cause of the bang. She ran round to the front of Gertie and checked the winch, remembering her incredulity all those months ago when she'd discovered Pete had added it. When she next saw him, she would kiss him. She climbed into the cab and started the engine. Gertie puttered into life and, for a second, Charlie felt calm. If she was with her bus, she could do anything: it was her and Gertie against the world. And now, they were facing their most important challenge of all.

She turned the bus round and drove off the beach, then gestured to Hugh to let her past, pointing at the winch until he understood and stood back. She kept her pace steady as she climbed. She knew the bus's weight would pull Daniel's car back to safety, but she didn't want it to make the cliff more unstable before she'd attached the winch. Her heart was in her throat, her palms slick on the steering wheel as she reached the crest of the hill.

Juliette and Lawrence stared at her open-mouthed, and Reenie was wide-eyed, clutching Marmite tightly. Charlie drove the bus as far as she dared, positioning it a good way back behind Daniel's car, and at an angle because the road wasn't wide enough to park horizontally across it. Then she climbed out of the driver's original door, the quickest route down.

'Here,' she said, yanking the disengage lever and pulling out the winch. 'We can attach this.'

'Charlie, you fucking genius!' Lawrence took the end of the winch and approached the back of the BMW.

'It's not perfect,' she said. 'I can't get the bus directly behind him because the road's too narrow, and we don't have time to set up a pivot point so, as it pulls, his car will twist to line up with the winch. But it should be enough to get him onto solid ground.'

'It's brilliant, Char,' Lawrence replied.

This time it was Juliette who called out to Daniel. 'We're going to winch you to safety, OK? If you feel a jolt, it's not that you're going over, it's that we're pulling you back. Hold on, Daniel!'

'Is he OK?' Charlie called, climbing back in the small door and behind the wheel. She found the winch button on the dashboard.

'As much as he can be!' Juliette shouted.

She could hear muttering from the others, standing around and doing nothing except telling her *not* to rescue him. She pushed down her anger. She had to focus. Afterwards, perhaps, she would tell them that it wasn't the man *they* cared about who'd been stuck on the edge of the cliff, and if it had been, they might have felt differently. But perhaps she wouldn't. Maybe she would be too busy holding onto Daniel and never letting go. Besides, she might accidentally push one of them over the edge, and she didn't want to snatch defeat from the jaws of victory. *Victory, victory, victory*, she said to herself. *This has to work.*

She watched as Lawrence spent several tense moments securing the end of the winch, the load hook, to Daniel's car, his movements slow and measured. Then he walked backwards, never taking his eyes off the BMW. He re-engaged the winch lever on the front of the bus.

'OK, Charlie!' he shouted, giving her the thumbs-up.

'Right,' Charlie said to herself. She thought of the first time she had seen Daniel in the pub, his insolent comments about Gertie, and the last time, in his office, when their kiss had been a promise, a prelude to something more. She could replay, easily, all the meetings in between; they stood out like stars, burning brightly in her memory. *Victory, victory, victory. This has to work.* And then, out loud, she said, 'Here goes.'

She pressed the winch button, heard a clunk as it swung into action, and then watched as slowly, slowly, the cord began reeling in.

There was a collectively held breath. She could feel it inside her and all around, as everyone watched the BMW creep slowly backwards, the silver winch cord gleaming in the evening light. It inched closer and closer, turning as it began to line up with the winch and Charlie's bus, the passenger side coming towards solid land first. The front left-hand wheel hit the edge of the cliff and bounced up, the driver's side of the car dipping precariously towards the sea, a long way below. Juliette squealed and Charlie gripped the steering wheel so tightly she couldn't feel her fingers. She thought, for a horrifying, time-stopping moment, that Daniel's weight would send it over, tumbling down the cliff, unravelling the winch as it went.

But then the car lurched up again and, a few seconds later, seconds that seemed like hours to Charlie, the driver's front side wheel rolled backwards onto the cliff. Then it was only the bonnet with a sheer drop beneath it. There were sighs and shouts of relief. Juliette wrapped her arms around Reenie, while the older woman looked on, aghast. But Charlie didn't dare breathe. She wouldn't until the whole car was at least five metres away from the edge.

The winch kept working, the BMW got closer to the bus, and by now everyone was clapping and cheering, Reenie pressing her head into Marmite's soft fur while the little dog scrabbled in her arms.

'You've done it!' Lawrence called, giving her another thumbs-up. 'You can switch it off now, Charlie! Charlie?' He patted the front of the bus and Charlie pressed the button. The winch stopped.

Reenie and Juliette rushed to Daniel's door and flung it open. Marmite jumped down inside the car and Juliette picked him up again, shushing him gently.

'Daniel, my God, are you OK?' With tears in her eyes, Reenie bent inside the car and, a moment later, Charlie saw feet on the ground; blue Converse, jeans; and then he was half pushing himself up, half being pulled by Reenie, until he was out and leaning against the side of the BMW. Dark hoodie, dark hair, face as white as a sheet.

Charlie finally let her breath go. She gulped air in as if she couldn't get enough, and then, her whole body trembling, she climbed out of the driver's door into the cool evening.

Daniel stepped away from the car, towards her. Reenie gripped his arm, but he patted her hand and she let go. He took another few steps, and she could see the rise and fall of his chest, his eyes bright with shock. He rubbed his hands together, as if loosening up his fingers. Had he been gripping the wheel, just as she had?

'I didn't know your skills extended to winching,' he said. He sounded only slightly less in control than she was used to. Relief and desire flooded through her.

'Are you OK?'

'Thanks to you,' he said. 'Charlie, I—'

'You're OK. Thank God you're OK.' She rushed forwards and put her hands up to his face. His skin was cold and she felt the graze of stubble under her palms. He searched her eyes, as if reminding himself that she was still there.

'Juliette said you were leaving.'

'I'm not,' she said. 'I had to make a decision, at the end of the summer, about my old job, but I'm not going. I chose to stay here. With you.'

He placed his hands over hers and pulled them gently away from his face, but didn't let go of them. 'I called you. I didn't understand, Charlie, after the other day—'

'It's all my fault,' Juliette said. 'I overheard Charlie on the phone and I misunderstood.' She had tears in her eyes, Lawrence's arm wrapped protectively around her waist. 'I am so, so sorry.'

'It's OK, Jules.' He turned to look at her. 'This was entirely my fault. I was going too fast, as usual. Especially fast, on this occasion.' He faced Charlie again. 'But you're not leaving. That's all that matters.' He brushed his hand over her hair, traced a finger down her cheek. Charlie shivered with delight.

'And that you're OK,' Charlie said. 'That matters too. Quite a lot, actually.'

His smile slipped. 'Because of you. I would like to tell you that I wasn't remotely scared in there, that I sat back and enjoyed the impressive view out of my windscreen, but it would be a massive lie. You saved my life, Charlie.'

She swallowed. 'I just . . . Pete, he—'

He put his finger on her lips. 'You did. You saved me. You and that bus.'

Charlie tried to speak past his finger. 'Gertie is—'

'Wonderful, I know.'

She could feel the emotion bubbling up inside her, uncorked now that Daniel was back on solid ground. She bit back a sob just as sirens pierced the air, the flash of blue lights filling the sky.

'Your rescue party,' Lawrence said quietly, and Charlie wondered if they were all thinking the same thing: if they'd waited, would the BMW still have been balanced on the cliff? She didn't want to consider the alternative.

'You should let them check you over, Daniel,' Reenie said. 'You must be in shock. Did you hit your chest against the wheel?'

'I'm fine, Reenie.' He bent to give her a hug. 'But I will get checked over, just to be sure.'

She scrunched his cheek. 'Oh, you ridiculous man! Imagine almost getting yourself killed for an extra five minutes off your journey.'

'It was an important journey, though. Even if, at the time, I was acting under false information. My intentions were good. Charlie and I have unfinished business.' He smiled, and Charlie could see a glimmer of his usual spark. The ember was still there, even if shock had temporarily dulled it.

She placed her hands flat on his chest, feeling him solid and warm beneath them. 'I couldn't leave you behind, Daniel. I love Porthgolow, Jules and Lawrence, Reenie, Jonah and his family. I could have come back and visited everyone, watched the sunsets, driven my bus around Cornwall, but I knew that if I left, if I only came back here occasionally, you wouldn't be in my life in the way I wanted. You'd be Daniel Harper, owner of Crystal Waters, dedicated businessman, warm and kind-hearted, often completely infuriating. And I love that you're all those things, but for me, you're so much more. I *want* you to be more.'

'Good,' he said. 'Because I want to be more than that, too.' His lips found hers, and his arms circled her waist until she was fully wrapped in his embrace. His kiss went through her, straight to her heart. She held onto him and kissed him back, and it was even sweeter, even sexier than the last time. He was here, he was alive, and he was hers. It was only the sirens that broke them apart, much louder now as the fire engine, ambulance and two police cars finally reached them, coming to a stop metres from the bus and the BMW.

Charlie stepped back, her smile mirroring Daniel's.

'We understood there was a person in trouble at the edge of the cliff. Could someone please explain what's happened?'

'Is there anyone in need of medical attention?'

Reenie pulled Daniel away and Charlie watched him introduce himself to the paramedic and the policeman, shake their hands and start to tell them what had happened. Even after such a terrifying experience, he was the epitome of professionalism. And then a fireman approached her, asking about the bus and the winch, and she explained everything – everything except the emotions that had raged through her as she decided she *was* going to risk it, that she couldn't wait for Daniel's car to crash over the edge of the cliff when there was something she could do about it.

By the time she'd finished, Daniel was sitting in the ambulance, his hoodie and T-shirt off while a paramedic checked his chest and breathing. Charlie hovered in the doorway, reasoning with herself that, under the circumstances, she shouldn't be enjoying the view quite so much.

'Is he OK?' she asked.

'I'm fine,' Daniel said.

She waited for confirmation from the paramedic. 'All his obs are normal,' he confirmed. 'But he's had a shock, so I'd like him to rest and book in with his GP next week for a check-up. If you start having pain or discomfort in the meantime,' he said to Daniel, 'then call 999.'

'Of course,' Daniel replied.

'I can make sure all of that happens,' Charlie said, smiling at Daniel's surprised expression.

'Oh you can, can you?'

'Especially the resting part.'

Daniel thanked the paramedic, pulled his T-shirt and hoodie back on and hopped down from the ambulance. 'Rest wasn't exactly what I had in mind.'

'What?' Charlie widened her eyes innocently. 'You don't think you're entitled to a hot tub session? I would have thought all the tension from sitting in that car, still as a statue, has wreaked havoc with your muscles.'

'Depends,' Daniel said. 'Will you be in there with me?'

'I think I'd have to be,' Charlie replied, 'to make sure you didn't succumb to any after-effects of all this.' She gestured at the flashing lights, the tow truck that had arrived to take Daniel's BMW to the garage. Its undercarriage was damaged, apparently. It would need a lot of work before it would be drivable again.

'You don't have much faith in my physical strength,' he said, as she took his hand and led him back to the others.

'We're going to the pub,' Lawrence announced. 'I don't know whether any of the food market guys will still be there, but we could all do with a stiff one.'

'I'm going to take Gertie back to the beach,' Charlie said, 'but—'

'You don't have to come, if you've got other things to do.' Juliette pulled her and Daniel into a hug. 'I'm so glad you're OK. You know, it *is* pretty romantic.' She stepped back and appraised them both. 'He comes rushing back because some

364

idiot tells him you're leaving, then goes over the edge and has to be rescued by the woman he loves.'

'*Juliette!*' Charlie's cheeks flamed.

'What?' Juliette smiled. 'Isn't it obvious? It is to me.'

'And me,' Reenie said, smirking. At least she was looking – and sounding – more like her old self.

'Come on,' Charlie said, taking Daniel's hand again. She couldn't meet his eye. 'We'll see you in the pub in ten minutes.'

Chapter Thirty-Two

By the time she'd parked her bus in its space on the beach, the sun was a burning orb hovering above the horizon, the water flaming pink and gold beneath, as if inviting it into its depths. Daniel was sitting at one of the downstairs tables, Marmite on his lap. He smiled when she approached, but she could see that the evening's events were catching up with him now that the sirens and adrenalin had been replaced by calm.

'We don't have to go to the pub,' she said, sitting opposite him.

He reached across the table and took her hands. 'I'd rather go home.'

'Of course. Is Jasper there?'

He nodded. 'My dad's allergic to dogs, so I left him with my neighbour over the weekend. I'm so glad he wasn't in the car this afternoon. When Juliette called to tell me you were leaving, and then I couldn't get an answer from you . . .'

'I'm so sorry that happened.' She ran her hand up the inside of his arm, sliding her fingers under the soft cotton of his hoodie. 'I was on the phone to my mum, telling her about looking for a place here, but not wanting to let Juliette know until I was definitely moving out, and Jules got the wrong idea. My old boss, at the café in Ross-on-Wye, had called to ask when I was coming back, and I'd talked to Juliette about it, so she knew it was on my mind. But then . . .'

'But then?'

'But then I came to see you at the hotel. I had decided that if you couldn't forgive me for accusing you of shutting Gertie down, then the choice would be harder. I love Porthgolow, and I love The Cornish Cream Tea Bus. I want this to be its home, to be *my* home, but I also knew that if you didn't feel the same way about me . . .'

'You must have known that I did,' Daniel said. 'And it started long before that night in the hot tub.'

'Because you kept antagonizing me?'

'Exactly,' he said, laughing softly. 'I couldn't leave you alone. With all my business knowledge and highly attuned understanding of what it means to be professional, I couldn't stop interfering. I may not have been enamoured with Gertie at the very beginning, but the very first time I met you . . . I wanted you to succeed, to stay, even if the bus wasn't my idea of a perfect café venue. Obviously, you have completely proved me wrong on that front.'

'And you've come to embrace the whole of Porthgolow a bit more too, if I'm not mistaken?'

He looked at her but didn't reply, just absent-mindedly stroked Marmite between the ears while the little dog sat in a state of bliss on his lap.

'You organized and paid for the car park upgrade, the

new streetlights – all those small changes that have made Porthgolow shine. And you arranged for Josie to come and cover the food market. I don't know what it took to convince her to give me a second chance, but thank you.'

'It was easy,' Daniel said. 'Your bus was making a name for itself, and as soon as I explained the situation to her, she understood. Besides, I think she liked seeing that drive and passion in you, even if, that evening, it was all directed at me.' He grinned.

'Don't remind me,' Charlie said, her cheeks flushing.

Daniel pushed her chin up with a finger, so she was forced to look at him. 'Charlie, your passion and determination are part of the reason I fell for you. You believed in The Cornish Cream Tea Bus, even when it was just an idea, and Gertie was battered and bruised and destined for the scrapheap. Look what's happened since. You were right.' He half-stood, clutching Marmite to him so the little dog wouldn't slide off his knee, pulled something out of his pocket and sat down again.

'Right about what?' Charlie watched as he opened a chocolate-coloured leather wallet and took out a small slip of paper, laying it flat on the table between them. When she realized what it was, she bit her lip.

'*Cornish Cream Tea Bus*,' he read from the ticket on the table. '*Grand opening, 4 May, Porthgolow.* You told me it would be a piece of history one day, but the moment you gave it to me, it felt significant. It took me a bit longer to realize quite how much you meant to me, but not that much longer.'

'You've carried this around with you?' She picked up the ticket, then took his hand.

'Every day. Like a talisman.'

Charlie shook her head and laughed.

'I have liked you from the day I met you, Charlie Quilter, and now I want you to come home with me.'

'Don't you want to rest?' She knew she should at least ask, after what he'd been through that evening, even though every part of her was screaming at her to simply agree.

Daniel shook his head. 'I'm not letting you go so soon after I've finally got you. Come back with me.'

She smiled. She felt as if her face might crack open with happiness.

She locked up the bus and they walked, hand in hand, along the road, Marmite scampering at their feet. The new streetlights burned brightly in the inky twilight. Even from a distance, she could hear the chords of music from inside The Seven Stars and remembered Hugh saying something about reassembling the Cornwall Cornflowers for the end of the bank holiday. Myrtle's pop-in was in darkness, the bright flowers in the hanging baskets eerie in the gloom, but Stella and Anton's B&B looked cosy, the rooms glowing behind closed curtains.

As they reached the bottom of the hill that led up to Juliette's house and then, a few roads back, Daniel's, he turned towards the jetty instead. They stopped at the end, gazing out at a sea bathed in silver-grey light.

'My house isn't like Crystal Waters,' Daniel said. 'It's small, fairly simple.'

'No hot tub in the garden?' Charlie squeezed his hand.

He laughed. 'You can get a bit bored with it, you know. The hot tub.'

'I doubt it – not with that view. But I don't care. I don't feel the way I do about you because of your hotel, or your hot tub, just as, I'm sure, you don't want me for my tables with cup-holders, tiny oven, or even Gertie's snazzy bell cord.'

'Gertie is great.'

'I can see why you have a new-found love of her after tonight. I do too, to be honest. God, I don't know what we would have done if—'

He pressed his forehead against hers. 'The fire engine would have turned up. It would have been fine. Please . . . don't think about it. I've decided not to. We're together, right now. That's what counts.'

'In the most perfect spot in the world.'

'It is, now that you're here.' He kissed her, and then added, 'Porthgolow is a special place, all things considered.' He wrapped his arms around her and she rested her head on his chest. She closed her eyes and listened to the thump of his heartbeat, in time with hers.

She wasn't sure how long they stayed like that, but eventually Marmite yelped up at them and Daniel scooped the dog into his arms.

Charlie turned towards the sea again, to the vista that would be her daily view. Not for the next few weeks, or months, but for as long as she wanted it to be. Porthgolow and its sunsets, Juliette and Lawrence, Reenie in her yellow house. They were her friends and this was her home, with Gertie standing proudly on the beach, and Crystal Waters looking over the cove like a glimmering guard dog.

She didn't need to hold back any more. She could plan more routes around Cornwall, taking in the sights of Penzance and Truro, Falmouth and Padstow, each with their own unique character. She could grow the food market; develop the idea with Amanda, Myrtle and the other villagers. They could find people to sell toffee apples and warming, spiced stews in autumn, Christmas puddings and mulled wine in winter. They could have more fireworks and another bonfire on the beach for Guy Fawkes. She could see Jonah grow into a bold, brilliant young man and take his first trip as a SeaKing Safaris skipper. She could watch Reenie's Instagram following grow, people flocking to the village because of the photographs she posted. She could find out, first-hand, what the future held for Juliette and Lawrence, and spend time with them whenever she wanted.

But, first thing in the morning, she had her meeting with the estate agent. She was committed to making a life for herself here, and she and Marmite needed their own space. She would go back to Cheltenham for a few days to see her mum and dad, pick up some more of her belongings, and then, once she was settled here, she would invite them to come and stay. She could see if Porthgolow had the same magical effect on them as it had on her.

'Ready to go?' Daniel asked.

'Lead the way.'

Charlie said a silent goodnight to her Cornish Cream Tea Bus, to the sea and the moon, the stars winking above them like the echoes of sparklers.

When they had reached his terraced house and collected Jasper from his neighbour, Daniel paused. 'I feel like, after such a momentous day, we need to mark the occasion somehow. What would Hal say?'

'I'm not sure he had any life lessons for this particular scenario,' Charlie said. 'Not any he shared with me, anyway.'

'Forget the mistake, remember the lesson?'

'Never, *ever* listen to someone else's conversation and think you know what's going on. That's the lesson – for Jules on this particular occasion, but it's important for us all.'

'Right, definitely need to remember that. What else?' He lowered his voice. 'Something about love and extra calories?'

371

Charlie laughed. 'How are you remembering all these?'

'Because you told them to me,' he said. 'They're an important part of who you are.'

'Spontaneous moments are always better than planned ones?' Her breath faltered as his gaze lingered on her lips.

'We had planned on seeing each other tonight,' Daniel murmured, 'and I'm not sure my unscheduled visit to the edge of Crumbling Cliff is going to be better than this, though my pulse was racing then – almost as quickly as it is now.'

'OK,' Charlie swallowed. 'Let me think.'

'Don't think for too much longer.' He kissed the side of her mouth, then opened the door and let the dogs go ahead.

'I've got it,' Charlie said. 'One of his simplest, but also his best. *Live life to the full, Charlie. You only get one chance.*'

Daniel smiled. 'Perfect. And I can absolutely guarantee that, with me, you will be living life to the full. I'm going to give you a taster as soon as we get inside.' He pulled her over the threshold and into his arms.

Charlie laughed, relieved and more than a little delighted that his confidence was firmly back in place.

As his lips met hers, silencing her laughter, and Charlie gave herself up to him; as she let Daniel Harper overwhelm her senses, promising herself she would give as good as she got just as soon as she could think straight, she knew she was exactly where she needed to be.

The bus hadn't just rescued Daniel; it had rescued her. Hal's gift to her, all those months ago, had been the start of her long road to happiness. Gertie, so forlorn-looking and lost when she had first driven it down the hill into Porthgolow, was now one of the highlights of the seaside village, and Charlie was more proud of her bus – and herself – than she had thought possible. Together, they had turned things around. And this, she realized – her last coherent thought before Daniel's touch took over her mind as well as her body – was just the beginning. She couldn't wait to embark on the next stage of the journey.

**Read on for an extract of Cressy's heart-warming
novel, *The House of Birds and Butterflies*…**

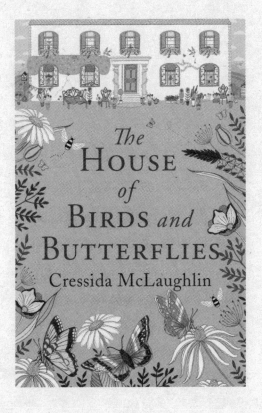

Chapter One

The robin is a small, brown bird with a red breast, that you often see on Christmas cards. It's very friendly, and likes to join in with whatever you're doing in the garden, especially if you're digging up its dinner. It has a beautiful, bubbly song that always stands out, much like its bright chest.

— Note from Abby's notebook

Abby Field was off the reserve.

She didn't know how it had happened, but one minute she was treading the well-worn woodland trail, intent on finding the perfect spot for the ladybird sculpture, the final creature in her nature treasure hunt, and the next she had pushed her way through the branches of the fallen elder and was standing at the side gate of Swallowtail House, looking up at the impressive, empty building. As always, she strained to see inside the grand windows, which remained free of any kind of boards, as if she could discover what Penelope's life had been like all those years ago.

She wasn't sure why she had ended up here now, deviating from her course and slipping away from the nature reserve, but something about this beautiful, deserted building captivated her, and not just because it belonged to her boss, and had been standing empty for over fifteen years. She wondered if any furniture remained, or if the large rooms had been stripped bare of everything except cobwebs. She passed the house's main gates on her way to and from work every day, could imagine the trail of cars that had, at one time, driven through them. But now they were kept secure, the huge padlock not to be messed with.

The house might be abandoned, but Penelope Hardinge was still intent on keeping people out.

She owned the Meadowsweet estate, the greater part of which was now the Meadowsweet Nature Reserve. Only Swallowtail House, abutting the reserve but secluded behind its redbrick wall, was off limits. The stories Abby had been told by long-term residents of Meadowgreen village varied, but it seemed that Penelope and her husband Al had started the reserve soon after their marriage, that Al's death sixteen years ago had been sudden, and that Penelope's flight from Swallowtail House had been equally hasty.

She had left it as if it was plagued, purchasing one of the mock-Tudor houses on the Harrier estate, a five-minute drive out of the village, leaving the grand, Georgian mansion to succumb to the nature she and her late husband loved so much, although she had continued his legacy. She had been running Meadowsweet Reserve with a firm grip ever since, showing no signs of slowing down even though she was now in her sixties.

For the last eighteen months, Abby had been a part of it. She had found a job that she was passionate about, and while she occasionally bore the brunt of Penelope's dissatisfaction, and sometimes felt her confidence shrinking in the older woman's presence, she could understand why Penelope had to be so strict, especially now the reserve was in trouble.

Abby closed her eyes against the September sun and listened to her surroundings. The wind rippled through the woodland, the dancing leaves sounding like the rhythmic churn of waves against sand. A robin was singing its unmistakable, bubbling song, and she wondered if it was the young one who, for the last few weeks, had been landing on the windowsill next to the reserve's reception desk, curiosity winning out over any fear of humans. He was a fluffy bird, his feathers never entirely flat, as if he hadn't quite got the hang of preening, and she and Rosa had named him Bob. But she wasn't sure he would stray this far out of his territory, and the reserve wasn't short of robins delighting the visitors with their upbeat chorus.

Somewhere in the house's overgrown grounds was the melodic trill of a warbler. It could be a blackcap or a garden warbler, their songs so similar that, even now, she found it hard to distinguish between them.

Opening her eyes, Abby turned away from the house and towards the laid-out trails of the nature reserve. She often wondered if Penelope ever returned, if she walked through the rooms of her old home and found it calming, or if her husband's death had forever tainted the place in her memories.

Abby didn't know why she was drawn to it, but ever since she had moved to the village she had found herself frequently staring up at the serene house, as if it held answers to questions she didn't yet know how to ask.

The swallowtail butterfly it was named after wasn't a regular visitor to north Suffolk, making its UK home exclusively in the Norfolk Broads, and this in itself was intriguing. She wondered if, at the time the house had been built, the population of large, yellow butterflies had been much more widespread; like so many other species, its numbers had declined, crowded out by the constant expansion of humans. Stephan, who ran the reserve's café, had told her that since Meadowsweet records had begun, there had only been two swallowtail butterfly sightings, and those were likely to be visitors from the continent. In some ways, it added to the house's mystery.

Threading her slender legs through the fallen elder and the tangle of brambles, she stepped onto a narrow track that led to the woodland trail. When she had first been shown round the reserve she had noticed the house, and as she found out more about its history, had decided that when Penelope and Al had lived there, this must have been their main route to the old visitor centre. She thought that the fallen tree might even have been left there on purpose – discouraging people from heading towards the abandoned building.

Back within the confines of the reserve, Abby turned her focus to her job, to the place she would now have to work so hard to rescue.

Meadowsweet wasn't the only nature reserve that looked after the lagoons and reed beds around Reston Marsh in north Suffolk. But whereas Penelope owned Meadowsweet, Reston Marsh Nature Reserve – already more identifiable because of its name – was run by a national charity. That the two were so closely situated had never been a problem up until now; the habitats were worth protecting, and while the visitor experience was a little less polished at Meadowsweet, it hadn't stopped people coming to enjoy the walks, weather and wildlife on offer. There was enough to go around, as Stephan always said, and Abby liked the slightly less kempt trails she walked along every day, the sense that nature was always on the verge of taking over completely.

But Meadowsweet didn't have a committee to make the

decisions, to test ideas collectively. Penelope kept everything close to her chest, and no amount of gentle encouragement or forcefulness could persuade her to share. Nobody had yet worked out how to chip away at her firm, upright exterior.

And now the reserve was in trouble. The last few months had seen falling visitor numbers, the damp summer not helping, and recently there had been another dark cloud hanging over it, something which Abby was convinced was the subject of the staff meeting Penelope had called for later that morning.

She was nearly finished. The ladybird was the final piece in her nature trail, a new activity she had devised for the school visits that would happen throughout the autumn term. She found a particularly gnarly root, easily visible from the wide walkway that cut a swathe through the woodland, and secured the ladybird beneath it, writing down its location in the notebook she always carried with her. The sculptures had been made by a local artist, Phyllis Drum, crafted from twigs and bound with twine. Abby liked the hedgehog best; it must have taken Phyllis hours – days, maybe – to put his spines in place.

When she got back to the visitor centre, she would create the map and the questions that would lead intrepid groups of children across the reserve to each of the crafted creatures.

It was the first week in September and the sun was still strong, sparkling on the surface of the coastal lagoons, but there was a faint chill to the air, a clarity that made Abby shiver with nostalgia for fireworks and bonfires, crunching through drives of shin-high leaves. She loved autumn; the sun bold but not stifling, the ripples of leafy scent and pungent sweetness of apples, the way everything burst forth in a blaze of colour, as if refusing to succumb to winter. She picked up her pace, hurrying along the trail that was one of the reserve's main arteries. Paths led off it down to the water, to the heron and kingfisher hides, to the forest hide, and along the meadow trail.

She greeted a couple in matching navy parkas, a tripod slung over the man's shoulder, the woman's rucksack bulky with extra camera lenses.

'Anything doing down at the heron hide?' the man asked, spotting Abby's reserve jacket, the logo of a sprig of meadowsweet and a peacock butterfly on the breast pocket.

'A little egret, and some bearded tits were in the reeds in front of the hide about half an hour ago.'

'Excellent, we'll head there first. Thank you.'

'No problem,' Abby said, and waved them off.

The visitor centre was a round, high-ceilinged building constructed out of wood and glass, the huge windows cleaned regularly, letting the weather encroach on the indoors. It was only eighteen months old, and was welcoming, modern and eco-friendly. Inside, it was split into four sections that reminded Abby of the Trivial Pursuit wedges. Penelope's office, the storeroom and the kitchen made up one wedge, the reception and enquiry desk made up another, the gift shop was the third and, leading out onto a grassy area with picnic tables that looked out over the lagoons, Stephan's café was the fourth.

When Abby walked in, Rosa was behind the reception desk, looking elegant in a loose-fitting teal top, her black, springy curls pulled away from her face in a large butterfly clip. She handed over day passes to two men dressed in camouflage and shouldering impressive telescopes.

'Busy so far?' Abby asked once they'd taken the map Rosa had offered them and headed out of the door.

'Not very,' Rosa admitted, her shoulders rising in a sigh. 'But it's still early. And lots of people go back to school and work this week so it's understandable that it's quieter than usual.'

'Of course it is,' Abby said, their false enthusiasm spurring each other on. 'Give it a few more days and we'll be heaving.'

'I truly hope so.' The voice came from behind Abby. It was smooth and calm, but with a steel to it that made her heart beat a little faster. 'How is the treasure hunt coming along?'

'I've placed everything along the trails,' Abby said, turning to face Penelope. 'I just need to finish the paperwork that goes with it.'

'Good.' Penelope raised an appraising eyebrow. 'When is our first school coming in?'

'Next week. The first week back was too soon for most of the teachers I spoke to, but they're also keen to come while the weather's still good. I think the possibility of forty children going home to their parents with muddy trousers was too much to bear.'

'And how's Gavin getting on with clearing the area around the heron hide?'

Abby's mouth opened but nothing came out, because she had no idea.

Penelope stood with her arms folded across her slender chest, her long grey hair, streaked with white like a heron's wing feathers, pulled back into a bun, waiting for the answer. She had used her usual tactic, lulling Abby into a false sense of security by asking her questions she could answer with confidence, then sneaking in the killer blow once she'd become complacent.

'He's been working since seven,' Rosa said, rescuing her. 'He told me he was making good progress when I saw him half an hour ago.'

'I wonder, though,' Penelope said, 'whether his version of *good progress* would be the same as mine?'

Neither Abby nor Rosa dared to answer that one, and Penelope pursed her lips and glanced in the direction of the café, from where the smell of cheese scones, as well as a rather ropey *a cappella* version of 'Bat out of Hell', was coming.

'I want you in my office in five minutes.' She spun on her heels and walked away, closing her office door firmly behind her.

Rosa leaned her elbows on the desk. 'Why do we put up with it?'

'Penelope's not *that* bad,' Abby said. 'She has the potential to be friendly – it's just that she's been on her own for so long, she's forgotten how.'

'She's not on her own though, is she? Her life is the reserve, and we're all here. You, me and Stephan, Gavin and Marek, the volunteers, the regular visitors. She probably sees more people on a daily basis than most other sixty-six-year-olds. My parents don't have as large a social circle as she does, and they're eternally happy.'

'Your mum and dad don't understand the meaning of the word miserable.'

Abby had met Rosa's parents several times since she'd started working at Meadowsweet, and they were the most cheerful people she'd ever encountered, living in a cosy bungalow in the Suffolk town of Stowmarket. Rosa's Jamaican mother was always laughing about something, and her dad had welcomed Abby with open arms, and was easy to talk to. Abby couldn't help feeling a pang of longing and envy that

Rosa had such a loving family close by. Not that Abby didn't have Tessa, her sister, but it wasn't the same as doting parents.

'My mum and dad don't take anything for granted,' Rosa said, 'which is the best way to live your life. Penelope has this whole estate, she has the houses – Peacock Cottage and that gorgeous, deteriorating pile that could be *so* wonderful, yet it's lying in tatters. And she still walks around as if she's sucking a rotten plum.'

'Yes,' Abby said, leaning over the reception desk and lowering her voice. 'But the reserve is in trouble, isn't it? We both know what this meeting's about.'

Rosa sighed in exasperation. Her dark eyes were sharp, inquisitive. She had spent several years in London, buying products for a department store, and had moved back to Suffolk when her mum had had a stroke – one which, thankfully, she was almost completely recovered from. A nature reserve gift shop was undoubtedly a backwards step, but Rosa had told Abby she liked being able to put her personal stamp on it, and the products she had sourced since being at Meadowsweet were good quality and highly desirable.

'Maybe it won't be as bad as all that,' she said. 'Maybe we're reading too much into it.'

Abby shrugged, hoping her friend was right but not believing it for a moment.

Ten minutes later, with Deborah, one of the volunteers, covering reception, Abby, Rosa, Stephan and head warden Gavin were seated in Penelope's office, in chairs crammed into the space between the door and her desk while she sat serenely behind it, her grey eyes unflinching.

'I think you know why I've called this meeting,' she said, without preamble.

'*Wild Wonders*,' Stephan replied quickly, and Rosa shot him a look.

'Gold star for you, mate.' Gavin crossed one overalled knee over the other.

'Thank you, Gavin,' Penelope said. 'And Stephan. Yes, you're right. I've had confirmation that *Wild Wonders* has chosen Reston Marsh Nature Reserve as their host venue for the next year.'

There was a collective exhalation, a sense of sad inevitability, but Abby's heart started racing.

'Year?' she blurted, because while she'd been expecting bad news, this was worse. 'They're going to be filming there for a whole *year*?'

'Got to cover all the seasons, haven't they?' Gavin said. 'Shit.'

'I don't need to tell you,' Penelope continued, 'that this is not good news for Meadowsweet. While it's not the most competitive industry, and many of our visitors frequent both reserves, the pull that *Wild Wonders* will have is considerable. It's prime time, and as I understand it, they will broadcast a live television programme twice a week, supported by a wealth of online coverage: webcams, competitions and social media. We need to be as proactive as we can.'

'In what way?' Rosa asked.

'In increasing our numbers, and our reach,' Penelope said. 'Making Meadowsweet at least as attractive a proposition for a day out as Reston Marsh, if not more, and becoming more visible. You all have your own areas of expertise, and you have to get thinking. We need visitors who will return again and again. It's not going to be easy, but as a small reserve with no regular funding, we, in this room, are the only ones who can make a difference.'

Abby ran her fingers over her lips. Up until that point the events she'd organized had been fairly standard: walks through the reserve and activities for schools, stargazing and bat watching, owl and raptor sessions, butterfly trails. They'd been well attended, but they weren't unique, eye-catching, untraditional. Maybe now was the time to start thinking a bit more radically.

'I have some thoughts,' she said. 'I was toying with the idea of—'

'Excellent, Abigail.' Penelope met her gaze easily. 'I'm encouraged that you have plans. After all, your remit is visitors and engagement, so the weight of responsibility is angled more in your direction. But don't tell me now; this is not the time for brainstorming. All of you go away, come back to me with written proposals and we'll take it from there. I need to see an almost instantaneous change.'

She indicated for them all to leave, which they did slowly, scraping their chairs back and filing out of her office, gravitating to the reception desk where Abby took up her post from Deborah and waited for an influx of visitors.

'Not a huge surprise,' Stephan said sadly.

Rosa shook her head. 'I've got some ideas, but it's still going to be a tiny shop in an independent nature reserve, without a national television show raising its profile.'

'That's the spirit,' Gavin said, giving her a playful punch on the shoulder. 'I'm sure your defeatist attitude is exactly what Penelope's after.'

'We just need to shake things up a bit,' Abby said, 'look at new ways of attracting people who would never ordinarily pick Meadowsweet as a day out. And if we can get the yearly memberships up, then we'll already be on the way to winning the battle.'

Stephan's smile was tentative. 'Exactly, Abby. And I can work on my recipes, expand my scone flavours.'

'See?' Abby said. 'Run a few more lines in the shop, Rosa, and concentrate on the online catalogue. That way we make money without anyone even stepping through the doors. There are lots of small things we can do.'

What Penelope was asking was straightforward. They had to attract more visitors, sell them more scones and sausage rolls, get them to walk away with bulging paper bags full of mugs and spotter books, boxes of fat balls. They all had their tasks, but, as Penelope had reminded her, Abby was doubly responsible because if she couldn't improve the reserve's popularity, then the café could have the best cheese scones in the world, but there would be nobody there to eat them.

She pushed down a bubble of panic. Would a few more walks, a few more members truly be able to make a difference against a television programme? In only eighteen months she had come to see Meadowgreen as her home, Meadowsweet Nature Reserve and its staff as her sanctuary and family. She didn't want anything to threaten the small, idyllic world she had carved out for herself.

The silence was morose, and as Stephan went to check on his trays of flapjacks and Rosa returned to the shop, Abby watched a young man with fair hair and a blue-and-white checked shirt walk through the door.

'Hello,' he said, bypassing the reception desk and going over to the binoculars before she'd had a chance to reply.

'Hi, Jonny,' Rosa called.

'Oh, hey.' Jonny turned uncertainly, as if Rosa was the last person he expected to see in the shop that she ran.

Abby had almost started a pool on when Jonny would actually buy a pair of binoculars, but then decided it was cruel, and that if he ever found out he'd be mortified. It was the regular customers who kept the reserve going, even if most of them only bought a day pass and a slice of carrot cake rather than a £300 pair of Helios Fieldmasters with high-transmission lenses and prism coatings.

'I need to fill up the feeders,' Abby said to Gavin, who was leaning on the desk alongside her, turning a reserve map into a paper aeroplane.

She went to the storeroom and lifted bags of seed, meal-worms and fat balls onto a small trolley, then wheeled it outside to the bank of feeders just beyond the main doors. It was often awash with small birds: blue tits, great tits, robins, chaffinches and greenfinches. Occasionally a marsh tit would find its way there, or a cloud of the dusky-pink and brown long-tailed tits, their high-pitched peeps insistent. Small flocks of starlings would swoop down, cause a couple of minutes of devastation and then leave again. Squirrels regu-larly chanced their luck, and rabbits and pheasants waited for fallen seed on the grass below.

Often, before visitors had even stepped through the auto-matic door of the visitor centre they had seen more wildlife than they found in their own back gardens, and once they were on the reserve, the possibilities were almost endless.

Abby waited for a male greenfinch to finish his lunch and fly away, then set to work.

Her job title, activity coordinator, didn't encompass all that she did for the reserve, but she didn't mind. There wasn't anywhere she'd rather spend her time, and her role mattered. She belonged at Meadowsweet, and if Penelope wanted her to get more creative, to double the number of visitors, then so be it.

Gavin had followed her out, pulling his reserve-issue

baseball cap on, and Abby noticed how muddy his ranger overalls were.

'That was a kick up the backside,' he said, speaking frankly now they were well out of Penelope's earshot.

'Not unexpected, though,' Abby replied. 'There have been rumours about *Wild Wonders* for ages, and taking a fresh look at how we run this place wouldn't be a bad thing, would it?'

'We could talk about it over a drink in the Skylark later, if you and the others are keen?'

'You've got a pub pass, then?'

'Jenna's taking the girls to her mum's for tea, so I'm jumping on the opportunity.'

'I'll see who I can round up,' Abby said.

'Grand. I heard it was someone's birthday at the beginning of the week. We should do a bit of celebrating.'

'How did you—?' Abby started, but Gavin placed a full feeder back on its hook, then grinned and sidled off, whistling.

She got back to her task, exchanging pleasantries with visitors as they strolled down from the car park. That was the thing about working on a nature reserve – nobody turned up grumpy. They were all coming for enjoyment, to stretch their legs and get a dose of fresh air, spot a species they loved or discover something new. There were the odd children who were brought under duress, but there was enough on offer to engage a young, curious mind once they gave it a chance.

On the whole, the reserve was a happy place, and she wished that Penelope would embody that a bit more. She had always been a strict, no-nonsense boss, but even so, Abby had noticed a distinct cooling over the last few months. She could put it down to the threat of *Wild Wonders,* but Abby had a feeling there were other things Penelope was worried about but had so far failed to share with her team.

But then, everybody had things that they wanted to keep to themselves. Abby had made friends here, but the thought of any of them – even Rosa – knowing her deepest insecurities, her past mistakes, made her feel sick. She hadn't even realized she'd told anyone when her birthday was. She liked to keep them quiet, but she had to concede that a few drinks at the pub would be nice, and nothing they didn't already do.

On Monday, the August bank holiday, Abby had turned thirty-one. Her sister Tessa, Tessa's husband Neil, and their two children Willow and Daisy had thrown Abby a birthday picnic in the garden of their modern house in Bury St Edmunds. Abby loved spending time with them. She was helping with the pond they were creating and had started trying to come up with ways to describe the wildlife that Willow, at eight, would be enthusiastic about, writing some of her ideas down in her notebook. Three-year-old Daisy was still a way off being converted, though Abby had her in her sights.

But thirty-one somehow felt even more of a milestone than thirty had. Abby had no children of her own, no husband or boyfriend or even a glimmer of romance on the horizon – not that, after her last relationship, she felt inclined to dive into something new. It had been a long time since she'd shared her bed with anyone besides a large husky with twitchy ears and icy-blue eyes. Raffle wasn't even supposed to go in her bedroom, but it had taken about five minutes from the moment she'd picked him up from the rescue centre for that rule to get broken.

Working on the reserve, and the long morning and evening walks that kept her husky exercised, meant that Abby was fit, her five-foot-four frame slender but not boyishly flat. Her dark-blonde hair was shoulder length, often in a ponytail, and she wore minimal make-up, usually only mascara to frame her hazel eyes. Being glamorous wasn't one of her job's remits, and the village pub didn't have much higher standards.

As she tidied up the visitor centre later that day, Abby decided an evening in the Skylark with her friends was just what she needed. She took her usual route home, knowing the land like the back of her hand.

The approach road that led from Meadowgreen village to the reserve's car park was long and meandering, forcing cars to slow down, twisting around the larger, established trees, and a single building. If Abby followed the road it would take her three times as long to get home, so instead she cut through the trees and came out halfway along it, opposite the building it curved around: Peacock Cottage.

Part of the Meadowsweet estate and therefore owned by Penelope, Peacock Cottage was a quaint thatched house with pristine white walls, a peacock-blue front door and four, front-facing windows – two up and two down – as if it had been drawn by a child. It was isolated, surrounded on three sides by trees, but also encountered regularly by visitors going to or from the reserve, the approach road passing within a hair's breadth of the low front gate. Abby didn't know who tended to the hanging basket – she'd never seen anyone go in or out of the cottage, though it still managed to look immaculate.

She wondered how many people driving past, or walking the less-trodden paths through the surrounding woodland came across the cottage and thought about who lived there. Was it Mrs Tiggywinkle? Red Riding Hood's grandma? Did the witch who lured Hansel and Gretel in hide inside, behind walls that appeared completely normal to adults, the true, confectionary nature of the house only visible to children? Abby had conjured up all kinds of interesting occupants, something that she'd never done when peering at Swallowtail House, perhaps because she knew Penelope had once lived there.

Once she'd left the cottage behind and emerged from the trees, Abby was in the middle of Meadowgreen village. She walked past the post box and the old chapel that had been converted into the library-cum-shop, and was run by her inquisitive next-door neighbour, Octavia Pilch, its graveyard garden looking out of place next to the newspaper bulletin board.

Then – as always – she crossed over the main road and walked along the outside of the tall, redbrick wall that shielded Swallowtail House and its overgrown gardens from the rest of the world. As she got to pass the main gates of the house twice a day, she didn't quite understand her need to visit it that morning, except that it had drawn her to it, as if it wanted to give up all its secrets.

She crossed back over as she came level with her road, unlocked the red front door of No. 1 Warbler Cottages, and was greeted enthusiastically by Raffle. The evening was warm so she discarded her reserve fleece, attached Raffle's lead and set off on one of her husky's favourite walks, neither she nor her dog ever tiring of being outdoors. Pounding through the countryside would help her think about how she could rescue Meadowsweet from the threat of closure, something that, until today, she hadn't even allowed herself to contemplate.

Also by Cressida McLaughlin

THE CANAL BOAT CAFÉ

THE ONCE IN A BLUE MOON GUESTHOUSE

A CHRISTMAS TAIL